threats *and* threads

A Sam and Bump Misadventure, Book 3

Also by N. Gemini Sasson:

The Sam and Bump Misadventures:
Memories and Matchsticks
Lies and Letters
Threats and Threads

The Faderville Novels:
Say No More
Say That Again
Say Something
Say When

The Bruce Trilogy:
The Crown in the Heather (Book I)
Worth Dying For (Book II)
The Honor Due a King (Book III)

The Isabella Books:
*Isabeau: A Novel of Queen Isabella
and Sir Roger Mortimer*

*The King Must Die:
A Novel of Edward III*

Standalones:
*Uneasy Lies the Crown:
A Novel of Owain Glyndwr*

In the Time of Kings

threats
and
threads

A Sam and Bump Misadventure, Book 3

N. GEMINI SASSON

cader idris press

THREATS AND THREADS
(A SAM AND BUMP MISADVENTURE, BOOK 3)

Copyright © 2019 N. Gemini Sasson

ISBN 978-1-939344-16-8 (paperback)

Library of Congress Control No. 2019909309

This is a work of fiction. The names, characters, and incidents portrayed in it are the work of the author's imagination. Any resemblance to actual persons, living or dead, events or localities is entirely coincidental.

All rights reserved. No part of this publication may be reproduced, stored in a retrieval system, or transmitted, in any form or by any means, electronic, mechanical, photocopying, recording or otherwise without the prior written permission of the Author.

For more details about N. Gemini Sasson and her books, go to:
www.ngeminisasson.com

Or become a 'fan' at:
www.facebook.com/NGeminiSasson

You can also sign up to learn about new releases via e-mail at:
http://eepurl.com/vSA6z

Cover art by Cheri Lasota at Author's Assembler
Editing by Cynthia Shepp

For Kirby and Pip,
who loved only me—and that was enough.

Lucky for us, dogs are good at being dogs.
If they were more human, they'd be less perfect.

THREATS AND THREADS

A Sam and Bump Misadventure, Book 3

There's a serial killer in the neighborhood, and Sam is being stalked. When she turns to her former boyfriend, Clint Chastain, an innocent encounter turns into a case of extortion.

Three months ago, sweet little Miley Harper was found suffocated by her own pillow. When reclusive neighbor Grace Hazelton turns up dead from carbon monoxide poisoning, Sam McNamee suspects a serial killer is at large in her neighborhood.

Then Sam starts getting fan mail that quickly turns threatening. Someone has figured out her secret identity. The only way to find out who is to infiltrate the ranks of the local book club.

When Sam gets the chance of a lifetime and needs a dog sitter for Bump, Clint volunteers. If things with him were complicated before they broke up, they're doubly so now—his ex-wife has baby plans, and he's the most likely baby daddy.

Then Bump disappears. And Sam is apparently next on the killer's list. This time, though, if she's going to survive, she'll have to save herself.

chapter 1

SNOWFLAKES AS BIG AS the paper cutout kind I used to make in elementary school meandered earthward, layering the quiet residential street where I lived in a downy blanket of purity. Not one car or living creature had gone down the road since the snow had begun falling an hour ago, so the only tracks visible were the ones my dog Bump and I were leaving behind on our nightly walk. We halted at a stop sign to take it all in.

"Sit, Bump." I looked down commandingly at Bump. He stared up at me, his cheeks bunched into a goofy grin of adoration. In reward, I scratched at his upright ear, the one nearest to me. "Those obedience lessons Clint gave you are paying off, huh, boy?"

At the mention of Clint's name, he wagged his hind end without breaking position. The plume of his tail cleared an arc on the sidewalk behind him. Soon, his front feet were tap dancing with anticipation. A few moments more, and he couldn't stand it any longer. His rear popped up, and he bounced in place with a playful *woof-woof.*

Before he could break into a run and pull me off my feet, I commanded him to sit again. He complied, but not without a sulky yodel. The Husky in him demanded that he comment frequently.

"Sorry, buddy, but he's not coming to take you for a run." Certainly not tonight. Not anytime soon, probably. Clint and I weren't exactly enemies, but we *were* history. I pinched Bump's jowls. "Archer's on his way, though. You like Archer, don't you?"

As if Bump had to think about it, he tilted his head, the gleam of a distant porch light catching in the pupil of his one blue eye. A crystalline flake alighted on the leather of his nose, melting with the warmth of his body. He went momentarily cross-eyed as he focused on it. His whiskers twitched. He sneezed—a sneeze so big and loud I half-expected his brains to splatter onto the sidewalk. Then he sprang to his feet and began snapping at the snowflakes falling around him. As exasperating as it was to have a dog with ADHD, it also kept life comical. Count on Bump to keep the joy of childlike wonderment alive.

Snow piled wet and heavy on the branches of crowded rows of arborvitae. Wherever there weren't fences, the evergreens served as barriers between the closely huddled bungalows of Bluebird Estates. Just over an inch had accumulated, but according to the forecast, that was about an inch more than we were supposed to get.

I wasn't normally a winter person—cold air hurt my face—but I sighed happily. It could snow a blizzard tonight, and I wouldn't mind. I wasn't going anywhere. My daughter, Tara, was spending the night with her best friend, Shannon Mullins, and Archer Malone, Chief of the Wilton Township Fire Department, was due at my house in half an hour. If Bump and I hoofed it, we'd be home in time to put a batch of oatmeal raisin cookies in the oven and a pot of chicken noodle on the stove. Archer was bringing the drinks and the classic movies. An intimate evening at home with my guy was long overdue.

Ever since Archer and I had started dating seriously, we'd been unable to coordinate our schedules consistently. Township budget cuts had forced him to put in extra hours with the fire department, which meant a lot of weekends. Meanwhile, I'd been on a self-imposed super-secret deadline. Usually, Tara was always home during the week, parked at the kitchen table studying. She had a compulsion to prove herself after the debacle a couple of months ago in the janitor's closet during the football game against Oil City. Tonight, however, she was away from home, and Archer *finally* had a weekend open. I'd been as giddy as a cheerleader before homecoming all week, just thinking about this evening.

After checking both ways, Bump and I crossed the street and continued. Except for the gentle *crunch-crunch* of our feet in the snow, the world was silent. Traffic on Route 379, less than half a mile away, couldn't even be heard. I'd never experienced anything so peaceful. It was like being set down inside a snow globe.

Two blocks down, a porch light went on. A small tan-and-white dog pranced across the street, laying fresh tracks. Thankfully, Bump had his head down, snorting the white stuff, because I really didn't know how he was around other dogs. Wilton didn't have a dog park, and people in this neighborhood tended to let their dogs out in fenced yards rather than take them on walks, so he rarely encountered one nose to nose.

A shrill but soft whistle cut the air, followed by, "Fancy! Faaaancy!"

At that point, I realized I was not the one in control.

Bump's head shot up. His ribs expanded as he took a deep whiff. Before I could brace myself, we were off to the races. No amount of verbal corrections or tugs on his leash could override his instincts. The hound in Bump meant his nose led him places; the Husky in him meant we got there at light speed, well before his brain could catch up. I wouldn't have minded the brisk jog, but the ground was slick. I wound the leash around my gloved hand an extra loop, figuring if I hit the ground, the extra weight would slow him down. Instead, he pulled harder, like I was just the load on the back of the sled and an entire town in the Alaskan wilderness depended on him toting a supply of vaccines to their rescue.

"Bump, stop." My glove loosened. I grappled at the leash with my other hand, figuring a two-fisted grip would work. "Stop. Stop, stop, stop!" Because he didn't hear me the first twenty times.

He pitched forward, his nails clawing at the snowy cement, his body arching with each powerful stride. The dog was on a mission. Nothing would deter him. But I tried anyway.

With all my strength, I yanked back. "Stooooop!"

I was fairly sure what *he* heard was "Mush," because at that exact moment, he ramped up his speed even more. My gloves—along with the leash and the dog—flew from my hands and down the street.

Lungs heaving for breath, I watched him go. The lactic acid burning in my thighs was crippling. I was used to taking Bump on daily walks, sometimes several times a day, but sprints hadn't been in our workout regimen.

As I watched Bump eat up the ground between him and the little dog now scurrying to reach its owner before the kamikaze mutt descended, my fear was less about Bump being loose and more about what he'd do to that poor creature. I forced myself onward, despite the fact I could barely breathe, hoping to reach him before he could grab the dog in his great big jaws and shake it like a flimsy tug toy.

Cleora Winkelman held her front door open wide. The little dog trotted up the steps, then jumped into her arms. She covered it with the loose sleeves of her oversized cardigan, admonishing it like a small child who had wandered away in a department store.

Upon noticing Cleora, Bump slowed to a trot. I doubled my efforts, sure that with the next step I'd hit a slick patch and my feet would go flying from beneath me. Somehow, though, I stayed upright. Bump glanced at me. His head went down, like he finally realized he was in a deep vat of doo-doo. Instead of running, he was now skulking. I slammed a foot down on the end of his leash, crushing my

THREATS AND THREADS

one still-attached glove into the snow. The other glove was somewhere behind us. I no sooner had the leash back in my hold than he was pulling me toward Cleora again.

"What were you thinking, running off like that?" Cleora rocked the little fluffball against her bosom, giving it a light squeeze. "Mommy was worried, Little Miss Fancy Pants. Do you know how worried Mommy was, sweetums?" The dog blinked a few times, then turned its face away like it was truly sorry. "No, no, of course you don't. But you can't just—"

Bump skidded to a halt in front of her house. Well, I skidded to a halt. Bump kind of boomeranged to me, because I'd finally summoned enough strength to halt his forward momentum. Inertia was a bitch to overcome. Bump had just discovered that science fact. He let out a strangled sound.

The rhinestones at the corners of Cleora's black-framed glasses twinkled in the wan glow of the porch light. She tipped her head to the left. "Sam McNamee, right?"

"Yep. Hi, Cleora."

My greeting was drowned out by a ghastly noise. Bump had started to gag, then cough, like I had a noose looped around his neck and was cutting off his air.

The other dog shivered, and Cleora unbuttoned her cardigan just far enough to tuck it inside. "I don't just let her out the front door to do her business, in case you were wondering. I put her out in the backyard—we have a chain-link fence—and the moment I saw someone had left the gate open, she was gone in a flash. She's a curious little lady. Bold as brass for her size."

Paws stretched before him, Bump retched. With his belly sucked up toward his spine, he arched his back and began heaving. The triumph swelling in my chest for having stopped him was quickly swallowed by guilt. I started to wonder if I'd hurt him somehow.

"Is he okay?" Cleora said.

On cue, Bump ejected a pool of radioactive-yellow bile onto the pristine snow.

"Oh, him? Sure, he just—"

Gulping air, Bump folded to the ground and coughed some more. I'd have been overcome with concern, except every other breath or so, he'd raise an eyebrow and glance to see if I was watching.

Cleora scurried down the steps, her furry bosom buddy peeking over the part in her sweater. "It sounds like his trachea may have collapsed."

I scoffed. Bump was also good at histrionics. "I don't think so."

Shock and dismay twisted Cleora's face. She was in her late sixties maybe, so every expression was exaggerated by the creases and folds of her skin. "How can you say that? He can't breathe, poor thing."

Fancy stuck her head out farther, and Bump lifted his nose ever so slightly. His tail twitched.

"Take a closer look," I urged.

She stooped over him, Fancy dangling above Bump. She yipped at him. Shooting up, Bump swiped his big, goobery tongue across the toy dog's head. Cleora stumbled backward, her imminent fall thwarted by the snowshoe-like quality of her Mukluks.

"Whenever he thinks he might get a little sympathy, he milks it for all it's worth." I stifled a giggle. Fancy's topskull was coated in frothy saliva. "Sorry he gave Fancy a spit bath."

"Don't worry about it. Dogs will be dogs." Cleora pulled a tissue from her pocket, then dabbed at Fancy's head. "At least he's friendly."

"You can say that again." Great for meeting people. Bad for running criminals off.

"Maybe we could arrange a playdate for them? Would tomorrow afternoon work? Fancy was attacked by an English Bulldog at a show last summer, and she's been skittish ever since."

"She's a show dog?" I didn't know my breeds that well, so I refrained from asking what kind of dog she was. I'd search Google images later: tiny dog, silky hair, fringe on ears, pencil legs, eyes that seemed like they might pop out of their sockets if someone squeezed too hard. All I knew was the purpose of her kind was to warm a lap and be coddled like a furry baby doll.

"She is," Cleora chimed proudly. "Grand Champion and a Best in Show winner twelve times over—and I only started campaigning her this year. But that all went to Helsinki in a handbasket after… *the incident*." She muttered it like it was a celebrity scandal. "She's shied a few times. Unfortunately, that doesn't go over well with the judges. She was *never* like that before. Her career's going to be put on hold here soon anyway, though. I found the perfect husband for her." Suddenly, she clutched Fancy tighter. "Your dog's not intact, is he?"

"Intact?" I blinked in response. He wasn't missing any parts that I— "Oh… Oh, no. He's been neutered." As far as I could tell, it hadn't made a difference in Bump's inclination to go exploring, but at least I didn't have to worry about him becoming anyone's baby daddy. Unlike Clint, seeing as how Danielle still hadn't left town yet. I had an inkling she still wanted his—

"Oh, nuts," Cleora exclaimed. "I left the teakettle on."

"No problem. I need to get home. I'm expecting company."

Lifting one of Fancy's paws in a goodbye wave, Cleora went up the steps, then turned around. "I didn't mean to be nosy about his… you know. But you have to be careful about these things. People in these parts don't understand there are those of us who actually plan the next generation of canines and that 'purebred dog breeder' isn't a dirty phrase. We put a lot of thought into health and genetics and…"

She wiped a dusting of snowflakes from Fancy's tiny face. "I'm sorry. I must be boring you. Sometimes, I forget not everyone lives and breathes dogs. I'll save it for the breed club meeting next month. I've enjoyed our little chat. You've lived here for months, and we've barely spoken. But I do need to go back in. Fancy's getting chills. Stop by again, and we'll let them meet more formally. It would be good for

Fancy to mingle with a friendly dog."

She shut the door behind her. I loved that she was proud of her… whatever Fancy was, yet still wasn't biased against my mutt.

I was about to leave when the door edged open again. A teakettle was whistling in the background. Cleora popped her head out one more time. "Say, you aren't missing a cat, are you?"

Bump's ears perked at the mention of feline snacks. Next to squirrels, Bump's greatest downfall was cats. It was the very reason we'd been forced to move out of Ida's house.

"Me? No. Bump here has a thing for… those. I could never have one, even though I like them just fine. Why?"

"I keep seeing a mostly black cat running loose lately. Almost flattened it with my car yesterday. Figured I knew everyone's cat around here. Must be a stray."

"Definitely not mine, but thanks for the warning. See you around."

She went back inside. Winding the loop of Bump's leash tighter around my hand, I scanned the street ahead for furry, whiskered critters. I didn't see the glove I'd lost, so I stuffed the other in my pocket, wet though it was. Thankfully, we were only a couple of blocks from home, so I didn't have to worry about frostbite.

When I started forward, Bump instantly took the lead, his pace much more casual this time. We made a hard left onto a cross street. Every so often, Bump would pounce on a little pile of snow, shove his nose into it, and snort. It was his first snowfall since I'd had him, and he'd never appeared more in his element. I tromped on, mindless of the snow melting in my shoes as the promise of Archer's visit quickened my steps.

In the distance, a dog barked. Fancy had a high-pitched relentless yap, and it wasn't coming from the direction of Cleora's house anyway. No, definitely not a small dog. More like a medium-sized one. I listened more closely. It was the plaintive bay of a hound. One of my pet peeves about this neighborhood was that no one seemed annoyed by their own dog's barking. Sometimes, people let them go on for hours. But that was the cost of living in a housing development—neighbors who existed in a bubble of oblivion.

Six months ago, I'd wanted to be anywhere but here in Wilton. Now… I didn't want to be anywhere else. And that had everything to do with Archer Malone—sandy-haired, hazel-eyed, broad-shouldered, heroic Archer. He'd never gone to college or lived in the big city. His job relied on the reckless courage to stand down danger. He wore plaid flannel and baseball caps, and he sang to country songs that would have otherwise shredded my nerves. He knew his way around a car engine, and how to use any power tool known to mankind.

He was Adonis to my Aphrodite. Romeo to my Juliet. Prince Charming to my—

"Batman?" called a voice from some unseen place.

More like Superman, but… Wait, no, that wasn't right.

I almost stumbled over Bump. He'd frozen in place in front of me. His ears were perked, nose quivering, eyes scanning the darkness.

Just ahead of us, a black cat with a patch of white on its chest shaped like a pair of wings hissed and arched its back, hair standing on end. Bump lifted a paw. I planted my feet wide in resistance.

A cat. Just… great. If Bump took off this time, I wasn't going to put my life at risk again. There was only so much I could do. I certainly couldn't keep up with him, and hoping he'd respond to my commands was a proven failure. If he ran off, at least he had a microchip to identify him. Unfortunately, that didn't help figuring out where he'd gone to. At the first chance I got, I was going to research getting him a GPS collar so I could track him down.

A warning growl rose from the cat's throat. Its eyes glowed kryptonite green. I was ready for Bump to lunge, but he sat there quivering instead. It was very unlike him.

Triumphantly, the cat flicked its tail, then trotted across the street, leaped over the curb, and bounded up a driveway. It disappeared between a set of trash cans before reappearing on the other side to race around a garage, a shadow in the darkness.

"Come inside," came the muffled voice.

A plaintive *meow* was followed by the click of a door shutting.

Bump whimpered. Then, in a belated show of bravado, he puffed out his chest and let out three shaky woofs that wouldn't have convinced a mouse of his fierceness.

I stood there a minute, studying the house, the vaguest sense of déjà vu tugging at my memory. What was it—

My chest tightened, squeezing my lungs. I remembered then—the cop cars, the neighbors all milling around, the crime scene tape, Leroy Roberds balling his eyes out... *That* was the house Miley Harper had been murdered in. I shuddered as I realized there was a killer still on the loose out there somewhere.

I hauled Bump to the other side of the street, then raced toward home to wait for Archer. Somewhere behind us, the baying of the hound turned to plaintive howls, shattering the calm of the snow-dusted night.

chapter 2

MY RIGHT INDEX FINGER twitched reflexively above the mouse. *Click.* I tapped the mouse again, waited three breaths, then tapped again.

Click, click, click.

It was worse than a slot machine addiction. Life in the digital age made it too easy to get hooked like this. If it wasn't porn or betting on professional sports, it was online shopping.

Click… Click.

Wait, how had I ended up browsing glittery sneakers? I redirected my efforts.

After ordering a GPS tracking collar for Bump, I'd put the soup on the stove and cookies in the oven, then returned to my computer to kill time. What had we all done before technology provided so much pointless amusement? Talk to each other? Read books? Exercise? Clean the house? I glanced at the clock in the lower right of my screen. Archer wasn't due for another ten minutes still.

A quick detour to my inbox resulted in one e-mail entitled 'Your Last Book'. I opened it. Short, sweet, and dripping with praise. Another case of random reinforcement. This was how Las Vegas casinos kept people glued to the blackjack tables. People only had to win once in a gazillion tries for that hit of dopamine to flood their neurons and give them a high.

dear s.a.

    started yur last book a few hours ago. ive read everthing uve ever written and this has to be the best. omg! i cant put it down!!! im not gonna sleep until im done with it. im adicted. what felicity has with her man is so real. thank u sooo much.

ur fan for life <3

    Aww. She was addicted. That gave me the warm fuzzies. Never mind the fact this person didn't seem to know that apostrophes existed. I'd thank her in the morning. At least I was assuming it was a her. There was no name in the signature, though, and the e-mail address was a generic account that said *TrueLuv2000@cheapmail.com*.

    I'd finally released the fourth book in my second romance series after a too-long hiatus. Moving away from Chicago, helping my dad sort through his belongings and then recover from the fire that decimated my childhood home had thrown a wrench in my plans and taken its toll on my nerves. Not much about my life the last six months had been what would be called normal, but things were finally settling into a routine.

    With my thumb, I stroked the ergonomically contoured sides of the mouse, wiggling my index finger above it. I moved the cursor and opened another tab, avoiding the rabbit hole of social media. Instead, I went to the website of the local newspaper to spy on my neighbors. *The Humboldt Messenger* only posted short teaser articles online, but it was enough to let me know whether the actual print version would be worth picking up at Garber's Groceries. It was usually mundane tidbits about the county fair, groundbreaking for a new gas station on Highway 379, or snapshots of animals for adoption at the nearest shelter. Occasionally, though, there'd be a mention of a local philanthropist passing, the marriage of the homecoming queen and king of four years ago, or an auto accident on an icy road.

I read the headline of the feature article and had to scroll over it again to make sure I hadn't misread it: *Investigation into Harper's Death Continues.*

How ironic, considering I'd just walked by her house, even though I normally didn't go down that road.

This past summer, they'd found sweet little Miley Harper dead just a few streets from where I lived now, suffocated in her own bed. It was the first night Clint and I had spent together at Melissa's house, which I'd since been renting from her. We'd awoken to sirens before going to investigate. So had the whole neighborhood. Uneasy about living so close to a murder scene, I'd delved into Miley's past and all her connections, chased a few leads, and ended up with more questions than answers in the end. Because no suspects had ever been named, I remained vigilant. My dog Bump might have been a source of comfort, given his size and big bark, but as a guard dog he was unreliable. He'd go berserk over a squirrel sitting atop the privacy fence, yet greet total strangers like favorite uncles with pockets full of candy.

With the toe of my damp sock, I nudged my big mutt in the shoulder. No response. He was lying at my feet, curled up next to the computer desk in my office. I nudged him harder. He went on snoring, dead to the world. Our walk had utterly exhausted him.

My phone dinged with a text. It was Archer.

Got off a little later than expected. On my way now.

Okay, I texted back. *Don't speed.*

I went upstairs for a dry pair of socks, then returned to the kitchen to check on the cookies and soup before the smoke alarm signaled they were past done. The soup hadn't yet come to a boil, and the cookies still looked gooey. After double-checking the timer, I went back to my office.

A car turned down the alley behind my house, going slowly, the beam of its headlamps broken into shimmering slats as their light speared the openings between the boards of the privacy fence. Probably just someone coming home from a late shift or drinking beers with their buddies.

I returned my attention to the glowing screen before me. The article didn't say much beyond the fact the investigation was ongoing. I didn't have much confidence in local law enforcement. Poor Miley might never be avenged.

The headlights in the alley went dead. The car had stopped. Someone was parked directly behind my house. Probably an amorous couple, stealing a clandestine moment. Never mind it was close to freezing out there.

Slipping my fleece hoodie on, I shuffled out to the kitchen and grabbed my trusty LED flashlight as I passed the junk drawer. As I lifted the blind from the window of the back door and pressed my nose to the glass, the fog of my breath steamed the window. I wiped at it with my sleeve, but all I could make out was the faint gray outline of a small car.

I was about to flip the light switch when I saw a shadow skulking behind the fence. Whoever it was had gotten out of the car. Guess that meant it wasn't a couple of teenagers necking. But what—

My back gate rattled. Now I was alarmed.

Someone wanted in.

My car was in the garage, so they wouldn't have seen it and might have thought no one was at home. Was someone trying to rob the place? Then it occurred to me—I'd had the kitchen light on, plus a small lamp in my office. That should've clued them in that someone was in the house. Then again, if they had a gun, they wouldn't care either way.

If I turned the floodlight on, they'd *know* I was here. Chances were they'd take off running before I got a good look at them. I'd had enough of the petty criminals in this town. If there was a chance of catching them red-handed, I was all for it.

I tiptoed back to my office to grab my cell. Halfway there, I realized I'd left it upstairs on my bedroom dresser after changing my socks. Thankfully, Dad had talked me into getting a landline and that phone was sitting on an end table in the living room. I crept out into the living room, then retrieved the phone.

A quick peek out the back window in my office revealed someone dangling over the gate. I ducked to the side. Crap! This was seriously worrying me. I crouched beneath the window, listening to the sound of my own breath growing louder and more ragged with fear. Were they really going to scale the fence? It was only six-foot tall. It wouldn't be that hard.

Breath held, I checked again. Nothing. It was pitch black out there—as in Stygian darkness. I crawled into the hallway, figuring once I got up the stairs, I could lock myself in the bedroom closet and call 9-1-1.

Outside, a car engine rumbled. But I couldn't tell if it was from out back or on the street in front of the house. Had the intruder left?

Still parked next to my desk, Bump groaned as he stretched his lanky antelope legs. I couldn't leave him there. I took a shoe off, then threw it at him through the doorway. It bounced off his thick skull. Groggy, he lifted his head, glanced around, and caught sight of me hunkered in the doorway to the hall. Before I could tell him 'easy,' he lumbered to his feet, shook the sleep off, and loped toward me with that goofy *I-love-you-I-love-you-I-love-you* expression of his.

"No," I whispered desperately, holding both hands in front of me as a barrier. "No, no, noooo—"

He slid to a halt three feet away. And kept sliding. My hands plowed into his wolfish mane. But they did no good stopping him. His front feet undercut me. The phone flew from my grasp. I folded into his body. Together, we skated across the hardwood floor of the hallway. Thankfully, the welcome mat next to the back door slowed our velocity just enough so when my back met the wall, it was with a soft thud.

He had me pinned.

"Get off," I growled.

Bump stood there, grinning ear to ear, his tongue lolling to the side, his tail slapping against the wall.

"Shh!" I swatted at his tail, which only made him waggle his hind end harder. "Quiet."

He tipped his head, one ear standing upright. His nose twitched. He leaned in closer, licked his lips.

"Don't you—"

Slurrrrp.

"—dare." I sighed.

A shadow hovered in the window of the back door. Bump must've seen it, too, because he gazed that way, his head tilting side to side like a bobblehead doll sitting on the dashboard of a moving vehicle.

Before I could hook my fingers in his collar, he lurched away, his nails clawing at the floor. The next few seconds were like watching a professional sports blooper play in slow motion. Bump lowered his head, aiming for the giant doggie door below the window. What Bump hadn't yet discerned was that I'd slid the solid barrier to the door down, then locked it in place several hours ago like I did every night. Bump's attention span would rival that of a maze rat on amphetamines. I witnessed the impending crash, powerless to stop him, his sixty-plus pounds of leanly muscled mass propelling him forward. His snout rammed into the closed door. His jaw folded to his neck. His body twisted sideways, colliding

THREATS AND THREADS

full-length with the door.

Thump.

The shadow retreated.

Bump let out a grunt of surprise, blinked a few times, then sprang at the blinds, shoving them aside. He barked. Harsh, bellowy barks that said, "Get the hell out of my yard!" Or maybe it was "Hey, where ya going? Come back!"

I reached him before he could launch himself through the plate glass. His collar in my grip, I hauled him off and flicked the outside light on. I could barely see through the trashed blinds.

The trespasser was clambering over the gate, one foot scrabbling for purchase against a support board. Whoever it was, they were pretty damn nimble. And not all that big, now I had a better view.

The faintest scent of smoke tickled my throat. Had they set something on fire? I couldn't see any flames. Maybe one of the neighbors was using their fireplace tonight, given the polar vortex that had descended on the area.

I dragged Bump to the office, shoved him inside it, and closed the door. Thirty seconds later, I had the phone in my hand and a dispatcher on the line. The voice was familiar.

"Hello. Can I help you?"

"Someone just tried to break into my house." I blurted out my address, followed by a stream of borderline nonsense.

A pause. Then, "Who is this?"

"Sam McNamee. Can you hurry? I'm not sure they're really gone, and they were just at my back door."

"Was it a person?"

"No, it was a zombie from the apocalypse. Yes, it was a person! What else would it be?"

"Knowing you... anything."

Then I remembered. This was the same dispatcher who'd

answered when I called to report a break-in at Ida's. It had turned out to be Bump chasing Ida's cats, Tiger Lily and Mr. Jeeves. In my defense, he'd sounded like a Kansas twister and done about as much damage.

The lid on the chicken soup banged and clattered. I whipped around to see boiling water splattering over the sides of the pot to hit the heating coil with a hiss. I rushed to it, the scent of smoke assaulting my lungs and stinging my eyes. The cookies!

Beep, beep, beep… Beep, beep, beep!

Smoke snaked out the sides of the oven door. No mistaking what that meant. Dinner was done—and had been for a while.

chapter 3

BY THE TIME I hung up, the dispatcher and I were on a first-name basis. Her name was Misty and she was somehow related to Russ Armentrout, the hardware store owner, through her mother's side.

Less than five minutes later, Deputy Strewing stopped by to take my report. Luckily, he'd been parked on Route 379, hoping to catch speeders on their way into town. All I could tell him was the burglar had been driving a small car and was shorter than average. If it was even a man, that was. I couldn't really tell.

Deputy Strewing made a visual sweep of the yard and came up with zero clues—not even a footprint, since the ground was frozen solid. His inspection had lasted less than three minutes. I insisted he check again. To appease me, he wandered around the perimeter once more, sweeping the beam of his flashlight from side to side.

Meanwhile, Archer texted me again.

Sorry it's taking so long. Stopped at the convenience store for drinks. Need anything?

Food.

Snacks, you mean?

More like dinner. I'll explain when you get here.

Okay. I'm not even going to guess. I have something to share, too.

What?

Gotta go. Tell you later.

I was slumped on a stool at the kitchen counter, a lukewarm mug of coffee pressed between my trembling hands, when the deputy returned. Bump nosed him in the kneecaps, then spit a slobbery ball onto his shiny black shoes. Grimacing, the deputy patted him on the head.

I set my mug down. "Any clues?"

"Nope, not a one."

"Are you sure? Positive? Nothing at all?"

He shook his head. "S'pose I can check around back one more time. If I find anything, I'll let you know, but people probably go up and down that alley all day long." He took his notebook from his coat pocket. "Meanwhile, can you think of anyone who might want to take something of yours in particular?"

Most of what was in the house belonged to the homeowner, Melissa, Clint's former receptionist. There were a few electronics of value, like the flat-screen TV and my computer, but the thief could have found those in any house along this street. "Not that I can think of."

"Anyone threaten you lately?"

"When you say *lately*, what kind of timeframe are we talking about?"

Tapping his pen on the page of his notebook, he shrugged. "In the last few weeks, maybe."

"Oh, no then. Not lately."

"Anyone who holds a grudge?"

"I think you know my history since I moved back to Wilton, deputy."

As far as I knew, Jake Taylor, Leroy Roberds, Lorraine Steinbrenner, and Deputy Halloway were all still in jail, awaiting trial. They did have friends and relatives on the outside, though. The evidence against Dawna Hawkins hadn't been sufficient for an indictment. Although I'd managed to avoid her lately, I didn't doubt she still held a grudge against me. Given all that, I frequently questioned why I was still even in this town.

Deputy Strewing jotted a few more notes, then returned it to his pocket. I offered to make a fresh cup of hot decaf for him, but he waved it off.

"Thanks, but if I drink any, I'll just have to make a pit stop. Several, actually. Prostate issues. Besides, I was due to get off when the call came in."

"Oh, sorry about that."

"Don't be. Part of the job. Meanwhile, is there someone you can call to come over?"

"I have a friend on the way."

"Want me to wait until they show up?"

"If you wouldn't mind..."

"No problem." He hooked a thumb over his shoulder. "I'll go search the alley now."

While he was poking around out back, I rang my best friend, Selma Paradiso.

"Selma, you'll never guess what just happened."

She sighed. An irritated, can't-be-bothered kind of sigh. "Is this important, Sam?"

It wasn't like Selma to brush me off, but I figured she was probably in the middle of dyeing her hair or color coordinating her wardrobe for the coming week. "You could say that. There's a deputy here. Someone just tried to break into my house."

"No joke, huh? You okay? Nothing stolen?"

"I'm totally fine. Just a little rattled. They scaled the fence and got as far as the back door, but Bump caused a ruckus and scared them off. Deputy Strewing's in the alley now, checking for—"

"Sorry, Sam," she interrupted, "but I *really* can't talk right now."

"Oh." I wasn't used to Selma brushing me off, so I didn't know what to make of it. "Okay, well, I'll call you back later, then. Or maybe we could meet tomorrow."

"Sure, Sam." Her tone was flat, like she didn't care one way or another. "Tomorrow."

Before I could even say goodbye, she hung up. I stood there, holding my phone, wondering if I should call her right back and insist she explain what had her so distracted. But if Selma had wanted to tell me something right then, she would have. For now, I had to respect that.

I grabbed a pecan blackberry muffin from the counter and devoured it. It didn't solve anything, but for thirty seconds, my taste buds had an orgy. I'd just set my coffee cup in the sink when Deputy Strewing came in.

"Anything?" I queried hopefully.

"Just this." He held up what appeared to be a strand of green yarn. "Not sure it's significant, but it was hanging from a splintered section of the back of the gate. Do you or your daughter own a green sweater?"

"I don't." I got up to take a closer look. About six inches long, it was forest green. Whoever'd lost it had a nasty snag in their fugly Christmas sweater or a partially unraveled knit cap. "I don't think it's Tara's, either. Not neon enough for her. But I'll ask her tomorrow if she's been near the gate and if it might be hers. Pretty sure not, though."

"Sounds good. I'll take it in for evidence. Meanwhile, I'll wait out front in my cruiser and fill the report out until your friend shows up." He dropped the strand in a plastic bag, then went for the front door. "We'll contact you if anything comes up, but chances are this was just some hood hoping to commit petty theft. I don't think you have anything to worry about."

I wasn't as confident as he was, but at least Archer was on his way. Holding onto Bump's collar, I went to see the deputy out. The moment the door swung open, I saw them—Maybelle and Harmon Purnell, Cleora Winkelman, and a couple of other neighbors whose names I didn't yet know. I was sure they all knew mine, though.

They muttered hellos at Deputy Strewing as he passed by, then returned their attention to me.

"Uh... hi." Arctic air wrapped around me. Teeth chattering, I waved at them from my doorway in an attempt to elicit a friendly response. Bump's tail thwapped against my legs. The neighbors glared judgmentally. I poked my thumb from my sleeve, then hitched it over my shoulder. "Just someone nosing around out back. Nothing stolen, though, and they didn't get in. The dog scared them off. But you might want to keep an eye out. I hear people in some neighborhoods serve as lookouts for theft rings, letting robbers know when others are away from their houses. Once the goods are stolen and sold on the black market, they take a cut of it." When they continued to gaze at me disbelievingly, I added. "I saw it in an internet meme."

Their faces shifted as they stole suspicious glances at each other.

Maybelle Purnell folded her flabby arms over the gray winter coat covering her flowery housecoat, harrumphing under her breath. She elbowed her husband in the ribs.

"You heard her, Harmon. Run on home. Make sure no one's stealing *our* stuff." Maybelle glared at me accusingly. "She might be tipping them off."

Shoulders rolled forward, Harmon gave me his trademark puppy-dog eyes. A sweet old guy like that didn't deserve a harpy like Maybelle cracking her whip at him in public.

Before I could rescue him, Harmon swung around and lumbered off, his oversized sneakers scuffing on the uneven cement of the sidewalk. As he ambled away, I noticed there were a few porch lights on now. Deputy Strewing hadn't had his lights or siren on when he arrived, but the presence of a patrol car in this neighborhood was like a dog whistle.

"Step it up, Harmon," Maybelle bellowed. "At that rate, by the time you get back there, they'll have cleaned out my book collection—and I'm holding you responsible if they do."

Without a backward glance, Harmon quickened his steps and disappeared around the corner.

The distant wail of a siren cut the air. Being so close to Route 379, no one paid sirens much heed. It was like living close to the airport and getting used to the roar of jet engines.

I stomped onto the front porch, then flung the door shut behind me. Deputy Strewing turned around, his hand already on the handle of his car door. Cleora's head sank between her shoulders. The two other women flanking Maybelle retreated a step as I approached.

I narrowed my glare on Maybelle. "Why do you treat him like that?"

"Harmon? Like what?"

"So, so..." I stopped two feet from her, right inside her personal bubble. "So *mean*."

She puffed her chest out. "Mean, huh? In case you haven't figured it out, Harmon isn't the brightest light bulb in the lamp store. He needs someone to tell him what to do, since he can't think for himself." Waddling closer, she jabbed a pudgy finger at my sternum. "So maybe you oughta just let me handle my husband the way I see fit, got it?"

"He's *not* dumb, Maybelle. He's just afraid to stick up for himself because you're always haranguing him."

Dispatch chatter erupted. Deputy Strewing ducked inside his car.

"If he really feels that way, then he should stand up for himself. I'm not stopping him. I'm just saying it like it is." By now, the siren was so loud Maybelle was practically yelling. "Why don't you mind your own beeswax?"

"I'll mind my own business when you start treating him like a human be—"

"Excuse me, Ms. McNamee?" Emerging from his car, Deputy Strewing cleared his throat. "You said someone was on their way, right?" He readjusted his holster like he was afraid this spat between Maybelle and me was going to turn into a fight to the death.

I backed away from Maybelle. It had felt good to give her a piece of my mind, but chances were she wasn't going to change.

"No, I'm good," I told him. "My friend will be here any minute."

"All righty, then. I need to go after all. Since your neighbors are here, too, that shouldn't be a problem. There's been a medical emergency over on Cardinal I need to look in on."

"Cardinal Drive?" Cleora flattened a hand over her heart. "That's just one road over from my house. Good heavens, any idea what happened?"

"Sounds like a case of carbon monoxide poisoning," the deputy relayed. "Happens sometimes this time of year when folks turn on their furnaces for the first time without having them checked out."

He dipped his head in a farewell nod, got into his cruiser, and backed down the driveway. Seconds later, Archer's truck rounded the corner. Relief surged through me. Neither Maybelle nor a thwarted robbery could ruin my mood now.

Archer pulled into the driveway. I went toward him, but was distracted by Maybelle stomping behind me. At the front bumper of Archer's truck, I pivoted. Judging by her scrunched-up face, she had something more to say. Then again, that was more or less her normal appearance. Still, I'd expected the crowd to scamper off toward Cardinal Drive, but no one budged.

I planted my hands on my hips. "What is it?"

Maybelle sucked her chin in. "What makes you think I was going to say anything? Maybe I was just leaving."

"You have that look. Something's on your mind. Out with it."

She glanced over one sloping shoulder, then the other. The two ladies behind her cocked their heads like a flock of hens hunting for insects in the barnyard. Cleora stood off to the side, appearing more apologetic than condemning. My guess was she didn't kowtow to Maybelle like the other two hens. She'd just shown up to make sure I was all right.

"You know, funny coincidence, but..." Maybelle scanned me up and down, a scowl twisting her lips. "Nothing ever happened in this neighborhood until you came along."

"That so?" I asked. Archer stepped from his truck, a grocery sack hugged to his side. I sashayed to him, hooking my arm around his free elbow. We walked to the front door, me clinging limply to him like seaweed on driftwood. "Now you'll have even more to talk about."

On the front porch, I twined my arms around Archer's neck and pulled him close to plant a kiss on his lips. His body stiff, he shot a sideways glance at our voyeurs. I slid my palm from his jaw to the back of his neck, then plowed my fingers through his tousled hair. Archer had a shy side to him and getting him to loosen up in front of an audience was proving to be a challenge, but I was determined. It didn't take much.

"Maybe we should take this inside?" he whispered between kisses.

"Love to." I grappled for the doorknob, then gave it a twist. My hand slid around the cold, unyielding knob. I twisted harder, thinking the cold had jammed it, but it wouldn't turn. Letting go of Archer, I rattled it. On the other side of the door, Bump stared at me innocently. Grabbing the knob, I put my full weight into the effort. Nothing. "No, just... no. Not now, damn it."

"What's wrong?" Archer murmured. He put a hand on the small of my back, which was the only thing that kept me from bursting into tears of frustration.

"I locked myself out."

The Gossip Patrol snickered behind us.

I whirled around, ready to go verbal-ninja on them.

THREATS AND THREADS

Archer gripped my shoulders to stop me from shaking. "Hey, hey, hey... I have a key, remember?"

"Oh, right." Again, he'd rescued me—this time from embarrassment. I slid to the side, waiting while he searched his key ring, then let us in. Bump barked twice in greeting, sniffed Archer's crotch, and meandered away to chew on a bone. I peered from behind the drapes while Maybelle and her buddies slithered away. Cleora, however, lingered at the edge of my property, almost like she wanted to tell me something but was afraid to, knowing Maybelle would see her. After a minute, Cleora crossed the street and headed home.

Rubbing my upper arms to chase away the chill, I leaned my forehead against the windowpane. Wilton was my hometown, but sometimes I didn't feel like I was welcomed here.

The feeling didn't last long, though. As I gazed off into the darkness, Archer came to stand behind me. His breath tickling the back of my neck, he pulled me into the comforting circle of his arms. Closing my eyes, I just breathed. Belly-deep breaths that filled me with serenity and carried away my fears. As scary as tonight had been, worse had happened to me. I hadn't been beaten, trapped in a burning building, stuck in an out-of-control car, or been shot at.

I was safe. In a place of my own. My car was paid for. My daughter was happy. Archer was with me. My widowed dad had a *girlfriend*, for Pete's sake. And I had adoring fans.

Life wasn't so bad, after all.

If only it would stay this way.

"Now," Archer said, "are you going to tell me what happened?"

ARCHER PULLED THE SHELL apart with artful precision. Egg hit the heated griddle with a sizzle. In the skillet next to it, bacon popped and crackled, the aroma of it filling the kitchen with heavenly goodness.

He was making breakfast for our late supper, since my cooking had been relegated to the trash.

"It's a good thing you happened to be sitting in your office." Archer slid the first egg aside with his spatula before adding another. He had one of Ida's old aprons on, and he couldn't have looked manlier in it. If Humboldt County ever put together a calendar of hunks, Archer would be the cover model. "I mean, if you'd been upstairs asleep, they could've gotten in and..." He shook his head. "I'm sorry I was late. If I'd been here—"

"Archer, don't." I hugged him from behind, my cheek pressed to his broad back. "You couldn't help it. Besides, there's no way you could've known this was going to happen."

"I know." He flipped the eggs. Over medium, just like I liked them. "Just thinking out loud. Maybe you should consider moving to another neighborhood. The house is fine, but the area does seem to be a draw for criminals lately."

"I totally would, but Melissa gave me a sweet deal on the rent. Someday, I'd like a place in the country." Someday seemed like forever away, though. I didn't need a big fancy house. Just peace and quiet. I set the table and filled our glasses, then slid into my seat and took a sip of juice. "Maybe I should have Tara stay with Dad and Ida?"

"Until when, Sam?" He flicked the pepper shaker over the eggs, added a pinch of salt, then put them on my plate. I had my fork poised for the first bite when he snatched my plate away to add the bacon. A few seconds later, he returned it. Three strips of bacon were arranged in a smiley face with the eggs as eyes. It was too cute to eat. He'd be the most awesome dad—

"Sam, did you hear me?"

"Oh, sorry. I forgot the question."

"I said until when?"

"Until they figure out who it is, I suppose."

Sitting across from me, he took a big gulp of milk. I watched him shovel in bites as I grazed absentmindedly. It seemed so normal, so ordinary, for him to be there at the table, eating with me. Like we did it every day, even though this was the first time in weeks we'd been together like this. I'd been independent for so long, and proud of it, that it hadn't occurred to me until that very moment that sharing my life with someone could enrich everything about it.

Archer waved a hand between us to break my trance. "And the chances of that are…"

I shook my thoughts loose. "I know, I know. But I do think she should stay there until I make this place more secure, don't you think?"

"And what about you? Are you going to stay with your dad?"

"You know I can't. The cats… Bump is obsessed with them."

"Right, I forgot about that." He tapped his fork on the table as he chewed the last of his bacon. "So what were you thinking of doing? An alarm system? Marco from the firehouse, he's in the business. Bet I could swing you a deal. Extra locks on the doors and windows?" He pointed his fork at me. "Or what about a security camera? They say just having them is enough to stop intruders sometimes."

"Those are all good ideas, but… but…" I faltered. None of it seemed like enough.

"But what?"

Then it occurred to me. "*You* could stay here."

His face almost froze. Not in shock. But in thought. Deep thought. Like the two of us getting that serious hadn't yet occurred *to him*.

Easing back in his chair, he studied me. "That's a big leap, Sam. Not that I wouldn't consider it. I mean, I almost suggested you stay at my place for a while. But it's an apartment complex that doesn't allow pets, and my buddy Ty is staying with me until the water damage from his burst pipes gets fixed. He's sleeping on the futon, as it is. I can't just kick him out. It's looking like a bigger project than he first—"

It must have been the disappointment on my face that made him stop talking. He scooted his chair next to mine, then took my hand.

"Sweetheart, I'm not ruling it out. But it would be a big step, me moving in here. We'd need to talk about it some more. Like... would it just be until you get an alarm system in—or something more permanent?"

"I know it's a lot to consider, Archer. And I wouldn't have suggested it if tonight hadn't happened. But I'm concerned they might come back."

"I know. I am, too." He tucked a strand of hair behind my ear, his thumb lingering to stroke my cheek. "We just have to think it all the way through—like how it would impact Tara and what would she think about it?"

Something about his reluctance didn't compute. When I'd had to move out of Ida's because of Bump's fascination with her cats, Clint had immediately invited Tara and me to stay with him. On a physically intimate level, things with Clint had moved at light speed, but there had been a lot about our personal relationship that hadn't fully developed, things about each other we hadn't known or understood at that point. With Archer, it felt like the opposite was true. That it was going slowly, sometimes excruciatingly so, but that what we had was a lot more profound and solid. We'd been friends first. Even now that we were exclusive, we spent more time talking than doing other things. Private things. Which begged a point—

"Archer..." I lowered my gaze. Clint had been all fire and passion, as prone to ignite as he was to consume. Archer was the guy next door, an all-American hero, and I'd like to think my Mr. Right. But I was beginning to wonder if his feelings for me were as strong as mine were for him. "Is this because we haven't... you know..." What was the best way to say it? Done the nasty? Had sex? Known each other in a biblical way? Good gosh, he was a *man*. Didn't they all want it? I certainly did. The anticipation was killing me. I raised my eyes to meet his, saw the depths of his soul in his pupils, felt the kindness of his touch. Saw the longing for a forever reflected in his eyes. "Because I want to, in case you weren't clear on that."

He let out an airy laugh. "Wow, Sam. You sure shoot straight from the hip, don't you?"

Before I could accuse him of Dr. Phil-speak, he cupped my jaw and leaned toward me. His gaze flicked to my lips. And just like that, his mouth was on mine, his tongue probing deep, exploring.

"I want the same thing, babe," he whispered.

Finally!

His breath tickled my neck as his kisses left a moist trail from my ear to the curve between my neck and shoulder. My heart rate ramped up. I melted at his touch, molded to the curve of his hands. Every inch of my skin tingled.

He pulled back to gaze into my eyes. "But making love and moving in together are two different things."

"Yes, but—"

He pressed a single finger to my lips. "I'll think about it. There's a lot we need to talk about. Right now, though, let's just enjoy each other's company. This is our first one-on-one date in how long?"

"Three weeks and four days." Okay, so I kept track of these things. "Wait, did you mean you'd think about moving in with me, or that you'd think about the other thing?"

An amused smile tilted his mouth, deepening the dimples in his cheeks. "We're alone, Sam. And we have all night." He pushed his chair back and stood. "Why don't I take a few minutes to make sure no one's lurking outside so you can be at ease, then we can finish what we started. Sound good?"

While he was outside, I checked on Bump. Sound asleep on Tara's bed, just like he was every night, whether she was home or not. Before shutting down the office computer for the night, I clicked on send/receive on my e-mail one more time out of habit. Three new messages dumped into my inbox—a piece of junk mail in Cyrillic, another entitled *Urgent: Speaker Needed,* and one more from TrueLuv2000. I deleted the first, ignored the second for the time being, then opened the third.

did it. finished book two in one sittin. never red a book so fast in my life!

Always good to hear. I read on.

really kept me gessin. but the ending…

My stomach tightened—and it wasn't because of the typos.

u just dont get it do u? alexander and felicity belong togethr. u cant keep rippin them apart!

Say what? It was what kept my readers hooked, wasn't it? Felicity and Alexander had an on again, off again, on again relationship. Sure, romance built anticipation. But without conflict, where was the tension? Without obstacles to overcome, what were they risking?

so disappointed in u. so so terribly disapointed.

I should've stopped reading then, but I just couldn't. I wasn't sure where this was going.

i expect better.

Well, that wasn't nice, but she was entitled to her opinion.

"Sam?" Archer leaned against the doorframe, arms crossed. "Everything okay?"

"Yeah, sure." I quickly exited out of everything. "Just shutting down for the night."

"Good, because I was watching for a minute and you didn't even notice I was here. You seem kind of worried."

"No, no, I'm good." The screen went blue, then winked off. After I went to him, I wrapped my arms around his waist. "Find anything?"

"Nope. I'll take a closer look in the morning, but all's quiet out there." He rested his cheek against the top of my head as he stroked my back.

I realized in that moment how lucky I was. Archer knew when I needed a hug or a sounding board. Our connection was far more than

THREATS AND THREADS

physical. And it was that very thing that made me want to be with him even more.

Maybe even forever.

chapter 4

IF THIS DATE WERE any hotter, we'd be sprawled naked on a sandy beach under a midday sun somewhere in the South Pacific next to a lava flow.

"You sure Tara's not coming home anytime soon?" Archer swept a strand of hair from my neck.

"Sure as I can be." I sank onto the couch. "She and Shannon went to the Winter Ball, then they're having a sleepover at the Mullinses. There was talk of a chick-flick marathon."

"You really want her watching those kinds of movies, Sam?" Gradually, he lowered himself to me. "I mean, she might get... *ideas*."

"Don't worry. They're from Judy Mullins' personal collection—and she's a strictly PG-13 kind of gal. Besides"—my heartbeat quickened as he teased my shirt upward, his fingers inching up my rib cage—"I think you're the only one with 'ideas' tonight."

He pulled his hand away. "If you're not ready—"

"Archer..." Grabbing his hand, I put it back. "Can't we just..." My breath caught as his fingers slid upward. "It feels right to me. Doesn't it feel right to you?"

"Oh, it more than feels right." He smiled, sweet and sincere. "But if it seems like I'm taking things slowly, it's because I have certain intentions toward you. Serious intentions."

"Serious? Serious how? Like… leaving a toothbrush in my bathroom serious? Or steady girlfriend serious? Or something more… permanent?"

"I think we ought to start with the steady girlfriend part, don't you?" He kissed me softly on the lips. "After all, that'll give us more time to get to know each other. I kinda like that part, don't you?"

"I do." I responded to his kiss, its intensity growing.

He tugged at my zipper. Pulled harder. I hurried to help him. But it was stuck. And these were the tightest skinny jeans I owned. I hooked both thumbs beneath my waistband and sucked in my stomach, thinking maybe I could slide my pants down over my hips to help him out.

"Can we"—I shimmied my hips some more, but my jeans weren't budging—"close the drapes, just in case? Harmon Purnell likes to walk past my house with his head craned in this direction. I don't want to give him a show."

"At midnight?"

"What can I say? My neighbors are nosy."

"Back in a second." He eased himself up. As he walked over to the window, he removed his shirt, then reached for the curtain edge, the muscles of his back flexing with the movement. I hadn't seen him bare-chested since that day at the lodge picnic this summer, when he'd volunteered for the dunk tank.

Perspiration trickled down my breastbone. Good, when he turned around and saw me glistening, he wouldn't be able to resist. I undid the top two buttons of my shirt, just enough to reveal the lace of my bra. Then I fiddled some more with my zipper. Still stuck. Since it wouldn't go down, I pulled it all the way back up. But when I tried unzipping it again, it wouldn't go at all.

Just great. Fantastic. Peachy keen. If I couldn't get out of these pants in the next ten seconds, I'd just have to excuse myself and go to the bathroom. Maybe in full light, I could figure out my wardrobe malfunction.

Archer pulled on the drapery cord. The curtains slid two-thirds of the way across the rod before halting abruptly. He gave the cord another tug. They moved two more inches, then stopped.

"Pull harder," I told him. "They get stuck like that all the time. They're just stubborn."

He yanked at the cord three more times. "Nope, not budging." He inspected the pulley, then flicked through the curtain rings one by one. Finally, he lifted the curtain back to inspect the backside of it. "I don't get where—"

The entire outfit—drapes, rod, and hardware—came crashing down. The *thunk* of a metal pole hitting a human skull sounded.

"Ow!"

He'd been steady enough on his feet to remain upright, but he was lost in a tangle of green jacquard. He flailed his arms, trying to find a part in the material. The brass rings clinked.

"Some idiot forgot to use drywall sinkers," he muttered.

That idiot would be me.

And I'd been so proud of myself for hanging my own curtains.

Leaping up to rescue him, I stifled a giggle and lifted the bottom hem. We worked him loose, and he tossed it all in a heap on the floor.

"Sorry about that." He glanced up at the gaping holes in the wall above the window where the rod had been secured. "I saw one screw was loose. Just didn't know the rest of them were."

"Not your fault." I pecked him on the lips. "I've been meaning to ask you to help me fix that—and maybe a few other things. I just didn't want to assume you'd—"

"Sam, you know I'd help you whenever you need me to. Don't ever hesitate to ask, okay?"

I tucked my chin down. "Okay." Then I remembered where we'd left off. "Say, there's a something-or-other in my bedroom I need

THREATS AND THREADS

you to check out. Maybe you could help me?"

"With what?"

Waggling my eyebrows, I tilted my head.

"Right. Something-or-other. Got it." His arms slid around my waist, and he pulled me to him. "I'll see what I can do. It might take me a while, though. I have to inspect everything very closely, then consult with the boss."

"So I get to be the boss tonight?"

In one swoop, he had me cradled in his arms. "Sam, honey, you are *always* the boss."

Every time he talked like that, it made me giddy. When he took me to the movies in Fullbright two weeks ago, he'd snuck his arm around me without me noticing. Just the gentle movement of his thumb over the top of my shoulder had sent chills down my spine. He held doors open for me and pulled out my chair when we went out to eat. He gazed at me like there was no one else in the world he'd rather be with.

Some days, when he had an extended shift at the firehouse, he invited me to share a meal of chili with the crew—his special recipe of three-bean chicken chili. My first visit there, he'd introduced me to everyone, the whole time holding my hand as if to say he wasn't letting go, not even for a moment, not ever.

After turning off the lights, he carried me to the stairs, my head tucked against his chest, my ear in just the right place to listen to the steady *thump-thump* of his heart. As he lifted a foot to take the first step, a shadow appeared at the top of the stairs, blocking the pale glow of the upstairs bathroom nightlight. The silhouette was Bump's. He studied us from above. Archer paused, his weight balanced on his back foot. I could feel him bracing for the inevitable tackle. But it never came.

With a drawn-out yawn, Bump turned around and padded across the second-floor hallway toward Tara's room, as if it was nothing out of the ordinary for Archer to be carrying me around like that. The gentle *plop* of Bump tossing himself in the middle of Tara's mattress drifted down, followed by a weary sigh.

"All clear," I told Archer, urging him on.

A grin played across his lips as he retreated to the bottom. "We don't have to go upstairs, you know."

"You're saying—"

He trailed kisses down my throat, lingering in the little hollow of my collarbone. "I'm saying we could start anywhere."

My head lolled back, waiting for more. "But the curtains—"

"I was thinking more like the kitchen. When's the last time you—"

I turned my head away. The last? A couple of months ago, maybe?

"Sam? Oh… right. Never mind. I don't want to know." He lowered my feet to the floor, but I still clung to his neck.

"Archer, don't…" I took his face in my hands, searching his eyes. "Clint isn't in my life anymore. You are. And I'm here. Right now. With *you*."

He leaned his forehead to mine. Took my hand in his. Grazed my knuckles with a whispery kiss. Every gesture tender and sincere. Several breaths passed before he spoke, his voice a murmur. "It's not that, Sam. It's… it's hard to explain."

I tightened my fingers around his. "Try."

His jaw worked back and forth. The creases in his forehead deepened. "I just keep waiting for… expecting something to change. Like I can't believe I'm lucky enough to have you. To be with you."

The sentiment was so sweet I forgave him his doubts. Even if circumstances kept preventing us from being together as much as we would have liked, the fact that he didn't take it for granted made me love him that much more. And I did. Love him. So I said so.

"I love you."

THREATS AND THREADS

For a few moments, he was silent. Disturbingly, worryingly silent. Then the corners of his mouth twitched and curved upward. "I love you, too, Sam. A lot. So much it scares the pants off me."

I touched a fingertip to his lower lip, kissed him there. "Isn't that what we were going for when Bump distracted you?"

He laughed. "Yeah, I had to say it, though. I know I've been… aloof. That I probably haven't moved fast enough. But I only wanted to be sure you felt the same way, too. You don't know how many times I almost blurted the words out."

"So what stopped you?"

"That you might not say them back."

I would've asked him how he couldn't have known, but feelings could be tricky things. They were complicated. They changed. When I came to Wilton, I had no intention of staying. I sure hadn't wanted to get involved with anyone. I was content being Tara's mother and immersing myself in my career. I hadn't needed a man to make my life complete. But I also learned that I shouldn't close myself off to the possibility, either.

He scooped me up again, then started up the steps. "Do you know when I knew?"

"That you loved me?"

"Yes, that I loved you. When I saw you in Garber's Groceries that first time. Your shirt was all crumpled, and your hair was going fifty different ways."

"How could you have fallen in love with that? I was helping my dad clean his house out. I must have looked a mess."

"Exactly. I figured if you were that pretty when you weren't even trying, then you'd sure be easy on the eyes in the mornings after just waking up. Besides"—we topped the last step, and he turned toward my bedroom—"you had this determination about you. A look. Like you weren't ever going to let anyone tell you what to do or how to do it."

"And you liked that?" The mattress sank beneath me as he lowered me onto it. "Sounds like a stubborn kind of woman to me."

"Or a woman who knows what she wants." And like that, he grabbed the hem of my jeans at the ankles and slid them off me, zipper be damned. He stepped out of his pants and stood before me, taking me in. The barest glow from a neighbor's floodlight outlined his exquisite form. Any trace of self-consciousness I might have felt was eclipsed by my desire to hold him, touch him, kiss him, accept him as a part of me. Nothing else existed at that moment.

Until the landline downstairs rang.

I glanced toward the open door. The phone rang three more times.

"Do you want to get that?" he asked.

"No, probably just Tara telling me what time to pick her up tomorrow."

"At midnight?"

"She knows I don't go to sleep until late. Let the answering machine get it."

At that moment, the ringing stopped. Archer sank beside me, parting my shirt all the way to kiss my stomach, my ribs, my—

The voice mail went on. I keened my hearing. It wasn't Tara's voice at all, but a woman's. She sounded alarmed. I sat up.

Archer rolled onto his back. "Who was it?"

The message ended, but I hadn't been able to make out the words from upstairs. "I don't know. Maybe it was someone from the sheriff's department."

Sitting up, Archer collected my jeans from the floor and handed them to me. "Go check."

Pants in hand, I ran down the stairs. I'd just made it to the kitchen when my cell phone upstairs began ringing.

"Sam?" Archer stood at the top of the stairs, holding my cell. "The caller ID says Judy Mullins. Should I answer it?"

THREATS AND THREADS

Judy Mullins was Shannon's mother. She wouldn't call at this hour unless it was an emergency.

"Yes." I flew up the stairs three at a time.

Archer answered the call. "Hello? Yes... Could you hold on a moment?" He handed the phone to me.

"Judy? What is it? Is Tara okay?"

"Sam, she'll be fine. But I think you'll need to come and get her—"

"Okay, okay. Be there in ten." I sat on the bed and tried to jam my foot into the leg of my pants while hugging the phone between my head and shoulder, but I kept missing. "Is she sick?"

"Not exactly. We're at the hospital, in emergency. Fullbright."

"What?" I let go of my pants. Archer turned them around for me and guided my foot into one leg, then the other while I fought hyperventilation. "Why? What's wrong?"

"They were just hanging out in the basement about an hour ago—Tara, Shannon, and two other girls. According to them, the dance was a total bore, so they all left early. There's a ping-pong table down there, a TV, of course, an old couch, and a recliner... but it's mostly an unfinished space where we store our junk. At some point, they discovered Shannon's hoverboard from a couple of Christmases ago. When we heard how dangerous they were, we took it away from her. Tom thought I'd thrown it out—and I assumed he'd thrown it out. We were both wrong. Anyway, they found it and started fooling around. On a cement floor, for goodness sake! And, well... Tara fell and broke her arm."

"Oh, no." I stood while Archer helped me finish dressing. "Left or right?"

"Right."

That was bad. Very bad. She was right-handed. I'd have to cut her meat for her. Wash her hair. Type out her homework. For weeks. My shoulders slumped forward. I cradled my head in my hands. "Radius, ulna, or humerus?"

"Upper arm, whichever bone that is."

"Oh, dear."

"I'm so sorry, Sam. I feel responsible somehow. Tom and I should have known better. That basement has been long overdue for a purging. And we should've kept a closer eye on them. But they're always so good, and they weren't being noisy. We were right above them in the living room with the door open. They were talking and laughing, then, suddenly, Shannon was screaming for us. Tara has handled it like a trooper so far, though."

Judy didn't have many more details to provide after that. A minute later, Archer and I were headed down the stairs. I started toward the garage, but he pulled me toward his truck.

"I'll drive," he offered.

"Yeah, that's probably best."

It was a huge relief to let him take the wheel. The snow had stopped a while ago, but the roads were just slick enough that I probably would've wrecked my car speeding to get there. I gazed out the window as we pulled onto Route 379, wishing I could leap into a wormhole and be at Tara's side in an instant.

"Sam..." Archer said quietly. "There's something I've been wanting to talk to you about."

I was taking so long to respond, he prompted me again.

"Sam?"

"Oh, sorry. Just distracted. I don't think I'd be a particularly good listener right now. Can it wait until later?"

"Sure," he muttered.

We were halfway there before I took a good hard look at Archer's face. I was generally good at reading people, but he was stoic sometimes. "Archer, you're not upset we got interrupted, are you?"

He scoffed lightly. "Sam, I'm a firefighter, remember? Getting interrupted is part of my everyday life. If there's one thing I've learned,

THREATS AND THREADS

it's to expect the unexpected." He darted a glance at me. "Especially with you."

I shrank in my seat. "I'm not so sure that's a good thing."

Flicking the wipers on, he returned his attention to the road. "Sure does keep life interesting."

chapter 5

ARCHER'S EYELIDS FLUTTERED SHUT. I poked him in the thigh and he sat up with a start, wiping his mouth like he was sure he'd started drooling.

"You never said what you were going to tell me," I said.

We were sitting in the waiting area of the emergency room at Fullbright Medical Center. Judy Mullins and her daughter Shannon had left shortly after we'd shown up. They hadn't wanted to leave but I'd insisted. That was an hour ago, and I was already eager to leave.

I'd been in this building twice in the last year. Once after my dad escaped the house fire, and again for myself later after said arsonist Jake Taylor kidnapped and beat the tar out of me. This was as much a place of healing as it was a cascade of nightmares. Although tonight's mishap had brought me here, thankfully it wasn't anything catastrophic. I'd been taken back to see Tara briefly. She was in pain, but the break was a simple one. She'd heal. In time. If nothing else, she was a little wiser and hopefully more cautious.

Tara had a minor accident. She was going to be okay. But she was hurting, and she was my baby. My heart ached for her. There wasn't much I could do for her until they released her, though. Until then, I had a question I needed answered.

THREATS AND THREADS

"Archer, what was it?"

He ran his palms down his pants legs. His eyes were baggy from lack of sleep after a grueling shift. "Don't worry about it. You have bigger things going on right now."

For a rural Indiana town, the emergency room had been full to overflowing since we'd arrived. I'd given up asking the receptionist how much longer it was going to be. Everybody else had been asking her the same thing.

To our right, an elderly couple waited. The wife clutched her stomach while the old man rubbed her back in slow, loving circles.

Leaning close to Archer, I nodded in their direction and whispered, "Look at them. They're so lucky, don't you think?"

He focused his weary eyes on them. "Why do you say that?"

"He's worried about her. And I bet right now, he's wondering what he'd ever do without her."

"That's kind of sad."

"Not really."

"How so?"

"Because right now, they have each other. And they've been there for each other for years and years. Through the courting and the honeymoon. The first child. The second and third. When they bought their first house and fixed it up. When he lost his job and she was the one who got a promotion. When his business thrived. When they moved into a bigger house…"

"How can you look at two strangers and imagine their whole story?" Archer curled his fingers over mine. His thumb caressed the vein in my wrist, as if he could tap into my heartbeat.

"Everyone has a story. The lucky ones have someone to share theirs with." I paused, imagining that elderly couple exchanging vows on their wedding day. "In sickness and in health."

"For better or worse," Archer murmured. "Richer or poorer."

"Through arsons and kidnappings."

"And cookies so badly burned they taste like charcoal briquettes."

"Hey." I slapped his arm teasingly. "Not my fault. None of it."

He grinned. "But it happened. And I'm here. In the middle of the night. Waiting for *hours*."

"You are. And that makes you amazing in so many ways." Gripping his fingers, I squared my body to face him. "Archer, you might as well tell me what it is you were going to say. We have plenty of time."

"Sam, I'd rather not. You have Tara to worry about."

"Tara's going to be fine. Relatively speaking. She's in good hands. Besides, I'm curious now. What could be so bad you don't want to tell me? Out with it, Arch."

He squirmed. "Sam, I…"

"Fess up."

He exhaled. Released my hand. Let his gaze wander everywhere except on me. Finally, he slipped me a sheepish glance. "All right. But you're not going to like hearing it."

Worry filled me. Was he sick, in need of surgery? It would be just like him to suffer in silence and not tell a soul. Was it something about his job? According to Ida, there'd been rumors of additional budget cuts. I rubbed his forearm. "You've been laid off? Oh, Archer. I knew the budget cuts had been deep, but—"

"That's not it. I'm the fire chief, remember? I'm the last one who'd get canned. I… I got a call last week… Cirrus Software had a new proposal regarding Everly's Foundation. I believe it could be even more impactful than what I did before. It's about more than just getting a message out. Drug addiction needs to be addressed directly. Taken to the streets, so to speak. There's some training involved that—"

"You said yes?" My voice rose so sharply it startled even me. I balled my fists. Took three deep breaths. But for some reason, I couldn't beat back a sense that everything was about to take a one-eighty just when I thought it was all finally going in the right direction.

He pressed his palms over his thighs. "I told them I'd think about it. I have plenty going on here in Wilton that needs my attention. Meanwhile, I've put in for a leave of absence from the department until I figure out—"

"We've been through this before. You told them no." I stood, trying to process it all.

"Sam, I know the timing on this isn't great. Things between us are just getting started and I want to be with you as much as possible, but—"

I held up the flat of my palm. That word—*but*. It canceled out everything before it.

Blindsided was how I felt. All night, he'd kept this from me, knowing we were going to take the next step. I tried to keep my tone level and my emotions in control. "You said a while ago the talk circuit wasn't what you wanted to do. That you wanted to stay here in Wilton. And I thought…" I gulped in a shallow breath. "I thought, just maybe, that was… in part… because of us."

"First of all, it isn't a talk circuit." He rose slowly. "You know, this is not a position I ever envisioned myself in, but you have to understand where I'm coming from. Did you ever believe in a cause so strongly you couldn't let go of it? Did you ever think *you* could make a difference in someone else's life?"

He had me there. I wasn't an activist. I wasn't even a classroom volunteer. I didn't do causes. It wasn't me. But I also didn't think there shouldn't be people who did want to do them. The most I ever did in the way of charity was donate old clothes to a battered women's shelter or drop my change in the kettle at Christmastime.

"Archer… please…" I couldn't help but feel like I was being left in the lurch. He'd led me to believe he'd be here indefinitely. "You can't…"

You can't go because I love you. Because I need you.

I wanted to say it, but it sounded so... desperate, so clingy.

"My daughter died because of her mother's addiction. And I knew it was happening, yet I didn't do enough to stop it. I've carried that guilt around for years, and it wasn't until lately that I found an outlet for it. A way to make something good out of something bad. So before you say I didn't think about you—about us—when they gave me the offer, think again. I did. I still am. And that's why I haven't answered them yet. Because I wanted to talk to you about it first."

It probably wouldn't have mattered right then what he said to justify that he was still considering it. I wanted to scream at him. Beat my fists against his chest in outrage. And I might have. But... everyone in that waiting room was watching us.

Emotionally, I was wounded. I felt on the verge of being abandoned. Again. Intellectually, I understood Archer just wanted to discuss this with me, just as I would if someone had offered me my dream job.

His voice had the slightest quaver when he spoke again.

"I was hoping... you'd support me, even if you didn't want me to go. Isn't that what people who love each other do?"

I could've walked beneath the belly of a lizard—I felt that small. I wanted my words back. Wanted to lock them up in a vault and never let them out again. But they were already out there.

Where was a time machine when I needed one? Or a rock. Because I really wanted to crawl under one.

I sank onto my chair. I hadn't noticed until then how hard and cold the seat was. How unnatural it seemed to sit there, my back against the rigid plastic, feet flat against the tiles, when minutes before I'd been leaning against Archer's shoulder. He sat rigidly next to me.

When I finally raised my eyes, the lady from the older couple offered a sympathetic smile. Her hand slid down to clasp her husband's, and he brought his other hand over to pat the back of her wrist. He also smiled at me, as if to say they'd had terse moments like ours, too.

"So…" I kept my voice low and even. "Is this our first fight?"

Archer shrugged. "I don't know. Is it? I'm not much of an expert at these things."

"Me, either."

He moved his hand toward mine.

"McNamee?" A nurse stood in the entranceway to the examining rooms, studying her clipboard. "Samantha McNamee?"

I rose to my feet. "Here."

She smiled, a forced one that did nothing to hide the jadedness in her eyes. "You can come on back. Your daughter should be ready to go very soon."

A PINK SUNRISE WAS edging away the inky blue of night as we arrived home. Archer walked us in, did another survey of the house and grounds, including the back alley, and declared an all clear.

Tara's shoulders sloped heavily to one side as she kept her injured arm close to her chest. Her feet barely cleared each tread as she trudged up the stairs. The entire ride home, she'd bleated like a wounded goat about how her life had been ruined twice in one school year already. Couldn't say I blamed her. The whole stink from the beginning of the school year, when she'd ratted out Dixie and LeAnne for smoking in the janitor's closet, then had weed planted in her school locker, was just beginning to blow over. Since then, she'd not only made one friend, but several. She'd made the honor roll two grading periods in a row, and she'd been voted in as French Club vice president. Two weeks ago, she'd started swimming practice, and while not a Katie Ledecky by any means, she showed promise. Life had been looking up for Tara. She was finding a balance of scholarly pursuits, athletics, and a real social life. In her eyes, that was all ruined now. Her right arm wouldn't be fully functional until well after the last meet was swum... or was that swam? There was a reason I hired an editor.

"Mooooom?" she whined from the upstairs bathroom. "I can't get the cap off the toothpaste with one hand. Did you have to screw it on so tight?" A drawer slammed, then another. A cup fell to the floor. Wire hangers scraped across the closet rod. Shoes hit the carpet in a series of thumps.

"I'll be there in a minute, pumpkin," I called.

"Poor kid." Archer pecked me on the forehead before heading for the door. "I think I'm going to go on home and get some shut-eye."

Following, I touched his arm before he could leave. "Arch, you don't have to go."

He turned around, the focus in his gaze long since gone.

I gestured toward the couch, the drapes still in a heap beside it. "You can crash here. I've got plenty of blankets and pillows. Tara won't mind. I'll just tell her it was too late for you to drive home. She'll understand. In the morning, when she's a little more lucid, I'll tell her about the attempted break-in. She'll be happy to have you around. It would make us both feel safer."

The first light of day was stabbing in through the big picture window. Archer blinked at the intrusion as he glanced that way. I could've knocked him over with a feather. He looked that beaten down.

"Moooom?" Tara wailed from upstairs. She sounded like an overly tired five-year-old on the brink of a meltdown. "Can you help me with my shirt? I think Bump needs to go out, too. And I could use a cup of hot chocolate, with some marshmallows and a candy cane... Pleeeease."

We both eyed the top of the stairs. Tara's pleas had eroded to blubbery mewls of helplessness. She wasn't going down for a nap without a fight.

"Thanks, Sam." Archer edged toward the door again. "I appreciate the offer, but I'd just be in the way. Anyway, I have to be back at the station in…" He glanced at his watch. "Ah, man… three hours? I really do have to go."

I opened the door for him. "I'm sorry this night turned out the way it did, Archer."

He wrapped me in a hug. "It wasn't your fault."

"I mean about our fight. Your news just sort of took me by surprise, that's all."

"I haven't had time to process it, either." He kissed me, our lips barely brushing. "We'll talk when Tara's feeling better, all right?"

"Sure." He was halfway out the door when I grabbed him and put my arms around him again. "It's selfish of me, I know, but I… I kind of wish they hadn't called you. I just want to know you're close by. Especially after last night."

"I understand, Sam. I do. Bye now."

"Goodbye, Archer."

And then… I let him go.

chapter 6

"HE REALLY HAD TO go, didn't he?" Cleora rubbed her mittened hands over her arms.

The second hand on my watch indicated Bump had been urinating for well over a minute. When Bump was finally done, Fancy ran up and curled around him, so they could exchange butt sniffs. Couldn't dogs just greet each other with a shoulder bump, since they couldn't shake hands? Or was it their way of sharing what they'd had for dinner last night and how their digestive habits were doing?

It had been a lazy Sunday until now. I was still groggy from last night. Tara was at the house binge-watching old Gene Kelly movies with Ida and my dad, who'd shown up with a bucket of fried chicken shortly after two o'clock, at which time I'd still been in my pajamas. I hadn't changed until ten minutes ago, when I finally remembered Bump's playdate with Fancy.

Although this was only Bump and Fancy's second meeting, they already had a romance brewing. Fancy licked the underside of his jaw, then shamelessly presented her lady parts to him. A few wags of his tail, and Bump was ready to get down to business.

"Bump, no!" I raced across Cleora's backyard to yank him off Fancy. "That's *not* why I brought you here. You don't even have the equipment to get the job done, buddy."

I pulled him away by his collar. "Maybe we should go. I thought being neutered, he wouldn't—"

Cleora snickered. "Don't be too hard on him. She's letting him know it's okay for him to be in charge for now. Nothing sexual. They're simply establishing the pecking order."

"If you say so, but he's like ten times her size. I don't want him to hurt her."

"I don't think you have to worry about that. Fancy may be small, but she'll let him know if he oversteps his bounds."

Reluctantly, I let go of Bump. Head down, tail low, he approached Fancy more cautiously. She pranced before him, circling one way, then the other. When he got to about two feet away, Bump promptly flopped over and rolled onto his back in the snow, legs sticking up in the air like the stiffened corpse of some unidentifiable roadkill.

"See, they've already got it figured out." Cleora clapped her hands. Fancy raced to her, then bounded into her outstretched arms. The little dog licked her face, then let out several gleeful yips before Cleora put her back on the ground. With all the zip of a hummingbird on diet pills, Fancy raced off in Bump's general direction, veering away just before she got within paw's reach. Soon, they were engaged in a game of chase. It wasn't clear who was pursuing who as they ran in tightening spirals and loops. Dainty, agile Fancy darted under and around leaf-bare bushes, then hid between the legs of a snow-dusted lawn chair. Gangly Bump ate up huge swaths of land as he gamboled and galumphed about, occasionally dipping his snout to plow it through the thin layer of snow.

This was good for him. He needed more of it.

"Why don't we go inside?" Cleora said. "We can keep an eye on them through the back window by my dining room table."

Since my cold tolerance had been exceeded on the walk here, I happily agreed. Inside, Cleora offered me a chair at her table, then put out a plate of oatmeal raisin cookies. While she was in the kitchen making coffee, I scanned for a cat. No signs of any that I could detect.

"So is Fancy an only child?" I asked just to make sure. The coffee maker gurgled in reply. I always hesitated to volunteer that Bump was obsessed with cats and rodents. Cleora was one of the few normal people I'd met in this town, and I wanted to stay on good terms with her.

A minute later, Cleora set a saucer in front of me with a spoon and mug. "Yes, just Fancy and me right now. Her grandmother died just a few months ago, but she was twelve. It was kind of expected. But then last year, I also lost her mother, Fiona. Which was odd, because Fancy's mother was only five. We never did figure out the cause of her death. I'd hoped to have one more litter out of her."

"That's sad. I'm so sorry. No wonder Fancy was eager for someone to play with."

"Which is why she approached the bulldog at the show. I'm usually more attentive to these things. I watch out for my own dogs because I know some have their personal space, just like people. But poor little Fancy was merely doing a play bow from three feet away. Then, just like that, the bulldog had her delicate neck in his great big jaws." She shuddered visibly. "I thought I was going to lose her, too. Good thing I had a wire slicker brush to beat the monster off."

After a quick glance outside to make sure everything was okay, Cleora returned to the kitchen. As she came back with the coffee pot, she said, "Fancy's been hesitant around other dogs ever since, which is why I was so surprised she took to Bump so readily. Maybe if she had better experiences, she could put the one bad one behind her."

I held my mug up for her to top off. "Well, I'm glad it's working out. Bump could use the outlet. I've been walking him twice a day, even though we have a fenced backyard, but he's wearing me out. Plus, I think I'm getting plantar fasciitis." I moved my right foot in a tiny circle. Pain flared in my heel.

"Likewise for Fancy. She doesn't need as much room as Bump to run, but she can be needy." As she sat and poured her own coffee, a frown tugged at her mouth. "She misses her family."

"Understandably. She's such an adorable little dog."

Cleora added enough cream and sugar to her coffee to stack up the calorie count significantly. "Fancy's the top-winning bitch in this region—or was until the incident. My Fuzzbuster kennel name is renowned for top-winning Papillons, even though I breed, on average, less than one litter every two years. Given the average size of a Papillon litter is about three puppies, that means my waiting list is long. We've also had numerous obedience and agility champions, both in America and Eur—" She stopped abruptly. "There I go again, off on a tangent. Whenever I start talking about dogs, I just assume that… Never mind." Cleora picked up the coffee pot. "More?"

I wasn't even halfway through mine, but I held it out anyway. "Your sister lives close?"

Steam rose in lazy spirals from my mug as she topped it off. "South end of Wilton. Cordelia Harper's her name. She's a real estate agent. We're twins. Fraternal, not identical. We bicker a lot, but we still love each other."

Harper? It was a common name, but I couldn't help but ask anyway. "Any relation to Miley Harper?"

"That would be her husband Hubert's first cousin, once removed, I believe."

I remembered Hubert from the lodge picnic. "The cat you mentioned roaming the neighborhood…"

Her eyebrows crept up. "Yes?"

"I think it lives at Miley's old house."

"Someone lives there now?"

"It seems so, although I don't remember ever seeing a 'For Sale' sign in the yard, but I don't go down that street often. Last night as we were going home, I heard someone calling the cat from that house. It went around the corner of it and disappeared."

"You don't say? Cordelia never said anything about that house being on the market, but sometimes property gets transferred to whoever's in the will or sold privately. I'll ask next time I talk to her. She might know who lives there now."

"It's not important, really."

The conversation turned to lighter subjects for a while. I'd kept my phone on vibrate in case Dad or Tara needed to reach me, but not a peep so far. It was great to have a little spare time to chat with a new friend.

While Cleora returned the empty mugs and saucers to the kitchen, I watched the dogs playing outside in the snow. Bump had found a giant stick, almost a log, that had fallen from a maple tree in the center of the yard and was offering it to Fancy. She barked at him. He dropped it and went off, then returned with a smaller and longer one. Fancy immediately took the skinny end and tugged. Without argument, Bump let her steal the stick. Rather than try to take it back, he fetched another, which Fancy again demanded—and was given.

Cleora joined me at the window. "They are having a grand ol' time, aren't they?"

"Sure are. We should make a regular appointment, just for them."

"Every Sunday?"

"Perfect!"

After exchanging phone numbers, I put my coat back on, although I was reluctant to detach Bump from his newfound best friend.

A wall of frigid air barreled in as Cleora opened the back door to call Fancy inside. Bump followed faithfully. I clipped his leash on, then followed Cleora to the front door.

"Say, I have an idea," she said. "We have a book club here in Wilton—the Apple Pie Bibliophile Society—and this week's meeting is here on Tuesday. I don't know if you read much, but..."

"Yeah, I read a little." Actually, it was my number-one hobby. An addiction, really. As much as I loved Cleora, the introvert in me wasn't sure about becoming part of a group, though. "Does it require, you know, speaking in front of people?"

"Not at all. Cordelia just shows up to get away from Hubert, since he retired and is always at home. She made him join the lodge just to get him out of the house. A couple of them just nod and say 'Uh-huh, uh-huh' whenever someone else talks. Speaking is entirely optional. And if you don't like the book we're reading at the time, you can just skip the meetings until we agree on something more to your liking. Our last pick was Orwell's *Animal Farm*. I'm afraid that was over some of the ladies' heads. They couldn't get past the talking pigs."

"What are you reading now?" I asked cautiously. Maybe folks in Wilton were a little more sophisticated than I'd first presumed.

"We'll be starting on an author who is new to me. Maybelle insisted."

I cringed to hear Maybelle was part of the group. But I also relished the opportunity to showcase my literary knowledge. Of course, that wouldn't do anything but irritate her. Which meant it would be a *lot* of fun.

"I'm only mentioning it because, well..." Cleora went on, "because Miley used to belong. A lot of us miss her. She kept things light and got along with everyone. Mostly everyone, anyway."

Her last comment piqued my curiosity. I couldn't understand what anyone would have against Miley Harper. It still bothered me that her killer was running loose out there. Chances were whoever killed Miley had known her. And if these women knew anything at all about Miley—

"So what *are* they reading next?" Bump was whining already, and we hadn't even left the house. I rubbed the leather of his floppy ear to console him. "James Patterson? Liane Moriarty? A bestseller... or another classic? *The Great Gatsby*, maybe?"

"No. Someone named... S.A. Macaw?"

"You mean Mack? S.A. Mack?"

"Yes, that's it."

My gut twisted. That was so... weird. I wasn't sure I wanted to know what people in this town thought of my life's work.

"I heard her Felicity series is like that *Fifty Shades* book, but I try to keep an open mind and haven't missed a meeting yet. I've read all sorts of things I never would have touched before. But you know what? Sometimes I discover I like things I never thought I would. And I do learn a lot about the ladies. Not to mention hear more gossip than I care to know about." Cleora scooped Fancy up, then tucked her inside her cardigan as she opened the front door for me. "It's all right if you don't want—"

"What time?"

She blinked, stunned. Then she smiled. "Seven PM. We end no later than nine."

"I'll be there." I stepped forward, but the dead weight on the end of my leash stopped me. Bump's legs were locked. Grabbing his collar, I lugged him across the threshold. His body was in full *rigor-mortis* mode. As we cleared the doorway, he started to shriek in protest. If the local humane society had happened by just then, I would've been charged with animal cruelty. Not to mention if this were to go on another minute, my ears might start to bleed. I gazed pleadingly at Cleora. She was more of a dog behavior expert than I was. "Help?"

She laughed, which was no help at all. "Just keep going, darling. He'll give up before his pads get scraped off."

I adored Cleora, but she didn't know Bump at all. He was not a regular dog. He was a drama queen in head-to-toe fur.

THREATS AND THREADS

IT TOOK TWO BLOCKS before Bump began trotting alongside me. I prayed no one was watching, but I avoided looking to find out for fear they might be. He still managed to deliver a full load of guilt by whining inconsolably the rest of the way.

Although it wasn't our ordinary route, we walked by the place Miley had lived. *Walked* was maybe not the right term. I strained to drag deadweight while Bump crabbed with his head screwed on backward to watch Cleora's house fade into the distance.

It wasn't until we stood in front of Miley's house that Bump's obsession was broken. He lurched to the right, toward Miley's yard, his nose quivering. There was no sign of anyone home. No car in the driveway. The drapes were even closed, which seemed unusual in the middle of the day. Then Bump sneezed several times in quick succession, shook so hard that a dab of slobber flew from his lips and spotted my jeans, and continued, this time leading the way.

I returned home to a blissfully napping teenager. Tara was curled up on the couch, her favorite blanket neatly arranged over her, and the final scene of a Dean Martin and Jerry Lewis movie playing quietly in the background.

Bump sniffed the back of her head, decided there were more interesting things to do, and disappeared out the doggie door.

"Did she fuss much before she dozed off?" I asked Ida. Despite a mild dose of painkillers, poor Tara had been so uncomfortable last night she'd hardly slept. She had school tomorrow, and I wasn't about to let her off the hook, broken arm or not, so the more rest she got, the better.

Ida turned the sound on the TV down even more. "Honestly? I think what upsets her most is being so helpless. If she'd broken her left arm, she might be able to manage, but... She's very independent." Ida gave me a sidelong glance. "Just like you."

"I'll take that as a compliment."

She patted my arm. "You should." She was almost a foot shorter than me, but she more than compensated for her size with her *live-life-large* personality.

"Should what?" Dad ambled into the living room, hugging a bag of potato chips. He popped one into his mouth, then crunched loudly.

"Shh." I motioned them both out to the kitchen. "Ida was just telling me Tara's upset about not being able to do everything for herself."

"Stubborn, huh?" He dug out a handful of chips, stuffed them in his mouth, and said, "Reminds me of somebody I know."

I turned my head away so Dad wouldn't see me roll my eyes.

"I heard that," he muttered.

"Heard what?"

"You rolled your eyes at me."

"How could you hear me roll my eyes? You could see me, if I'd been looking at you, but you can't *hear* someone roll their eyes."

"So you did?"

I clamped my mouth shut. I wasn't going to admit to it.

Nodding, he tucked his thumb in his belt. "I know you, Sam. Don't think I haven't been paying attention all these years."

Ida helped me put away some of the dishes. "That's right, Sam. Walter *does* pay attention. He just chooses to ignore us most of the time."

"Don't you two gang up on me!"

Tara stirred, grumbling. I slapped Dad on the arm. "Keep it down, would you?"

He snatched a clean plate from the dishwasher and handed it to Ida. Then he flicked on the TV on the kitchen counter, stopped on a football game that was only in the first quarter, and whispered, "Geesh, the estrogen level here is enough to drown a man."

Ida and I rolled our eyes simultaneously, but Dad's attention was fixed on the game. Having said his piece, he'd already tuned us out.

"Truce then," I said. "You two are welcome to stay for dinner. I put a roast in the crockpot earlier. Should be done in an hour. Meanwhile, I need to do a few work-related things. I'll be in the office if you need me."

"What?" Dad slapped the counter. Startled by his own outburst, he muttered an apology, then cursed at the refs under his breath.

"Thanks, Samantha." Ida continued to empty the dishwasher. "Dinner sounds great. I don't think we're going anywhere until the game is over."

I ducked into my office then booted up the computer. Fifteen e-mails dumped into my inbox. *Must be an influx of junk mail*, I told myself. But it wasn't.

Because fourteen of them were from TrueLuv2000.

why havnt u ansered me? do u ignor all your fans? well im not a fan anymor...

I read it to the last period. All five hundred flaming, lowercase, misspelled words.

I quickly went on to read the next one. And the next.

dont u care about the time peeple like me have put into readin yur books???

It was like watching a fifty-car pileup on an icy freeway. I couldn't look away.

ive read every dam one of your stories. some twice. what a waist of my time! not to mention the time u waisted rightin them...

By the time I got to the last one, I was drained. The first few had been lengthier, expressing her disappointment in how the book had ended. But from there, they got shorter, more caustic, and were peppered with so much profanity it felt like I needed to scrub the filth from my eyeballs with a scouring pad.

A knock behind me made my heart jump.

"Hey, Sam?" Dad stood in the doorway, his knuckles resting on the frame. "Don't mean to interrupt, but can you come to the kitchen?"

"Sure. Just let me finish up here. It'll only take a minute."

"No hurry. Ida and I just wanted to tell you something. Whenever you're ready."

He walked off before I could say anything else. He'd sounded so *serious*. Were they going to announce their engagement? Oh, what if they were? Just the thought of it made me delirious with joy. I loved Ida beyond belief. She'd made my dad happy, transformed him from a sour-faced curmudgeon into an intermittently grumpy, yet sometimes agreeable, old man. Best of all, she kept him in line.

I deleted the nasty-grams, then opened the last e-mail. It was from another author whose name I recognized, but as far as I could recall, I'd never corresponded directly with her.

Dear S.A.,

Greetings from sunny Miami! I hope this finds you well.

Sure, rub it in. At least this message was starting off with an upbeat overtone.

I'll get straight to the point. I'm in charge of a panel on romantic triangles at the upcoming RomNovCon in Chicago next weekend. We've had a last-minute cancellation from one of our panelists. Margaret Markley broke her femur on a ski trip, so she won't be able to make it. I've long admired your Felicity series. Could you possibly take her place, pretty please? I would be so honored! We'll cover your accommodations, gas or flight expenses, and throw in a modest speaking fee of three thousand dollars to help cover lost work time.

Sincerely,
Summer Monroe

Three grand? That might be modest to some mega bestselling novelists, but it was a healthy chunk of change to me. Enough to cover the down payment on a new car, seeing as how my beloved Subaru Forester had been acting sickly lately. How could I refuse? I planned to talk Dad into staying here for the weekend with Bump and

THREATS AND THREADS

Tara. Meanwhile, Archer's friend Marco could install an alarm system.

And I could clear out my storage locker while I was up that way. Perfect!

I shot back my acceptance, telling her I'd be driving up since it was only a few hours away.

Then I hurried into the kitchen. Bump was gnawing on a bone Ida had brought for him. She always came bearing gifts for Tara and the dog. Sometimes even me. Not that we needed more stuff—ever since the move and the fire, I'd sort of taken to the minimalist way of life—but it was nice to know someone was thinking of us.

Dad nodded at Ida. "Go ahead," he said to her. "You tell her. I get butterflies just thinking about it."

"Oh, Walt, you're being absurd. People do it all the time. It's nothing out of the ordinary."

I clasped my hands together, ready to slap them over my mouth. My dad getting married! They hadn't known each other all that long, just a few months, but they weren't getting any younger.

But for news this big, why hadn't they waited for Tara to wake up from her nap? Surely they'd want to tell her, too? But then, maybe they wanted to run it by me first. It *had* been a little shocking to learn they were an item. Since then, though, we'd all gotten used to them living together. Marriage was just the natural progression of things.

Or maybe they'd already told her.

"It's the getting there that makes me queasy, dear heart," Dad said to Ida. "And what happens afterward."

What? Had she proposed a hot air balloon ride to the church? A bungee jump off the New River Gorge Bridge in West Virginia after they said their vows?

"Fine, Walt. I'll tell her." Ida took my hands. Her face was radiant, her words ebullient. That was the look of a bride-to-be. "Walt and I are going to South America. Lima, Machu Picchu, Buenos Aires, Patagonia... It's been my life's dream, and there's no one I'd rather go with than Walt. We'll be gone for almost a month—twenty-six days altogether—but I have so much vacation time built up at work that they've been pressuring me to take it so they don't have to fork it all over when I retire from the township government office eventually. A lot of people think secretaries don't do anything complicated, but I can assure you that place would grind to a halt without me. Besides, I like knowing what's going on in this town. Anyway, I know it's sudden, but a couple of days ago, I found a great deal on plane tickets and we've been scrambling to make plans ever since. Cleora's going to drop by to take care of Mr. Jeeves and Tiger Lily for me and..." Her smile dipped, then melted. She touched my cheek. "Sam, is there a problem?"

I was unable to form words. This simply didn't compute. I knew Ida had traveled a lot over the years, but this was a little exotic even for her. And my dad? I couldn't even recall the last time he'd been on an airplane, let alone stayed in a hotel. He was firmly entrenched in his rut and seemed content to stay that way. Did Ida have any idea of what twenty-six days of traveling abroad with my dad might do to their relationship? I'd read somewhere that a quarter of couples quarreled and broke up while on vacation—and here she was toting him off on a month-long adventure to the Southern Hemisphere?

"Sam?" she prompted, her face pinched with concern.

"But P-p-Patagonia? Machu Picchu? They're so far away from civilization. Do you even speak Spanish or Portuguese? They might not even speak that where you're going. It's probably some indigenous language. How will you even ask directions?"

"Oh, we're not winging it, sweetheart. We'll have a guide. Plus, we'll be part of a senior citizen's tour group, so we'll get to know some people while we're there. Safety in numbers, right?"

"But..." I wanted to be happy for them, but this wasn't the news I'd been expecting. It was so crazy, like something a nineteen-year-old would do on a gap year, not a couple of senior lovebirds. "How will I get in touch with you? They don't exactly have cell phone towers down there."

"In the cities, they do. And we'll check in as often as we can and send you a copy of our itinerary. Anyway, it's just vacation. A little farther away and longer than normal, but we'll be back before the holidays and—"

"The holidays?" I stumbled backward until my butt hit a bar stool, then planted myself on its cushion for anchor. "You said you'd be gone a month. It's November already."

Dad put an arm around Ida to let me know they were together on this and weren't budging.

"We leave on Friday," he said.

"Friday?" I echoed. Mumbling, Tara kicked a foot from under her blanket. I lowered my voice to a growl. "Why so soon?"

"We got a bargain, that's why," Dad said. "One of those last-minute internet deals."

That alone would've raised red flags with the Walter Schimmoller I knew. Or thought I knew, anyway.

Ida folded her hands together pleadingly. "Sam, dear, aren't you happy for us? It wasn't easy to talk your dad into this."

"So how did you?"

"She told me she'd go without me," Dad answered. "No way I was going to let my honeybunch go traipsing off to some third-world country without a bodyguard."

If I hadn't already been stunned beyond belief, I would've snorted to think my dad could hold off any attackers. He was in his seventies.

There were moments when you realized the world you grew up in was no longer the same one you saw before you. This was one of those moments. I had to reframe my image of Walter David Schimmoller. He was no longer a bitter, predictable recluse. He was impulsive, even reckless to a degree, and occasionally agreeable and easy to be around. I should've been happy, but I was just so... jarred.

"*Is* there a problem, Sam?" Ida repeated.

Still reeling, I looked outside. Another gray drab day. The wind had picked up since I'd come back from Cleora's. I could feel the draft sneaking in around the closest window. Slumping, I held back a sigh. "No, no problem. You two have fun. It's just that I have an opportunity for an impromptu trip to Chicago this weekend. A work-related thing. Figured I'd empty my storage unit while I was up that way. I was hoping, Dad, that you could stay here and watch Tara and Bump."

"I wish we could help," Ida said, "but we have to be at the airport early on Friday. One of my co-workers has a brother who lives just southwest of Indianapolis, so she's dropping us off on her way, that way I don't have to leave my car in the airport parking lot. There are several connections, not to mention a five-hour layover in Miami. It's going to be a long day for us."

"Sorry." Dad clapped me on the arm, seeming genuinely regretful. "You know I'd do it any other time. Can't Tara stay with the Mullinses?"

"I suppose. But I can't send Bump with her. She can't handle him with her broken arm."

"What about that friend of yours?" Ida said. "The one with the weird hair and all the ink. She likes the dog, doesn't she?"

"Selma, you mean? I hadn't thought of her, but I could ask." It was worth a try. Selma didn't have a lot of dog savvy, but I could probably trust her to let him outside and feed him twice a day.

After Dad returned to his football game and Ida settled in the recliner in the living room with a book, I shot Selma a text.

Hey, Sel! Want to meet for lunch tmrw? I have that book I promised you.

I was about to join the family when my phone dinged with a reply.

Heck yeah! Suds and Grub. Noon.

Great. See ya.

THREATS AND THREADS

BTW. Got something to tell you. Big secret.
What?
A minute went by before she replied.
Can't say. It's a SECRET.
But you will, right???
She didn't answer.
Damn it. I hated when people did that. Cliffhangers were cruel.

chapter 7

ONE HAND ON HER hip, the other swinging her sequined handbag, Selma Paradiso sashayed through the door of Suds and Grub and then bounced across the yellowed linoleum floor with all the flair of a drag queen at Mardi Gras. She had a rainbow of beads on. Lots and lots of shiny beads. The multifaceted reflection was enough to temporarily blind a person.

"How's my bestest bestie today?" she asked, her floral-print sneakers squeaking on the linoleum.

"You're colorful today." It was the best I could come up with. In truth, she looked like an industrial-sized package of Skittles had exploded. That or confetti vomit.

"Why, thank you!" She twirled around next to the table. "I couldn't decide what color mood I was in today, so I wore the whole speculum."

It would take hours for me to get that image out of my mind. I slid the tray with her lunch on it across to her. Selma and I had a system—whenever we met for lunch, we traded off on who paid. By now, we'd shared the ritual often enough to know who ordered what where.

"Gawd, I missed you!" She flung her purse down, grabbed my

hands, and leaned in to give me a great big noisy smooch. Right on the lips. If that wasn't enough exhibitionism, she smooshed my head to her double-Ds and held it there. "You and I need to spend more girl-on-girl time."

I wasn't sure that was quite what she meant.

The couple with six children seated closest to us stopped in mid-chew to gawk. The mother intensified her judgmental glare. Several seconds passed. Not only was I wilting with embarrassment, but I was having trouble breathing.

I slapped the table to signal for help. "I need air!"

"Oh, geez. Sorry, Sam." She released me. Planting her rump down in the booth, she wiggled into a comfortable position. "Did you bring the goods? I've been working so much lately—I'm feeling sex-starved."

The oldest of the couple's kids, a lanky dark-haired boy of about fourteen, stared at Selma, both of his hands still clamped on his hamburger. Mayo was oozing out the sides to fall in drips and globs onto the table. His mom jabbed an elbow into his ribs. He winced.

"Stop staring at that hussy and eat your lunch," she barked.

His face went scarlet red. All the other children kept their eyes on their meals. But the husband slipped Selma a smile and waggled his eyebrows.

"Hey there, darlin'." Selma blew him a kiss. "Nice to see ya. Been a while, hasn't it?"

The man's wife cleared her throat. When her husband feigned an innocent look, she kicked him in the shin. He stifled a grunt of pain.

"Do you actually know him?" I whispered. "Or were you just teasing?"

"Honey, I never tease. That would be mean. That's the assistant pastor at the Baptist church over in Oil City. Only reason I know is 'cause I was a bridesmaid in one of my old classmate's weddings. It was her fourth trip down the aisle. But yep, that's Bartholomew

Esterline. He married Taylor and Taylor in July last year."

"Taylor and Taylor? Sounds like a fashion brand. That must be confusing."

"No, what's confusing is that they just had a baby—little Taylor."

"Boy or girl?"

"I don't remember. Coulda been either, I s'pose. Anywho, you got what I came for?"

"Sure do." I pulled the bag to me. Selma put her hands out. "But first you need to tell me your"—I used the air quotes—"*big* secret."

Pouting, she pulled her hands to her chest. "No fair, Sam. You promised me that book *months* ago. I've been awfully darn patient."

I peeked inside the bag. "Mmm, I don't know."

"C'mon, Sam."

"How bad do you want it?"

"You *know* I want it."

"How bad?" I bit my lower lip.

"Really bad, Sam. Now c'mon."

I slid my hand inside the bag, then pulled it back out.

"Give it to me—now!" she shouted so loud even the chick behind the counter with the nose piercing turned to stare. Eyes narrowed, Selma planted the tips of her fake nails on the table, fingers curled. One slash and she'd leave a mark like Wolverine. "You *owe* me."

All the conversation in the place had stopped dead. Simon & Garfunkel's "The Sound of Silence" was playing over the speaker system.

I slid the book across the table to her, face down. "Here you go."

She snatched it to her, then flipped the cover open. "Signed?"

I pointed to my illegible scrawl. "As promised."

"We're good then." Selma flipped to page one, immediately starting to read. Eventually, people stopped staring. Another family came in, and the chick behind the counter took their order.

THREATS AND THREADS

I tapped my paper-wrapped straw on the page to get her attention. "And now *your* secret."

She scrunched her eyebrows. "Here? Now?"

"Well, yeah."

"I can't."

"Why not?"

"First of all, you promised me this book months ago. You were ablated."

I blinked. "Excuse me. I was what?"

"Ablated."

Pretty sure the last time I heard that word it had a medical connotation. I took my phone out, connected to the Wi-Fi, and searched *ablated*, which led me to *ablation—to remove by surgery, melting, or erosion*. I pondered that one some more. *Ablated, ablated*. Sounds like... amalgamated? No, that didn't make sense. Abated? Maybe I could ask her to use it in a sentence again.

This was driving me nuts. I tried to focus on the sounds coming out of her mouth.

"Sam, I thought you were getting me an autographed copy of S.A. Mack's book because we were friends, not because you wanted to bribe me. A promise is a promise."

Obligated!

If deciphering Selma's malapropisms was a game show, I'd be out in the first few rounds, but I was slowly catching on.

"You're the one who told me you had a secret to share," I pointed out.

She twisted the beads of her necklace around two fingers. "Okay, okay. Just not..."—her gaze slid around the room—"here. You know how the grapevine is in this town."

True. Wilton was one giant, twisty grapevine. Sneeze at noon and the rumor mill had you dead of pneumonia before sundown. Get audited? By the time that tidbit made a full round, word on the street was that you'd been indicted for tax evasion and money laundering. Go to the doctor to have a wart removed? Must be herpes—and you probably got it from working in a secret bordello in a room above the donut shop.

"Okay, then when?" I asked.

"Next time we're alone, 'kay? I promise I'll tell you."

"How alone? Like, could you tell me out in the parking lot after we're done here?"

Taking a humongous bite of her sandwich, she stared me down. She wasn't leaking anything. At least not right now.

"All right. Later then." I added a packet of sugar to my iced tea, then stirred with my now-unwrapped straw. "How's Dylan?"

She half-coughed, half-choked on her food.

"Are you okay?"

"I'm..."—she coughed again, then dragged in a lungful of air—"fine."

I waited until she was breathing normally again, or almost. "And Dylan? How's he doing?"

She averted her eyes.

Aha! I'd hit the nail on the head. I couldn't remember a moment in the last several months that Selma hadn't gushed about her tattooed, muscle-shirted, biker sugar daddy. If the saying 'Love is blind' had a poster child, it was Selma. Dylan Hawkins was a womanizer. He had a roving eye and my run-in with him at the lodge was proof of that. But if you pointed out his flaws to Selma, she'd usually just defend him all the more. Secretly, I hoped their relationship was on the rocks because she'd finally wised up, but I couldn't say anything of the sort.

"Have you not seen him lately?"

She shrugged. "I'd rather not talk about him right now."

This was baffling. "What *do* you want to talk about then?"

She thought about it. Which took a while. Finally, a tiny smile lit her face. "I heard you were joining Cleora's book club."

"Just thinking about it. Anyway, how did you hear? Cleora just told me about it yesterday."

"This is Wilton, remember?"

"Right. So do you belong to it?"

"Heck no! Too uppity for me. But since they're going to talk about Mack's books, I was thinking about jumping in. Just for a little bit." She took a few more bites of her sandwich. "Hey, wanna carpool?"

I hated pointing out the obvious, but— "Cleora lives just a few streets over from me. I was going to walk there if I—"

"Great! I'll save you a seat then. It'll be fun, Sam. Us two besties, talking love stories."

"Sounds like a barrel of monkeys."

"How well do you know Mack, Sam? Like… is she nice or stuck-up? Does she have a sense of humor or is she all business? Does she have big hair and wear stylish clothes, like me"—I had to bite my tongue on that point— "or does she wear her hair in a bun and dress like a librarian? And I'm not talking about the kind you see in porn flicks with the tight blouses unbuttoned down to here"—she held her hand just above her navel—"and the short, short skirts that come up to here." She moved her hand to an inch below where a modest person's panty line would be.

"Guess I'd say she dresses casually." I tugged the zipper up higher on my well-worn hoodie. It was chilly in here. Thank goodness I had on my thickest sweatpants and an old pair of leggings underneath.

"And? What else?"

"She's… nice. I'm not sure what else to tell you, Sel. Except she's serious about her work and loves her readers. S.A. Mack believes in true love."

Even as I hoped that would satisfy her, the irony of using the words 'true love' struck me. Those e-mails had been disturbing. Even though there hadn't been any additional ones this morning, I dreaded hitting send/receive now.

"What does S.A. stand for? Give me a clue, will you? Let's start with the 'S'—Suzanne, Suzy, Saffron, Stacy, Sophia, Serenity, Shalonda… Tell me if I'm getting warm."

"Could be anything. Might not even be her real name, you know. She's very close-mouthed about her private life."

"Hey! Your first name's Samantha. Maybe that's hers, too. Say, did you ever tell me what your middle name is?"

"No, and I don't think you ever told me yours."

"I don't have one. Momma said she couldn't come up with anything on the spot. Can you believe that? She had nine months to think about it. Well, five actually, since she didn't know she was pregnant until she couldn't get her bell bottoms on anymore. Anyway, I bet *you* have a middle name, right? Tell me what letter it starts with, and I'll try to guess. Go ahead."

Before she could badger it out of me and put two and two together, I drained my iced tea and steered the conversation in another direction. "Hey, I have a favor to ask."

"You know I'd do anything for my BFF. What is it?"

Thank goodness she was easily distracted. "I'm going out of town this weekend. Back to Chicago to empty out my storage unit. I need someone to watch Bump. Do you suppose—"

"Nope, can't."

"Oh." Her abrupt refusal left me momentarily reeling. It wasn't like Selma to turn down a friend in need, especially not twice in as many days. She had to have a good reason. "Why not? I figured you liked Bump."

"Honey, I love that dog of yours. You know I do. And if he weren't a walking dust bunny, I'd have one just like him. But my work schedule is crazy lately. I'm pulling twelve-hour shifts. It wouldn't be fair to him." She jerked her head to the left and down a little to peer at the clock in the grill area of the restaurant. "Oh no, I'm going to be late. Sorry, gotta go." She wrapped her sandwich in a napkin, dropped it in her purse, and grabbed her drink.

As she shimmied from the booth, I glanced at the clock, too. It hadn't even been fifteen minutes. "Go where?"

"Work. Where else would I go?"

"But isn't this Jourdane's shift?"

"She quit."

"Quit?"

"Yeah, just up and quit. Over the phone. No notice. Turns out that dressing up in leather and chainmail for Coma Con pays more than being a grocery clerk."

"You mean Comic Con?"

"That's what I said."

I'd clearly heard her say *Coma* Con.

With a flourish of her hands, Selma tossed her unfinished meal in the trash and clomped out the door.

Fine. I'd just stalk her at work and catch her in the back alley while she was having a smoke break.

Meanwhile, I still had to figure out what to do with Bump this weekend. My dad was jaunting off on a romantic holiday, Selma was working overtime, and Tara couldn't care for him with her broken arm. There wasn't a kennel in this county that I knew of.

I perused the contacts on my phone. Asking Cleora would be presumptuous, given that we barely knew each other. I was sure Clint would watch him, but I was trying to keep my distance from him out of respect for Archer.

Archer, of course. He could stay at my house while he kept an eye on Bump. I dialed him. It immediately went to voice mail. Then I remembered he was still on shift. If he was on a call, he wouldn't even have his phone with him.

I had four days to find a dog sitter. Plenty of time.

chapter 8

"Archer?" Phone glued to my ear, I flopped onto the couch. Tara was upstairs getting ready for bed after a long session of me typing up an essay for her government class as she dictated it to me. I figured I had a less than a five-minute reprieve before she called for me to help her into her pajamas. "Sorry about leaving so many messages, but I was hoping you'd be able to check them during a break. I know it's a big favor to ask, but it would mean a lot to—"

"I... I can't, Sam," he said. A pause, during which a brittle silence extended to something very, very fragile. "I'd be happy to dog sit, but, unfortunately, I won't be in town."

I sat up. Stared out the picture window. Saw nothing but darkness. "Why not? I mean, where are you going?"

"The big guys at Cirrus Software want me to sit in on a conference this weekend that the foundation is associated with. It has to do with approaching the opioid problem at a community level, figuring out how it even starts, what factors play into it, what sectors are the most vulnerable... and also what to do about it, like opening up treatment centers."

He went on to explain how there would be other conferences and meetings, visits to centers and communities grappling with the issue around the country. The more he talked, the more I realized this wasn't just a weekend thing like my conference.

So I pointed out the obvious. Because he seemed to be avoiding it. "But your job at the fire department? A weekend is one thing. This sounds like something more permanent."

"Maybe. It all depends..." Another silence descended. Stayed there so long the chasm between us just got wider and deeper. He finally bridged it. "Sam, I know how unhappy you'd be about me being gone a lot. That's what makes this so hard. I know I turned them down before when they asked me to speak on a circuit, but this... well, it made me realize I don't want to just stand behind a podium and talk to strangers—I want to help *people*. People whose names and stories I'd come to know."

"So you feel pretty strongly about this?"

"If there was just me to consider, I wouldn't hesitate. But things are different now. There's you. I want to know what you think."

He'd struggled with it, I could tell. I was struggling, too.

"Archer, honey... you *need* to do this. I know you do. And I'd follow you around the world. I can take my work anywhere. But I can't do that to Tara. I uprooted her just this summer. She needs to stay in one place for a while." If I had to choose between my family and my boyfriend, the choice was clear. Still, that didn't make deciding any easier. "I'll be here whenever you come home. And I'll join you when I can. Maybe not as often as I'd like, but..."

"If it goes well, I'm thinking of quitting the fire department altogether and making the development of treatment centers my full-time job."

"Oh." It was almost like someone had just punched me in the gut. I found it so hard to breathe I had to force the words out. "I'd hoped this was going to be temporary. That you'd just be taking a leave of absence. Why quit the department? I thought you loved your work there."

He didn't hesitate. "Something happened today."

That 'something' had caused a shift in his outlook. Knowing how much pride he took in his work, it had to be big.

After a heavy pause, he explained, "We were called to an apartment complex on the east side of town this morning. You know the place? The ones over by Liberty Drive?"

"On the side street between the car wash and the used car lot?"

"That one, yeah. Sometimes, they'll call us if it's a medical emergency and the closest ambulances are tied up elsewhere. Which they were. So we went, Marco and me, because we're both trained in CPR and trauma, and... You don't expect things like that in Wilton. I mean, you pass people on the street, see them in the grocery store, and you never think that kind of thing is going on here. But it is. And it's getting worse and worse. Everywhere. Even here."

There was so much angst in his voice I couldn't help but feel his pain, too. "What is? What's getting worse, Archer?"

"Heroin, Fentanyl..."

I'd seen segments on the Fort Wayne and Indianapolis news stations about the growing epidemic and how it was reaching into rural and small-town America. The effects were devastating and often deadly.

"A neighbor had called because he heard the two kids crying. He could see them through the window, but one was a baby and the other maybe only two. He was positive he'd seen both parents return home a few hours earlier, but nobody would answer the door. The manager couldn't get in because the deadbolt was locked. We had to break the door open. The kids had dirty diapers, hadn't eaten..." His words trailed away.

"Did you find the parents, Archer?"

A somber pause. "In the bathroom. One dead, one almost. The dad... the guy—I don't know if he was their dad or not—he'll live. But he's pretty messed up. Funny thing is, I remember him from high school. He was a couple of years younger than me, so you probably wouldn't have known him. But he was just a regular guy. Played in the band, got decent grades, ran track."

"Any idea what happened along the way?"

"We spoke to some neighbors afterward. He'd gotten painkillers a few years ago for a work-related back injury. Got hooked on them. And when the doctor wouldn't give him any more, he got what he needed on the streets."

Sadly, it wasn't a unique story. Archer knew better than anyone how drugs changed people, robbing them of reason. "Where are the kids now?"

"Foster care. At least until social services locates some decent relatives."

I knew it was the kids who affected Archer most of all. He'd lost his own daughter, Everly, as a result of his ex's addictions, and he'd spent every day of his life since then trying to save lives because he somehow felt responsible.

"Archer, you were there for the kids. But you can't save everyone. Don't beat yourself up about it."

"I'm not. And you're right about not being able to save everyone, but—"

Here it came. The locomotive. The avalanche of regrets and guilt.

"I have to do *something*. And I know what it is. As a first responder, sure, I save people. But sometimes, I get there too late. After the fact. I want to keep it from ever happening in the first place. I *have* to do this. For all the Everlys out there."

I couldn't fight this anymore. Even as much as I'd tried to wish it away. "Archer?"

"Yes, Sam?"

"I hate that you're going. I wish you could stay. But I understand, I really do. And I'm proud of you for doing it."

Because what good was it being in love with a hero if he didn't have someone to save?

A faint sniff. An indrawn breath. He cleared his throat. "Thanks, Sam. That means more than you could ever know."

And that was what I would have to remember when I was sitting here all alone in the months to come.

I was still holding the phone after Archer had hung up when Tara came blazing down the stairs. Her hair might as well have been on fire.

"Why didn't you tell me?" she screeched.

"What?"

She clasped a hand to her throat, gulping in air. Before I could get to her, she crumpled to her knees, her forehead touching the floor.

I rushed to her, then laid a hand on her back. "What do you mean, Tara? Tell me."

"The... robber." Her breaths were coming in rapid pants, her words becoming more and more spaced. "Cooper John... told me... that someone... tried... to..."

We were on the verge of a meltdown. I had to break through before I completely lost her.

"Tell you what?" I asked, although I already suspected what she'd say. Pressing my hands to either side of her face, I lifted it. Her eyes had that far-off gaze. "Tara, look at me. Look. At. Me."

She stared blankly into my eyes.

"Stay with me, pumpkin. Stay with me." I smoothed a stray lock from her face to tuck it behind her ear. "Can you understand me?"

No response.

"Tara!"

She blinked once, twice.

She was hanging on by a thread. If I let her go there, slip all the way, it would take an awfully long time to get her back. These panic attacks, her childhood therapist had speculated, were a symptom of post-traumatic stress—the result of when she'd been in the backseat of the car during the accident that had killed her father.

THREATS AND THREADS

I placed a hand underneath her chin, pulling down gently to open her mouth more. "Tara, Tara... I want you to take a deep breath, okay? Can you do that, pumpkin?"

She took a longer breath. Not deeper yet, but she was trying.

"Again, deep breath," I told her. "Deeper now, deeper."

She took a big breath, held it.

"Don't forget to breathe out."

She blew air out so forcefully it almost seemed to startle her.

It was five minutes later before she was back with me.

"You heard someone tried to break in here?"

Tara nodded faintly.

"And you're afraid they'll come back?"

"Y-y-yes."

I wanted to tell her they wouldn't, that the police had them locked up in prison. But I couldn't tell her any of that. I couldn't even tell her not to be afraid, because I was, too.

Bump, who'd been doing his business in the backyard, squeezed through the doggie door, took one look at Tara, and galloped toward her, pulling up just in time to avoid a wipeout. He snuffled at Tara's head, her ears, her eyes, then licked great slobbery licks all over her face and the hand of her good arm.

The tiniest of smiles lifted the corners of Tara's mouth.

"Whoever it was," I said. "Bump scared them away. They didn't hurt me or take anything. Bump did his job."

She wrapped her arms around his neck and hugged him hard. "You'll always protect us, won't you, buddy?"

Bump woofed.

"I love you, you big goof."

He gave that half-yodel, half-moan kind of Husky sound. But I swear he said "I love you" back.

Then Tara giggled, and together they collapsed in a wrestling heap of fur and limbs.

I DIDN'T SLEEP WELL that night. Tara's panic attacks, if given reason to return in force, could be debilitating for her. Although I knew I couldn't shield her from the world forever, she was still my baby. Always would be.

Then there was my relationship with Archer. As much as I tried to tell myself that he and I were the grown-up equivalent of two high school sweethearts going off to different colleges who would reunite after graduation, there was too much about our situation that was open-ended. When was he leaving? For how long and how often? When would he be back for good? So like any imaginative worrywart, I feared the worst—that he might never return to sleepy little Wilton.

Unwilling to let myself think about it one minute longer, I took Bump for a walk earlier than usual the next morning, letting him lead the way. Tara was at school, probably garnering sympathy from her teachers and getting out of a few tests. Usually at this point in the day, I'd still be in my PJs, frumping at the computer with a strong cup of a coffee and a piece of well-done toast slathered in Nutella, trying to gather the motivation to get in the shower. Today, however, I'd awoken with a sense of urgency. To do what, I had no idea, but lying in bed wouldn't accomplish anything.

Bump took us straight to Fancy's doorstep.

"Aww, pining for your girlfriend? Sorry, buddy." I stroked his back. He studied me with hopeful eyes. "We can't just show up here whenever we please. But Cleora said you and Fancy can romp around in the backyard every Sunday, as well as when the book club meeting is going on, okay? I'll stay as long as I can bear it—just for you."

I tugged him along. Somehow, he managed to walk forward while gazing longingly backward for almost a block.

My phone rang. The number wasn't in my contacts, but I

answered anyway.

"Miss McNamee? This is Deputy Strewing, checking in. Have you had any more trouble?"

I contemplated whether to tell him about the strange e-mails, but I decided not to. As disturbing as they were, there was nothing criminal about them. "No, been pretty quiet, thankfully."

"Good to hear."

"My daughter doesn't own any knit clothes in dark green, so the piece of yarn you found couldn't have been hers. Any other leads?"

"Coming up empty, unfortunately. No neighbors have come forward to report anything unusual and no other break-ins in the area recently."

I thanked him for touching bases, and we said goodbye. Bump and I turned a corner, heading for home.

Temperatures had stayed low enough there was still snow on the ground. Snow was pretty, but I was more than over it now. My fingers were so cold I could barely bend them. It hurt to breathe. And my nose felt like it would snap off if I so much as wiped it. If I didn't *have* to walk the dog, I'd be in hibernation.

"Pssst."

A shiver tickled my spine. I swiveled my head around, but I didn't see anybody.

"Pssssssstttt!"

I walked faster.

"Hey, it's me," came a loud whisper.

Against my better judgment, I stole a glance.

The dry branches of a nearby hedge rustled. A black-clad figure squeezed through a thin patch.

Relief flooded my chest. "Harmon?"

Looking over his shoulder, he pressed a finger to his lips. "Shh. I don't want Maybelle to know I'm talking to you."

I lowered my voice. "Oh, right. Sorry. How are you doing,

Harmon?"

"Good enough, considering that witch I have to put up with." It seemed a little out of character for him to speak so boldly about her, but then again, maybe he was beginning to feel more at ease with me. That or he'd finally had enough of Maybelle's browbeating. "Did they ever figure out who tried to rob your place?"

I shook my head. "I just got off the phone with the deputy who took the report. He figures it was probably a one-off. I'm guessing someone looking for money for drugs. Unfortunately, no leads and no suspects yet. Which is probably more disturbing than the fact that it happened at all."

"I bet. Someone stole a sweatshirt of mine from the Y once. I could never look at folks the same way afterward. Anyway, I hope the hoodlum ends up in jail. Terrible thing to happen to a nice gal like you." He stared at me for an uncomfortably long time. I reminded myself that what Harmon lacked in social graces, he made up for in sentiment.

"Thanks, Harmon." I angled away from him, trying desperately through body language to indicate I had places to go, things to do. It wasn't that I didn't like the guy. I did. He was just so odd, in a sad but loveable way. "I'll, uh, see you around, then. Tara should be home from school soon, so..."

He shuffled closer. "Didn't mean to interrupt. Just wanted to have a look at the dog, seeing as how I'm not allowed to have one myself." Crouching, he extended his hand to Bump. "Mind if I say hi?"

Bump had already curled around to present his butt to Harmon. I was stuck until they greeted each other properly.

"No, go right ahead."

Which commenced a five-minute session of butt scratches by Harmon and a medley of monkey sounds from Bump. The guy really did like dogs. And Bump *really* liked him. Which made me think—

THREATS AND THREADS

"Say, Harmon. I'm kind of in a bind and... and I'm wondering if you could help me out? I have to go away this weekend, and I don't have anyone to watch Bump. He'd be fine in the house by himself most of the day, but I could really use someone to feed him in the morning and at night... Oh, and make sure the doggie door is closed at night. Someone is supposed to be installing an alarm system. I'm not exactly sure when that's going to happen, but until then, I'd also need you to do a walk-through of the house when you're there, just to make sure no one has broken in. If you see anything fishy at all, call me right away. Oh... you do have a cell phone, don't you? I never thought to ask."

Harmon was still crouching before Bump, staring at him with a glazed look. The hand he'd used to scratch Bump's neck was still, positioned over his collar.

"Harmon?" When the use of his name brought no reaction, I touched him lightly on the shoulder. "Harmon, did you hear any of what I said?"

Sputtering, he stood. "Y-y-yes. I heard it. All of it."

"And? Can you?"

"I'd... love to..." He eyes flicked to mine, then fell away.

"But?" I prompted.

"Maybelle." Standing, he huffed out several exasperated breaths. His forehead was beaded with sweat, even though it couldn't have been more than thirty degrees outside.

Right, Maybelle. Which begged a question— "Harmon, why wouldn't Maybelle let you take care of my dog for a few days? We're neighbors. I'll pay you thirty dollars a day. And if you guys ever go away, I'd be more than happy to check your mailbox and take care of Maybelle's bird. Or let you borrow anything you need—loan you a cup of sugar, a yard tool, my lawnmower. Isn't that what neighbors do? I'm not trying to make you feel guilty, honest. Just trying to figure out why she keeps you on such a short leash."

He studied his scuffed-up black sneakers with a confused sort of intensity. Like the answer to my question was written on his laces in Sanskrit.

When he finally spoke, it was barely above a whisper. "Because you're a... you know."

"No, I don't. What am I?"

"A... w-w-woman."

I looked up and down the street. "At least half the people in this neighborhood are women. Are you not allowed to talk to any of them?"

He gave a weak shrug. "Just... not the pretty ones."

My heart halfway melted. Still, it wasn't right. Not even remotely. "Harmon, don't you think you should be able to talk to whomever you want to? We're just friends after all, right?"

His mouth twitched with the faintest of smiles. "Sure."

"You like Bump, and Bump likes you." To be fair, Bump liked everybody. Some more than others maybe, but he wasn't very particular. I often wished he was more discerning. At least he barked at anything that moved. "You'd like a chance to spend some time with him, wouldn't you?"

He nodded again.

"Could you, maybe, do it without Maybelle knowing?"

His head swiveled. "Oh, no. No, no, no. I don't think so. What if someone saw me at your place and told her?"

"Someone could see us right now."

"That's different. We're on the street. Not meeting in private."

"I won't be at my house when you let him out and feed him."

He pondered it. "Oh, right."

Then Bump tapped him with a paw. When Harmon glanced down, Bump dipped his front end in a play bow and wiggled his butt, before giving a little playful leap. Harmon laughed at his antics as Bump let out a long *A-roo-roo-rooooo*.

THREATS AND THREADS

"Okay," he said, "I'll do it."

"Great!" Although relieved, I was still a little worried. Harmon may have liked Bump, but he certainly wasn't experienced in caring for dogs. I probably should've gone to more effort, checked with one of those online odd job services under 'pet care,' but it was too late to withdraw my offer now. Harmon was practically beaming with anticipation.

"I'm leaving early Friday. I'll put the key under a box on the top shelf just inside the garage. There's only one box, so you won't have to hunt for it. Top shelf, under the cardboard box, okay?" Then I told him when to stop by, morning and night, and started in on other instructions. I hadn't even gotten to how much to feed Bump or where I kept his food when I realized Harmon was becoming thoroughly confused.

"Let me back up a second, all right?" I began.

Harmon nodded slowly.

"You remember where the key is?"

He pulled at his lower lip. Then his pointer finger drifted into the air. "Top shelf. Under the box."

"Right, yes. Okay, when you come later on Friday, get the key, let yourself in the house. I'll leave instructions on the kitchen table. Everything will be written down. Everything. Sound good?"

"Yeah, yeah, I can handle that. But what if there's a problem? I don't have one of those smartphones. I can't call you from my house. Maybelle might find out."

"I'll write my number down on the instruction sheet. Tara's too, in case you need someone closer. Call me from the phone in my kitchen every time you stop by, and if I don't answer, just leave a message. If you use my phone, Maybelle won't know you've called me."

After repeating everything yet again, Harmon and I said goodbye. Before I dropped Tara off at the Mullinses on Thursday night, I'd fill her in and tell her to call Clint in case an emergency arose with Bump. But only as a last resort.

Tara's situation was taken care of. Bump had a dog sitter. And some guy named Marco was coming to install an alarm system eventually. All I needed to do was rent a small trailer in Chicago after I cleared my storage out to tow my stuff home with. Easy-peasy pumpkin pie.

At home, I called the storage facility and confirmed the code for getting onto the property. Then I searched trailer rentals on the internet. I booked one from a place just a few miles from the storage unit. After that, I went over the topics for the panel discussion on Saturday, making sure I had plenty of witty and meaningful material at hand to leave a lasting impression. I'd spoken at a couple of retreats before, but nothing this big. I was as excited as I was terrified.

I even managed to pack a suitcase—because it was good to stay busy. As long as I was busy, my mind didn't have a chance to roam. Everything was in order. What an odd feeling that was. It almost seemed like I had to be forgetting something, but no matter how many times I ran through everything in my head, I came up empty.

chapter 9

I STARED INTO AN empty coffee cup, willing it to spontaneously refill itself. Nope, didn't work. Admitting defeat, I crammed my feet into a pair of Tara's fuzzy slippers and trudged from my office to the kitchen. On autopilot, I scooped the coffee grounds into the paper filter and filled up the reservoir. Ten seconds later, my life force began flowing into the coffee pot. As soon as it reached the two-cup level, I filled my mug and inhaled, my senses awakening fully.

Archer had called a couple of nights ago, apologetically explaining that everything with Everly's Foundation was now on fast forward. They'd booked him on a flight bound for San Francisco for today. I'd tried to sound happy for him, but I doubt he was any more convinced than I was. Since he was due to end his shift at the firehouse in less than an hour, I'd gotten up early so I could raid Wilton's one and only donut store to join him in a celebratory send-off.

While I sipped and waited for my brain to wake up, I partook of my usual morning ritual—checking and purging my messages, then a dose of online surfing to catch up with the happenings of the world outside my tranquil bit of domesticity. Working at home was both a blessing and a curse. I got to set my own hours, yes. The problem was that nobody ever thought twice about interrupting my schedule.

Which I discovered for the thousandth time as Tara appeared in the doorway to my office in a state of bourgeoning panic.

"I'm going to be late," she whined.

"Why?" My point was she should've gotten up earlier, given her circumstances, but, clearly, she hadn't quite figured this all out yet.

"Because I'm broken, that's why." Her shoulders sloped dramatically to the right. She glanced down at her cast, sniffed, and wiped a tear from her cheek. "And I need help."

"I'll be up in five minutes to help you into your clothes."

"Great. Another day in sweats. I'll fit right in with the trailer trash of Wilton's west side."

"I could help you into your jeans. But then, you couldn't go to the bathroom all day long. Unless Shannon wants to help zip you up every time you take a potty break."

"We're not *that* close." Tara didn't move. Just jutted her lip out. "And my hair. I can't do anything with my hair. Will you do a French braid for me?"

"How about a regular braid? My manual dexterity's not all that good."

"You type for a living, Mom."

It took all my self-restraint not to correct her. I usually didn't become fully civil until after two cups of coffee, a hot shower, and a walk around the block with Bump. But she was my only child and out of sorts because of her broken arm, so I cut her some slack and put on a cheery face, my cheeks almost cracking with the strain. "Trust me, you don't want me doing anything complicated with your hair. It would look like a cornrow job performed by an uncoordinated octopus."

Tara blew out a puff of air, lifting her overgrown bangs back from her forehead. "Fine. But you'll at least apply some eyeshadow for me? I look like Casper the Unfriendly Ghost."

"Sure, pumpkin. But since when did you start wearing makeup?"

THREATS AND THREADS

"Months ago, Mom. You'd know if you were paying any attention."

Right. About the same time Cooper John entered the picture. I saw the two of them talking when I picked her up from the French Club meeting last week. He was standing awfully close to her at the time. Of course, when I'd questioned her about him, she'd denied everything. I still contended that her being a freshman and him a senior was too much of an age difference at this stage.

Before she left to go upstairs, she added, "Oh, I think I'm going to miss the bus, by the way. Can you drop me off at school?"

"Sure." After all, I had nothing else to do besides type all day. I could pick up the donuts after that.

Once she schlepped off, I downloaded my messages, dreading to look at my inbox as it filled up. Turned out, there was nothing out of the ordinary. I was both relieved and wary that I hadn't heard from TrueLuv2000 in a couple of days. Maybe she'd moved on to trolling someone else.

After I added a couple of ice cubes to my coffee so I could chug it, I hopped in the shower and got dressed. I helped Tara into the same oversized sweatshirt I'd worn when Jake Taylor had trampled my wrist, then twisted her hair into a semi-neat braid. After letting Bump back inside and double-checking that the dog door was securely shut, I grabbed my purse to leave.

An urgent chirp rang out. I twirled around, searching for the source. It took a few seconds for it to register that it was the landline, since we'd gone several months without a home phone. I'd only added it because my dad insisted I get one, saying I purposely avoided answering him on my cell phone. That wasn't really true. I didn't always carry it on me when I was at home, because I liked not being enslaved by it twenty-four-seven. In the end, I'd caved. Some things weren't worth the fight.

The caller ID said 'Unavailable'. Even though I was in a hurry, I picked it up on the off chance the readout was an error and it was my dad after all.

"Hello?"

Silence echoed. I almost hung up, but thought I heard the faintest indrawn breath on the other end.

"Dad, is that you? Is everything okay?"

"No, it's not."

The voice... it definitely wasn't my dad's. It didn't even sound like anyone I could place. "Who is this, and what are you talking about?"

"It's me... and you know what."

That didn't help at all. I honestly couldn't tell if it was a man or woman. They sounded like they were talking underwater. "'Me who?"

A long pause. Static.

Finally, in a forlorn voice, "Why didn't you ever write back?"

My heart thumped. It was TrueLuv. I wanted to ask how she'd gotten this number and why she was calling me, but I decided to play dumb. "I... I don't know what you're talking about. Write you? Can you be more specific?"

A psychotic laugh bored into my eardrum. "Good one."

It was a woman. Or a man who could imitate one very well. "Who is this again?"

"Every reader you ever screwed," she said bitterly.

"I still don't know what you're talking about." *Deny, deny, deny.* The three elements to evading the truth. "Who are you trying to reach?"

"You, Samantha."

A shockwave of cold fear hit me. Of course. If she'd figured out my home phone number, she had to know who it belonged to. But how? There were only a couple of people in the world who could connect my name with what I did.

I could hang up now and call the sheriff to let him know I had a certifiably insane stalker, or I could figure this out myself. So far, it was just some disgruntled, slightly unhinged fan. My life hadn't been threatened. I decided not to blow it out of proportion. "Look, I still have no idea who you are, but what exactly do you want?"

"A better ending."

Before I could interrogate her further, she hung up.

I stared at my reflection in the window above the sink. The bride of Frankenstein stared back. I flipped up the lever on the spigot, then splashed warm water on my face. Not that I needed waking up. I just didn't want Tara to see how near death I looked.

"IT WOULD BE EASIER if you spent tonight and tomorrow at the Mullinses," I told Tara. We'd finally worked our way up in the drop-off lane at school.

She picked her backpack up from the floor of the car one-handed. "Why? I thought you weren't leaving until the end of the week."

A truck honked from behind us. I resisted flashing the bird in my rearview. Tara did it for me, right out in full view.

"Don't do that," I snapped. "Haven't you ever heard of road rage?"

"Mom, it's the school parking lot, not I-90 at rush hour in Chicago. Anyway, you know you wanted to do it."

"That's beside the point. You could get in trouble for doing that on school grounds."

"They'd have to give half the school detention then. Besides, it's just Nelson Hooten and his alcoholic dad. Nelson's always getting in fights. Nobody would believe him."

"Just ask Shannon if it's okay," I said, attempting to get back to the subject. "I have a lot to do between now and then." I couldn't tell her the real reason why, but she'd totally buy me needing some free time to get stuff done.

"Sure, Mom." She fought a sneer. "I love you, too."

"Love you, pumpkin." I blew her a kiss, then motioned for her to shut the door.

She slung the backpack over her good shoulder, rolled her eyes at me, then bumped the door shut with her hip.

Nelson Hooten's dad honked his truck horn again. I shifted into reverse, purposefully tapping his bumper. Then, prepping for my getaway, I shifted back into drive. Window down, I stuck an arm out and yelled, "Sorry!"

Letting off the brake, I punched the accelerator. The engine revved, but the car didn't move. Behind me, the truck's gears clunked into place. I moved the shifter, just to make sure I'd put it in drive and not park. Same damn thing. Frick.

Knuckles beat at my passenger window. My heart nearly stopped. It was Nelson Hooten's dad—camouflage hunting vest, short sleeves rolled up to his shoulders, tattooed biceps, and the requisite Wilton-style boxy baseball cap, complete with grease stains.

"You're flooding it, sweetheart," he said in a beer-laden drawl. "Give it a sec, then slowly depress the accelerator. Might also want to have your transmission checked if it keeps acting up."

"Uh, thanks." I smiled nervously.

"No problem."

I was about to roll the window up when he stuck his hand through the open crack to grasp the window's edge.

"Oh, and next time... don't dally in the drop-off lane. Never know who you'll tick off."

He wasn't smiling.

Eyes ahead, I did as he'd told me. The car crept forward, the RPMs way above what they should have been. I was half a mile from the school when the car finally started picking up steam. By then, I was only a block from Donnie's Donuts, so I coasted into the parking lot. I ran inside and loaded up with an assortment of two dozen sugar bombs, as Dad called them.

It took a few encouraging pats and a 'C'mon baby, you know I still love you' before the engine sputtered to life. I'd written off my car's recent temperamental issues on the cold snap. Now I was beginning to wonder if there wasn't something more serious going on under the hood. I sure hoped not. A new car might delay me making an offer on the house we were renting from Melissa.

At any rate, since I didn't have time to drive the car to Fullbright and have it looked at before my trip, or Dan's Tire Service even, I'd just have to hope for the best and do it once I returned next week.

After I pulled into the fire station, I reluctantly put the wagon in park and switched it off.

"Just stay with me the next few days, all right?" I stroked the dashboard like an old lover, recalling all the memories we'd shared—the move from a rundown apartment to one in a more respectable neighborhood, then to an upscale suburban development, the drive-in movies, the soccer and T-ball games I'd insisted Tara try her hand at, the Midwest snowstorms… This bucket of rust and I had a history of being faithful to one another. I wasn't ready to leave all that behind yet.

Gathering my faith, I shoved the door open and went inside, the two donut boxes clutched protectively to my chest.

"Heeeyyy. 'Bout time you showed up with the goods." A man with a shaved head pulled me into a hug. Then he twirled me around, flipped the lid of one box up, and grabbed a donut in each hand. "Ah, you remembered—my favorite!"

"What kind is that, Marco?" Archer asked as he mopped the sweat from his forehead with a hand towel, then draped it around his neck.

"All of them." Marco winked, taking a bite of chocolate-covered cake donut. "Never met a donut I didn't love."

I gave Archer a WTF-look, and he laughed under his breath. "Marco, this is Sam. Sam, Marco. I told him you were bringing breakfast. He's been hangry all morning."

"Marco, huh? So you're the part-time alarm installer?" I steadied myself with a hand against the wall. I was still dizzy from his moves.

He wolfed down half a Bismark in two bites. "Yeah, I do all that kind of stuff. Locks, doors, security systems, cameras. Archer here was telling me you need some work done?"

"I do. How much for a basic alarm system?"

In between bites, Marco proceeded to query me about how many windows and doors I had and what kind of system I needed. The quote he gave was more than reasonable. By the time he'd finished off six donuts, I actually liked him. After I gave him a spare key, Marco told me he'd stop by the house over the weekend in between some other projects for a preview.

A cluster of Mylar balloons was tied to a leg of the dining table in the break room and a hand-painted banner that said, 'Good luck, Boss-man!' hung on the wall next to the fridge. On the counter beneath it lay a card with a dozen signatures.

Two other firefighters ambled into the room, then offered handshakes to Archer. After a series of awkward, yet sentimental exchanges and some backslapping, Archer escorted me into a small office. He turned the lock before drawing down the blinds.

I sat in the chair behind the desk. He sat in the one beside it. For a long while, we stared at each other, neither knowing what to say. Words weren't enough.

Archer scooted his chair closer to mine, leaned in to kiss me, and brushed his lips against mine. It was his breath I was aware of more than anything. A whisper of air—invisible, gentle, and life-giving. The warmth of it. The promises unspoken. I wanted to draw his breath inside me. Hold it there forever.

THREATS AND THREADS

Breaking away, he got up and flicked the overhead light off. Returned to his chair. Then, in the muted indoor light that pried between the slats of the blinds, I felt… his fingertips light across my cheek, my chin, my throat. He kissed me below my collarbone. It was like making out in the basement with your parents upstairs. The excitement was heightened by the danger of discovery. Vaguely aware of men's voices outside in the common area, I kept watching the door for shadows to indicate movement in the hallway, until it became nothing more than background noise of laughter and friendly banter, the clang of equipment being repositioned, and rustle and heft of gear being moved.

There was camaraderie here in concord with purpose. It was hard to imagine him leaving this. But Archer was going to change lives, and, today, he would start a new chapter of his.

Maybe if it had been earlier in our relationship, before we'd realized what we meant to each other, then this wouldn't be so hard. Or maybe if it had been later, when our history was already underway and our roles established, I'd feel more secure about it.

This time, right now, it was fragile and explosive all at once.

As much as I wanted to be with him, in every sense, this wasn't how I'd imagined it being. "Archer, I don't think—"

He silenced me with a kiss, then inclined his head toward the wall behind me. "I only have half an hour before I need to leave for the airport, and I got this wild hair that maybe we could go in there and…"

"In there?" I looked behind me. It took a few moments for my eyes to focus in the dim light. There was a door there, big and bold as the sun, solid, no windows. When we first came in here, it had barely registered in my brain. I suppose I'd assumed it was a closet. "What is that—a supply room?"

"Bunk room. *Private* bunk room. One of the perks of being chief, not that I have many, but I sure do appreciate that one."

I poked a finger at his sternum. "Do you take women in there often?"

"You'd be the first." He was sitting back in his chair now, seeming disappointed we didn't have more time or privacy.

I mirrored his position. "Half an hour, huh?"

He nodded sadly.

I stood. Took his hand. Curled a finger at him. "Then we'd better hurry up."

"I DIDN'T THINK IT would be this hard." He held me to him, his hands stroking my back.

"Again already?" Pulling back, I slapped him playfully on the arm. "We just got done not five minutes ago."

We were now standing in the parking lot of the firehouse, saying our final goodbyes. The guys had snickered when we strolled by hand in hand a few minutes before, keeping their farewells to fist bumps and 'Don't be a stranger, dude.'

"I meant leaving you, Sam." After a kiss on top of my head, he let go. Wintry air sliced between us. "I thought, knowing it wasn't permanent, that it's just for now, that I'd be okay going off on my own for a few weeks… or months. I don't really know how long yet. But now that it's here, I can't imagine, can't believe…" His face twisted with confusion.

I didn't want him to go. But I had to *let* him go. "I'll come see you sometime, make a long weekend of it. Okay?"

"Okay."

Seconds plodded by, each one precious and irretrievable.

"Sam, I, I…"

"What?"

"I love you."

THREATS AND THREADS

Three words, eight letters. But so powerful, eternal. They transcended *everything*. How had we arrived here so quickly, after such a crazy start?

My head on his chest, I placed a hand over his heart. "I love you, too, Archer."

I hadn't said those words to a man in over fifteen years. Before Kyle died. And even then, I couldn't remember the exact day or where we'd been or what we'd been doing the last time I'd spoken them aloud.

But this... I would never forget this moment.

chapter 10

I WAS ONLY HALFWAY home on Route 379 when the engine started to sputter and cough.

"Not now," I pleaded. "Please not now."

This clunker was a veteran. Although, it had served me well, its age was catching up with it. It lurched so hard the back of my skull bopped against the headrest. The lights of the dashboard flickered, flashed, then went out. Instinctively, I glanced from one mirror to another, making sure there were no eighteen-wheelers bearing down on me. Nope, nothing but a pickup that had already passed me going in the other direction and a small car in my lane about a mile back.

While the engine may have gulped its last breath, the steering and brakes still seemed to be in order. Easing down on the brakes, I guided the car over onto the gravel shoulder. When it finally came to a full stop, I listened to the resolute silence of its once-vigorous engine. I turned the key several times, pumped the gas lightly, waited, and tried again. Nothing.

So I did what any person who didn't know a carburetor from a carbuncle would do—I flipped the latch on the hood, got out, and inspected the guts of my car. It was dark. And dirty. And full of hoses and wires and… metal thingies. A manual would've helped, but I'd tossed it years ago when Tara was a toddler and had colored all the pages with magic marker.

The only thing to do now was call a tow truck.

I paused beside the left front tire and, in lieu of cursing, kicked it hard. Just as a car pulled up behind me.

Pain throbbed through my foot. I steadied myself against the driver's side door, plastered on a fake smile, and waited to greet my Good Samaritan. The door of the car behind me opened.

"Aww, shit," I mumbled.

Dr. Danielle Townsley, my former boyfriend's ex-wife, stepped out of her sports car, looking supermodel sexy in her waist-length lab coat. She pulled it tight across her silky salmon-colored blouse to ward off the bite of the wind.

"Car trouble?" She clicked toward me in her silver stilettos. The wind teased at her hair. Instead of whipping it into a tangled mess, it gave her that frolicking bikini-calendar girl look. "Mind if I take a peek?"

I hadn't even answered before she strode past me to brace both hands above the grill and began to study the engine.

"Uh, hi, Danielle." I watched over her shoulder as she unscrewed a cap, then pulled out an oily metal stick. "I'm sorry, but I don't have the manual."

"Not necessary. This car was manufactured before computer chips became the norm." She wiped the stick on a tissue from her pocket, put it back in, then pulled it out again. She returned it before checking another fluid level. "Basic stuff, really, if you understand rudimentary mechanics."

Not a frickin' clue. But I smiled and nodded anyway.

"Your transmission fluid and oil levels are adequate. When is the last time you had them topped off?"

"Uh..." I hadn't had an oil change since I'd moved here, but then, I didn't do much driving on a daily basis. "A couple of thousand miles ago." I said it more like a question, but if she'd picked up on that, she didn't let on.

She glanced underneath the car. "No leaks, so that's not your problem." After jiggling a few wires, she stepped back. "It's like diagnosing a patient. Start with the most likely causes, then by process of elimination, narrow it down. What kind of problems have you been having? Any difficulties with steering, braking, ignition, shifting, etc.?"

"Steering and braking seem to be fine. It starts up okay... unless it's been really cold, in which case it's like waking the dead."

"But once it's warmed up, what then?"

"It's good for a while. If I stop to go into the store and come right out, no problem."

"Shifting?"

"No issues with reverse, but when I first shift into drive... yeah, it struggles. Sticks between gears unless I really gun it."

Her perfectly plucked eyebrows lifted ever so slightly. "Hmm."

That wasn't the good kind of 'hmm'. "What's wrong with it?"

"How many miles on the car?"

"Two hundred and seventeen thousand."

"Ah."

Not the good kind of 'ah' either. Tucking my hands into my armpits, I braced myself for the worst. "Tell me the truth. Is it going to die?"

"Not going to. Is. Partly, anyway."

"Partly?"

"It's your transmission. Look, I opened more than a few manuals and read them before ever going to a mechanic. When those hacks first see a woman, they smell money, figuring most of them don't know a dildo from a dipstick. I may not own all the tools to repair an automobile, but when I seek the services of a professional, I want to know whether they're indeed telling me the truth or are trying to swindle me. But given what you've told me, chances are that if a routine flushing of the transmission doesn't fix it, you're in for a complete overhaul."

"And what's that going to run me?"

"Upward of four grand. Which I'd surmise is more than the vehicle is worth even if it were running properly."

And she would be guessing right. Which ate me up. This is why I hated running into her. She was the prom queen, the student council president, and the class valedictorian all rolled up in one. She probably even had head cheerleader credentials.

Defeated, I slumped against the rear door and covered my face with my hands. The metal was cold against my rump, but it shocked me into clarity of thinking. I had to figure this out. And fast.

"I'm sorry," she said. "Contrary to popular belief, I always hate delivering bad news. But sometimes, there's no other way than to just do it. Unexpected expenses like this can cause undue financial hardship."

Prying my fingers apart, I studied her a moment before lowering my hands. "I have some money saved up, so it's not that, really. Although I had other plans for it. It's more sentimental than anything."

"I understand some people do form attachments to their automobiles."

I glanced at her car. "What, you're not? Like if a semi came along right now, hit a patch of ice, and ran that sparkly toy of yours off the road and crushed it like an aluminum can, you wouldn't be the teensiest bit upset?"

"I'd seek monetary compensation, of course, but there are thousands of other cars just like it. So no, not really. It's replaceable."

This chick was part Vulcan. Or a very convincing android. Not that I was into sports cars, but if someone wrecked a car of mine that cost as much as my first house, I'd shed a few tears. Right now, I was just trying to figure out how to make my schedule work. This had put a real crimp in matters.

I pulled out my phone, then started flipping through contacts.

"Calling a tow truck?" she asked.

"Eventually. Right now, I just need a ride home."

After waiting for a car to pass, she walked toward the driver's side door of her car and motioned to me. "Get in then. I'm headed your way. This road is too busy, and the day is too cold to stand out here and wait."

"Danielle, I—"

"Sam, I saved your life once before, remember? I don't think me offering you a ride home is too farfetched."

I couldn't fight logic, so after closing the hood and locking up, I got in her car. My bum was so frozen I almost melted in the buttery-soft heated leather seats. The difference in the get-up-and-go between my car and hers was like comparing an overloaded chuckwagon to Star Trek's Enterprise.

We headed down the road. It took her a few minutes to work up to it, but she eventually shot me a sympathetic frown. "It's a good thing you work at home. If you decide to replace your transmission, you'll be without a car for at least a week."

She said that like I had nowhere to go.

I shrugged. "There's always Bucky's Auto Wrecking."

"That graveyard of twisted metal south of town?"

"I prefer to think of it as a recycling center, but yes, that's the place. My real problem, though, is that I had somewhere else to be this weekend." I waited for her to ask where, but she didn't. Maybe that was her way of saying we'd talked enough for one day. So to irritate her, I told her anyway. "I'm due in Chicago on Saturday morning. I was supposed to leave day after tomorrow."

"Chicago, huh?" she said flatly.

"Yes."

That was when she was supposed to ask *why* I was going there.

THREATS AND THREADS

Only she didn't.

I waited another minute before saying, "For a meeting with the publisher I proofread for. Boring stuff, really. Business. But I figured while I was up there, I'd clean out my storage locker. Only without my car, I can't. So now I have to figure out not only how to get there, but also if I can get my stuff at all."

"I can help."

"You have a truck you can loan me?" I joked.

Her face maintained its usual stoic façade. "No, why would you think I have a truck?"

"Forget I said it."

"I can't help transporting your belongings, but I can get you to Chicago and back, if returning later on Sunday works for you."

"Say what?"

"I said I can—"

"I heard you. Just... why?"

"Coincidence. I'm going to a convention for people with HSAM."

"Sorry, I don't know that acronym. What's HSAM stand for?"

"Highly Superior Autobiographical Memory."

"So, like a photographic memory?"

"In a way, but that's oversimplification. Individuals with HSAM can access our memories far more readily. Like it's all in a filing system. For instance, if you ask me what happened on a certain date, even years ago, I can recall it as if it just happened yesterday."

So, of course, I spent the next five minutes quizzing her on decades past. After fact-checking her on a few events on my phone, I was convinced of her mental superpowers. "Must've been great for college. Bet you hardly studied at all." She shrugged lightly, so I asked her a question. "What do HSAMs talk about at a convention, anyway?"

"Convention makes it sound like a bigger event than it is. It's a small gathering, really. Less than a hundred. There's a young woman named Bellamy Larson giving a talk on the results of her PhD dissertation about the autism spectrum that I'm particularly interested in, since I occasionally have patients with the disorder. There aren't many of us who have HSAM, but getting together and sharing our knowledge helps us understand not only what we have to offer the scientific community, but also our unique situation from a sociological standpoint and brainstorm about ways in which we can assist society as a whole. They've used studies on HSAM to better understand what goes wrong in the neurological landscape of Alzheimer's patients. In other words, we're lab mice."

"Wow. This all gives me a whole new level of respect for you."

"Don't be too impressed. We also need the chance to be among our own kind. You have no concept of how aggravating it is to quiz patients at the clinic on their medical history when they can't even remember what they had for breakfast that morning."

"I'll bet. Speaking of the clinic—I thought that was just a temporary position. Weren't you applying for other positions?" Okay, so maybe that was a hint. While her ex, Clint Chastain, and I were no longer an item, she'd been in town more than long enough and having her around was just *Aaawkward* with a capitol A.

"It's more a matter of deciding on the right position at this point than having options." The turn signal clicked as she waited at the intersection for an oncoming car to pass. "I've narrowed it down to two, but the better of those doesn't start until next summer. Besides, I have other matters to attend to right now. Moving would only complicate things."

"Oh." If I wasn't mistaken, her lip had twitched in a sneer. There was no love lost between us, although I had to wonder what we would've ever thought of each other if Clint hadn't complicated things. Probably, I'd see her as some snooty, slightly intimidating bitch. And she'd probably dismiss me as an uninformed peon, just like she did everybody else.

Ten excruciatingly long minutes later, she pulled into my driveway. She didn't turn the engine off and I didn't ask her to come in. We understood each other perfectly.

"Should I pick you up at ten on Friday?" she said.

"Sure, that works." Although I had my hand on the door handle, I couldn't go the next two days without knowing something. "Are you and Clint…"

"We're not dating, if that's what you want to know."

"Oh, okay. I was just curious. Not that it's any of my business."

"It's not, but there's no reason I shouldn't tell you the full story. We're not romantically involved. However, he has agreed to help me out with my conception difficulties."

Oh, I mouthed. Then, half a minute later, the engine still idling, Bump standing inside with his front feet on the sill of the picture window and his muffled barks booming across the panes of glass, I said, "What does that mean, exactly?"

"It turns out my uterus and ova are not as healthy as they need to be. I found a surrogate. Clinton offered to be a father to the child." She studied her fingernails for a moment. "Part of the reason I'm going to Chicago is to meet with the prospective birth mother."

Wow. Okay, then. Danielle was not exactly having Clint's baby after all. She was just incubating his spawn in another hatchery. That made it so much better.

Should have, anyway. What it really did was add layers of complication. Because now, I actually felt sorry for Danielle. I'd had a child with a man I loved deeply without a specialist getting involved. Tara was the light of my life. If I only ever accomplished one thing during my time on Earth, she was it. I couldn't begrudge that pride and joy of anyone. Not even Danielle.

"I hope it goes well," I unbuckled myself, then opened the door. "See you Friday afternoon."

chapter 11

MY LOYAL SUBARU WAS towed to the nearest mechanic that afternoon. Dan of Dan's Tire Service duly confirmed what Mr. Hooten and Danielle had said. I could replace the transmission, he told me, but it would cost more than the trade-in value of the vehicle. If I sold it to Bucky's for parts, I could get five hundred dollars.

I opted for DNR—*do not resuscitate*. It was time for a new vehicle and a new chapter in *my* life. I'd worry about replacing it when I got back next week. The storage unit could be cleared out some other time, even though there was something in there I'd been itching to get a hold of ever since I'd gotten the DNA test about my paternity back. Meanwhile, I double checked my plans for the weekend and crammed in as much work as I could in a few hours' time. Tara was already squared away for an extended visit at the Mullinses. I was more grateful than ever to them, and I made a point of letting Judy Mullins know it.

After I ate my dinner alone, Archer called. He'd landed in San Francisco, having slept through most of the flight. I missed him sorely, but if I said that too soon, it would sound like I was already begging him to come back. I needed to let him do his own thing, just like I'd want him to do for me. If we were meant to be together, we could survive this.

I told myself that. But living it was a different matter altogether.

We said goodbye, then I must've sat there at the kitchen counter staring at the 1970's avocado-green backsplash tiles for fifteen minutes. I was lost without him. Totally and utterly adrift.

When I finally snapped to, I had just ten minutes to hoof it to Cleora's for the book club meeting. I whipped my hair into a ponytail before pulling on a fresh sweatshirt. The moment I grabbed Bump's leash, he was spinning circles and making excited monkey sounds.

Three blocks away, I could see that Cleora's driveway and all available parking spots in front of her house were full. I'd been counting on a low turnout. Who knew Wilton residents were so literate? Since Bump had caught on to the fact we were paying his girlfriend a visit, I couldn't back out now. In the hierarchy of loves of his life, I was now a distant second to Fancy. Actually, I may have been third behind Clint. No, make that fourth or fifth if you threw in Tara and my dad. I was in the top ten, anyway.

Since that morning, my thoughts had been mostly on Archer and where our relationship would go from here, but the closer the hour had drawn to the Apple Pie Bibliophile Society meeting, the more my thoughts had turned to it instead. I'd told myself it was no big deal, that I was merely showing up undercover to glean some reader reactions and help determine the course of my series. Yet, with every step, my dread increased and my pace slowed. Bump, however, pulled harder.

"Bump, no." I checked the leash repeatedly. His ears flicked back. He dug in harder. "Easy, buddy. Easy."

Whimpering, he lowered his head, ears flat. His steps slowed. Which didn't buy me nearly enough time. Why had I agreed to this? What if they hated the book?

Selma stepped out of her ageing Camaro, then waved at me. I'd been so lost in thought I hadn't noticed her car on the opposite side of the street. She clacked across the pavement in a pair of over-the-knee brown leather boots, avoiding a wide puddle as she came to me. The snow had melted. Overnight, a steady rain had soaked the earth in a mantle of sogginess. She was sporting hunter-green leggings and a hound's-tooth cropped jacket over a beige turtleneck. In one hand, she carried a canvas messenger bag. Her hair was pulled into a loose bun to show off a pair of plain pearl earrings.

The look was shockingly tame. I gawked openly.

"Selma, you look so... Gosh, I don't know how to describe it."

"Hang on. Maybe this'll help." She dipped her hand into her small brown cross-body purse, then put on a pair of tortoiseshell reading glasses. "What do you think?"

"Hmm, very—"

"Smart-looking? Nerdy? Brainy?"

Bump barked in agreement. Laughing, she petted him.

"I was going to say nice, but sure, all those things, too. You look like a totally different person. More intellectual." Oh, dear, that came out wrong. Selma beamed a smile, indicating she hadn't taken it as an insult. "Why the change?"

She covered her eyes briefly with the back of her hand. "Man, these are giving me a migrant." Then she whipped the specs off, shimmied her shoulders, and patted at her bun. "Anyway, thanks. I had to go to the Goodwill store over in Oil City to find these gems. I figured since I was attending my first book club, I might as well look the part."

"Well, you nailed it." We walked across the street. "I'm glad you're here, Selma. I can't say this is my idea of a good time, but I figured it might be a way to get to know more people in the area."

"You're a better person than I am, Sam. I heard there was free food and that someone spiked the punch last month. That's why I came." As we started up the front steps, she tapped her purse, where a notable bulge protruded. "Just in case the crowd looks kinda stodgy,

I brought something to loosen 'em all up."

I snickered. "The hell with spiking the punch. Can I have a drink? I'm going to need it."

She handed me a tiny bottle of rum, similar to the kind they gave out on an airplane. I'd had an unhealthy relationship with alcohol in the past and tried to avoid it entirely, but I needed something to calm my nerves. I unscrewed the cap and took a gulp. Just as the door opened.

Smirking, Maybelle stared at the bottle. "That would explain a lot about you. The shady characters hanging around. The loose behavior. The rise in crime."

"Nice to see you too, Maybelle." I replaced the cap and handed it back to Selma, who wedged her way past Maybelle while blowing her a kiss. A floaty feeling washing over me, I followed her. Actually, Bump pulled me along, aiming for the back door.

As Maybelle turned to watch us, Selma performed an abbreviated version of the Macarena, hugging her messenger bag to her. "Guess who has a signed copy?" She twirled around, continuing her dance into the middle of the living room. Three older ladies sitting on the couch glanced up. Selma tapped one of them on the knee. It was Gladys Detwiler.

"Guess." Selma pointed to her own face with both index fingers.

"Oh my. Oh my, oh my." Gladys clamped both hands over her heart. "You, Selma dear? How on earth?"

I let Bump out back, and he and Fancy greeted each other effusively. Cleora's yard appeared to be well drained, so it wasn't too muddy.

While the rum warmed my insides and brought on a sense of calm, I pretended to study the assortment of appetizers laid out on the sideboard in the tiny foyer, because I knew Selma was watching to see if I'd react to her announcement. Keeping my secret was killing her.

"I just happen to know someone who knows *the* S.A. Mack." She spun around once more, then flopped into a rocking chair. "In real life."

Cleora introduced me to a few of the women, including Selma's former BFF, Amy Sue, and Cleora's twin Cordelia, who was a good four inches shorter than her. Their height difference and dissimilar facial structures suggested they were fraternal twins, not identical.

Amy Sue gave Selma a sideways glance. They locked eyes.

Selma's eyebrows twitched. "Miss Bradley."

"Miss Paradiso," Amy Sue replied flatly.

And then they both averted their eyes.

Everything about Amy Sue was very rigid and formal—from the way she crossed her legs and sat up stick straight, to the ironed lapels of her baby-blue blouse. She seemed like the kind of person you had to work to get to know. I was never sure why they'd fallen out. Maybe they'd just drifted apart and gone in different directions. It happened. Whatever the reason, she and Selma seemed like they would've been an odd couple, but so were Selma and me.

"Are you sure it's an authentic autographed copy, Selma?" A petite thirtyish woman came from the dining room and went straight to Selma. She dressed like a teenager—faded jeans with holes in the knees, an oversized Mighty Mouse T-shirt, and a pair of navy Keds minus the laces. "You do know S.A. Mack is a pseudonym, right?"

"Of course I know that, Birdie." Selma flapped her hand dismissively.

"How did you make the connection then?"

"Sorry, I can't reveal my sources."

Birdie persisted. "But she keeps her identity super secret. Do you know her?"

Selma pretend-zipped her lips. As soon as I got the chance, I'd remind her why it was critical that no one in this town knew my secret. Anonymity was my only chance at normalcy. Selma might not yet have figured out that I was S.A. Mack, but someone a little more astute

THREATS AND THREADS

just might. TrueLuv had.

A younger woman with a baby strapped to her back spoke. "I heard S.A. Mack is actually a *man* and it's short for Sidney Andrew MacDonald."

A bit off the mark, but they were onto something. If anyone ever found out my middle name and connected the dots…

The mother bounced on the balls of her feet while the baby giggled. "He was a newspaper columnist and was jilted by his socialite New York lover, who told him he wasn't sophisticated or rich enough for her. So he moved to a cabin outside of Montpelier, then didn't leave for six months until he'd written his first romance novel. Now he's a multimillionaire, and they're talking about making some of his books into movies."

"Movies?" several voices exclaimed.

"Are you sure about that?" Cordelia asked. "I'm not fond of watching movies made from novels. The book is always so much better."

Sounded like they were confusing S.A. Mack with Nicholas Sparks. Anyway, no one had ever contacted me about movie rights. I wished they would.

"Yes, movies!" the young mother answered. "And the best part is the woman who dumped him tried to win him back after he became an overnight success, but he'd since reconnected with his high school crush and married her. Isn't that priceless?" The baby started to fuss, so she popped a pacifier in its mouth and swayed side to side.

Gladys whispered to me, "Is Ida with you?"

"No, sorry. She and Dad are headed to South America later this week, and they have some loose ends to tie up first."

"South America, you say? Ida was always adventurous. But Walter? How did she talk him into it?"

"Heck if I know. I can't imagine the stories he'll have when he gets back."

Theories on who S.A. Mack really was included a professor of psychology at an Ivy League college, a bedridden truck driver who'd been injured in a highway accident, and a former writer of children's books. So I added my own theory, just to stoke the outlandish creativity in the room.

"I heard it was a twenty-six-year-old Mormon mother of twelve from Salt Lake City."

"Mother of twelve?" Cleora echoed, setting a tray of cheese and crackers on the coffee table. "And she's how old?"

"Twenty-six. Maybe twenty-seven by now. I read that last year sometime. Heck, she's probably had kid number thirteen by now."

"Good Heavens," Gladys said, ladling herself a cup of punch from a crystal bowl, "the poor woman barely had time to heal from the episiotomy before her husband was…"

Three women seated next to each other on folding chairs simultaneously crossed their legs, and a generalized grumbling rolled through the room.

"I'd have beat Hubert off with a meat tenderizer," Cordelia said, "if he so much as touched me the first six weeks after I gave birth to little Phillip. How about you, Stacy?"

Stacy? I wondered if that was Stacy from the BMV, a friend of Ida's. Probably.

Stacy, the infant's mother, stooped to grab a handful of crackers. "Don't ask me. I had a C-section."

Cleora clapped her hands together. "Remember what we're here for, everyone. We only have an hour-and-a-half."

"Minus fifteen," Amy Sue muttered.

Cleora tipped her head in question.

"We have only seventy-five minutes now"—Amy Sue checked her watch—"seeing as how some of us arrived late."

Flipping to page one, I pretended to read. Showing up at a book club incognito wasn't the brightest idea I'd ever had.

THREATS AND THREADS

Selma rose, the book clasped to her chest. "Has anyone gotten to Chapter Seventeen yet? Did Alexander really do it with Marissa in his law office after hours—or were they just discussing the terms of her divorce? I got confused, what with all the talk about how well-rounded her assets were."

A collective groan went around the room.

"You're not supposed to read that far ahead," Gladys informed her.

Birdie planted her hands on her hips, elbows jutting out. "Plus, you broke the first rule of the Apple Pie Bibliophile Society."

"Did I?" Selma batted her eyelashes. "I didn't know. What rule?"

"No spoilers unless you warn us all ahead of time." Birdie pointed to the kitchen. "And then you have to announce a coffee and pastry break, to give time for anyone who doesn't want to hear it to leave the room."

"Oh, sorry. I'm new here. I just wanted to know why he referred to a certain part of her anatomy if he didn't want to fornicate."

"That's called innuendo, Selma," Amy Sue explained patronizingly. "He was just hinting that her healthy financial portfolio was as generous as her—"

"La la la la la la…" Stacy had both fingers stuck in her ears and her eyes closed.

"Forget I mentioned it," Amy Sue said. "I'd never dream of telling you how it *really* is."

For the life of me, I couldn't see what Selma could have ever seen in Amy Sue. It was a good thing she'd moved on.

"Could someone tell Stacy she can stop now?" Maybelle said.

Cordelia leaned across the woman seated between her and Stacy, then tapped Stacy's arm. When Stacy's eyes snapped open, Cordelia gave her the *okay* sign.

"We were supposed to read as far as Chapter Four," Cleora reminded everyone. "If you would, please, open your books to page twenty-three, which is the end of Chapter Two... Perhaps Gladys will give us a recap on the first two chapters, and we can talk about Felicity's inhibitions instead."

Inhibitions? Just because she started off the series as a virgin did not mean she had psychological problems. She just hadn't met the right man.

After Gladys Detwiler gave her fourth-grade interpretation of Felicity's 'uptightness,' the conversation then veered abruptly to Alexander's backstory. Meanwhile, Maybelle kept slathering crackers with goat cheese to stuff in her mouth, a fact I was grateful for.

"Can you imagine losing your mother at the age of five?" Cordelia offered. "And to know that she was murdered—"

"Alexander's mother wasn't murdered," Stacy insisted. "It was an accident. A terrible accident. It could happen to anyone."

To be accurate, I'd never said either way. It was amazing how real a fictional world could be to readers and the different conclusions each of them reached. Maybe coming here wasn't such a bad idea after all. It gave me a whole new perspective.

"Accident, huh? Kind of like Grace Hazelton over on Cardinal Drive the other night?" Birdie's thin eyebrows crept high onto her oversized forehead, a feature disproportionate to the rest of her diminutive frame. The woman could rent billboard space between her eyebrows and hairline.

"She was murdered? Oh, my." Gladys scanned the room. "I wondered why she wasn't here tonight, but then, she never said much."

"Not murdered, no," Selma chimed in. "Misty the dispatcher bought groceries this morning and told me it was a gas leak."

Stacy frowned. "How terrible! She may have kept to herself mostly, but I liked her."

"Yes, what a pity." Gladys rotated the growing yarn creation in her lap. "She was only in her thirties."

THREATS AND THREADS

Everyone nodded, many of them echoing how tragic the event was.

But not Maybelle. "That blasted beagle of hers used to bark all night. I hear she took sleeping pills every night. Probably put him out, forgot about it, and snoozed right through it while the rest of us suffered."

The night I'd been out walking with Bump when it snowed, the beagle had been crying for a while. For months, I'd been taking Bump on evening walks at varying times. Never once had I heard her beagle carry on in that manner.

Cleora glared at Maybelle. "Most women I know need a little help getting a good night's rest from time to time. So stop spreading rumors about Grace having a sleeping pill addiction."

"Amen," Stacy said, holding the now-sleeping baby in her arms.

They all nodded again, many of them sharing stories about how they couldn't get to sleep at night, or fell asleep instantly, then woke in the middle of the night. Tales of sleep deprivation then morphed into shared misery of menopause, perimenopause, monthly cycles, childbirth, lactation, rearing children, and how to be properly fitted for a bra. The estrogen in the room was palpable. Too much for me even. Back in Chicago when I was actually surrounded by other women in the workplace, I never even asked a co-worker for Pamprin, much less talked about feminine product failures or whether bio-identical hormones were an option.

While they all commiserated about what it was to be female, my mind kept going back to Grace Hazelton. A healthy thirty-something falls asleep in her home as her furnace leaks toxic fumes? Sure, accidents happened, but that would've been an easy scenario for a murderer to fake. Not so long ago, someone had tried to stage Miley's death as an accidental overdose. The autopsy had proven otherwise.

I looked around the room, trying to gauge whether this Grace Hazelton, who I'd never met, had any true enemies. Maybelle took complaining to a professional level and wouldn't think twice of speaking poorly of the dead, so it was hard to know whether to take her seriously. As for the rest, I couldn't discern any contempt for Grace.

Cleora tried to lasso the discussion back to the book, but the gossip herd was on a stampede. There was no stopping it now.

Knitting needles working furiously, Gladys started talking to herself. "Poor sweet little Pythagoras. He was such a good boy."

I grabbed a thread of yarn as it unraveled from her skein. "Was?"

She blinked at me. "Was what, dear?"

"You keep saying Pythagoras was a good dog. So Grace died a couple of days ago. What happened to her dog since then?"

She frowned. "He died, too."

"Probably of a broken heart," Cordelia added.

"More likely heart failure," Cleora said. When I gave her a questioning glance, she explained, "Pythagoras was thirty pounds overweight. And he was sixteen years old. She'd had him since she was a teenager, I heard."

"When did Grace die?"

Cleora shrugged. "No one knows for sure exactly. Sometime Saturday."

"She lived alone, right?"

"Yes, why?"

"How did anyone know she was dead, then?"

Stacy raised her hand. Everyone went silent. "I heard the dog barking, so I went to check on her. When she didn't answer the door or her phone, I called 9-1-1. They found her."

"And the dog?" I asked.

Stacy shook her head. "I heard one of the paramedics say they were calling Dr. Chastain about Pythagoras."

"For a dead dog?"

"Oh, he wasn't dead yet."

THREATS AND THREADS

"Yet?"

"No, just dying. I suppose they thought Dr. Chastain might be able to save him. But apparently, he couldn't."

Someone mumbled about how touching it was the owner and dog had both passed so peacefully and so close together, but that maybe it was for the best. I, on the other hand, couldn't put it all out of my mind so easily. Tomorrow, I'd call Clint and ask him about the dog.

Gladys's knitting needles whipped furiously back and forth, her fingers weaving yarn in intricate patterns. When the discussion got back around to Chapters Three and Four, which was mostly Cleora giving recaps and a few others nodding, Gladys was the only one not participating or even pretending to listen.

I watched with fascination. A tiny yellow sweater was taking shape in her lap.

"What are you making?" I asked.

A beaming smile lit her face. "A sweater for Stacy's baby."

"It's beautiful. Do you knit often?"

"Every day. This is the fifth sweater I've made for her little ones. Handmade gifts are the best, don't you agree? And if I don't have someone to knit for, I give things away to charity."

"Knit any green sweaters lately?"

"Not that I can recall."

So much for chasing that clue. The green thread Deputy Strewing found on my gate might've been hanging there for weeks. I only ever went out that way to put the trash cans in the alley on trash day—and I certainly didn't inspect the boards for stray pieces of cloth.

Gladys set down her needles and lifted the little sweater up for everyone to admire.

Stacy clapped her hands. "I'm going to put it on Aster for church this Sunday, so I can take her picture in it."

Over the next fifteen minutes, rather than the book, they talked more about the weather, the new department store in Oil City, and whether Wilton Memorial could afford to replace the roof on the high school. The meeting broke up. As they all began to filter out, Gladys caught me on the way to the back door, where I was headed to collect Bump.

She tapped at her temple. "You know, I did make some green and red scarves last Christmas for the church bazaar."

"You did? Who bought them?"

"I wouldn't have the slightest idea, honey. They were part of a silent auction. Would you like me to make you one? Is green your favorite color?" She stood close, squinting, and surveyed me up and down, finally settling on my face. "Of course it is, just look at your eyes."

Then she proceeded to measure me for a scarf. Because I was tall. And apparently there were fashion rules as to how many times a scarf should be wrapped and how long it should be.

When I finally retrieved Bump from the backyard, he was visibly exhausted. Fancy, thankfully, looked none the worse for wear. It was evident in the way she pranced about and held her head high that she'd established herself as the boss.

I crouched to clip the leash on Bump while he stared longingly at Fancy, as if they were about to part from one another for a very long time. It was hard to tear them away from each other. Fancy sidled over to me, her white silky tail wagging gently.

"Don't worry, sweetie." I scratched between her ears. "We'll come back. I promise."

She climbed into my lap. Closing my eyes, I hugged her to my chest. She snuggled close, laying her chin on my shoulder. Not to be left out of the love-fest, Bump put a paw on each of my shoulders and leaned his head into mine, pressing Fancy between us in a group hug. The fringe of Fancy's ears tickled my neck. She licked my earlobes. I felt as giddy as a schoolgirl in love for the first time.

I also felt small and close to the ground. Detached from the

THREATS AND THREADS

moment I'd just been experiencing and slipping into another one of my...

My legs churned rapidly. All four of them. Periodically, I lowered my tiny snout to the ground and inhaled. The air smelled of cut grass and... cleaning solution? I sneezed to clear my nostrils of the overpowering scents. I was wearing a lightweight harness to keep the pressure of a collar off my throat. Beside me, a pair of sensible shoes shuffled along—Cleora's. We were walking the neighborhood sidewalks on what was unmistakably a summer evening. From my low perspective, the hedges bordering the yard we were passing looked like a towering canopy of tropical forest.

I warned you not to go there, didn't I?

Cleora's steps slowed. The voice had come from the house behind some bushes. Harsh. Accusatory.

Another voice replied, but the words were muted by the garble of a TV playing loudly. I tried to separate the voices out, but it was hard. I wasn't sure who was saying what.

You know exactly what I'm talking about, came the first voice. *Admit it.*

I didn't do nothing. Honest.

If you're lying, so help me—

Two pairs of feet stomped inside the house, like one was being pursued by the other. There was a thump and the feet stopped.

Cleora halted in her tracks. I bolted to the end of the leash, ducking between the clumped stems of the hedge. The flickering light of the TV glowed through the picture window. But no one moved across that square of wavering light. The two distinct voices were gone. Only the TV played on.

The pressure of the harness around my shoulders tightened as

Cleora reeled the leash in, pulling me back to her. I tried to scramble beneath the hedge to watch, my nails scraping the concrete, but my determination was no match for her size and strength.

"Sweetheart, what are you doing down there?"

chapter 12

HURTLED BACK INTO MY own human body, I opened my eyes to see Cleora gazing down on me. My legs were sprawled before me. My back was pressed against a cool surface. It took a few moments for me to realize I was sitting against her fridge and that both dogs were snuffling at my face.

I blinked, waiting for my brain fog to evaporate. "What…"

"You dropped to your knees and started crawling across the floor," Gladys said, a satchel full of yarn skeins and knitting needles on the floor next to her. "Then you got this dazed look, and Cleora and I sat you back against the fridge before you could fall over."

Cleora lowered herself to my level, her knees cracking. She tilted my chin up to peer into my eyes. "Do you have epilepsy, Sam?"

"No, no, I…" I pressed the back of my hand to my forehead, my head throbbing as I tried to figure out how to explain my unusual condition. It had happened several times before, but I'd always seen the world through Bump's eyes, not some other dog's. "I just have a killer headache, that's all. Happens sometimes. I see… colors, lights. I get confused."

"Oh, migraines. I get those," Gladys sympathized. "Makes me want to turn out all the lights and crawl into a hole, too."

Giving me her hand, Cleora helped me to my feet. The dogs circled me, concerned. Fancy even stood on her hind legs, trying to get closer.

"Are you going to be all right, dear?" Cleora asked.

I took one step, then two. The lightheadedness faded away. The floor grew firm beneath me.

"I'll be fine. The walk home will help."

"Maybe someone can go with you?" Cleora suggested. "Selma," she called into the living room, "are you still here?"

"I am indeed!" Selma bounded through the doorway, her shoulders pulled back and her fake reading glasses perched on her nose. "Oh, honey pie, you look woozy. Did you spike the punch after all?"

"No, I just—"

"Damn good thing you didn't drive here, girl. Last thing you need is a DUI to give folks something else to talk about." She handed Bump's leash to me before guiding me to the front door. Cleora and Gladys bid us goodbye as Selma escorted me cautiously down the front steps, Bump leading the way.

We were half a block away before I loosed my elbow from Selma's iron grip. "I'm fine, Sel. I can walk myself."

"I overheard them saying they picked you up off the floor. That's not normal."

She had that right, but I wasn't about to explain my dog-centered visions to her. Even I had trouble believing them and this last one had really thrown me for a loop. I knew they meant something. I was just never sure what until after something really big happened—which made me apprehensive. The last two times I'd had bouts of visions from Bump, I'd ended up getting kidnapped and having the tar beaten out of me, then both my dog and me being kidnapped and nearly killed. I wanted the visions to stop. I hated they happened at all. But I also couldn't help but think if I only understood them better, I could avoid all the trouble to begin with.

"It was just a migraine," I told her. "It's gone now."

She gave me a dubious glance. "Well, I suppose if you can make it back to your place without me scooping you up, then I'll take your word for it. But I have to leave right after that. I have somewhere to go."

"A date with Dylan?"

We rounded a corner. For a minute, Selma didn't say anything, like she was trying to work out how to answer me.

Then, "No, not with Dylan."

"Someone else then?" My voice had probably brightened too much. She had to know by now that I was no fan of Dylan Hawkins.

"Yeah, someone else."

"Who?"

Her shoulders twitched in a shrug. "I'm not ready to say."

My mind raced through the possibilities. I'd find a way to milk this out of her. "Clint? Because if it's Clint, you don't have to hide it from me. We're long done. He's fair game."

Honestly, I couldn't imagine Dr. Clinton Chastain being her type, or her his, but she was determined to hide this mystery man's identity from me.

"Honey, he is definitely one hot number, and I'll admit I was more than a little jealous you'd snagged him your first week back in town, but no, my date is not with Clint."

We turned left and went another block. Except for the lights on inside some of the homes and a few porch lights, there was little sign of life in the neighborhood—no dogs barking, no cats on the prowl, no neighbors out for a walk on this chilly late autumn night, and no sound of cars except for the highway traffic in the distance.

I thought hard about how to get her to spill the beans. Since I didn't have any clues so far, it came down to a process of elimination. "Oh... I get it."

"Get what?"

"You're involved with a married man, aren't you? I just want you to know, Selma, that I won't judge you. Just because two people are married doesn't mean they're still emotionally invested in each—"

"You're wrong, Sam. I learned my lesson with Dylan. He cheated on Dawna, and I know he cheated on me."

I didn't look at her. Did she know Dylan had tried to pressure me in the back room of the lodge? Did she think I'd welcomed his advances or even enticed him?

"Do you know why Jourdane left town?" she said suddenly.

Ah, she must've found out about Dylan flirting with *her*. Still, I had to find out where she was going with this. "I thought she was modeling chain mail."

"Yeah, she is, although it's only part time, but she's hoping it'll pick up. In a way, I'm glad it worked out for her, because it got that bitch out of my hair, but I finally had to admit that Dylan was cheating on me with her. But anyway, the real reason she left town was because she found out Dylan was cheating on us both."

"What?" My surprise probably sounded as fake as Selma's hair color *du jour*. "With whom?"

"Some other chick living in a trailer between here and Fullbright. That's all I know. Look, it's not really important who. I just wish I'd known what kind of scumbag he was sooner."

"But you were head over heels, Selma. If someone had told you before, would you have believed them?"

Stone-faced, she stared straight ahead as we crossed the last street and came to the block I lived on. "I suppose not." She didn't look sad, or even mad. She seemed like someone whose view of the world had undergone a seismic shift—for the better. "And to think, I thought about having a baby with him at one time. I can't even imagine."

Slowing to a halt, I slung an arm around her in a half-hug and she leaned against me briefly. We resumed our walk, going the length of that last block without either of us saying a word, which was unusual, but there were moments you needed to let solidify.

Then, I couldn't stand it any longer. I had to know one more thing. "So that was Amy Sue, huh?"

"Yep." The undertone of a growl tainted her voice.

"What was her problem, anyway?"

She rolled her eyes. "Look, I'm not responsible for Amy Sue's attitude, 'kay? She thinks everyone should just do as she says. I'm so glad you're not like that, Sam."

Whatever had gone on between her and Amy Sue was still raw. I decided not to push her on the matter, because, frankly, it wasn't that important. I had my own problems to deal with.

When we got to my house, Selma stopped at the end of the driveway.

"Go on inside," she insisted, "then give me the okay sign if everything's all right in there. If it's not, tug on your earlobe or something."

"You want to come in, Selma? I bought Tara a stash of Cheetos, and I know you like them, too. I'm sure she wouldn't mind."

"I really do have to go, Sam."

"Ah, yes. The secret date. So are you going to tell me who you're seeing? Is it Ryan Gosling? Did he finally answer one of your DMs on Twitter?"

She blushed. "That would be nice, but no."

"Then who? Come on. We *are* besties, aren't we?"

"I wish I could, but we're not ready to go public."

I needed leverage. And I did have something of my own I needed to share with someone. "What if I told you a huge secret of mine?"

Her eyes widened, then gradually lowered to my midsection. "Are you and hunky fireman going to have a—"

"No!" I smacked her lightly on the arm, then brushed it apologetically. "Of course not. This is something completely different.

It doesn't have anything to do with Archer." I teasingly tugged at her sleeve. "So if I tell you, will you tell me your secret?"

She hedged. "Give me a hint."

"It's about S.A. Mack."

The temptation was too great to resist. "'Kay. Shoot."

I looked around. Random front porch lights threw patches of light across the street at intervals. As far as I could tell, no one had followed us. And since I'd read one too many high-tech thrillers lately, I glanced skyward to check for drones. Nothing there either. Leaning in close, I lowered my voice. "I know her true identity."

"S.A. Mack's, you mean?"

"Yes."

She gripped me by the shoulders. "You mean you lied to me? You do know the real S.A. Mack?"

"Shh, shh." I waved both hands at her, even though no one was around. "Okay, so, you going to tell me or not?"

She crossed her arms. "You go first."

"It's me."

She burst out in laughter. The reverse-snorting kind. "Really, Sam? That's hard to believe. You're a little too… what's the word?" Hands flapping, she cast her eyes upward. "Don't help me, don't help me. It's on the tip of my tongue."

I wasn't about to help her, because I couldn't wait to see what she would come up with.

"Got it!" She held a finger up. "Repressed."

"Me, repressed?"

"I was gonna say chaste, but I know you're not that much of a prude. Just shy or maybe confused about… you know"—she lowered her voice to a whisper—"your sexuality."

"Selma, I'm telling you the truth." Hooking her elbow, I reeled her in close. "I *am* S.A. Mack. Samantha Ann McNamee… get it? S for Samantha. A for Ann. Mack for McNamee."

THREATS AND THREADS

For a few moments, she stared blankly at me. Then, loudly, "Get. Out. Of. Town!" She slapped a hand over her mouth. Between her fingers, she muttered, "She's you? Or are you her? How's that work?"

"We're the same person. I use a pen name because I don't want anyone to know I write romance." I inclined my head toward the house. "After all, I have a teenage daughter. It would be kind of awkward at the parent-teacher conferences if they ever asked what I did for a living. I'd rather people didn't know."

She gave me a skeptical look. "Can you prove it?"

"If you come inside, I'll show you the files on my computer of my WIP."

"Why would I want to see pictures of your whip? Are you into S and M? Oh, honey, I didn't peg you for one of—"

"Not whip—WIP. W-I-P. Work in progress."

"Don't bother. I believe you. I kinda suspected it, anyway."

I wasn't sure if that was true or if she was saying it because she didn't want me to think I'd been duping her all along. "You do... did?"

"Sure. I just had a hunch. I'm highly impunitive, you know."

I wasn't even sure what impunitive meant, something legal maybe, but my guess was it had nothing to do with gut feelings.

"Anyway," she went on, "now that I know for sure, it'll just take a little getting used to. Here I thought you were just some stuck-up academic, going crazy with your red pen. It's going to be weird for a while. Not all those ladies in the club wanted to read your book, you know."

"Truthfully, I'm not shocked. But who was it?"

She shrugged. "I can't remember who—I was occupied in the ladies' room when they were taking the vote—but somebody said trash like that was smut. Lady porn. That it was responsible for the demoralization of American society, rising adultery, and sex trafficking."

Why did everyone in this town think that romance stories had to involve leather and chains or illegal acts? Didn't anyone understand it could simply be about falling in and out of love and back in again?

"Selma, do you think anyone hated my books enough to, I don't know, want to give me a scare?"

"Why would they do that? If I don't like a book, I just stop reading it."

"I don't know. It's just that, well, I've been getting fan mail in my inbox lately. Not fan mail, really. I mean it started out that way. But then, when they got to the end of the last book, they were upset. And I do mean *really* upset. Like they could kill me for letting them down."

"Seriously? That's nuts. I've read books that made me cry or laugh out loud. One even made me pee my pants. But when I'm done with the story, I know it's *just* a book. Someone would have to be completely off their rails to do something like that. It was just e-mails, right? People write all kinds of crazy things on their computers they'd never say or do in person. You use a pen name, so you're safe. They can't know where you live."

"I wish that were true. I got a phone call this morning. Someone knows who I am."

"You have to report that to Sheriff Driscoll, honey. ASAP!"

"I know I should. It's just that once I do, I'm afraid my secret's going to come out."

She tipped her head. "Apparently, it already has."

"True. But I still don't want the whole town to know. You're the only one in Wilton who does. Not even my family knows. Or Archer. Selma, you can't tell anyone."

"Don't worry. I won't," she said, and I believed her. Then, she added, "But what are you going to do about this person?"

"Right now, I don't know, but I'll figure it out. I just had to tell someone, though." Amazingly, talking to her *was* helping. Not that I was getting any practical answers. It just felt good to unload my troubles on a caring ear. "Okay, so I've told you my secret. Now what's yours?"

"I... I'm seeing..." Screwing her face up like she was wringing it from the inside out, she pulled her coat tight. "I have feelings for... Good heavens, I don't know how to say it. It's just so... I can't describe it."

"Try." I gripped her shoulders. "Name."

After casting a look around and behind her, she whispered, "Newt."

"Newton Tipton?"

This time, she covered *my* mouth with her hands. My nostrils also. I yanked her hands down, coughing, and Bump jumped up, planting both paws on my chest. He licked my face.

"What? How?" Pushing Bump off with my knee, I dragged a coat sleeve across my face. I patted his head to let him know I was okay. "And *why*?"

"Why? Sam, you of all people should know. Look at Felicity and Alexander. They're from different worlds. Who would've ever thought they'd fall in love?"

"Love? You're *in love* with Newt Tipton?"

Newton Tipton had been her boss at Garber's Groceries for years, and they were just now figuring out there was a spark there? Newt was the sort of guy who got so nervous talking to women, even his customers, that he needed medical-grade antiperspirant.

"I don't know. Maybe?" A heavy sigh of exasperation bellowed out of her, forming little clouds of ice that hung suspended in the chilly air. "See now, this is why I didn't want to tell anyone. Not even you. He's a good man, Sam. He really is. A much better man than Dylan Hawkins will ever be."

A centipede could've jumped over the bar Dylan Hawkins had set in the boyfriend department. As for Newt, yes, I'd always judged him as lacking in social graces, but that by no means made him a bad person.

I took a deep breath. They said there was someone for everyone. If Selma was falling for Newt because of the person he was deep down inside—a person I'd never taken the time to get to know—then I had to trust her on that.

"Selma, I'm sorry. I didn't mean it to come out like that. I just didn't think he was your type, that's all." Honestly, I didn't think he was anyone's type. I remembered Newt from as far back as elementary school. He'd never had a girlfriend, never gone to a dance, never had a date that I could recall. He was the type of guy who might arrange a meet-up with a girl through an online dating site, only to get jilted when she 'went to the ladies' room. "Look, just give me a little time for it to sink in. You know him better than I do. After all, he's been your boss for how many years?"

"Six. Almost seven. I know it's weird, but looking back, I always knew there was something there. Maybe it was the way he complimented me on how I bagged groceries, grouping like items together, or told me he appreciated the fact my uniform shirt was always so clean. Dylan never complimented me unless it was to get under my skirt. Newt is a gentleman. He notices things, little things." Her phone dinged with a text. She pressed a couple of buttons, then slipped it back inside her purse. "I really do have to go. I'm already late."

"I'd offer to drive you back to Cleora's, but the Subaru's transmission is gone and I probably need to just replace the car altogether."

"Sorry about your car, but that's actually exciting! We could go new car shopping together. You'd look great in a Cadillac."

I shuddered at the thought of driving around in a boat on wheels. Tara would probably refuse to acknowledge me in the drop-off lane at school.

"Anywho, don't worry about it. The walk will give me time to think." Selma pulled out her phone again, a little smile of delight curling her mouth. "Oh, lookie there. He sent me a note—*Please remember to park behind the house, not to the side or in front.*"

"That's it?"

Her face was radiant. "Yeah. Sneaking around adds to the excitement. That's why I'm not supposed to tell anyone. And before you ask, we both agreed to it. So if I find out you told even a single soul, I'm going to call up *TMZ* or *Entertainment Tonight* or one of those tabloids we park in the rack right next to the candy and gum and tell them all about you."

I held my hands up in surrender. "Fair enough."

"Let me know you're safe in that house of yours once you get inside. If you figure out later there's anything out of place, call me. I can drive back and blind 'em with this." She whipped out a can of pepper spray from her purse.

I gave her a thumbs-up. "All right, but it'll probably be too late to rescue me by then."

"Say, why don't I just loan this one to you? I've got a spare under my front seat."

I took the canister from her. It looked like all I'd have to do is aim and press down on the button. "Thanks."

"I'll wait here on the sidewalk until you give me the signal." When I didn't budge, she waved. "'Kay, bye now."

"Bye, Sel." Reining in my fear, I went up the sidewalk, Bump ambling beside me, and had my foot on the first step when I wheeled around. "Wait." I ran back down the sidewalk, then hugged her. "I really am happy for you, Selma. I am."

"Thanks, sweetie pie. Me too. Now quit stalling and go inside. I need to skedaddle."

I did as she ordered, but not until I'd inspected the front door for signs of forced entry. Looked normal to me. After I unlocked the door, I let myself in. Bump immediately tore away from me before galloping into the kitchen. Deep slurping sounds ensued.

The can of pepper spray gripped in my hand, I tiptoed through the house. A quick inspection of every room revealed nothing was amiss.

I went to the picture window. Selma was there, punching a text into her phone. I tapped on the glass, giving her the thumbs-up. She blew me a kiss, then hurried off faster than we'd come. A spark of jealousy kindled inside me. Selma had found someone who treated her like she deserved. Newt wasn't going anywhere. They had their entire future together if things worked out.

And just this morning, I'd watched the man of my dreams jet off on new adventures that didn't include me.

As strange as it was to think it, for once, I wanted to be Selma instead of me.

chapter 13

"YOU COULD DRIVE THIS beast clear across the country, Sam," my dad said with inflated pride. "It's already made it two-hundred-forty-thousand. Sure, I've replaced a few parts along the way, but what a workhorse, huh? They don't make trucks like this anymore."

And a good thing that was, too. The only AC Dad's truck had was to drive at top speed with the windows open—and even those had to be rolled down with a crank. The thing didn't have an auxiliary jack or even a CD player. The cassette player was long dead. Only the AM stations worked on the radio.

"What about the muffler, Dad? I think it needs a new muffler." I'd heard him coming half a mile away.

"Oh, eventually, maybe. But it'll do for now."

"It needs a new muffler, Walt." Ida shut her car door, then joined us in the driveway. She'd followed behind to take him home after he dropped the truck off at my house for me to borrow. "What if it falls off and the sparks set it on fire as she's driving it down the highway?"

"It's not going to fall off while she's driving, Ida dear." He walked behind the truck, pressed down on the bumper as if testing it, then stooped to peer beneath. "Yup, got three wire hangers fastening it to the frame. That muffler's not going anywhere."

It might not be going anywhere, but it was still spewing toxic fumes. I'd make sure to keep the windows cracked for ventilation, no matter how cold or rainy it was, just so I didn't asphyxiate myself.

Dad put the keys in my palm. "You take care of my girl, hear me?"

Aw, he was being sentimental about the old bucket of rust.

"Will do." I gave him a quick hug. "I appreciate the loan."

I wasn't trying to impress anyone; I just needed it for last-minute errands and emergencies until I had time to find a good deal on a newer vehicle.

Ida embraced me, telling me how much she was going to miss me. A tiny lump formed in my throat.

"You two lovebirds have a wonderful time, okay?" Then I added, only half-jokingly, "You aren't eloping, are you?"

"What if we are?" Dad said.

Ida slapped his arm. "No, of course not, Sam. We'd tell you if we were going to do something like that. Wouldn't we, Walt?"

He looked toward the house. Bump was inside, his front paws planted on the sill of the picture window. His furry cheeks puffing with air, he woofed at Dad.

"Mind if I say goodbye to the dog?" he asked.

Hmm, was he avoiding Ida's question or just distracted by Bump's plea for attention?

"Go right ahead." The moment he was inside, I turned back to Ida. "Is something going on with you two—something I should know about?"

Pulling the hood of her coat up to ward off the chilly breeze, Ida shook her head. "Sam, dear... neither of us wants to rush things. We're both set in our ways. Me as much as Walt. We just need time to see if this is going to work out."

"And what better way to test it than a month-long getaway? Gotta hand it to you—you are a brave, brave woman. Don't know that I could handle a week on the road with him, let alone a month. If you can survive this, you're definitely meant for each other."

"I'll be fine. If anyone can handle your father, I can."

"One-hundred-percent true." I hugged her again. "And of all the women in the world, I'm glad he ended up with you. I hope it all works out. I really, really do."

I seemed to be saying that to other people a lot lately, even as my own relationship was strained by the distance. If Archer came home tomorrow, it wouldn't be soon enough.

Five minutes later, Dad and Ida were in her Camry and on their way back to Ida's house to finish packing. They were headed to Indianapolis in the afternoon to spend the night before embarking on the first leg of their international journey. True to her nature, Ida had every detail planned out. Dad's job, apparently, was to speculate about every possible thing that could go wrong.

I had just settled back into a rhythm at my keyboard when a horn beeped from outside. A brown box truck was idling in the driveway. I opened the side door off the kitchen to a forced smile.

"Sign here." The delivery man's smile dropped immediately as he held the electronic clipboard out. He wore an expression somewhere between intense boredom and perpetual irritation.

I signed with a fat stylus in a signature that didn't even remotely resemble my real one. He handed me a small box in exchange.

"Thank you," I chirped in fake cheerfulness. But he wasn't buying it.

He grunted 'Have a good day' as he turned away and climbed up into the driver's seat.

Inside, I opened the package. It was Bump's tracking collar. It wasn't as bulky as I expected, so I decided he should wear it all the time. That way, whether he got loose from me out on a walk again or dug out of the backyard, he'd always have it on. Squirrels were his nemeses, and they were ubiquitous, so I chose to err on the side of caution.

I grabbed some of Bump's essentials, put the tracking collar in my pocket, and loaded him up in the car.

"Want to go see Dr. Clint, Bumparoo?"

Evoking the name of the Beloved One pitched Bump into a frenzy. Spinning in a circle in the backseat, he gave a few earsplitting high-pitched yips.

Hot saliva dripped onto my shoulder. I elbowed Bump in the sternum. "Stay in the back, will you? We're just going to pick up some heartworm medicine."

And to ask a favor. A big one.

WE WALKED INTO THE clinic—or, rather, I walked, while Bump pogoed like a kangaroo—and straight up to the counter. A new receptionist, maybe in her sixties, was manning the desk. Her pinched face and thin lips were as unwelcoming as a TSA security officer the day before Thanksgiving. Dark-rimmed glasses accentuated her laser stare. I felt guilty, unworthy, and bothersome before I even opened my mouth.

I smiled. "Hi, I need to pick up a six-month supply of Have-A-Heart."

"Does your dog have a negative heartworm test on file dated within the past month?"

"No, I—"

"Are you a client here?"

"Yes, I—"

"Your name and the dog's?"

"Bump McNamee... and Sam."

She blinked at me a few times, before I corrected myself. "Sorry, I'm Sam McNamee. My dog's name is Bump."

THREATS AND THREADS

"Weight?"

"Mine or the dog's?" I joked.

"Have-A-Heart is approved for canine use only," she said with deadpan seriousness. "The dog's, please."

"The same as last time he was here."

She typed my name into the database. "Are you sure? He's right on the border between dosages."

"Actually, he's probably a couple of pounds lighter." I forced a smile, hoping to convince her. "We've been walking twice a day."

Pushing her glasses up higher onto her nose, she gave me a dubious look. A few taps of the keyboard later, she said, "Have a seat." Then, to my relief, she rolled her swivel chair back and went into the supply room.

Even though there were a couple of other cars in the parking lot, no one was in the lobby. Soon, the unhappy yowl of a cat and soothing tones of an owner confirmed Clint was with a patient. I could hear him calmly explaining feline idiopathic cystitis to the owner. A minute later, cat and owner emerged from the exam room just as the receptionist emerged with the heartworm medicine. I let the man finish paying his bill before I returned to the counter.

I paid up, deposited the medicine in my purse, and waited for her to look back up at me.

It took a good solid two minutes.

Finally, chin still down, she slid her glasses lower on her nose with a fingertip to peer over the top of the frames at me. "Yes?"

As badly as I wanted to suggest some courses in customer service, I resisted. "I need to ask Dr. Clint something. It will only take a moment."

"Do you have an appointment?"

There was no one else in the lobby. And unless another patient had walked here with their pet, I was now the only one.

From down the hallway, Clint's voice drifted. It sounded like he was returning a patient's phone call. He ended the message, then opened and shut a couple of cabinet doors.

"No, I—"

"Would you like to make one? We have an opening at three."

"At three? You can't be—"

At that point, Bump—who was at the end of his leash, staring down the hallway—started making his delirious monkey whoops and tap dancing on the linoleum.

"I don't really need one. It's kind of—"

"He's on his lunch hour."

"Important and I'm going out of—"

"He's not available at the moment."

I stopped in the middle of my sentence. She may have intimidated me when I first walked in, but I'd had enough. Time to push back.

"Listen up... *you*!" I almost said 'lady,' but that would've been giving her too much credit. "Clint and I are good friends. He used to be my boyfriend, if you need to know. And he helped nurse this dog back to health after Bump was hit by a car. Then again, after he almost died of smoke inhalation. I don't think I need an appointment just to pop in and ask Clint a question that'll take him less than a minute to answer. So if you don't go back there and tell him his friend Sam is here, I'll just march right past you and—"

"Sam, is there a problem with Bump?" Clint stood at the end of the hallway, a concerned expression on his face.

I should've known from the way Bump was twisting in circles that he was there, but I'd been intent on putting the new receptionist—whatever her name was—in her place.

The moment Clint knelt, I let go of Bump before he could rip my arm out of socket. He bounded into Clint's waiting embrace.

"Hey there, buddy!" Clint greeted. Bump slathered him in wet kisses. "All right, all right. Back on all fours. I've missed you, too, Bumparoo."

THREATS AND THREADS

This was why I avoided Clint. Not because he and I had broken up after a whirlwind fling, but because it melted my heart when Bump went out of his mind around him. It almost seemed cruel keeping them apart. And seeing the affection Clint had for the dog, well, it was easy to imagine him being someone's father.

"Oh, hey," Clint said, finally remembering I was there. "What brings you here? Bump seems fine."

I darted a glance at the frontline guard. "Can we go in the back?"

"Sure, follow me." He pushed Bump gently away, and the three of us went into one of the examining rooms.

I closed the door behind me. "Where did you find *her*?"

"Efficient, isn't she?"

"Is that what you call it? I felt like I was being interrogated by border patrol."

"Why's that?" He honestly appeared confused. Bump proceeded to sniff every surface of the room.

"She was—how do I put it?—brusque. No, no, that's not quite right. Rude is a better word."

"Really?"

"Really. Are the pickings that slim in the work pool around here? You couldn't find anyone a little… friendlier?"

"She's my aunt."

"Your what?"

"My dad's sister. Aunt Janelle. She was a surgical nurse for thirty-four years. She's been retired from that for just over a year and offered to help me out here until…"

I noticed then that he'd been avoiding my gaze pretty much since we came in here. He'd jump over the moon for my dog, but apparently would've preferred I stayed away. "Until what?"

"Until Melissa moves back."

It was Melissa's house I was renting. I'd been under the impression she wasn't coming back anytime in the foreseeable future.

It had only been a few months since she'd left to help take care of her sister's baby in Nashville. "When will that be?"

"June, she hopes. July at the latest." He went on to tell me how Melissa's mom was a widow now and had offered to move in with her sister, freeing her up, and that Melissa wasn't liking city life all that much.

"So she'll want her house back, I take it."

He hesitated. "I'm sorry. I know how much you and Tara like the place."

As unexpected as it was, I tried to find the good in it. "That's probably for the best. We love the house. I'd even thought about offering to buy it. But lately, the neighborhood…" A sigh escaped me. Maybelle was right. Strange things *had* been happening ever since I'd shown up. I'd kept hoping that each incident was just a one-off, but a pattern was clearly emerging. Maybe this was a blessing in disguise. If Melissa was going to reclaim the house, Tara and I could find a different house, in a safer neighborhood. Then life would settle down.

I steered the conversation to the real reason I'd come here. "I want to ask you about Grace Hazelton's dog, Pythagoras. You know she was found dead the night he was brought to you?"

One hand cupping his elbow, the other stroking his chin, he nodded. "I did later, but at the time, no."

"Doesn't it seem odd to you the dog died the very same day?"

"I suppose it is unusual."

"What did you conclude he died of?"

He tipped his head thoughtfully. "Indications were renal failure."

"You didn't run blood tests?"

"Sam, he was sixteen years old. She'd had him since high school. By the time he got here, he was in major distress and having convulsions. He'd been vomiting, there was blood in his urine… It all pointed to his kidneys giving out. Like I said, it wasn't until that afternoon I learned about Grace's death."

THREATS AND THREADS

Obviously, he hadn't done lab tests *or* an autopsy. This trip had gotten me nowhere.

"Can they dig his body up and run the tests post mortem?"

"You've been watching too much CSI."

"NCIS actually," I corrected. "But could you? What would they show?"

"A few things: heavy metals, pesticides, drugs. But for some substances, it would be too late. The longer you wait, the more some chemicals break down. Anyway, tests like that are expensive. Nobody's going to pay for them without having a good reason for doing them. So, even if I wanted to, unless law enforcement suspects criminal activity—and even so, we're talking about a dog, not a human being—well… Anyway, it's all a moot point, doing an autopsy. He was cremated."

So much for that. I took my line of questioning in a slightly different direction. "Could some of his symptoms have been a result of poisoning?"

"They could, I suppose. But again, why are you asking?"

My stomach clenched. If Pythagoras had been poisoned to silence him, that meant there was a dog killer in the neighborhood. Leaving Bump at home alone with just Harmon to take care of him didn't seem like such a good idea.

"No reason. Just a strange coincidence—both of them dying, that is."

"You have quite the imagination, Sam," he said.

"So I've been told." The more I thought about it, though, the weirder the coincidence was. That little intuitive worm of worry writhed in my gut. "Clint, can Bump stay with you this weekend? I have a… work thing to go to back in Chicago."

"Sure, he's always welcome."

"Shall I drop him off later? What time?"

"Save yourself the trip and leave him here. I'll take him on a walk at lunchtime."

"Thanks for doing this for me. I wouldn't have asked last minute, but I'm kind of in a bind. Harmon Purnell was going to drop by, but I don't like leaving him alone all day and I don't want to unload him at a boarding kennel."

"Not a problem. Like I said—I'm glad you trust me to keep him, but I'd have thought Walt would want to take care of him. I know how much he loves him."

"He and Ida are going out of town."

"Ah. So what kind of 'work thing' are you doing?"

"Just... meetings," I said. Which was mostly true. Kind of. "I was going to clean out my storage unit while I'm up that way, but I can't because my car's given up the ghost, so I'm going up with..." I stalled, deciding last second I didn't want to visit that topic with him. "Say, did you redecorate in here?"

"If you call swapping out the flea life cycle poster for one on nematodes, yes. Who are you hitching a ride with?"

"Danielle," I mumbled.

"Did you say Danielle?"

I shrugged. "I might have."

"You and Danielle in the same car? That'll be interesting." He switched the soap dispenser with the cotton swab jar on the counter, then the cotton swab jar with the biscuit tin. Evidently, the mention of Danielle's name made him uncomfortable, but he was also curious. "What are you going to talk about for four hours each way?"

"We'll have plenty to talk about." I tapped him on the shoulder. "I know about the baby plans, Clint."

He paused with his hand in the biscuit tin. Several seconds later, he pulled out a handful. One at a time, he fed them to Bump. "I gave it a lot of thought, Sam. I almost called to talk to you about it, but you and I barely seemed to be on speaking terms, so..."

"You don't owe me an explanation, Clint. I'm okay with it. I'm happy for you both. I hope it works out."

That phrase again. It drained me. Trying to spread good karma was taxing.

He gave me a skeptical look. "Are we talking about the same thing, Sam? Because I'm surprised you'd say that, given our history—yours and mine, that is."

"Danielle told me everything. And no matter the hurt we may have caused each other before, it's time we both got on with our lives." I handed Bump's leash to him. I may not have trusted him with my heart anymore, but I did trust him with my dog. "I'll check in regularly. And, of course, if anything happens, call me. Oh, and here." I took the tracking collar and charger from my pocket, then handed it to him. "Can you put this on him once it's charged? It's new and I haven't had a chance to read the manual yet, but just in case… I'm afraid if he gets loose and out of earshot…"

"If it'll make you feel better, sure, I'll make sure he has it on at all times."

"Thanks, Clint. I can't tell you how much I appreciate this." I took the manual out of my purse, then set it on the counter. "There's an app you can download to follow him if you need it. Website's listed on the cover, along with my password."

"Okay, great. I'll download it after work."

Bump was staring at Clint, his eyes on the last biscuit in his hand. The dog didn't even notice me putting my hand on the doorknob he was so enamored with Clint.

Clint tossed the biscuit in the air for Bump to catch, then dug a few more out of the tin. "Sam, Danielle could end up moving away, far away, and then… I don't know. She keeps telling me I'm under no obligation to participate in the kid's upbringing and have no financial responsibilities. But the more I think about it… I really just don't know. It would seem wrong not to play a part in his or her whole life once I've started."

He shook his head, his expression changing from one of contemplation to apology. "Sorry, didn't mean to get personal. Have a great weekend, work or not."

"Thanks, I'll try." I opened the door. Bump glanced at me, his ears flattening. I went to him and kissed him on the head, then stood up. "You're a good guy, Clint. You really are."

"Thank you." He smiled. "I was starting to think you didn't like me very much anymore."

I'd never stopped, I wanted to tell him. I cared about him. A lot. But it takes more than being head over heels in lust with someone to make a relationship work.

"Say, uh…" He paused. "How are you and Archer getting along these days?"

"Great." What I wanted to say was 'complicated,' but that would've invited more questions. I suspected Clint wanted to know if there was any possibility of us ever getting back together again. So I made it clear. "I think he may be *the* one, Clint."

His smile sank. He didn't even try to hide it. "Then he's a lucky guy."

I ducked out before things could go any further. When I got out to Dad's truck, I texted Archer.

Miss you bunches. Hope your meetings are going well.

I was still digging in my purse for the keys when a text dinged. It was Archer.

Miss you too. Terribly. Can't wait to be with you again. I'll come back as soon as I can.

When? I asked.

Soon. Very soon. Promise. I have plans for us!

I stared at the screen until it went dark, then pressed the phone to my chest. A hollow feeling welled inside me, crowding my lungs from the inside. I struggled for air. Tears stung my eyes.

That was when you knew you were in love. When without them,

the emptiness was so crushing you could barely breathe and you sat in a parking lot crying like a baby.

Bunching up the collar of my shirt, I wiped the tears away and typed out a reply.

I can't wait to hold you again, Arch. I don't want to be without you. Ever.

It's only for a little while, he texted. *Just think how lucky it is we found each other.*

So everyone kept saying. But at the moment, I sure didn't feel lucky.

chapter 14

SINCE IT WAS ON my way, I stopped at Garber's so I could say hi to Selma one last time before leaving town—that and see if I could pick up on any sparks between her and Newt, now that I knew they were an item.

"So, what is it that you see in him?" I placed my shampoo on the conveyor belt, along with a package of M&Ms, a trial-sized tube of toothpaste, and a mega bottle of vitamin water.

Selma waved the shampoo bottle over the scanner. It didn't ring up. She waved it again. Nothing. "Blast it! Thing's been acting up all day." A tilt of the bottle, a few more swipes, and, finally, the machine beeped. A drawn-out irritating beep that signaled rejection.

With a huff, she typed the code into the register. A price popped up. She dropped the bottle into a plastic bag on the bagging carousel.

"What did you say?" she asked. Clearly, she wasn't having a good day.

"Newt. You said he complimented you, but what else? Is it the way he treats his customers? Does he have a nice house? Is it his eyes? I mean, there's always something about a guy that..." The whole time I'd been speaking, her eyes had been roaming from one aisle to another. I'd made certain not to come up to the checkout until there weren't any other customers standing in line, but she looked like she was waiting for someone to jump out at her. "Selma?"

She snapped her head back in my direction. "Sorry. I haven't had a cigarette lately. It's starting to get to me."

"You quit?"

"Trying to."

"Well, I admire that." Now that she mentioned it, she was kind of twitchy. "So, what is it about Newt?"

Quietly, she said, "He's the opposite of Dylan. Isn't that enough?"

Depends on what your criteria is, I almost said. Anyway, she could do a lot worse than Newton Tipton. And she had. But maybe I shouldn't get obsessed with her relationships. I had my own to worry about.

"You can start on aisle twelve," she directed loudly. "And hurry up. You're behind."

A man I didn't recognize stood at the end of aisle eleven, pushing a half-full cart of cardboard boxes filled with soup cans. He was tall and athletic-looking, maybe in his early thirties, and dark-complexioned, possibly part African-American.

A warm smile spread across his features as he nodded in greeting. I smiled back. My heart might've fluttered a little, too. I may have been in a committed relationship, but I hadn't gone blind yet.

"Who's that?" I asked as he rounded the corner and went down to the far end of the aisle.

"Lionel Monroe," she growled. "He lives in your neighborhood, by the way. Says he knew that chick who died of carbohydrate poisoning."

Unless Grace Hazelton had stuffed herself to the point of asphyxiation on pasta, that wasn't quite right. "You mean carbon monoxide?"

"All carbs are bad, Sam. Anywho, he started here three days ago. Things have gotten nothing but worse since he showed up."

"Is he a slacker or something? You don't seem too happy with him."

Selma pulled the M&Ms across the screen. The scanner protested again. She pounded the code in. "Hardly a slacker. He's always on time, works after hours, and catches on to everything the first time. I think Newt's considering him for shift manager."

Seemed pointless to have tiered management in a store that employed less than half-a-dozen people. Lionel already had half the boxes unpacked and the cans lined up perfectly. Newt appeared from the supply room and clapped him on the back.

"Ah." I looked back at Selma. "You were hoping he'd make you shift manager?"

"That's what he hinted last week, when..." Frowning, she passed another item in front of the scanner. It buzzed. "Damn it."

She stepped away from the register, then hailed Newt with both arms. He took his glasses from his pocket, moving to put them on as he approached.

"Problem, Selma?"

She readjusted the apron over her uniform shirt, tugging it downward to reveal the top of a black lacy bra and bursting cleavage. Squinting, Newt seemed not to notice. Her dark hair was streaked with orange. She tugged a lock behind her ear, from which dangled a gold hoop earring. A trio of thick gold chains hung around her neck. Her press-on nails alternated black and orange. Ah, tiger theme with bling today. Selma Paradiso could give the trendiest big-city drag queens a run for their money.

Biting her lower lip, she traced a fingertip over Newt's bicep. Or where a bicep would've been if he'd had any muscles. It was hard to tell under that starched, one-size-too-big, button-up shirt of his. "That dumb ol' machine's not cooperating again. I just can't figure it out. Can you... help me?"

From under the register, he took out a chamois and some spray cleaner. A few spritzes from the bottle, a couple of wipes, and he had the last two items scanned and bagged. "Anything else while I'm here?" he said to Selma.

"Naw. But I might need you later." She poked a finger at his sternum. "Don't go too far, 'kay?"

With a perfunctory nod, he left, going down an empty aisle to return to the supply room.

"What was that about?" I prompted, handing her a check for the exact amount.

She dropped my receipt in one of the bags. "He likes to be needed. Boosts his Eggo."

I couldn't resist. "Hey, Tara likes those frozen waffles. What do you call them? Leggo my... something-or-other?"

She blinked at me. "No idea, Sam, but they're in aisle eight if you want to leave your bags here and have a look-see."

"Thanks, I'll do that." I passed the frozen foods where the waffles were, then went a few more aisles. Lionel Monroe had just finished arranging all the soup cans. Perfectly spaced, labels facing out, alphabetical order.

He flashed the friendliest smile at me. "Can I help you find something?"

"You must be Lionel," I announced.

"Ah, no, I just put his name tag on today because I left mine at home." He laughed. I laughed, too. "Just joshing. That's me."

I stuck my hand out. "Hi, I'm Sam. Sam McNamee. A friend of Selma's."

Lionel shook my hand. "Nice to meet you, Sam McNamee, friend of Selma's. Now what can I do for you, miss?"

He'd called me 'miss'. And here I thought I'd crossed that bridge a decade ago. He may as well have handed me a dozen roses. "Selma tells me you live in Bluebird Estates."

"I do."

"Me too. Terrible what happened with that woman over the weekend, isn't it?" When he gave me a blank look, I got more specific. "Grace Hazelton. They say her furnace wasn't operating properly and leaked gas. She died of carbon monoxide poisoning."

"Oh, yeah, terrible. I heard the ambulance."

"You did?" Now I was on to something. "Do you live close to her?"

"Yeah, across the street and a few doors down. Always sad to hear about someone who died so young. We'd talked once or twice, but I didn't know her name until after that night. I'm kinda new to the neighborhood."

"How long ago did you move in?"

"Been there since the first of September. First house I ever owned. Hopefully not my last, though."

"September, huh? I walk the streets a lot—" I realized that didn't sound quite like I meant, so I reworded it. "I mean, I walk my dog around the neighborhood a lot, and I can't recall seeing you out."

"Probably 'cause I work sixty or seventy hours a week. This here's my second job. Plus, I'm taking night classes to get my degree. Just need to finish up two more courses and I'll have it. Then, I can get a better gig than this." He pointed a finger at me. "You didn't hear that from me."

"I won't say a word." I winked. "Say, did you hear Grace Hazelton's dog died practically the same day?"

"Huh. That right? Come to think of it, I haven't heard him carry on this week."

"Did he bark or howl a lot? Did she leave him out all the time? That must've been annoying."

"No, he didn't bark or howl *all* the time. Just most of the time when she let him out. Usually, it wasn't for long. Just long enough to wake me up. Some cat was always standing right outside her fence, bugging the tar out of that dog. The dog was just being a dog. But man, that dog's complaining sure wrecked a lot of good nights' sleep for me. Nothing against dogs—I'd have one myself if I had the time."

Lionel didn't seem like the sort to gas a neighbor out of spite, even if he did have a reason to. But another neighbor… "Who owns the cat?"

"The one her dog kept barking at? Beats me. Could be a stray, for all I know. Thin, but healthy-looking. I put out some tuna for it once, but after that, it never came back."

"Was it a black cat with a little patch of white on its chest?"

"One of those tuxedo cats? I guess. Why?"

"Just that I noticed one like that near her house when I was out that way not too long ago." With a turn of my wrist, I checked my watch. "Anyway, nice to meet you, Lionel. I have to run now."

"Nice meeting you as well, miss."

On the way out, I grabbed my bags and darted for the exit.

"Were we out of the waffles?" Selma asked.

"I forgot," I told her. "Tara's on a gluten-free kick. She won't touch wheat products anymore."

"Honey, you don't have to get the whole-wheat kind. They still sell the regular ones."

"Made out of flour?"

"I suppose."

"Which is made out of wheat, right?"

"How should I know?"

"Uh, thanks anyway." Unless they'd started stocking rice flour waffles, they were wheat, which meant they had wheat gluten, but I wasn't getting into that argument. "See you around."

I DROVE PAST HARMON and Maybelle Purnell's house four times, hoping to find Harmon out before I remembered he'd be working at the school until it let out around three. So I went home, Selma's can of pepper spray in hand as I opened the door into the kitchen. Once again, nothing was out of place. No messages on the phone and no threatening e-mails.

For an hour, I busied myself going over my notes for the panel discussion, but when I attempted to resume my WIP, the words were elusive. I doubted every twist and turn. Even simple plot points and scene settings. This was the worst case of writer's block I'd ever had. The outline I'd been working from no longer seemed to fit. Especially since TrueLuv was breathing down my neck about how I'd tossed my hero and heroine in separate directions.

Instead of working, I cleaned the house. At a quarter to four, I stowed the vacuum in the linen closet and got ready for a solo walk. Instinctively, I reached to lift Bump's leash off the hook by the side door, but it was gone.

The house was empty. Deathly quiet. Bump was with Clint and Tara was at the Mullinses'—both out of harm's way. While I didn't like the prospect of staying here another night by myself, by the time I came home at the end of the weekend, Marco would have the alarm system all planned out and would start installing it Monday. I'd even asked him to put up two security cameras—one in the back of the house and one in front.

Alone, I stepped outside. It was warmer today. The leaves were almost all gone from the trees, and the grass had turned a dull yellow. Winter wasn't far off, though. I strolled past Harmon's house again, but I didn't see him. I didn't even notice Maybelle peeking out from behind the drapes. I went around the block. Twice. Still no sign of him. I finally decided if I didn't run into him on the way back, I'd just leave him a note in the kitchen.

Since my main goal of talking to Harmon hadn't materialized, I went by Cleora's house. She, fortunately, was home.

"Sam." She waved at me from her front porch. "Where's your

walking partner today?"

I went to stand at the base of her steps. "I left him with his best buddy, Dr. Clint, so Bump could get some exercise while I'm gone over the weekend."

"Fancy loves Dr. Clint! We're lucky to have such a knowledgeable vet in a small town like this. You tell him he's free to bring Bump by this weekend for a playdate with Fancy. Interacting with Bump has improved her confidence around other dogs tremendously. It also tuckers her out. You should have seen how hard she slept after book club."

"Hey, if you have a chance at any point, would you keep an eye out on my house and call me if you see anything suspicious? Since someone tried to break in last week, I'm afraid if they figure out I'm not there, they'll try again."

"Of course. Fancy and I can do that on our daily walk." At the sound of her name, Fancy peeked from behind Cleora's ankles. Her tail wagged at seeing me, but after realizing Bump wasn't with me, she disappeared back inside. Cleora pulled her cardigan closed. "How rude of me. It's still a little nippy out here. Come inside, Sam."

"I can't. I have a lot to do before I go. I just wanted to ask, though... Is the book club meeting at the same time next week?"

"We are. You'll be coming back, I trust?"

"Oh, yes."

"Do you like the book then?"

"Love it. I'm almost done."

"Good, because not everyone wanted to read it."

That confirmed what Selma had said.

"Like who?" I blurted. I wanted to slap myself. I did not need to know exactly who hated my book. That was like asking friends what they *really* thought of my wardrobe, my hairstyle, my boyfriend, or my decorating choices. Most of the time, I'd be better off *not* knowing.

"About half, I'd say."

Geez, that was way worse than I thought.

"Then again," Cleora added, "that's the case every time we try to pick a book. It's never unanimous. Grace Hazelton was particularly against it, though. When she came into the library, she only ever wanted to read depressing books, mostly dystopian and post-apocalyptic stories. Sometimes epic family sagas where everyone turns against each other in a power bid. Her suggestions got voted down at the meeting. She never talked much, so I'm not even sure why she came to the book club, except, maybe, like the rest of us, she just needed to belong to something."

"Did anybody in the book club have a gripe with her?"

"Not that I'm aware of. She may have had different tastes, but she was always polite. Pleasant, too. Mostly she kept to herself. Why do you ask?"

"Just trying to figure out if her death was an accident or not."

She frowned. "What a shame. She was so young. She was divorced, you know. Maybe her ex or a beneficiary wanted to collect on her life insurance?"

"Did she have a big policy? Relatives who needed money?"

"I'm only guessing, Sam. I didn't know her well enough to say. I do know she hasn't lived in Wilton that long. Less than a year, maybe. She never volunteered much information about herself."

"Any idea where she worked?"

"No, it never came up. Say, why don't you come inside for some hot chocolate, please?"

"That sounds heavenly, but I really ought to go. Again, if you see anything—"

Behind her, Fancy barked for attention. "Just a minute, baby doll." Then, to me, "Should I let anyone else know you'll be out of town—sort of a neighborhood watch—or not?"

"Mmm, no. I don't want to alert the world, so if you could keep it under wraps..."

THREATS AND THREADS

"I certainly will. Have a wonderful time, Sam. We'll see you at the next meeting."

Fancy gave a few parting barks before Cleora shut the door.

I picked up the pace on the way home, going down the street Harmon's house was on, bypassing the street where Miley's old house was. I spotted Maybelle getting out of her car and waddling inside with a few bags of groceries. I was one step away from pivoting around and reversing course when she stopped dead and stared me down.

"Lose your dog?" Maybelle asked, almost sounding hopeful.

"Haha," I said, faking laughter. "Actually, I loaned him to a friend to run with."

She hit the automatic lock on her remote key. A barely audible click sounded. She punched the button with her thumb again. The car beeped twice and flashed its lights. "I can never tell if that thing's working or not," she grumbled.

Setting the bags down beside the front door, she unlocked the door and opened it. Then she placed the bags inside and turned to me. "And yet, you figured you needed to walk past my house anyway. What for?"

"Why not? I just took a walk, went down a street. Is that a crime?"

"With people like you, it oughta be."

Before I could ask her what the hell that meant, she went inside and locked the door. I stood there speechless, wondering why on earth she had it out for me and had ever since I showed up in this neighborhood. There had to be some answer, but it probably wasn't worth worrying about.

I took my time getting home. There wasn't anything, or anyone, to go home to.

chapter 15

"Did I tell you where the key to the safe deposit box is?" Dad asked.

"Where are you, Dad?" The phone squeezed between my left ear and shoulder, I rifled through my closet and dug out my dress-up shoes—a pair of open-toed silver flats that went with everything fancy I owned.

"Miami. Been here five hours, waiting to get on the next flight. Five blinking hours. Five. Ida made me walk around the concourse, so I don't get blood clots. Did you know you can get blood clots in your legs from sitting folded up like an accordion for too long? Now did I tell you where the—"

"You did—and for the fourth time, it's inside the mateless, blue-striped tube sock at the back right of your sock drawer." I put my phone on speaker while I tossed the last few clothing items in my suitcase.

"Okay, okay. But if the house burns down—"

"Then Gladys Detwiler has an extra, although she doesn't know it. You hid it in her spare tire compartment when you changed a tire for her after the lodge picnic."

"I checked the safe deposit box two days ago, just to make sure she hadn't gotten into it. Everything was still there, thank God."

My dad was a member of the E and C Church—Easter and Christmas. He called on God to damn things ten times more often than he thanked Him for anything. I stepped into the upstairs bathroom to grab my toothpaste and toothbrush, then returned to put them inside my suitcase. "Pretty sure she'd have to show ID at the bank to do that, Dad. And anyway, even if she found the key, how would she know what it was for? Or what bank to go to? Or which safe deposit box it went to?"

As I searched through my underwear drawer for my no-show panties, I realized he hadn't replied. I picked up the phone to make sure I hadn't run out of battery. "Dad, are you still there?"

"What if she threw it away, Sam?"

"Threw what away? And who?"

"Gladys! The key!"

His voice nearly punctured a hole in my eardrum. I set the phone down on the bed and zipped up my luggage. "Pretty sure she hasn't changed a tire herself since then, Dad. Look, don't worry. I'm sure everything's fine. If worse comes to worse and you do die, I know Ernie down at the bank will let me into the safe deposit box once I show him the obituary. But, just in case that happens, is there a million dollars in stocks in there I should know about?"

"Funny, Sam. You shouldn't joke about me dying when I'm about to take a plane over the Gulf of Mexico."

"Just being practical. Anyway, you're the one who keeps bringing up your last will and testament."

"Do you have me on speakerphone, Sam?"

I switched the speaker off, then tucked the phone to my ear as I headed downstairs. "No, Dad, I don't." Not now, anyway.

"You know how I hate being on speakerphone. Might as well have it on a bullhorn. Anyone could overhear both sides of our conversation."

"I'm at home, Dad." I walked into the kitchen, checking to see that the coffee maker and toaster were unplugged.

"You do know they're spying on people through their computers and TVs now, right?"

"Who's 'they'?"

"CIA, FBI, ICE, NSA, DHS, DEA…"

He may as well have been reciting the alphabet backward. My father was sure that federal intelligence had an interest in checking up on Average Joes like him.

"Oh, hey, my ride's here." It wasn't, but I didn't want to get into spy surveillance with him because that was an argument I couldn't win. "Gotta go. Call me when you get there."

"I'm not sure I'll be able to, Sam. Remember we're visiting a third-world country."

"You're flying in to Buenos Aires, Dad. They do have internet and phone service there. Have Ida message me. Just let me know you're safe, all right?"

"If you don't hear from us in forty-eight hours, assume the worst. I pre-paid for funerals for myself and Ida, just in case. That way you don't have to worry about financing it when you're grieving for us."

As much as I hated being a sounding board for his pre-vacation doomsday phase, I knew he was putting up a much braver front for Ida. The fact he was taking this step at all for her was monumental. All I could do was hope he had some fun while he was there, and he came back a changed person for it.

It was either that… or Ida would end up dumping him. Which meant he'd want to move in with me.

"Dad, can I talk to Ida now?"

"She's indisposed. Been drinking a lot of water so she doesn't get dehydrated on the flight, but all that's doing is making her have to—"

"Can you tell her as soon as she's done that I want *her* to contact me first chance she has when you guys get there?"

THREATS AND THREADS

"I will, I will... Oh, hey, I think they just called for us to board. And I see Ida now. She's over at the ticket counter waving at me and everybody's lined up, jockeying for position. It's like a cattle call."

"Bye, Dad. I'll miss you." Strangely, that was true. For most of my life—ever since my mom left us—he'd been the bitter, barely there single parent. But after I came home last summer, I'd developed more empathy for him. I understood what he'd been through with Mom—how she'd jilted him to jet off to France with an old lover, how she'd kept the secret of my paternity from him, how he'd struggled with loneliness and depression while trying to raise a little girl all on his own. In short, he'd become less villain and more hero in my eyes.

The sexy hum of a sports car sounded outside. One last time, I checked that the back door was locked and the doggie door securely shut. Leaving the house unattended left me uneasy, but I couldn't back out on this obligation now. I was destined for Chicago where hundreds of romance fans and aspiring writers were gathering to hear their favorite authors speak—and I was one of those authors. The thought of it was both exhilarating and terrifying by equal measures.

Danielle knocked at the front door. No one ever came to the front door who'd been here before.

I opened it and motioned her in, grabbing a stack of yesterday's mail from the counter. "Hi. I'm running behind. Just let me check one more time that I've unplugged everything that needs unplugged."

She was dressed as casually as I'd ever seen her, with tailored navy-blue ankle pants and a gunmetal-gray crop jacket with more zippered pockets than any person could possibly have use for. She'd ditched the three-inch strappy heels in favor of closed-toe pumps. I glanced down at my traveling attire of fuzzy Ugg boot knockoffs and comfy leggings. Even on her day off from work, Danielle still looked like she'd just walked out of Ann Taylor on Chicago's Magnificent Mile. I, on the other hand, looked like I'd raided the fifty-cent discount rack at Salvation Army.

Danielle glanced around the house, no hint of judgment in her gaze. "Actually, I should apologize for being early. Having lived much of my life where traffic congestion is a daily problem, it's ingrained in my habits to depart early for a destination. I forget the only traffic around here is school busses and tractors. Considering the children have already been picked up for the day and it's past harvest season, I should know better. Again, my apologies."

"No problem. I'm usually a little behind getting out the door, just to warn you."

She didn't say anything out loud, but I could see her stiffen at the prospect of having to hurry me along at every departure. It was hard to imagine this woman with a young child. Did she think they weren't going to spit up or soil their diaper five minutes before leaving for an appointment? Babies, in particular, operated on their own schedule. Maybe her maternal side would override her punctual one. Maybe.

While she loitered in the living room, I scribbled a note for Harmon:

Dear Harmon,

Scratch that. What if he tucked the note in his pocket and Maybelle found it? Addressing him as 'Dear' Harmon was likely to land him crotch deep in manure. I crumpled the note up and tossed it in the wastebasket, then wrote another.

Tried to get a hold of you yesterday. Dr. Clint has the dog, so you don't need to worry about him. Thanks anyway. Lock the door behind you. Talk to you later.

Short and to the point. He couldn't possibly get confused. The dog wasn't here. He didn't need to come back. I tried to think of ways to omit Clint's name and mentioning the dog at all, but I figured that would be too vague. I did leave my signature off, just in case. I placed the note squarely on the kitchen counter where I'd shown him, then weighted the corner down with a plate of freshly baked brownies to draw his attention there, just in case.

As soon as I was assured my hair dryer, all the TVs, and the desktop were unplugged, I grabbed my suitcase from upstairs, stuffing the mail in the side pocket for later. I joined Danielle in her car, and we hit the road.

Our small talk lasted less than five minutes. Which meant a dreadfully long trip ahead. Reading to pass the time seemed like a passive-aggressive way of rudely shutting her out and the GPS had stolen possible navigation duties, so I pretended to nap for the first hour as we wound our way through rural Indiana.

Mile after mile of stubbled grain stalks rolled by. Occasionally, we passed a herd of cattle grazing on the remnants of cornfields. Leaning barns with missing planks and old farm houses with peeling paint characterized the landscape that most thought of as Midwest Americana—the sleepy heartland of a nation. The state highway we were on dipped and curved erratically, following the outlines of vast tracts of private property.

"Before we get to the beltway," Danielle broached halfway to Valparaiso, "I suppose I should know where exactly to drop you off."

I roused myself out of semi-sleep to process her words. I would've stretched my legs, but it was impossible to do folded up in this jet engine toy car. A yawn burgeoned up, and I let it out before answering. "The Walden Conference Center in Oak Brook, just off—"

"Just off I-88. Yes, I know the place. You're practically across the street from me. My conference is at the Marriott. But I thought you said you were meeting with your publishing company about work? I assumed that was downtown."

Dang, I hadn't thought this out. So I made up a flimsy half-truth on the fly about meeting up with the editing team at a publishers' conference there.

We were somewhere on I-65 now. I offered Danielle a dip into my bag of pretzels, hoping some munchies would prevent either of us from talking. To my dismay, she waved them off and spoke anyway.

"Tell me about your daughter," she said.

Polite and not too intrusive. I could handle it.

"Tara? Well, she's fifteen going on fifty." After I pulled out a pretzel, I licked the salt off before taking a bite. I needed a minute to think about how to describe her. For some reason, my brain worked better when my mouth was busy. Maybe because it gave me a chance to actually think things through before speaking. "She just discovered boys. Kind of a late bloomer, but I'm okay with that." Then I went on to list the activities she was involved in, including how she'd had her hopes of making a swim relay team dashed.

"She sounds like a wonderful young lady."

"Snarky at times, but I wouldn't trade her for anything. She's wiser than her years. Even if she is having trouble fitting in because she's not the popular type, her maturity will pay off in the long run."

It was always hard to read Danielle's expressions, but her silence was telling. Her lips parted as if to speak, but then she snapped them shut.

"What is it?" I prompted.

Flipping the turn signal on for a lane change, she shook her head. "I'm sorry. What's what?"

"When I mentioned Tara not being popular, it looked like you were going to say something."

Her eyelids twitched. "There's an assumption that being popular is a gift granted to the genetically blessed. But popularity isn't about looks, is it? It's about how others perceive you. It's about being liked."

"I wouldn't know." I bit off a piece of pretzel, then munched away.

Her mouth slanted with a smirk. "Neither would I."

We both broke into smiles. We understood being different. My reaction had been to retreat into books where I could inhabit the world of my choosing. Hers had been to study medicine. We both gave back to the world in vastly different ways.

THREATS AND THREADS

I had to be careful. If I spent much more time with Danielle Townsley, we might just end up being friends.

CHICAGO TRAFFIC BEING WHAT it normally was at rush hour on a Friday, we arrived right on time—meaning an hour and fifteen minutes later than we should have. But having lived here before, I always factored that in ahead of time.

Stuffed from my bag of pretzels, I hadn't asked to stop and eat. By the time Danielle dropped me off at my hotel, I was so thirsty I could have drained a lake. Checked in, unpacked, and supperless without a dinner date, I did the next best thing—I ordered room service and called Archer while I waited for my food.

"Hey, Sam..." His voice trailed away wearily. I was afraid he was going to proclaim an early night and beg out of the conversation. Instead, his voice took on a wistful tone. "I can't tell you how much I wish you were here with me... or that I was there with you."

Having drained bottled water number two since arriving, I lay back on the bed, tired from the drive. "Me too. I'd like to be anywhere with you."

"Anywhere?"

"Sure, anywhere."

"Huddled on a set of metal bleachers at a high school football game, freezing our buns off?"

"I'd do that—with you." And he knew I hated football. But if he wanted me there, I'd go.

"Camping under the stars in the desert?"

"As long as you promise to slay all the rattlesnakes before they strike. I can't imagine anything more heavenly than you telling me all the names of the constellations."

"You're assuming I know them."

"Do you?"

"Sure do. I was an Eagle Scout." Of course he had been. "How about backpacking on a dirt mountain road in Nepal?"

"Sounds exotic. But why would you be there?"

"Some sort of pilgrimage, I suppose. Play along."

Closing my eyes, I focused on the sound of his breathing and imagined him beside me. I saw him clutching a walking stick, a worn canvas backpack drooping from his shoulders. There were creases at the corners of his eyes from squinting into the sun and the barest touch of gray at his temples. Every once in a while, he'd gaze at me, smile, and offer an encouraging word. It was easy to imagine growing old with him and doing all sorts of unusual and exciting things. Just like Dad and Ida were doing right now. The difference was that Archer and I had a couple of extra decades in which to do all those things. Even though we weren't old, we still weren't young. Time was too precious to be spending it apart. I thought about how good it would feel to hold him again, to look into his eyes...

But when I opened my eyes, all I saw was the lumpy popcorn ceiling above me and a sprinkler nozzle. That last thing reminded me of him.

"Archer, you are coming back to Wilton eventually, aren't you?"

"You're there," he said. "I have to come back."

"When?" I shouldn't have pressed the matter, but the question flew out of my mouth involuntarily.

"As soon as I can. Promise. I have projects to finish in Wilton."

As much as I wanted to believe 'soon' meant days, not weeks or months, I wasn't so sure about that.

Then he said something even better. Something that was less promise, more substance.

"Sam, do you ever think about... us, you know, not just a few weeks or months down the road, but years?"

"Sometimes, yeah. How about you?"

THREATS AND THREADS

"More and more each day."

"What do you think about?"

"How nice it would be to come home to you at the end of each day. How we'd sit on a porch swing—our own porch swing—on summer evenings and listen to the bullfrogs while the fireflies lit up the fields. How we'd rake leaves together, sit by the fireplace on dark winter nights, and listen to the spring rain as we lay in a bed on a lazy Saturday."

"I'd love that. Very much." Although neither of us owned a home in the country in which to do all those things.

But it didn't hurt to have something to dream about.

chapter 16

WHEN I GLANCED IN the mirror the next morning, I knew this day was off to a bad start. I blinked hard, rubbed my eyeballs, and blinked again. Leaning in closer, I took another look. My eyelids were puffed up so bad there weren't enough cucumber slices in the world to get the swelling down. The whites of my eyes were more shocking pink than anything, underlain by a mapwork of snaky blood vessels. I'd rubbed them so hard before getting out of bed I'd apparently ruptured blood vessels in both eyes. Between falling asleep with my eye makeup on, staying up late, and a bag full of salt-laden pretzels, I'd retained enough water to be a body-double for Shamu the Killer Whale.

After a quick shower, I checked my texts, hoping for a message from Archer, even though I knew it was still early in his time zone. The only message, one from Ida, simply said, *We're here!*

Attached was a selfie of her and Dad in front of a posh hotel in Buenos Aires. Off to the side was a sleek silver tour bus and what I assumed was their travel group, maybe twenty people total, all over sixty. Ida had on a white peasant-style top and a flouncy skirt in a flower pattern. Large dark sunglasses hid her eyes, but there was a smile on her lips as big as Brazil. Dad, although appearing a little more haggard from the overnight flight, was smiling, too. His face was shaded by a flat-topped almost cowboy-style black hat with a wide brim. All he needed was a pair of boots and gaucho pants to complete the look.

Just as I was about to set the phone back down, another text came through.

This is your father, Walter David Schimmoller, it said. *Pilot almost took us down over the Gulf. Later, we nearly crash-landed in the jungle. Some foreigner named Emilio is now dragging us on a tour of the slums of this godforsaken city. Criminals everywhere. If you don't hear from me ever again, I was either kidnapped or arrested for a crime I didn't commit.*

If they kidnap you, I texted back, *tell them your family is broke and they are stuck with you. If you get arrested and end up in jail, remember to make friends with the guards. I hear they are good for smuggling candy bars and cigarettes inside.*

You know I don't smoke, he replied.

I texted, *After a few years in the slammer, you may want to start.*

I replaced the phone on the nightstand, then sat on the edge of the bed. Achingly aware of how alone I was, I searched for the remote to the TV, finally finding it under a pillow. I turned it on, and the sound blared so loudly I almost didn't hear the next text come in.

Ida here. He's exaggerating, as usual. Turbulence over the Gulf. He had to use the sick bag. Flew over the Amazon rain forest at sunrise after a storm—it was breathtaking. The locals have been wonderful. And Emilio is from Miami.

I smiled as I typed my reply: *Looking forward to pictures. Prison or otherwise.*

P.S., I added a minute later, *tell him to look out for the Chupacabra.*

Only if I want to get rid of him for good.

Right, I replied. *In that case, your call.*

TWENTY MINUTES TILL NOON. If there was ever a time for an anxiety attack, it was now.

Mustering what little courage I could, I stepped out of my room for the first time since yesterday afternoon. I'd been using the time without distractions to work on my novel and had gotten an amazing amount done.

Voices sounded nearby. I grabbed the doorknob and turned, but it was locked. Panic overwhelmed me. I shoved a hand inside my jacket pocket and found my key card, but before I could insert it into the slot, a group of women appeared from around the corner about four doors down. Several had a small stack of books cradled in their arms. One even had an oversized bag bursting with books. They were engrossed in chatter about that morning's signing event, which I'd missed on account of my puffy eyes and face.

"I can't believe you scored a signed copy from Octavia Bloomsdale."

"Me either! I got one from Rooby Hart, too. Can you believe *that?* I stood in line for thirty minutes and when I got to her, she made me feel like I was the only person in the room with her. I even took this." She touched the screen of her phone, then held it toward her friend.

"Well, I'll be. Lucky you. Better make that your profile picture."

"Already have!"

As they walked toward me, I took out my phone to check for texts. Nothing. I turned the volume off so it wouldn't ring in the middle of my panel session.

"Hey," came a small, mousy voice.

I met the big brown eyes of a Hispanic-looking young woman holding a single paperback. She smiled warmly in a way that made it appear she was about to ask a favor.

"Hey," I said back. Was she going to ask for my autograph? I didn't have a pen—

A few feet from me, she looked away. I glanced at the spine of her book. It wasn't mine. A little bubble of pride burst inside me as I reminded myself there was no way she could have known who I was.

THREATS AND THREADS

I hadn't been at the book signing, having instead just sent a box of already-signed books, and had never put my picture in the back of my novels. Anonymity did afford me privacy, but it also meant being, well… anonymous.

Blast. She was just being nice to a stranger. I wasn't sure if I was relieved or disappointed.

The women walked to the end of the hallway, then gathered before the elevator doors. With just fifteen minutes to go, I decided now was as good a time as any to march toward my fate. I hurried after them. The doors whooshed open, and ten of us filed into the tiny six-by-six box suspended from a cable in a dark shaft twelve floors aboveground.

Safely wedged in the back corner, I peered over the shoulder of one of the women at the book on top of her pile. Adorning the front cover was a busty redhead in a strapless leather getup, shorty shorts, and biker boots with a sword in one hand and her other resting on the withers of a golden-eyed wolf. Ah, the paranormal urban fantasy crowd. I had to admit, badass crossbow-wielding chicks who mated with shapeshifters was intriguing. I may have read a few in my day. Purely for comparative market research.

The bell dinged, and the doors slid open. En masse, we swarmed into the lobby. After checking the closest room number plaque on the wall, I turned left. As I walked, I shuffled my stack of note cards from hand to hand.

I could already feel the cotton mouth setting in. A zip tie of dread had tightened around my intestines. Stopping, I leaned a shoulder against the wall and began to read my cards. The type was all blurry. I'd left my reading glasses back in the room. Squinting, I held the cards out at arm's length. My slanted scrawl sharpened just enough to be legible.

"Excuse me," a vaguely familiar voice interrupted. "Do you know which room the—"

I glanced up. Birdie Swinson came at me, a conference folder tucked against her sleeveless black denim vest. Red leggings with printed roses and black glittery high-tops drew attention to her pencil-thin legs. Pushing her glasses higher on the bridge of her nose, she slowed. Recognition was setting in.

Five feet away, she ground to a halt, blinking like she had a bug stuck on her eyeball.

Remarkably, I had on a business suit—and yes, I did own one—two if the one I wore to funerals counted. I even had on jewelry, even if just an interlinking silver necklace and dangly earrings. My hair was also pulled into a French twist, taming my unruly curls. In short, from a distance, I was probably unrecognizable, but up close—

"You're the new person," she said, scrutinizing me.

I played dumb. "You must be thinking of someone else."

"In the book club. Sam McNamee, isn't it?"

Cornered, I went belly up. "Yep, that's me. So… you're a romance fan, huh?"

A set of double doors about thirty feet down the corridor opened, and women dressed in flouncy gowns and fake wigs began trickling out. It was a historical romance session entitled: *History vs. Story. Where Do You Draw the Line?*

"I don't read anything else." She pulled her chin back. "Actually, I used to. But literary fiction was too snooty. Who wants to think that hard? Mysteries always seem contrived. Who cares whodunit? Gather the evidence and slap them in jail. When it comes to science fiction, I'd rather see a movie. No matter how they describe a starship, it's never as good as what the special effects people can conjure up. Don't get me started on fantasy. I mean elves, dragons, magic… really? And suspense—forget it. Makes me paranoid someone's stalking me. Puts ideas in people's heads, too."

A chill zipped up my spine. How was it that someone I knew—sort of—from a town as tiny as Wilton, Indiana would be at *this*

THREATS AND THREADS

conference? I'd have bet my life against it. Otherwise, I would've turned it down. If a fear of public speaking had me rattled before, now I was hurtling straight into panic mode.

"Did you come alone?" I hid my index cards behind my back.

Her eyes narrowed. "That's a creepy question to ask."

It was creepy she'd turned up here. Maybe Birdie was my stalker.

"I mean, did anyone from the book club come with you?"

"Of course not. Most of them aren't *real* readers. They just skim and stop on the juicy parts. None of them understand a thing about mounting tension or climax." She stepped uncomfortably close. "Except for Cleora, they don't even know the difference between a protagonist and a protozoan."

Someone jostled my elbow and I stepped to the side, thankful for an excuse to put another foot of distance between Birdie and me. I wasn't sure what to make of her. She seemed harmless, but I'd been fooled before.

People were filing past us in droves now, a sea of them—readers, writers, agents, editors. I wondered which talk they were going to. In any given fifty-minute slot, there were as many as six different ones scheduled.

Birdie studied me. I must have looked as out of place as a cat at a dog show.

Eager to escape, I checked my watch. "Oh, dear, only ten minutes until the next session. You'd better hurry so you don't miss it."

She didn't budge. "Which one are you going to?"

So much for dissing her. She wanted to tag along. "I haven't decided yet. I might just skip this one and go back to my room for a nap."

She shrugged. "Suit yourself. See you around."

Stepping away, I waved goodbye. "See ya."

I waited until the crowd swallowed her. When I thought I saw her duck into Room 103, I resumed my journey down the corridor, now thick with people. The stream turned into an oozing sludge as the doors of a conference room swung open and another talk let out. Now twice as many people were crammed into the same hallway, going in opposing directions. The poster board on the easel outside the room said: *Bestselling Author Rooby Hart Tells All—What My Life as a Call Girl Taught Me About Love.*

At least three dozen fans were milling around Rooby Hart. She juggled signing copies of her books as they barraged her with questions and smiled for selfies. I admired her multitasking abilities, and I was thoroughly jealous of her sales numbers. I may have managed a living off my books in a short span of time, but Rooby Hart had built herself an empire over her twenty-year career.

The blond ahead of me stopped abruptly, blocked by the logjam. She flinched as the corner of my index cards jabbed her in the back. Her elbow swung around in a defensive move.

I jerked back, my hand clipping the briefcase of an editor type to the left of me. Index cards slipped from my grasp, scattering onto the floor. I ducked to retrieve them, only to get whacked in the noggin by aforementioned briefcase.

Stars exploded across my vision. My knees buckled beneath me, dropping me to the floor. Franticly, I scooped up the note cards, plucking several from beneath the soles of nearby oblivious people. The only thing that kept me from getting trampled was that the flow of traffic had stopped entirely. The lady carrying the briefcase set it down, then helped me to my feet.

"I'm so sorry," she said, staring at my forehead. Or maybe she was looking me in the eye. I still couldn't see straight. "Can I get you a bandage?"

I touched my free hand to my face, probing above my eyebrow until I located a tender spot. Ah, yes. She *had* been staring at my forehead. There was a small cut there from the metal corner of her briefcase. A thin trickle of blood traced its way over my temple. "Do you have one on you? I have to be in Room 107 in a few minutes."

A grimace twisted her mouth. "Uh, no, sorry, I don't. But I could fetch one from the concierge and bring it to you, if you let me know where you'll be sitting."

I wiped at the blood with my thumb. It wasn't much. Then I remembered I'd stuffed a tissue in the pocket of my blazer. I pulled it out, then pressed it to the cut. "That's okay. I think I'll be fine in a few minutes."

Although now I had a killer headache to go with the roughed-up look. After I wedged my way past her, I wove around a dozen others until I found the wall. With about fifty more "Excuse me's," I was at the door of my assigned room. I opened it, saw nothing but wall-to-wall people blocking my view of the dais, and stepped back out.

"This can't be right," I muttered to myself.

Putting the tissue back in my pocket, I took out the slip of paper with the schedule on it. I read the plaque again, glanced down at the paper, back at the plaque. Oh, crap. This *was* the right room.

Moths swarmed in my stomach, fluttered at the back of my throat, and tickled my gag reflex. Stuffing the schedule in my pocket, I slapped a hand over my mouth to keep from hurling.

Breathe, Sam. Breathe.

I swallowed, opened my mouth, and pulled in air. Then I went in. A din of conversation immediately overcame my senses. Row upon row of chairs were filled. So full it was standing-room only. Faces turned to gawk. I lowered my eyes and forged on once more, glancing up only often enough to pick a path through the throng. Five years later—it seemed that long, anyway—I made it to the dais.

Summer Monroe, the one who'd invited me to be on the panel, sat front and center. She waved at me. I waved back. On wobbly knees, I mounted the steps to the top of the stage and walked behind the long table until I found the place card with swirly loops and dips of calligraphy I was fairly sure said S. A. Mack. If it wasn't, someone would let me know I was sitting in their chair. Scooting the chair back, I sat my rump down. A bouquet of daisies and dahlias temporarily blocked my view of the audience. Good, maybe I could hide in plain view.

Then the septuagenarian beside me removed the vase, setting it on a round table behind us. When she sat back down and smiled, I went from flummoxed to awestruck. It was Octavia Bloomsdale, the queen of billionaire jetsetter romance. Her books had dominated the *New York Times Bestseller* lists for almost four decades—even been made into TV movies and feature films. I felt like a speck of stardust next to a supernova.

"Good afternoon," she said. Her voice had that soft purr to it with a slightly gravelly texture, like an old recording of Greta Garbo. "Lovely to meet you, Ms…"—she tilted my nameplate toward her, then faced it forward again—"Mack, is it?"

"Yes," I heard myself say, amazed I was able to speak, I was so mesmerized. "Nice to meet you, too." I wanted to tell her to call me Sam, but I wasn't sure sitting next to each other in a room with five hundred other people constituted being on a first name basis. Besides, I was here as S.A. Mack, the author, not Sam McNamee, the private citizen.

I tapped my cards on the table to even the edges. As I took the first one from the top of the stack, I realized they were totally out of order, some of them backward, some upside down, some both. I hadn't taken the time to number them. They were useless.

I glanced at Octavia Bloomsdale. The only thing in front of her was a champagne glass of ice water and a pack of Tic-Tacs. Farther down the table, the other six authors had either no notes or only a single sheet of paper. The only digital device was a laptop situated between the two lead panelists. I hastily set my index cards under my chair.

Octavia patted my hand. "It's all right, dear. We were all virgins at one time or another."

Heat fanned up my neck. I blushed with embarrassment.

"Just smile and nod until it's your turn," she whispered. "And don't worry—I'll rescue you, if you need it."

Placing my other hand over hers, I gave a light squeeze. "Thank you," I mouthed.

"Sing my praises every chance you get though, sweetheart. I could always use an ally." She winked playfully. "Some of these fans will turn on you in a heartbeat."

Wasn't that the truth?

Braving a look at the crowd, I saw nothing but indistinct features amidst a forest of wildly varying hairstyles and fashions. For once, I considered it a blessing my vision wasn't what it used to be.

The next thirty minutes were a blur. The two lead panelists alternated speaking about the several types of love triangles and their possible complications, while overheads flashed on the giant screen behind them. Then we went down the line, thankfully starting at the other end, and gave examples from our own stories.

Right before it was my turn to speak, Octavia dazzled the audience with anecdotes about her own colorful love life and how that helped her evolve as a storyteller.

"… In the end, your heart should always decide which lover to choose, not your head, and not some contrived plotline. A true genius understands that." She turned to me, a conspiratorial twinkle in her eyes. "Don't you agree, Ms. Mack?"

"Absolutely!" I nodded and smiled—and nodded some more, vaguely aware all eyes were on me now. "I mean it's not about which man is the richest or handsomest or most reliable."

I paused, not for effect, but to grapple for something I'd written on one of those notecards on the floor behind me. None of them seemed relevant or worth saying. So instead, I thought of the choices I'd been faced with and what exactly it was I felt for Archer Malone.

"It's about that connecting of the souls… that vibration of molecules that stirs in the hero or heroine when a certain someone walks in the room. Sometimes, there's no logic to it. That playboy can't be right for her; that recent divorcée with the bruised psyche can't be right for him. But they are. They are meant to be, even though their relationship isn't easy. Because if it was, would it really mean as much? How else does love grow, if not through adversity? People love in each other what they lack in themselves. They discover in that other person, not only what they are missing, but also what they aspire to. Both hunger for approval, wanting to be needed, reaching out, and needing to be reached."

The silence that followed was palpable. I could make out faces in the first few rows now that my headache was fading. What I saw was not polite boredom, but rapt attention. They were hanging on my every word. I had connected with a roomful of strangers.

"There's a myth that romance is about feeding our sexual cravings," I continued, growing more confident with each passing second. "That we want to be desired and blown away by orgasm. But at heart, it isn't that at all. A woman doesn't need a man or even a partner for the physical thrill. But we all desire… no, we all *need* love. So we turn to stories to assure ourselves there is someone out there for each of us. And there is, trust me, there is. Just remember that true love isn't always easy—it's hard. But it *is* worth the struggle. We read romance to remind us of that. Hopefully, then, when we emerge from that story on the page, we see the world a little differently—and treasure those we love a lot more."

I waited for the applause, but the crowd simply sat there gaping at me—waiting to hear more. Someone in the front row sniffed. I spotted the woman just in time to see her take out a tissue and dab at her eyes. A few rows behind her, someone else blew their nose. Then a pair of hands came together.

Soon, the whole room clattered with applause.

THREATS AND THREADS

"And I think we'll end our session on that wonderful note," Summer Monroe said. "Thank you all for coming. Refreshments are in back. For those who signed up for it, the luncheon begins in fifteen minutes."

"I KNEW YOU'D EMERGE a star, sweetheart." Octavia Bloomsdale pinched my cheek hard enough to make it sting. "I could see the twinkle in your eyes."

Too stunned to react, I let her flounce my hair and flip my shirt collar out from beneath my jacket. The talk over, we were standing at the foot of the dais. I'd already deposited my note cards in the trash can and had been headed for the door when she'd tapped me on the shoulder. "Th-th-thanks, Octavia."

"You bet. Anytime you need a favor"—she rearranged the drapes of her infinity scarf, then dipped a hand into her pocket— "look me up."

Into my clammy hands, she pressed a business card. Scrawled on the back of it was her phone number. With a wink, she strutted away, her fans flocking to her like lost chicks to a mother hen.

I shuffled out of the conference room, feeling buoyed but also hoping to make it back to the isolation of my hotel room without being intercepted. The attention had left me inexplicably drained.

Birdie Swinson blocked my path. "That was so, so, so..."—her voice dropped to a whisper—"moving." She wiped at the corner of her eye. "I cried. Real tears. Sobbed, actually. Blew my nose in front of total strangers. And it wasn't because of my sinuses—although I have been a little stuffed up."

"That was you in the front row?"

"You didn't see me?" She took a tissue from her pocket, then daintily blew her nose again. Her eyes were watery and her nose chafed, like she was getting a cold.

"I probably looked right at you. But everyone's face was kind of blurry. It was all so surreal. I'm not used to speaking in front of so many people. I was terrified."

"Really? I couldn't tell. I had no idea you wrote love stories. I *love* your books—and I'm not just saying that to be nice. I really do!"

If I'd thought that TrueLuv might be Birdie's alias when I ran into her before the session, I wasn't so sure anymore. People couldn't fake being as pleasantly starstruck as she was. Like it or not, my secret was out. Somehow, I had to turn her into an ally.

I pressed a hand over my heart. "I'm flattered."

"I know you didn't say much until the end, but you were the best speaker of the bunch. The only one who touched my heart." She pressed her tissue to her nose once more before putting it back in her pocket. "You expressed exactly why I read romance."

"Thank you."

"No, thank *you*." She yanked me into a hug. An uncomfortably long hug, during which I could only manage the shallowest of breaths.

I had to peel her arms off me. "You're welcome, Birdie. But promise me you won't tell anyone in Wilton who I am. I try to keep my professional life and my private life separate. For my daughter's sake." *And mine*, I wanted to add, but so many people couldn't understand shying from fame. Not that authors were constantly trailed by paparazzi, but how did people live a normal life, let alone get any work done, when random strangers were interrupting a family dinner outing?

Looking like the kid on the playground who'd been left out of a game of kickball, Birdie flapped her eyelids. "I see. Sure. No problem. Will do. I won't tell a soul I saw you—except maybe my cat, Harpo. But then she won't be impressed. Your name won't mean anything to her."

Oh, that smarted. "Birdie, I'm sorry. I didn't mean you couldn't talk to me about this. I just don't want everyone in town knowing."

She lifted her chin, looking me square in the eye. "You have a nice day, Sam McNamee—or S.A. Mack, whatever you're calling yourself."

Then she pivoted and marched off, her brown ponytail swinging behind her.

My heart sank for Birdie. I'd hurt her, but I'd have to figure out how to do damage control later. Right now, I needed to regroup.

"Coming to the luncheon, honey?" Summer Monroe asked in a deep Southern accent. "I'll save you a seat beside me."

"Uh, actually, I'm not feeling all that well." *Mentally, that is.* "I just didn't want to skip out on my commitment, so I came."

"Oh, bless your heart then. Well, you rest up and get better now, hear?"

"Thanks. I will."

Before she'd gone three steps, she turned back. "By the way, I'll send someone up to your room later with a check for the speaking fee. Thanks again for stepping in at the last minute. We'd love to have you back again sometime."

"I'd love that," I told her. While the publicity from the engagement was a double-edged sword, the money couldn't have come at a better time. I could put a down payment on a new vehicle.

Then she was gone, and I was alone in a crowd of hundreds, maybe thousands.

People bustled past me, a few pausing to say how much they agreed with what I'd said. I didn't feel worthy of their admiration, but I thanked them anyway. Desperate for an escape, I scooted over to the wall and took my phone out. The little bubble on the text icon said I had... fourteen? No, that couldn't be right. I squinted harder, holding the phone at arm's length. Yes, a one and a four. Fourteen texts.

Had Tara had a panic attack at school yesterday? It was standardized testing week, after all. Or was it a problem with Bump?

Gastric torsion? He was known to empty the garbage can on occasion to help himself to a smorgasbord. Something gone wrong in South America with Dad and Ida, maybe?

The longer I stood there, propped up by the wall, the more my mind swirled with tragic scenarios. Ribs tightening, I sipped in a breath, then drew a longer, deeper one.

I didn't want to look. But I had to.

I opened my messages. Most were from Cleora, but there were a few interspersed ones from Clint. I knew if I read the most recent one first, they wouldn't make much sense. So to get the full context, I started at the beginning with Cleora's first text.

Sam, there are sheriff's cars surrounding your house. Can you call me right away?

chapter 17

TUNING OUT THE BUZZ in the hotel corridor, I skipped the rest of the messages and dialed Cleora back.

Ring... ring...

"C'mon." I pressed my free hand to my forehead to keep my brains from exploding. What on earth could be happening at my house?

Ring...

"Pick up, pick up, pick up," I chanted, the back of my skull thudding against the wall with each phrase.

Someone tapped me on the shoulder. My first instincts were to either slug them or spew profanity, but I restrained myself and pulled my hand down.

"Is everything okay, Ms. Mack?" a woman with a blond-streaked crew cut asked.

"Probably not," I said. Another ring sounded faintly. "Trouble at home."

"Oh. Can I do anything to help?"

"I doubt it," I lashed back.

Ring...

Instead of getting an offended look from her, she frowned in sympathy. "Goodness, dear. My family's like that, too. Can't function without me there, turning and oiling the cogs constantly. I once came home from a weekend visiting my sister in Mississippi to find my hubby had gone out and bought eight different sizes of diapers for baby Elroy because he didn't know which ones would fit. Heaven forbid he should weigh the baby to figure it out—or ask, but you know men."

Ring...

"Excuse me." I held a finger up to stop her. "It's an emergency. I have to take care of this."

She nodded several times. "Don't we all know it."

When she left, I slammed my head back against the wall with an audible bang. Several people nearby turned to look. Any other time, I might have felt a flush of embarrassment, but hysteria was in the driver's seat right now.

My call had gone to voice mail. Pushing away from the wall, I dodged through the crowd and hurried in the direction of the lobby, leaving a breathless message as I clip-clopped over the marble tiles.

"Cleora, it's me. Call me back ASAP. Please!"

I veered right to avoid the revolving doors and extended a hand to push the other door open, but my approach triggered the automatic function and it *slid* open... slowly. I pulled my hand back in the nick of time to avoid putting it through the plate glass. Wedging myself sideways, I squeezed out, but misjudged the timing and clipped the metal frame with my right elbow. A bolt of pain tore through that arm. My phone flew from my grasp, then clattered onto the concrete. But I kept going. Onto the sidewalk. Out into the light. Into the fresh air. *Cold* air.

The blast to my lungs yanked me out of flight syndrome and landed me squarely back in the present. Clear-headed enough to see my phone was in two pieces. Nothing to hold me up, I crashed to my knees.

THREATS AND THREADS

A pair of shiny black shoes stepped into the perimeter of my vision. White-gloved hands retrieved the two halves of my phone. A moment later, the doorman was kneeling before me. "A little scratched up," he said, "but not broken." He snapped the case back onto my phone and handed it to me, then helped me to my feet.

I vaguely remembered Tara insisting I get a case for it when I first brought it home. I'd had to take her to the store with me to fit it properly.

Before I could even thank him, the ringtone started playing *Call Me Maybe*. My daughter had been at it again, changing up my ringtone. It was both annoying and amusing. A tiny pang pricked a hole in my heart. I answered.

"Cleora, what the hell is going on there?" My voice was terse from the throbbing in my elbow and knees.

"Wow, hello," Clint said. "Maybe I should be asking you that."

"Is this important, Clint? Because I need to talk to Cleora right now."

"In that case, hang on. She's right here."

I could hear voices in the background. But not normal conversation—shouts. And above them, the dying wail of a siren.

"Oh, thank goodness," Cleora said. "I thought you'd be out of touch the entire day, and I realized I forgot to ask where you were staying."

The doorman assisted me over to a stone bench. I gave him a thumbs-up to let him know I was okay, relatively speaking, then returned my attention to Cleora. "Explain. Why is the sheriff at my house?"

"We were hoping you could clear things up. You see, the alarm went off, apparently. Only it's not one of those high-pitched screeching alarms. It just notifies local law enforcement directly that there's been some sort of break-in. So they showed up and when they got there, they found Harmon Purnell. He was in a dither, talking nonsense. Having a breakdown, by the looks of it. Maybelle showed up when all the neighbors started gathering, and that only made him worse."

Marco must've shown up early and installed the alarm. Only I'd figured he would've called first to let me know how to turn it off before I came home and accidentally set it off.

I rubbed my arm to chase away the goose bumps, but that only made my elbow throb more. "Put him on the phone."

"Who, dear?"

"Harmon. Let me talk to Harmon."

"I don't know if that's possible right now."

"Why?"

"It looks like they're reading him his rights."

"What? Why? Never mind. Who's there—Deputy Strewing?"

"I'm not certain. I do see a shorter, blond female officer."

"That's Deputy Ecklund. Let me talk to her."

"I'll speak to her for you. You sound a bit... frantic. Studies show that people having an emotional crisis don't think rationally. Meanwhile, I think Dr. Clint wants to talk."

Frantic was an understatement. At any rate, she was probably right. I waited while she passed the phone off.

"Sam," Clint began, "they found him in your house. Upstairs in your bedroom."

"Upstairs?" I thought about it a moment. I knew it looked bad, but... "Wait, no. I told him to look for Bump up there if he didn't come out right away when he went to let him out."

"Why would he show up at your house to let the dog out if I—"

"Because I'd asked him to let Bump out before I went to you, then I couldn't call or text to let him know you were taking Bump. I thought I'd be able to talk to him before I left, but I never did. He was afraid of Maybelle finding out and giving him a tongue-lashing. So I left a written message on the counter that you had the dog. He must not've seen it."

"So Harmon had your permission to go inside your house while you were gone?"

"Yes!" I shouted. "I told him where the extra key was!"

"Whoa, there. Volume control, please. Listen, why don't you just take a few deep breaths while I handle this, all right? Everything will be fine."

"No, it won't. Marco wasn't supposed to be there until tomorrow, and now Harmon's suffering the wrath of Hera—and I bet half the Humboldt County Sheriff's Department is there in my front yard."

"More like all of it."

"What?" I started to hyperventilate.

The doorman rushed to me again. "Ma'am, are you having an asthma attack? Would you like me to call a doctor?" He stooped forward in front of me, way inside my personal bubble. "Ma'am?"

"Don't call me that!" I yelled so forcefully his bangs lifted off his forehead.

Slowly, warily, he straightened and took a step back. "J-j-just making sure you could breathe all right. Clearly you can. Sorry."

Behind him, a crowd of onlookers had gathered. I recognized a few of the faces from the session I'd just spoken at. A pit formed in my stomach. A very big, prickly pit of shame and guilt.

I reached out. He stared at my hand, shook his head.

"No," I told him, "*I'm* sorry. You weren't doing anything wrong. There's been an emergency at home, you see. It's crazy... I just... There was..." What could I say? The Humboldt County SWAT team was surrounding my house? My front yard looked like a production set for a gunman standoff episode of *Blue Bloods*?

I had to downplay it. "My neighbor set off my alarm by accident when he came to take care of the dog. Silly, really. Whole neighborhood showed up... and it was nothing. Absolutely nothing. These kinds of things happen to me all the time. Well, not *all* the time. Just lately. Ever since I moved to—" I almost blurted out 'Wilton,' but stopped myself just in time. I already had one stalker. I didn't need an army of them.

Shrugging, I laughed, but it sounded like someone tripping on nitrous oxide at the dentist's office before a root canal. "Everything's going to be fine. Absolutely fine. I'm just trying to get it all sorted out. Thanks for your concern, though. Very thoughtful of you."

"Oh, okay then. That's good." He retreated a few more steps. The crowd behind him relaxed, a few drifting back inside. When I gave the rest of them the 'okay' sign, they reluctantly disappeared. The doorman seemed like he wanted to go with them and forget I was there entirely. "Let me know if you need anything, though."

What he meant was 'Please get your head together and don't do this again.'

"I'm good for now. Thanks."

When he'd gone far enough away I was sure he couldn't overhear, I spoke to Clint again. "Why is the whole sheriff's department there? Even if they thought it was a break-in—"

"Um, less one squad car now. Make that two. Looks like it's wrapping up."

"They let him go, right? Cleora found Sheriff Driscoll and told him, didn't she?"

"I... I don't know. I lost track of her in the crowd. But no, I don't think she talked to anyone in time."

"Why do you say that?"

"Because Harmon was in the back of one of the cruisers."

Rats. This was going downhill faster than an Olympic skier. "And the other one?"

"I couldn't tell, because whoever it was had a coat pulled over their head. Hang on. I'll find out."

I shivered as I waited, the cold of the stone bench leeching into my bones. I desperately wanted to go back inside, but there were tons of people in the lobby peering out at me through the glass doors. Out here, there was only the doorman now, standing as rigid as a Buckingham Palace guard in his brass-buttoned coat.

Clint said something unintelligible as the phone changed hands.

"Oh, dear." It was Cleora on the line now. "This has turned out to be quite the mess."

"What happened?"

"They've taken Maybelle away, too. Reports are she struck Harmon upside the head with a blunt object and gave him a slight concussion. He might even need stitches. That would explain the ambulance."

Lovely. Not only were the cops swarming my house, but the medics were there, too.

"No," I said wishfully, "she didn't."

"She *did*."

All this because I couldn't call Harmon directly to let him know Bump was with Clint. I should never have asked the poor guy to take care of my dog in the first place. Maybe there was something I could do to patch things up. I didn't know what, but on a four-hour drive, I could figure something out. "I should come home. I'll call Danielle, ask if—"

"I'd advise you to stay there for now, Sam. And when you do return, stay in your house. Don't go out in public."

"Why would I do that? I need to talk to Harmon. Tell him this wasn't his fault."

She sighed, stalling. "Trust me, you don't want to be seen in town if you can help it."

"I don't follow."

"Maybelle Purnell accused her husband of having an affair with you."

I laughed so hard I snorted. The doorman stole a glance at me, and I slapped a hand over my mouth until I regained control. "That's ludicrous. Me and Harmon? What would ever make her think that?"

"Who knows, Sam? This is Maybelle we're talking about. I try to keep my distance, but she's always butting in wherever she can, book club included."

"I'll talk to her and tell her that—"

"No, stay out of it… please. Let Harmon and Maybelle work out their own problems. You don't need to get tangled up with the two of them, especially Maybelle."

What was there about Maybelle to be scared of? She was nothing but a sandbox bully. Still, there was something odd about Cleora's insistence I back off. "Cleora, is there something you're not telling me?"

"I'm merely advising caution, Sam. That woman is a black cloud. Stay far away. Anyway, Sheriff Driscoll said he'd call you soon and get your story, but he has a lot to take care of first, so don't call him. I'm sure they won't charge Harmon with anything concerning your house, but the situation between Maybelle and him goes well beyond what happened here this morning, you have to understand that. You do understand, don't you?"

"Sure, I guess. But I can't help but feel somehow responsible."

"Don't. Couples fight all the time. Some have bigger problems than others. When Joseph and I were married, we used to fight over the dumbest things. Little things. Big things. But I'd give anything to have my Joseph back."

"I'm sorry, Cleora. I didn't know you were a widow." Turned out we had more in common than just a love for dogs and books.

"Technically, I'm not, I suppose. We were divorced before he died."

"Oh." I wasn't sure if I should dig deeper. It seemed like too personal a matter, and Cleora and I hadn't known each other all that long. So I redirected the conversation. "Tell the sheriff to call me as soon as he can, so we can clear things up. Meanwhile, let me talk to Clint."

She put Clint back on the line. "Hey, Sam. Bump's doing great, by the way. We went on a run this morning. I was on my way to drop him off at Cleora's for a play session with Fancy when I came across, well, the scene at your house."

He was doing his best to take my mind off the fiasco at my house, I knew. It did make me feel the tiniest bit better. "Thanks, Clint. I can't tell you how much I appreciate you taking care of my dog."

"You know I'm happy to do it anytime. It's the best of both worlds, really. Like being a favorite uncle. I get to hang out with him on occasion, then hand him back to you and not feel guilty when I'm busy working. The side benefits aren't bad, either."

"Like having a running partner?"

"Yeah, that, but also getting to talk to you. Even when strange things like today happen. Makes me realize how much I miss you."

This was why I'd avoided talking to him the last couple of months. Because I knew he still had feelings. As for me, it wasn't that I didn't still care for him. I did. But the situation was complicated. "Clint…"

"I had to say it, Sam. But if you want, we can just pretend I never said any such thing."

If he was going to say it at all, I was grateful he'd said it over the phone, though. That way, he couldn't see how mixed up I felt.

Because I'd moved on, damn it. I had.

"I have to go now, Clint."

"Okay. I'll see you tomorrow."

"Um, I—"

"You have to get Bump back. Listen, Sam, you don't have to say anything back now. Not even tomorrow. Or ever."

Before I could respond, he ended the call.

Emotionally spent, I went back to my room. To be alone so I could think. Not that I expected to figure anything out anytime soon.

I just needed for nothing to happen for a change—no threats, no lurking burglars, no suspicious deaths, no emergencies at home. Just… nothing.

By the time Sheriff Driscoll called, I'd been in my room for nearly two hours. I'd changed out of my fancy clothes and into my stretchy jeans and an oversized sweatshirt. My plan was to stay here by myself, until Danielle picked me up tomorrow afternoon.

Only twenty-two more hours of self-imposed isolation to go.

"Ms. McNamee?" the sheriff began. "Harmon Purnell says you gave him permission to enter your home in your absence, is that correct?"

"It is, sheriff." I then explained the situation with Harmon and that Clint had Bump. "So he's not being held, right? You let him go?"

"Are you aware he was upstairs in your bedroom when Deputy Ecklund arrived?"

"He was probably just looking for Bump. Sometimes, the dog falls asleep on Tara's bed. I can't remember if I told him which room was hers or not."

"So you don't want to press charges?" Even when he was speaking about crime, his voice had the liquid gold tenor of Cary Grant.

"For what?"

"Breaking and entering? Trespassing?"

"Heavens, no. Harmon Purnell is a sweet old man who wouldn't hurt a fly. Not even one of those nasty biting deer flies."

"All right. I'll let him know he's clear on that."

I thought about asking the sheriff if he'd gotten my house key back from Harmon, but it was possible Harmon had left it in the house. I made a mental note to check when I got home.

"Since he's been here at the station," the sheriff continued, "we've been trying to get a statement out of him regarding the altercation with his wife, but he won't say a harsh word about her. He was actually being detained in your kitchen by the first deputies on the scene when his wife showed up. Well, barged in is more like it. She went through several cabinets before she found an oversized ceramic coffee mug—"

"Wait, did it look kind of like a frog, with a pair of eyes on the side?"

Papers rustled. "Just says here it was lime green and likely handmade."

"Tara made that in third grade art class." It was one of the few things we'd brought with us from Chicago and had later been able to salvage from the fire at my dad's house. She'd been so proud of that frog. When one of the other kids told her it looked like a pile of dog puke, she'd called him a 'bombastic imbecile'. Unfortunately, the other kid started crying and she'd said he was being 'hypersensitive'. When he asked what that meant, she reinterpreted it as a 'limp wiener'. That got her landed in the principal's office, and they called me in with a report that she was sexually harassing a fellow student. After working so hard to teach her to use her words properly, it had been even harder trying to explain that sometimes it was best not to use them at all if they might hurt others' feelings.

By now, Tara had probably heard about the cop convention at her house. Maybe it was time to move after all. Away from Wilton. If Ida and Dad's relationship survived their trip, I could be reasonably assured their relationship was long term, and I wouldn't have to worry about someone looking after him. Melissa would be booting us out of our home in the near future anyway, so—

"Maybelle bludgeoned her husband with the mug repeatedly," Sheriff Driscoll continued. "For a bigger woman, she is amazingly quick and strong. It took three deputies to peel her off Harmon, whom she'd plowed to the floor and was straddling as she clobbered him. It took one more to hold Harmon back once she was restrained. He did get one good strike in with a wooden spoon first, though."

"Wow, really? He fought back? Good for him."

"These things can escalate, Samantha. People without any criminal record or history of abuse have been known to snap in the heat of passion. Unfortunately, once the situation cooled down, we couldn't get Harmon to incriminate her. He was almost defending her, sticking up for her. He refused counseling. Said he just wanted to go back home and apologize to her."

"That's so wrong! He needs to dump her ass. I'm going to tell him that, as soon as I—"

"Samantha, Sam… you can't. It's his decision. You showing up at his house would only aggravate an already-delicate situation."

"Delicate? How is a husband-beating wife delicate? She has that poor man so far whipped he might as well be topping for pumpkin pie."

"While I appreciate your concern for his welfare, the fact is intervening at this point could put Harmon in danger. Let them work it out. If he's had enough, he'll leave her. Or maybe she'll kick him out."

"That would be a blessing."

"I agree. Then again, they may just patch things up. It is their call. Meanwhile, we would reset your alarm for you, but we don't know how. So for now, we just turned off the power to the unit. I know that's not ideal, but until we get the code… If you'll just let me know what it is…"

Right. The alarm. The whole situation had been so chaotic I hadn't even thought about that. "I don't have it, yet, but I'll contact Marco and have him reset it."

"Marco?"

"One of the firefighters in Wilton. A friend of Archer's. He installed the alarm system."

"Good. Let us know when that's squared away. Is there anything else I can do for you?"

"Maybe... I don't know. Do you mean *anything*?"

"Anything and everything within my powers, as long as it entails law enforcement."

If I trusted anyone in all of Wilton, it was Sheriff Driscoll. I needed someone on my side.

"How much time do you have?" I asked.

"All the time you need."

So I told him about my stalker. Everything.

chapter 18

SITTING AT THE FOOT of my bed late the next morning, I balanced my brunch plate on my lap—a sun-dried tomato and basil frittata with maple bacon on the side. Forkful after forkful, I ate without really tasting any of it. A gardening show was on TV, and I watched with dulled interest the mounds of colorful perennials and abundant shrub roses. I'd always dreamed of having a garden like that. It made me sad that Tara and I might have to relocate to an apartment or modest condo before we could ever think of moving into a house of our own.

Unless I found some money…

Suddenly remembering the mail I'd brought along, I retrieved it from the side pocket of my suitcase. The electric bill, two credit card offers, a pack of coupons, and a hand-addressed envelope with no return address. Probably some kind of spam designed to look like a personal letter.

I put the bill back in the pocket and moved toward the wastebasket, ready to toss the rest. A postmark on the envelope caught my eye—Wilton, IN. I tore it open. Inside was a simple piece of plain copy paper with a mere few sentences sloppily printed:

i know everything about u. where u live. where ur dauter goes to school. ur passwords.

THREATS AND THREADS

u have until wensday to get out of town. or ur dog is a gonner.

TL

TL. TrueLuv. Wednesday was only three days from now. Why was she suddenly insisting I leave town? And why threaten to steal my mutt if she could clean out all my bank accounts and max out my cards? It didn't make sense. So far, this had been about her disappointment in my story. Why the sudden shift—unless this was somehow more personal than she'd originally let on?

My first urge was to laugh it off as an empty threat. My second was to change all my passwords, which I began doing immediately.

Then I texted Clint.

Need to talk to you when I pick up Bump.

A few minutes later, he responded.

Don't keep me in suspense. Hint?

Just then, Danielle messaged me to tell me she was waiting at the curb. I texted Clint back.

Too complicated. Gotta go. I'll explain later. And keep an eye on my dog. Please.

I buried the envelope deep in my suitcase and crammed my belongings inside, then headed downstairs to meet Danielle.

LAST NIGHT, I'D SLEPT in fits and starts, awoken by nightmares of angry fans heckling me at a book signing and then bludgeoning me with e-readers and hardbacks. When I opened the car door and plopped myself into the passenger's seat, Danielle didn't even ask why I looked like a zombie. Along the way, a gloomy drizzle turned into a relentless downpour.

I'd been meaning to go to the storage unit ever since Dad had given me that box of letters from my mom. I could've kept putting it off indefinitely, but I knew it would always bother me if I didn't retrieve one thing in particular. Something that could solve my immediate problems—or prove to be worth nothing at all.

Danielle turned into the storage property, then stopped before the iron gate. The wipers slapped against the windshield in a monotonous rhythm.

"Are you sure you don't mind?" I said.

"Honestly? I could think of better things to do. But being this close, it would have been senseless not to come here if you need something."

If anyone else had said those things, I would've thought they were just being polite. But we were talking about Danielle Townsley, M.D. She was part Vulcan. It was all about the logic. She also couldn't tell a lie. If she'd needed to get home in a hurry, she would've said so.

"Thanks, Danielle. I really appreciate it." I burst out of the car, punched in the code, and hopped back in, half-soaked. The gate opened with a squeal and we drove through, the bumper barely clearing the gate before it swung shut again.

"Which one?" she asked.

I checked the piece of scrap paper that had been tucked in the inside zippered pocket of my purse for almost six months now. "Number two-six-two."

Four rows and three turns later, we were parked in front of my storage unit. The business was located at the edge of an industrial park less than ten minutes from my hotel. Being a Sunday, the area was practically deserted. If TrueLuv was trailing me, this would be the perfect place for an ambush.

"Do you want me to go inside with you?' Danielle asked.

Seeing as how I needed a lookout, that was out of the question. "Oh, no. I'm sure it's a cluttered mess. I crammed most of what I own in there. Stacked it to the rafters. Probably full of dust, mold, cockroaches... rats even."

"I still have my gun in the glove compartment."

"That's a little extreme for a rodent, don't you think?"

"My marksmanship is excellent."

"Yes, I remember. Anyway, I'll leave the door open. Shouldn't take more than five minutes. Ten tops. If you hear me scream, come to my rescue."

Nodding, she glanced at her watch. "Affirmative. Time: 2:45 p.m.... Mark."

If I hadn't known better, I would've thought she was treating this like a covert operation.

Gathering my courage, I got out of the car and stood in the rain while dampness seeped into my bones. Half a minute later, I still didn't feel any braver, just colder and wetter. Eventually, I moved one foot, then another, until I stood before the overhead door. I unlocked it and lifted. I let my eyes adjust, but it was still hard to see much beyond the first row of bins and boxes. Somewhere in the back of this heap was that black leather sofa on which Kyle and I had created Tara.

I groped along the wall until I found the lightswitch, then flicked it on. Glaringly bright light flooded the space.

Two-hundred-and-fifty square feet of memories. In other words, a lot of junk.

Funny how you could save for and look forward to a purchase, make good use of it—a dinette set for the breakfast nook, a CD player, a fancy dress for a special occasion—and then a day came when you set it aside for something trendier, less worn, with more bells and whistles, and then you wondered what it was that ever made you love that thing so much in the first place.

Once I got a new car, I'd bring Tara up here on a weekend, let her go through it all and decide what to bring back, what to give away to charity, and what to toss. As far as I was concerned, I already had everything I needed.

Except for one item.

I wedged sideways between a mini fridge and a teetering stack of boxes labeled 'Books', 'Movies', and 'Winter clothes'. I'd been wondering where I'd left my blue ski jacket for the last month. I pulled the clothes box out of the pile, then set it behind me to pick up on the way out.

When I reached the scratched-up mahogany desk, I knelt and opened the bottom drawer. A dusty bottle of cabernet sauvignon rolled forward. After Kyle died, I'd often drowned my sorrows while alone in the bathroom after Tara had gone to sleep. Realizing I couldn't raise a child in that condition, I'd poured all but this one bottle down the drain. Kyle and I had been saving it for our next anniversary. It was time to either empty it, too, or drink it in celebration of our love.

I set the bottle on top of the desk, then pulled open the center drawer. Beyond a logjam of broken pencils and dried-up pens, beneath an empty stapler and the good pair of scissors I'd thought I lost years ago, there lay a faded manila envelope. I pulled it free. There was no writing on the outside. It was so lightweight that, for a moment, I thought it was empty. My mother's parents had given it to me when I turned eighteen, telling me to read it when I was ready. I'd been so angry at her at the time that I'd hidden it away. I shivered, cold to my core. For a long time, I crouched there, staring at what I held, acutely aware of how the unknown could affect our world.

I unwound the string that held it shut and peeked inside—another envelope.

Still there. The answer to my past.

Sometimes in order to move forward, you had to look back.

But not today. Not here.

Later. Soon maybe. But not now.

I returned to the box I'd set aside, then undid the cardboard flaps. Deep inside, under several layers of clothes, I hid the manila envelope and the wine bottle, then closed the box.

Just as I aimed for the exit, something caught my eye. On top of Tara's old changing table was a jewelry box. I climbed over a row of bins and a box filled with sporting equipment to get to it. I took an old baby blanket from the changing table and wiped the dust from the outside of the box. Maple or some other fine-grained wood, faux stained glass in the little doors, brass knobs... inexpensive but made to look fancy. I opened each of the bottom drawers, finding some rings with semi-precious stones, lapel pins, and a few sets of earrings. When I opened the doors, there were slots with more rings and hooks on which hung necklaces. Most of it was costume jewelry, the kind found at any Goodwill—and that was where I intended to take the contents when Tara and I returned at some later point.

I closed the little doors and turned away, but didn't move. The jewelry box had been my mother's. More sentimental than valuable, really. Something tugged at my inner conscience. As a young girl, I'd wrestled with my mother's abandonment every day. The odd thing was, the older I got, the less I hated her for it. Time had fostered forgiveness. It was freeing. Because along with the resentment I'd held onto for so long, I also remembered good things about her. She hadn't been all bad.

I took the jewelry box, then carried it back to the clothes box, where I wedged it inside. Lights off, I shut the overhead door and locked it as a frigid rain pelted me and soaked into my clothes.

Inside the car, the heater kicked out toasty warm air onto my wet shoes. Droplets of rain fell from my chin onto the box sitting on my lap.

"Get what you came for?" Danielle asked.

"I think so."

"Need to go back in and double check? It's no problem if—"

"No."

She gripped the key, but didn't turn it. "Would you like to put that in the backseat?"

"Oh, sure." I squeezed it between the seats to set it on top of our luggage in the back. "Now, let's get out of here, okay? I want to go home."

As good as that sounded, I no longer felt safe there.

A week ago, everything had seemed right on track. My career was taking off. Tara had found a place where she fit in. My dad had a steady girl. And my relationship with Archer had been on solid ground. I'd been hopeful for the future. But now…

Now it was all falling apart like a popsicle-stick house in a tornado.

I'd survived worse than this before. I'd do it again.

"SO HOW DID THE meeting with the surrogate go?" I asked. She hadn't exactly sworn me to secrecy, but I wasn't going to mention I'd talked to Clint about their plans.

Danielle stared ahead. Construction barrels narrowed the road to pinball alleys. In typical Chicago fashion, some drivers were weaving in and out of lanes recklessly. With Danielle at the wheel, however, I felt as safe as I possibly could.

"Not well," she finally answered. "It seems she's suffered from a severe bout of endometriosis recently."

"So…"

"So she can't—shouldn't—get pregnant. Not anymore. I mean, she could, actually. But her chances of conception are much, much lower. The risks are greater, too." She smiled wryly. "Her gestational days are behind her, unfortunately."

A semi rumbled by. I waited until it was far enough ahead that she could hear me better. "I'm sorry, Danielle. I am."

She nodded dully. "Thank you." Her words came out flat, in the way a person would thank someone who offered condolences at a funeral. She was, in a way, grieving over the life that would never be.

"What will you do—or have you even thought about it?"

"Nothing right now. It has to sink in." After a few moments, she added, "I also need to analyze the feasibility of my alternative solutions—or whether I should pursue any at all."

I didn't suggest adoption or offer worthless platitudes. She needed to search her own heart before she could pour it out to a friend—and that was what we'd become—friends. Not intentionally, of course, but she *had* saved my life once. And the more I learned about Danielle, the more human she became.

I turned the conversation to lighter matters. "How was your conference?"

"Productive. Informative… It was good. I met the young lady named Bellamy Larson who was giving a talk on her graduate thesis paper about autistic children who are gifted in various areas. At the end of her summary, she mentioned she was from a small town in Kentucky called Faderville. A few years back, I'd treated a young girl from there who'd been submerged underwater in an icy river for forty minutes. Using a procedure where we gradually warmed her, I was able to save her life. But the most amazing thing—a miracle, some might call it—was that she suffered no brain damage from the event. Once she was fully recovered, she went off with her family. A follow-up confirmed she was healthy and well. I didn't think much about her after that.

"Anyway, after Miss Larson gave her talk, I approached her and asked if she knew the girl well. She did, she said. That same girl, Hannah McHugh, was the one who'd inspired her interest in teaching methods regarding autism."

"Wow, small world, huh?"

She gave me a sideways glance. After a look in the rearview mirror and another over her shoulder, she flicked the turn signal and changed lanes. "A highly unlikely coincidence we should both know of Hannah, yes. But even more intriguing is that Miss Larson, who calls herself Beam, said Hannah claims to understand animal's thoughts. That she 'hears' them."

This conversation had taken an unexpected turn. I didn't tell people I sometimes had visions I could only surmise came from an animal's memories. No one would've believed me. I laughed nervously. "Sounds like that little girl has an active imagination."

Danielle scrunched up her mouth. "I'm not so certain it *is* a fabrication."

"What do you mean? There's no way people can know an animal's thoughts." I'd wanted to convince myself of that many times. It was disturbing to have my mind taken over, especially when what I saw or heard didn't make sense.

"And yet, animals so often seem to know ours," Danielle speculated. "Or at least our moods. Dogs in particular are good at reading facial expressions. They can also sniff out any pheromones or other biochemicals we release with stunning accuracy. They can detect danger, even before it happens, like earthquakes or epileptic seizures. Who's to say that they—or we—don't posses senses beyond our comprehension?"

"Come on. What proof is there of any of that, besides the sniffing part?"

"Samantha, lack of scientific proof does not prove an absence of something. It simply means we don't know either way. And just because we can't explain something… well, that doesn't make it any less real or valuable."

Mind blown. Danielle was a deeper thinker than I'd realized.

The vacant fields of northern Indiana rolled by, vast stretches of tilled earth and stubbled stalks. Small towns with ageing factories and rusted grain-storage elevators interrupted the monotony. Billboards promising fast food bargains and cheap motel rooms blurred past. I hadn't slept well for over a week. The lack of rest had left me frazzled and short on patience. But the *whoosh-whoosh* of passing cars, rhythmic slap of wipers, and hum of rubber on wet asphalt lulled me into a more relaxed state. Eyelids heavy, I drifted toward napping bliss. Until—

"So how was your work meeting?"

My eyelids popped open wide. A tidal wave of embarrassment and panic rushed back. "My meeting? Um… boring. Really, really, *really* boring. You know, bunch of four-eyes sitting around debating the Oxford comma, semi-colons, overuse of adverbs, gender-neutral pronouns. That sort of thing. Total snooze-fest."

"So it wasn't as beneficial as you'd hoped?"

"Not even close."

"I'm sorry it wasn't more productive. Maybe the next time…"

"No, I don't think there'll be a next time. I'll just do all my work from home from now on—wherever that might be."

"What do you mean?"

"Melissa—the woman who owns the house we're renting—"

"Clinton's former receptionist?"

"Yes, her. Originally, she'd been planning on staying in Nashville permanently. But it turns out she didn't like it there, so she wants to move back to Wilton."

"And she wants her house back, and you're not sure where to go."

"Right."

"But you don't have the money for a down payment."

Damn mind reader. "I *did*. Before I came back to Wilton, I'd sold my home in Naperville and was going to buy a house in the Florida Keys. But when I realized I'd need to stay here because of Dad, and because Tara liked it here, well, I put part of the money in an investment plan for Tara's college and the rest in an IRA to build my retirement savings. If I touch that money anytime soon, I'll lose thousands. I'd figured I had a couple of years to build some savings back up. Plus, there's the car situation..."

"And you can't move into an apartment because of the dog."

"That does eliminate a lot of options. And it would mean giving up a backyard. I could walk Bump ten times a day, but it wouldn't be enough. I love having him around, but if he can't retreat into his own space, he's always underfoot. And before you mention it, I have checked into renting other houses. They'd all cost considerably more than what I'm paying now—the decent places, anyway."

Before today, I'd thought I had time to figure everything out. Now, TrueLuv wanted me out of town for reasons I didn't know. Not that I was going to jump just because she'd threatened me, but—

"I wasn't going to mention it," Danielle said.

"You lost me. Mention what?"

"That you should just find another house to rent. I wouldn't do that. People think you can just go somewhere else—a different house, a different town, different place of employment—and it will all work out the same, but that isn't necessarily true. I know."

It took me a minute to piece together where she was coming from. "Or a different surrogate."

Nodding, she relaxed her grip on the steering wheel. "That, too."

"Danielle... who was the surrogate?"

"My sister. I wouldn't entrust the development and care of my unborn child to just anyone. And she already has three children of her own. Her family was all on board with the arrangement. But now... They were almost as sad about the news as I was."

Wow, fancy that. Dr. Danielle Townsley suffered disappointment just like the rest of us.

She did have a soul after all.

I wanted to wrap her in a hug, but seeing as how she was driving and we were on the interstate, I said two simple words instead, "I'm sorry."

chapter 19

HOME WAS USUALLY WHERE I went when I wanted to unwind. But if I'd thought coming home was going to allow me to recover from a stressful weekend, I sure hadn't thought that through.

After Danielle deposited me at my doorstep and drove away, my anxiety returned in force.

Especially when I noticed the package sitting on my front porch.

Early evening sunlight bathed the box in an almost radioactive-yellow glow. As I walked up the sidewalk, my angle changing, I realized it was nothing but a glare cast upon the waxed brown packaging paper covering it. I paused at the base of the porch steps.

Today was Sunday. If it had been delivered yesterday or the day before, surely Cleora would have collected it for me, rather than let it sit out, free to any passersby.

I approached cautiously—almost as if I were afraid the thing was going to detonate. But it was just a box. A regular-looking box. Not even big enough to put a pair of boots in.

It was sitting in front of the storm door. Whoever had set it there wanted to make sure I didn't miss it. My name was printed in lowercase letters just like—

No, just no, no, no.

She'd been here. TrueLuv had been to my house while I was gone.

I yanked a little metal pole out of my raggedy flower bed, on which hung a silk banner with a ribbon of butterflies fluttering over a cottage garden. I poked at the box. It slid easily. Whatever was inside didn't weigh much.

I walked around it. No other writing on it. Nothing to indicate where it came from or what was inside. It didn't even have my address on it—which meant TrueLuv had delivered it herself, not a courier company.

Oh, what the hell.

I unlocked the door, picked the package up, and took it inside, quickly tapping in the security code Marco had texted me. For peace of mind, I checked the readout on the main unit. All good.

For five minutes, I circled that box, wondering whether to call the cops or to just throw it in the trash unopened. I was pretty sure Wilton didn't have a bomb-detonating robot on the force. If I called them, or even the sheriff, that would mean a fleet of patrol cars in my driveway… and the neighborhood flock of gossipers would convene in my front yard like the paparazzi.

What were the chances TrueLuv had bomb-building skills? If she could track me down and break into my online accounts, chances were good she could research that on the internet. I had to think this through, but the suspense was killing me.

So, of course, I did the not-so-smart thing.

I shook it.

No rattle or clunk, but something definitely shifted inside. My middle and last name had been misspelled: 'samantha anne macknamee'. The middle name was probably a mistake with the extra 'e', but I had no doubt the error in my last name was to emphasize the fact TrueLuv knew my pen name.

I checked the outside of the box for signs of a powdery

substance. Nothing. Definitely a shoe box though. What were the chances TrueLuv had sent me a pair of shoes? After loosening the brown wrapping, I flipped the lid open.

Inside was a short length of rope. Tied into the shape of a noose.

Beneath it was a piece of paper. The message had been computer printed.

might as well end yur career for good. far as im concernd yur ded anyways.

No signature, but I had no doubt who'd written it. TrueLuv2000 knew where I lived *and* what my real name was. If her threats didn't kill me, TrueLuv's grammar and punctuation just might.

But who was TrueLuv? Birdie Swinson, maybe? She was a fan who knew my identity now. She could've beaten me back to Wilton. She could've easily figured out where I lived.

And if not Birdie, then who?

I could call the sheriff right now, but if I did that, then Maybelle and all her cronies would show up. Then it would only be a matter of time before Tara would find out everything.

My phone dinged with a text. It was Tara—talk about ESP—telling me she was ready to come home. After I trucked upstairs, I stuffed some extra clothes for her in a shopping bag. I had ten minutes driving time to figure out how I was going to explain she couldn't come home just yet.

I paused at the top of the stairs. There was no way I could stay here, either. Where was I going to go, though? Ida's cats were still at her house. I could sleep on Selma's couch, but there wasn't room in her trailer for a Chihuahua, let alone a dog Bump's size. I didn't know anyone else well enough to impose on them. In a pinch, I supposed I could make up some story and ask Cleora for a favor. At least for a few days. I'd noticed a spare bedroom at her place during the book club meeting.

Hands shaking, I put the box on the floor behind the driver's seat of Dad's truck and drove all the way to the Mullinses' in a swirling fog.

By the time I was parked in their driveway, I still didn't have any answers.

Tara bounded down the front steps, waving goodbye to Shannon. The moment she slid into the passenger's seat, the pieces snapped into place. I stared straight ahead, my fingers pinching the key as it rested in the ignition.

Selma. Selma was the only one who knew what I did and where I lived.

Not that I believed for a second she was TrueLuv. But would Selma accidentally leak sensitive personal information?

Yes, yes, that was entirely possible.

Tara gave me a peck on the cheek, then looked behind the front seat, frowning. "You didn't bring Bump along for the ride? Has he been digging again?"

Her questions barely registered in my brain. "Huh?"

"Bump. Where's Bump? Is he a muddy mess?"

"Oh, him." I stared out the windshield to avoid her gaze. "Yeah... I mean, no, not digging. He's still at Dr. Clint's. I'm supposed to pick him up on the way home."

"That's cool. I bet they had fun." Tara waved a hand in front of my face until I focused on her. "Say, why do you have Gramps' truck? Did he loan it to you to pick up some stuff from the hardware store tomorrow? Are we starting a project on the house?"

"No, uh, my car... It died just before I left."

"So it's getting fixed?"

"No. Died as in dead. They towed it off to the junkyard."

"Oh." She scrunched her face in disappointment. A second later, excitement flashed across her features. "You're getting a new car?"

"Well, I don't know about new, but new to me."

"Awesome! Just don't get a minivan, okay? Because you're too cool for a minivan. Have you thought about a Jeep?"

Before I could respond, she tipped the shopping bag her way and peeked inside. "Why did you bring my clothes, Mom? You aren't donating these, are you? Because I still wear them. I know I told you I'd go through my stuff before—"

"The plumbing's busted," I interrupted. "It's leaking. Everywhere."

"Gross." Her face twisted in disgust. "Does it smell like sewage water?"

"Yes!" I said a little too enthusiastically. Then, more calmly, "Not sewage, maybe, but it does stink. It's leaking into the crawl space. The plumber can't come until tomorrow, or maybe the day after. You should probably stay here again tonight."

Her backpack was still sitting on her lap. It wasn't until then I realized she hadn't complained about her arm once, and she was managing miraculously well with it. She shrugged. "I'm sure Shannon's parents won't mind. But what about you?"

"Me?"

"Yeah, what are you going to do for a toilet? Want me to ask if you can stay here? The couch is pretty comfy."

"No, I'll manage. It's only a night. I can stop at the gas station on the corner on the way home. Plus, there's a spare bucket in the garage if I—"

She flipped her palm at me. "I don't even want to know."

"What do you suppose people did a hundred years ago before we all had indoor plumbing?"

"Considering they didn't even have deodorant back then, their olfactory senses were probably immune to the stench. Anyway, I bet they were too exhausted from walking five miles to school uphill, backward, and in the snow to care."

"You're sounding like your grandfather."

"Thanks!" She laughed. "Hey, guess what? Gramps friended me on Facebook."

"What? He has a Facebook account? Why didn't I know this?"

"I think Ida helped him set one up so she could tag him. She posted pictures of them in Buenos Aires with their tour group. It's crazy. I miss them."

"Me too," I said. "I hope they're having a good time. Bet Gramps will have some interesting stories to tell when he gets back. Of course, after he tells them, we'll have to get Ida to give us the low-down on what *really* happened."

"Yeah, but I'm sure his version will be entertaining. You know, when I'm their age, I want to be just like them. Going on adventures, like a cruise down the Nile or climbing Mt. Everest. But not alone. I'd want to do it with the person I love. Because that would make it all so much better."

She was right. What you did didn't matter as much as who you did it with.

"Do you think they're soulmates, Mom—Gramps and Ida?"

I thought about it. For years, Dad had doted on my mother. Even after she left him, he'd pined for her privately. But it had been unrequited love. When a person didn't love you back, they couldn't really be your soulmate. Without a doubt, Kyle had been mine. Our relationship hadn't been perfect—our last fight had been a doozey—but we'd grown together and supported each other, and the day he died... I'd died a little inside, too. I still hadn't gotten over it. But could a person have more than one soulmate in a lifetime?

"Yeah, I hope so," I said as much to Tara as I did to myself.

Leaning over, she pecked me on the cheek and heaved the truck door open. It groaned on its rusty hinges. "Bye, Mom. Just hang around a minute while I explain to Mrs. Mullins. I promised her I'd do dishes for a month once I get my cast off to repay her for putting up with me. She said I didn't have to, but I intend to anyway. Shannon and I were in the middle of binge-watching *The Handmaid's Tale* and she promised she wouldn't watch the rest without me, so I know she'll be glad to have me stay."

"Are you sure you should be watching that? It's kind of a grown-up's story."

"It's literature, Mom. We have serious discussions about it. Besides, I'm a young woman now, not a little girl. Say, should I take the bus home tomorrow?"

"I'll text you about that, all right?"

"Sure. See you." With a wink, she hopped out of the truck, shopping bag in tow. "Eventually."

I hoped she was right about that, too.

chapter 20

My stomach roiling, I held the box out for Clint.

"What's this?" The barest glow from the porch light fell across his face. His wavy hair glinted with droplets of water like he'd just stepped out of the shower. He took it from me. "You know I'll dog sit for free anytime. You really didn't have to get me anything."

"I didn't." I stepped through Clint's front door, the sound of galloping paws and chortling barks of glee greeting me. I braced myself. From six feet away, Bump leaped into the air. I flipped up both palms as a stop sign. He twisted in midair, hit the floor, and settled obediently at my feet on all fours. I grabbed his jowls, then leaned over to plant a kiss on top of his head. An abnormally long tongue flicked out and swiped across my right eyeball, temporarily blinding me. Slapping a hand over that eye, I stumbled toward Clint's couch.

"Then what is this?" Clint followed me to where I'd flopped down, then sat gently beside me.

"Open it." After I slipped my coat off, I placed it over the couch arm. Bump rested his chin on my knees, those big mismatched eyes studying me with concern.

Clint lifted the lid. Took out the note. "Sam… when did you

get this?"

"At home just now. It was on the front porch. Before I went to get Tara. Only I left her at the Mullinses, because..." I sighed. I didn't need to say it. Didn't want to think it. "Look at the rest."

He lifted up the noose.

Confused, he shook his head. "What does it mean? I don't get it." He set the box on the table and scooted closer, took my hand. The touch of his skin sent old familiar feelings coursing through me. He leveled a concerned gaze at me. "Sam, is this a death threat?"

I shrugged. "I don't know. Maybe?"

"Do you have any idea who sent it?"

Pulling my hand free, I scoffed. "Well, yeah... I mean no. Just a fake name."

"But there wasn't any signature." After looking at the note again, he placed it and the rope back inside the box. "This isn't the first threat you've received, I take it?"

"No." I got up, then drifted to the bay window. A pink ribbon of sunset striped the horizon. His neighborhood was more spread out than mine, single-level brick homes on one- to three-acre carefully landscaped plots, versus ageing Cape Cods on postage-stamp-sized patches of dirt hemmed in by rickety board fences. Here, everyone had a two-car garage and a long asphalt driveway. In my area, roadside parking was a necessity if you owned more than one car.

Clint came to stand beside me. "Want to elaborate?"

"I have a cyber stalker." Arms crossed, I turned toward him. "It was just e-mails at first, but then they got my home phone number, and, and now, now they..."

Whimpering, Bump nosed at my pant leg and snorted. There was already a drool stain on my jeans. I fixated on it, still fishing for the words to finish what I'd started to say.

"Now they know where you live," Clint said for me.

All my walls collapsed with an exhaled breath. I couldn't hold it in any longer. Tears sprang to my eyes. Blubbery sobs broke from my throat. I was the little girl in the mall, crying for my daddy, afraid and alone. Clint's arms went around me, pulling me to him. I melted into his touch. Let it mend the parts of me that were breaking.

"Sam, I'm here for you," Clint whispered, placing the lightest of kisses on the rim of my ear. Then one of his hands slipped lower to rest on the curve of my hips, his fingers grazing my back pocket as he held me tight.

Confusion churned inside me. His words... did they mean something other than reassurance? Or was it me who was reading more into them?

I pulled back from him. Searched his eyes. They were hazy, unfocused.

He brought a hand to my cheek.

"No." With a thrust of my palm, I pushed him back.

Confusion twisted his face, then insult. "Sam... I..."

Waving my hands, I stepped back. "I shouldn't have come here."

I should've called Archer, told *him* everything. Just because he wasn't here in Wilton right now and my life was in shambles didn't give me cause to run into Clint's arms. I had to get out of here. Go somewhere—

Clint latched onto my wrist before I could run out the door. "Sam, first of all—I have your dog. You came here to get him, remember?"

A bewildered Husky mix stared up at me, his tail curled under, his head dipped low. Bump, of course. I'd missed the big galoot. My weekend hadn't been the same without him as my alarm clock, hyper-speed walking partner, and confidante.

"Secondly, I think you misunderstood me. I wasn't trying to... I just wanted to let you know, as a friend, that I'm here to support you. Have you called the sheriff about the threat?"

I tugged my wrist from his hold, and he willingly let go. "Previous contacts, yes. But not this one. Not yet."

"Sam, this is serious. You have to report it."

"I know, I know, but...."

"What?"

It wasn't that easy.

"Sam..."

"I don't want her to hurt someone I care about, okay? Besides, I don't know *who* she is or who she's after, all right?"

He rose, then walked a broad circle until he was in front of me. "Any suspects?"

I shook my head. As much as I wanted to point a finger at Birdie, I didn't have anything concrete on her. It could've been any one of nineteen other women in the Apple Pie Bibliophile Society. Or someone I'd never met.

He held his hands up, as if to reinforce he was not going to sweep me into a romantic embrace after all. "Look, you obviously feel threatened, right?"

Mortally so. TrueLuv's messages had crossed the line days ago. A noose, even if she wasn't the murderous sort, was meant to strike terror.

"I'm afraid to go home, Clint. I made up some story about the plumbing to keep Tara at the Mullinses another night, but I'm not sure how long I can keep coming up with excuses. I'm afraid for her safety. And kind of glad my dad and Ida aren't in town right now." I put my hands over my eyes like I could shut it all out. "I just want it to stop."

"I know you do. How did it start?"

"Online. E-mails at first."

"When?"

I thought back. "A week and a half ago?"

It seemed like so much longer.

"Is your address anywhere online?"

"No, I've made sure it isn't. Although, obviously, they were able to figure it out anyway. The e-mails were just bitter at first. It wasn't until I got a call on my landline that things turned really bad."

"But when they e-mailed you—it wasn't anything random?"

"Definitely not. They knew my name. Well, names, that is. Real name *and* pen name."

"How..."

"No idea. The only two people who know what I do are you and Selma."

He gazed out the window like he was searching his memory. Then he shook his head. "If your address isn't searchable online, then somehow they tracked you down. It has to be someone who knows you, Sam. A friend of Jake Taylor's. Someone connected to Deputy Halloway, Lorraine Steinbrenner, or Leroy Roberds... You *have* ticked off quite a few people in this town in a very short time, you know."

I had—and those were just the obvious ones. Back when I was living in Naperville and commuting to Chicago, I'd felt anonymous. I had neither friends nor enemies. Here in Wilton, I'd fallen hard for Clint—in lust, anyway—found love with Archer, made a friend in Selma, formed new connections with Ida and Cleora—even Sheriff Driscoll. I had roots, people I could rely on. And yet, I might as well have had a bright red bull's-eye painted on the front of my shirt.

"You can't protect Tara without the law on your side, Sam."

Damn it. Why did he have to be right all the time?

"Tomorrow," I said. "I'll call the sheriff."

"Promise?"

"Yeah."

"Stay here tonight then." Before I could protest, he added, "I won't come within ten feet of you, if that'll make you feel more comfortable. And call Archer and tell him you're here. If he can't understand I'm just looking out for you and there's nothing going on between us, well... that's due to his own insecurities."

Would Archer be jealous, or would he understand? If I told him everything—including my identity and why I'd never purposely told anyone about it, except for Clint and Selma—

Selma. I could go to her place... except I still couldn't get the thought out of my head that somehow she'd let slip who I was. But it hadn't been that long ago that I'd told her. TrueLuv's first e-mail had come before my revelation to Selma.

My head was spinning. I needed to hear Archer's comforting voice. Tell him I was staying at Clint's for the night before the Wilton grapevine twisted it into something it wasn't.

"I'm going to call Archer now," I said. "Mind if I take the couch?"

"I have a spare bedroom."

"The couch is fine."

He disappeared into the main bathroom, then returned with a set of sheets and a spare blanket. Instead of just handing them to me, he made me a bed on the couch, even turning the sheet back so I could slip right inside that tidy cocoon. Then he brought out a bowl of fresh water and a carrot stick for Bump.

"Thanks for everything, Clint." Sitting on the couch, I hugged a throw pillow to my chest. "Goodnight."

"There's something else I wanted to talk to you about, Sam." He pulled a hand down over his chin and neck. "Danielle called me yesterday. Did she tell you the surrogate was going to have *my* child?"

"Not in so many words, but—"

"She's not," he said bluntly, almost defensively. Then, he added, "She can't, anyway."

Untucking the bedding, I slid my feet beneath the cool sheets. "I know. Danielle told me on the way home." I turned sideways to prop myself on my elbow. "I'm sorry, Clint. I know you were looking forward to having your own child and to being a father."

"For the record, I didn't... donate."

"But—"

"The way you were acting, it occurred to me that you thought I was going to be the biological father. That was never the case. But I wanted to be there for him or her. Kind of the backup whenever Danielle needed help. Something more permanent than a babysitter. I kind of figured the kid would need a father figure, and I was willing to be that. Danielle and I agreed I'd be called 'Uncle Clint'. That doesn't mean I was ever going to bail on the kid out of convenience, or if Danielle and I had a disagreement, though."

This was a side of him I hadn't known before we broke up. Then again, maybe it was a side of him that hadn't existed until recently.

"Anyway," he continued, his gaze direct, "I realize this doesn't change anything between us, but I just wanted you to know everything. I've learned the hard way that it's not worth keeping things from the people you care about."

It was like he knew I hadn't told Archer the whole story of what was happening lately. Or was he just trying to come clean with me? I was never sure where I stood with Clint, given our history. It was always so complicated.

He stood there not six feet from me in just a tee and shorts, his hair slightly rumpled, my dog staring at him with love and adoration, a man who'd just volunteered to be a father to a child not his own. And to cap it all off, he hadn't given any indication he and Danielle were even so much as friends with benefits.

I realized then I'd been staring. It hadn't been intentional. I'd just been lost in thought, but he probably assumed I was entertaining thoughts of us. So I decided to make it clear I wasn't.

"That's very selfless of you, Clint. Really. Say, if you don't mind. I'd like to call Archer now. I'm sure he's still up, seeing as how it's three hours earlier there." I took my phone from my purse, then tapped at the screen as a hint.

A cone of light bathed his face as he turned on the small lamp sitting on the end table. Then he hit the wall switch to turn off the overhead light. "I'll double check all the locks on the doors and the windows before I hit the sack. Goodnight, Sam."

"Night," I whispered as he walked away. After he closed the living room drapes and locked the front door, Bump started to follow him out of the room, but I called my dog. He looked from Clint to me and back to Clint. Then he came to me, his nails dragging over the hardwood, head down, clearly confused.

Clint made a quick but thorough check of all the doors and windows throughout the house. After the click of the deadbolt on the back door sounded, he went into his bedroom, leaving the door open a crack.

Turning off the lamp, I dialed Archer. It went to voice mail.

"Archer, hey… It's Sam." I hesitated. "Call me back as soon as you can, okay? I'll be up for a while."

For half an hour, I stayed awake, flipping through the TV channels, the sound on mute and the closed captioning on so I wouldn't wake Clint. I checked my phone twice to make sure I hadn't silenced it, but Archer hadn't returned my call. He would, though. I was sure of it. I upped the volume on the ringer before laying my phone beside my pillow.

Bump put a paw on the edge of the couch. I rubbed under his chin, and he stretched his neck for more. "Sorry, bud. I don't think it's big enough up here for the two of us. But you can sleep right next to me, okay?"

With a heavy sigh, he circled twice and lay down, his spine pressed along the length of the couch, his head facing the front door for extra vigilance.

My hand dangling over the edge to brush against the fur of his withers, I fell asleep to the steady rhythm of his breathing.

IN MY DREAM, A bird sitting on a low-hanging branch chirped. A pleasant, musical chirp. A persistent, unvaried chirp. Slightly... mechanical.

Dog snot sprayed my wrist. A furry snout rooted at my palm.

Aww, Bump. He was trying to tell me 'good morning'.

Before I could open my eyes, a tunnel of darkness closed around me. It was as if the solidness beneath me gave way and I was somewhere else...

TV LIGHT FLICKERED IN the darkness. I stretched my legs and yawned, paws extended. Fingers scratched behind my ears, then made their way down my neck and spine. Gentle laughter bubbled from behind me.

Feet shuffled from the kitchen and across the living room. Walt moved across the TV glow, temporarily blocking the view. *Whatcha watching, pumpkin?*

Some movie about a dog that gets lost and finds his way home. Tara tucked her feet up so he could squeeze onto the end of the couch. *Kinda sappy, but we're bonding over it.*

A snack bowl rested on Walt's lap, salted buttery goodness wafting over the rim. I stood, then went to sit at his feet.

Watch this. Walt tossed a puffed kernel. I snapped it out of the air. He threw several more—high, low, sideways, fast.

Tara clapped. *Wow, that's good!*

Pretty impressive, I'd say.

She wrapped an arm around me, giving me a big smooch on the head. *Gramps, you know what the best thing about him is?*

What's that?

He loves us sooo much. I don't know what I'd do without him.

I felt the love then. From both of them. As big as the world.

THREATS AND THREADS

I closed my eyes. Felt Tara's hands smoothing down my fur. Her cheek smooshed to mine. Heard the steady rhythm of her breathing. The garbled sounds coming from the TV—human voices, a dog's bark, and the chirp of a bird... Bird?

I SNAPPED UPRIGHT, HUMAN again. I'd expected morning light, but there was only a faint glow coming from a nightlight in the kitchen. I waited for my eyes to adjust fully as a fuzzy silhouette took shape before me. A pair of ears came into focus, one upright, one sideways. Bump sat in front of me, seeming pleased with himself. The chirping—

No. Not chirping. It was the ding of texts. Was it coming from *inside* him?

"Bump, what did you do? You didn't eat my phone, did you?"

He thumped his tail on the wood planks of the floor. Apparently, Clint had removed Danielle's alpaca rug and decided not to replace it.

It wasn't possible for him to swallow a phone whole... was it?

I peered into the kitchen, remembering a clock somewhere in there. The digital readout on the microwave read '5:42 AM'. It had to be Archer. But why would he be answering me at this time of night? That wasn't like him at all.

A jolt of panic rushed through me. What if it was Tara? Had something happened to her?

I flicked the table lamp on, then grabbed Bump's jaws to pry them apart. He twisted in my grip, his abnormally long tongue blocking my view of his esophagus as I craned his head toward the light. Nothing. I opened his jaws wider. He wiggled. All I could see was teeth and tongue.

"Stop it," I commanded lowly. The phone dinged again. Faintly. "Nooooo, no, no, no..." With each denial, the desperation and volume in my voice mounted. "You did *not* eat my phone!"

The hallway light came on. Clint stood framed in his bedroom doorway, bleary-eyed and with the worst case of bedhead imaginable. In nothing but his briefs. Not the shorts and T-shirt he'd retired in. Not frumpy boxers. Tight, revealing briefs.

Those shoulders. Those abs. That... *package*.

"Sam, is everything all right?"

I touched my jaw to make sure it wasn't hanging open.

Stretching his neck, Bump retched. I let go before he could eject a pool of bile into my lap. But he merely coughed, licked his lips, then flopped over sideways. Just beneath his rump lay my phone. He'd been sitting on it. I must've knocked it to the floor while dreaming.

"Everything's fine," I squeaked. "Just... fine."

Clint shuffled closer. Even with his hair all mussy, it just gave him that sweet, innocent quality. "I thought I heard you talking to someone and—"

"I was. I, uh, woke up to check my texts and couldn't find my phone. I was trying to get Bump to move. Sorry. Didn't mean to wake you up." I dug my phone from beneath Bump's inert derriere, then raised it in the air. "Ah, see. Found it."

Clint stifled a yawn behind his hand, then ran it around the back of his neck. "No problem. Just wanted to make sure you were okay."

"Very okay," I said.

With a lopsided smile, he turned and went back to his bedroom. The retreating view wasn't bad, either.

I slapped myself. No, this was not okay. I couldn't stay here again. Not ever. It had been a bad idea.

I turned my phone on and read:

ill make sure of it

Make sure of what? It took a moment for it to sink in that I'd read the last text first. I glimpsed at the number. It wasn't Archer at all. The number said 'Unavailable' so it had to be TrueLuv. Scrolling up,

THREATS AND THREADS

I started at the beginning.

u think u can just make ur troubles disapear by ignorin me?
uve ruined my life and now ur gonna pay for it
i know where you were last nite
and I know what you were doin with that animal docter
ur firefiter boyfriends gonna find out 2
ill make sure of it

What the… How exactly had I ruined her life? More like she was ruining mine. Who was this chick and why did she have it out for me?

I typed out a reply, erased it, typed another, erased that one. No, I shouldn't answer. She was a troll. Sick people like that got an adrenaline rush from arguing. Besides, if I did turn all this over to the police, it was probably better to just let her dig her own grave. She'd already escalated without me ever engaging. Heaven knew what I'd be in for if I gave her the satisfaction of fighting back.

Then, one more text popped up.

get out of town—now! or else

Or else what? Did I really want to find out? And if I did leave, where would I go?

I was vaguely aware of Bump moving away from me, drifting down the hallway. He was probably going to lie down in front of Clint's door—or, if it was still open, invite himself in to sleep on Clint's bed, hoping in the morning they'd go for a run.

My hand started to cramp I was holding my phone so tightly. I set it beside me and concentrated on taking deep breaths, but it felt like I had a corset on and someone had cinched it tight enough to break all my ribs. I told myself to calm down. That she was only a cyber bully, trying to scare me. Anyway, I'd left a message for Archer. First thing in the morning, I'd call again and tell him everything. Including who I really was. Then after I'd told him about all the messages TrueLuv had sent, he'd understand. Completely. Archer Malone was a reasonable guy. Not the jealous sort at all.

Ding!

Another text. My hand shot out to my phone, hovered over it. I was afraid to look. Didn't want to hear from her again. And yet... I had to know.

I flipped the phone over in my palm. No words. Just... a picture.

Of me in Clint's arms. My face buried in his chest. His fingers spread across the top of my ass. His lips next to my ear.

How was I going to explain *that?*

chapter 21

"SAM... WHERE DID THAT come from?"

At the sound of Clint's voice, I slapped my phone to my chest. "Where what?"

"I saw it, Sam. It was a picture of us from last night." He came from behind the couch, his face half shadowed from the light in the hallway. "Who took it?"

Even as innocent as the moment had been, I knew that by not having told Archer everything beforehand, I'd handed TrueLuv the perfect piece of blackmail.

Clint settled himself in the recliner, elbows on his knees, hands clasped. He had on a pair of heather-gray sweatpants and a crumpled pale blue shirt now. "The picture—did your cyber stalker send it?"

I nodded.

"You know what we have to do?"

I nodded again. "Can it wait until after coffee and a shower, though? I need to clear my head."

"If that's what you want... I could stand to go for a quick run, too." He pushed himself up, went into the kitchen and made some coffee. "But you realize you're going to have to come clean with Sheriff Driscoll about everything, so it doesn't just look like we're trying to cover up our own indiscretions."

My thoughts exactly. But it wasn't the sheriff I was worried about explaining things to.

"WHAT ARE YOU GOING to do?" Clint eventually asked as he handed me a cup of fresh coffee. He sat at the kitchen table across from me. The sun was only hinting about breaking above the horizon, but he looked ready to hit the road in his running clothes.

It had been nearly an hour since Clint had discovered me with the blackmail photo. I stared into my coffee cup, wondering what I expected from him at this stage. Archer would have pulled me into his arms and told me everything was going to be okay.

And Clint? He'd already done just that and look where it had gotten us.

"You aren't going back to your house, are you?" Clint lifted his cup as if to take a drink, but then set it down. "You can't."

"Guess not. Not right now, anyway. But at some point, I have to. I don't know how long I can ask the Mullinses to look after Tara."

"If you need any help, let me know. I'll follow you to the station and go in with you. I'm sure they'll want to talk to me, too."

"Yeah, I suppose you're right. Meanwhile, I'll try to get a hold of Archer again."

"You mean he didn't call you back?"

I shook my head.

His jaw muscles tensed. "What kind of loser—"

"It was late, all right?" I snapped. How dare he call Archer a loser? There had to be some logical explanation for him not calling back. Had to be.

I shot up and paced a few times in front of the window before it occurred to me that TrueLuv could be out there now, skulking behind the bushes with her zoom lens equipped with infrared capabilities. I sat, my chair tucked into a corner by the wall. "Besides, I didn't go into any details in my voice mail. Just said I needed for him to call me back. He might not have understood it was urgent."

Grumbling under his breath, Clint set his coffee cup aside. He'd barely touched it. "Look, I don't know why you're hesitant to tell him about last night—we don't have anything to hide, after all—but don't you think he needs to know you're in danger?"

"He doesn't know... about me."

"Doesn't know... I don't understand. Doesn't know what?"

"That I write romances."

"Why wouldn't he know that? I understand you don't want everyone to know, but you and Archer are—"

"It just never came up, okay? I guess before we got involved, he knew me the same way everyone else did—as a textbook proofreader—and, well, it just never came up lately." After some thought, I added, "Seems like we were always talking about *his* work, when we talked about work, that is."

I expected him to say something critical of Archer, but he didn't. What I hadn't told him was the reason I'd been so reluctant to share that part of my life with Archer was because, after breaking up with Clint, I was trying to guard some part of myself... just in case we parted ways, too. But if I was thinking that way, then I really wasn't all in.

"I suppose it's time you did," Clint said.

"Yeah, I suppose so." Once again, he was right. "So you don't think it's... weird or kinky that a mother of a teenager writes romances?"

"If you wrote psychological thrillers, I wouldn't think you were a serial killer. As for it being 'kinky'—no, not even close. As long as there's no bestiality or incest or S and M or—" His brows drew tight. "There isn't any of that, is there?"

"No!"

He fought a grin. "Maybe I'll pick up one of your books, just for research, and find out for myself."

When Clint and I first met, I'd told him I was a romance writer, but I was pretty certain I hadn't told him my pen name. I tested him. "They aren't under my real name."

"Then you'll have to tell me what name that would be."

So he didn't know. Good. I'd hate to think he was the traitor. "Sorry, I can't."

He shrugged. "Okay."

I waited for him to pry more, but instead he got up, carried his cup to the sink, then poured it out. "I don't even know why I made myself a cup. I rarely touch caffeine, and I only keep it in the cupboard for guests. I usually go for a run to wake up."

At the word 'run,' Bump emerged from beneath the table and began looking around franticly for his leash, going from room to room as he cast his nose to the floor and explored every crack and crevice for the umbilical cord that would attach him to his beloved.

Clint laughed. "Let's see how long—"

Bump ran past the front closet, spun a one-eighty, and rammed his nose under the closet door. He inhaled, snorted, inhaled again. Then he sat back on his haunches, scratched once at the door, and let out a great bellowing *woof!*

"I take it you hung it in there," I said.

Clint nodded. "Normally, I just set it on the sideboard in the front hallway, but since we've been out of the routine lately, I put it away. How on earth..."

"He's a retired drug dog, remember? Well, he flunked out—I'm guessing because he has ADHD whenever squirrels show up—but still, they wouldn't have let him in the program in the first place if he didn't have a good nose."

"I've noticed. Yesterday, he found an almond that had rolled under the couch."

"When did you lose it?"

"Months ago. Or last year maybe." Clint went to the closet, then took out the leash. Bump started doing pirouettes. "On second thought, it doesn't feel right leaving you here alone. Not after you got that package. No, I'm staying here."

Clint hung the leash back up in the closet. In a fit of hysteria, Bump took a couple of laps around the room. Thirty seconds later, he side-skidded to a halt at Clint's feet and hacked up a tennis ball. Clint scooped it up before it rolled away. "Okay, okay, buddy." He looked at me. "Mind if we go out back and…"

"Go."

"Thanks. Ten minutes should do it. If I stay over in the corner, I can see the whole yard from there. No one could get to the front door without me knowing."

I stood to stretch my arms. "Care if I hop in the shower while you two play outside?"

"Make yourself at home. You know where everything is." He waved toward the hallway as he opened the back door. Bump let out a few yips of excitement.

I peeked outside to see my dog racing over the frosted grass, his eyes on the ball as it arced through the pre-dawn sky. Leave it to a dog to bring a little sense of normalcy to an otherwise-abnormal day.

TWENTY MINUTES LATER, THE road grime rinsed away, I felt like a new woman, except for the manly deodorant. My hair hanging wet down my back, I opened the bathroom door to the smell of maple-flavored bacon and blueberry muffins.

Led by my nose, I tiptoed out into the kitchen. There was already a plate sitting at the high counter for me. Next to it was a glass of white, not red, grape juice. In the guest bathroom just off the kitchen, I could hear the water running. Clint was taking a shower now. Bump lay just outside the door, his treasured tennis ball tucked beneath a paw as he snoozed away. I slid onto the stool to wolf breakfast down. It wasn't until I'd snarfed down the last crumb and drained my glass that I realized I hadn't had supper last night. Having your life threatened tended to change one's priorities—survival first, sustenance later.

Morning sunlight beamed in through a tall window situated in the breakfast nook. Outside, frost sparkled on the grass and glinted off leafless branches. Now and then, a car went down the road. It was peaceful here, less crowded than my own neighborhood. Lawns wide enough to accommodate polo matches stretched between rambling brick homes.

There was no TV on Clint's kitchen counter like on mine, but he did have an iPod docked within arm's reach. I turned it on, then stopped on a selection of songs by Adele. The longer I listened to them, the more melancholy I became. By the fourth song, I felt like I'd been cheated on, dumped the bastard, and gone unemployed for months.

The water in the guest bathroom stopped running. A minute later, Clint's electric razor began buzzing away. I clicked the iPod off and listened to the simple sounds of a man's morning grooming routine—the drip and splash of water, the toothbrush being tapped on the sink edge, and a drawer gliding on its tracks as he put the toothpaste away.

The sounds of normalcy. Maybe even companionship.

I needed that in my life. Now more than ever.

chapter 22

HUMBOLDT COUNTY WAS LUCKY to have Sheriff Driscoll. Being in his presence was like truth serum: if you had anything to feel guilty for, you'd have a hard time hiding it—and if you didn't, you had every confidence he'd deliver justice like the small town superhero he was.

After he finished jotting down his notes, Sheriff Driscoll tidied his stack of papers. "We'll do our best to get to the bottom of this, Ms. McNamee. I'll put Deputy Strewing on the case, since he was out at your place recently... Speaking of which, we haven't had any similar activity since then—or before, for that matter. My guess is that whoever tried to break in was targeting you specifically."

Next to me, Clint shifted uneasily in his chair. He'd been fidgety the whole time we'd been at the station, even though it was mostly me who'd done the talking over the past hour and a half. He'd also been checking his watch obsessively.

"I'd advise against going back to your house." The sheriff's gaze shifted to Clint. "Especially if you're alone."

"I just need to pick up a few things," I said. "I don't plan on staying."

"Will you be staying at Dr. Chastain's then?"

Clint and I stared at each other.

"I have to go to work, Sam," Clint said hastily. "I have four surgeries scheduled for today. One could wait, but the others…"

"It's all right." I patted his hand, but didn't let my touch linger. "I'll give Selma a call. I know she won't turn me down at a time like this. Plus, her landlord is flexible. Her next-door neighbor took in a Florida relative with three kids and two dogs earlier this fall for almost a month after their home got flooded in a hurricane. I'm sure death threats count as dire circumstances."

When I said the word 'death threats,' I could see Clint's protective nature flare. He grabbed my wrist. "Sam, I'm not turning you away. I just don't think it's safe for you to be alone during the day while I'm at the clinic. If you want, you can hang out there. That way, I can keep an eye—"

"No, no, I'll be fine. Just let me ring up Selma. Trust me, it shouldn't be a problem. Besides," I lowered my voice, even though the sheriff was just a few feet away from us, "I think we've already given this town enough to talk about, don't you?"

"Right," he muttered.

Standing, Sheriff Driscoll scooped up the papers. "I'll have our secretary enter my notes into the system. If you could forward those emails and texts to Deputy Strewing today, that would help. Meanwhile, I'm going to have a patrol car swing through your neighborhood and by your friend's house, just in case your stalker makes a move."

A few moments later, Clint and I were left alone. An expectant silence opened, waiting to be filled.

Finally, Clint spoke. "You were going to call Selma, right?"

"Oh… yeah." I took out my phone, then checked for messages before dialing. Nothing from Archer still.

"What is it?" he asked.

"Nothing, it's just that… This is so unlike him, not to call back. I'm starting to worry."

THREATS AND THREADS

As we walked out of the room and down the hallway, my mind spun a thousand scenarios, none of them good.

"Is there anyone you could call that might have heard from him?"

"The guys at the firehouse, maybe. I need to call Selma first, though."

While he made a pit stop, I settled down on a hard wooden bench in the wide corridor across from the restrooms.

Selma answered on the fourth ring. "This must be important. You know I don't get up before nine, Sam."

"I wouldn't wake you if it wasn't." I gave her the lowdown, including how I'd spent the night at Clint's and why I was sitting at the sheriff's station right now.

She yawned. "Wow, you sure do live an exciting life for a Wiltonite—or is that a Wiltonian? Wiltoner, maybe?"

"I honestly don't know. But yeah, more exciting than I'd like. So is it okay if I hang out with you today? I remembered you told me last week this would be your first day off since—"

"Um, today? Gee, I wasn't really expecting company so…"

"I wouldn't ask, but—"

"I wasn't dissing you, Sam. Just trying to figure out the linguistics."

Ah, logistics. By now, my brain had been trained to translate Selmanese. "Sure, I understand." Although I tried to mask it, my words dripped with disappointment.

"Aww, Sam. I'm not gonna let you down, honest. Meet you at my place in half an hour?"

"Meet me?" Meaning she wasn't at her place right now. "Where are—"

"I'll explain when you get there, 'kay?"

"Okay, sure."

She didn't have to explain. I had a pretty good idea where she'd been last night.

For the fifth time in as many minutes, Clint checked his watch.

I grabbed a handful of panties and bras and stuffed them in my gym bag. "What time is your first surgery scheduled for?"

Standing in the doorway to my bedroom, Clint grimaced. "Don't worry about it, Sam. I called Aunt Janelle on the way. We'll just work through lunch to catch up."

"What time?"

He half-shrugged. "Fifteen minutes ago?"

"Go," I urged. I tossed a few shirts into my bag and trotted out of the bedroom and down the stairs, Clint a step behind. Bump shoved his way past us to bounce across the living room floor. At the front door, he spun a one-eighty, verbalizing his excitement. I had to raise my voice so Clint could hear me above the yodeling. "I'll be out of here in less than ten. And besides, all the neighbors are awake now." I glared at Bump, but he was practicing his drunk-kangaroo moves.

"I don't know, Sam." Clint followed me into my office like he was afraid my stalker might be hiding under my desk. "I don't feel comfortable leaving you alone after last night. That was a serious threat. Sheriff Driscoll even thinks so."

After I ripped the cord of my laptop from the outlet, I placed it in my bag, too. I hadn't even bothered to check e-mail when we arrived. I'd forward the emails to Deputy Strewing later.

I'd done a cursory search for the house key I'd left for Harmon, but hadn't seen it. In the kitchen, I grabbed the phone charger off the counter, added it to my hobo stash, and zipped my bag. How did people fleeing a wildfire or hurricane decide what to take with them and what to leave behind? It was overwhelming. I spun around so fast I collided with Clint's chest.

He caught me by the waist. "Whoa there. Slow down, slow

down."

I stiffened in his hold. I had to get my stuff, get out of here... But first, I needed Clint to leave.

His phone rang. Letting go of me, he answered the call.

"I'm sorry," he said to me. "I do have to go now. Heather Bartholomew just brought her Dane in. He's running a fever of a hundred and five, and he's refusing food and water."

"Go. I only need five more minutes. What can happen in five minutes?"

His eyes narrowed skeptically.

"Okay, don't answer." Bump barked. I pointed at him. "See, my security guard is alert and ready for business."

Torn, Clint headed for the door. "You'll text me—"

"As soon as I get to Selma's," I finished.

At the door, he hesitated. Whatever had gone wrong between us, I was thankful we could still be friends. He lifted his hand in a wave, then, nudging Bump aside with his foot, he slipped out the door. Bump rushed to the picture window and watched as he drove away.

Across the street, a neighbor I only vaguely recognized got into their car and left for work. A school bus trundled down the road, making me think of Tara. How long before I could safely bring her home again?

Dashing upstairs, I collected my suitcase, complete with my dirty laundry from the weekend, and tossed in the manila envelope I'd retrieved from the storage unit. One last look around proved there wasn't a belonging in the world important enough to risk staying here one minute longer for. Downstairs, I made sure the alarm was set and put Bump's leash on. Just as I stepped out the side door from the kitchen and locked it behind me, a slow-driving car came down the road. I plunged down beside the trash cans, assaulted by the stink of two-weeks' worth of fermenting garbage. Bump strained toward the truck, his nails raking at the concrete. He didn't understand the point of lying low.

"Bump," I whispered tersely. "Come *here*."

His ears flattened. He pulled harder, insistent. The car came closer, slowed more. I gave a sharp tug of his leash. Slowly, reluctantly, he slunk back to me. I wrapped an arm around him and scratched at his chest. He leaned into my touch, momentarily content.

The car turned somewhere. The engine stopped. If only I had a weapon... Maybe I should've taken Dad up on his suggestion several months ago to get a gun. If I had one, I wouldn't feel so vulnerable at times like this.

A door slammed. Feet thudded on pavement. I took my phone out, my thumb hovering over the keypad, ready to hit 9-1-1.

Then I remembered—Selma had given me her pepper spray. My hand flew to my side for my purse. But it was in the truck. Maybe I could creep to the door, open it—

The footsteps had stopped. Across the street, a screen door squealed on rusty hinges. I peeked around the corner of the trash cans to see another neighbor across the street going inside through her front door. I exhaled in relief.

Bump took a step toward the truck.

"Yeah, we're going." I opened the passenger side door for him, then went around and climbed in. As I fit the key in its slot, something caught my eye. Mounted on the underside corner of the soffit toward the back of the house was a tiny camera. Marco must have put that there when he installed the alarm. He'd mentioned adding a security camera, but I hadn't known that he had. If there was footage of who'd left the package, it could solve everything.

I opened my contacts, but before I could bring his name up, my phone dinged with a text. Archer maybe?

The moment I opened it, I wished I hadn't.

It was from TrueLuv.

this is the last yull here from me. i want a new story with a better ending. send

THREATS AND THREADS

it back to me by next satrday. not a day later.

An empty threat. Had to be.

At least I wanted to believe that was true. Besides, if I sent my work off to some incognito bully, who was to say she wouldn't post a spoiler online? Or maybe even pirate my book? It had happened to others.

Yet, there was an even worse possibility. She knew everything about me—my phone number, where I lived, the people in my life... She had the power and the motivation to ruin me or harm someone close to me. I had to know what she intended to do.

I typed: *Or what?*

I stared at the message box. It remained blank for an eternity. Had she gone away?

And then—

or someone close to u will go away... forever

Who? Tell me! I demanded.

But TrueLuv was gone.

Hands shaking, I took a screenshot of the exchange and sent it to Deputy Strewing.

I crumpled over the steering wheel. I couldn't live like this. Couldn't handle it all by myself, even as much as I wanted to be independent. But how was I supposed to admit to Archer or anyone else that I needed someone to lean on, to prop me up when I'd tried so hard since Kyle's death to stand on my own? Needing that made me feel weak. Like some stuffed animal being trampled and pulled upon until my stitches were stretched and frayed.

Bump snuffled at my ear. Soon, he was licking the side of my head, his soft whimpers an attempt to comfort me. But it wasn't the same as having a human being there who could pull me into a hug and tell me everything was going to be all right. I had a crazy person lobbing death threats at me, damn it. I couldn't sleep or function, let alone whip out an entirely new novel with a contrived ending in just over a week. It was impossible to conjure up a plot while I fretted over who TrueLuv was going to strike at. A friend? Family member? Archer?

It took a while, but I pulled myself together and backed out of the driveway. On the way to Selma's, I called Tara. Just to talk. When she didn't answer, I realized she was probably in class, so I voice-texted her to call me back ASAP.

She returned my call from the bathroom just a few minutes later, her voice noticeably hushed. I asked how school was going and what was new with Shannon. At first, she talked willingly—Tara was never one to hide her life from me. But the more questions I asked, the more guarded she became.

"Mom… is everything okay with you? You called me at school, so I figured something was up. You didn't call just because you missed me."

My daughter was intuitive, just like me.

"Just doing too much thinking lately, I suppose."

"About what?"

"About how lucky I am to have you as a daughter." I had to bite my lip to keep from bursting into tears. I didn't want her to hear the fear in my voice.

"Aww." She sniffled. Her voice went soft and sentimental. "I feel lucky to have you as a mom." Then she cleared her throat and with her usual precocious maturity, said, "But don't get annoyed at me if I text you multiple times a day when I go off to college. You have to answer back, even if it's just with an emoji so I know you're thinking of me, okay?"

"Of course I will."

Sometimes, I wasn't sure which of us was the parent.

chapter 23

SELMA'S MOBILE HOME HAD never looked as inviting as it did that day. Since she wasn't home yet, I texted Ida.

Hope you're enjoying your trip. Any new adventures?

While I waited, I angled all my rearview mirrors to survey the neighborhood. Except for a Honda puttering down the lane and pulling into a home about four doors down, the area appeared vacant. Ida's reply came a minute later.

Having the time of our lives! Walt insisted we take a balloon ride over the foothills of the Andes. Got some fabulous photos. After that, we watched wild alpacas and drank from a mountain stream. Walt is having a few stomach issues. Probably just something he ate. He's been trying all sorts of new foods.

Can't wait to see the photos, I texted back. *Post them when you have a chance.*

Will do! I have to go. We're going off-roading this evening, then taking a moonlit walk around the lake.

You two sure get around, I said. *Miss you both—hurry home.*

We miss you too, Sam. I'm looking forward to getting home to quiet little Wilton so I can recover from all the excitement.

I only wished I could say she was right about this town being dull. There were things going on here that would've shocked the most cosmopolitan socialite.

Still no sign of Selma. I called Marco.

"Hello! MarVan Security Services. Marco Vandegrift here." His East Coast accent came through loud and clear. Or maybe it was Canadian. Or New England. "How can I help you?"

"Marco, this is Sam McNamee. We met at Archer's going-away party. You installed an alarm system at my place this weekend."

"Oh, yeah! Hey, my apologies about the miscommunication. I'd just finished putting it in and was going to call you when my mom's gout started flaring up and—"

"Don't worry about it. I need to know something."

"Okay, what?"

"The camera you put up. I need to see the footage."

"Footage?"

"Yes, someone delivered a package to my place while I was gone. If I could see the footage, I'd know who—"

"Sorry, sweetcakes. There's no footage. I was going to come back next weekend to get that up and running. The camera feed needs to be wired into your computer and I didn't have access, what with you being out of town. Cool thing is there's a program where you can watch it remotely once it's all set up. I'm on shift today and tomorrow, but I can come out in a few days if you want."

Too little, too late, I wanted to say.

"Sorry about not getting to it sooner," he said, "but time is at a premium lately. I've finally convinced my mom to let me move back in with her. Won't solve her health problems, but at least I won't have to take care of two places."

I thanked Marco and told him it was fine. Since I was still a few minutes early and Selma hadn't arrived yet, I tried Archer one last time.

To my amazement, he answered.

"Oh, hey, Sam… what time is it?" He sounded groggy.

"Seven-thirty your time. Did I wake you up?"

"No, I've been up for about an hour. Just really tired."

"I left you a message last night…" I broached.

"Yeah, I know. I just got it this morning. My battery died yesterday while we were in a marathon brainstorming session."

Who held meetings on a Sunday?

Then he yawned, sounding utterly and truly exhausted. "I must've crashed on the bed less than five minutes after I got back to my room."

A little bubble of sympathy welled inside me. Archer was one of those guys who threw every cell of his being into a project until it was done. That was probably why Cirrus had been so relentless about getting him on board.

The very reason I loved him was what was keeping us apart.

Still… what could keep him so busy he didn't have a few seconds during the day to text 'What's up?' And if his phone had died, he could've borrowed someone else's.

"Busy, huh?" Whatever the reason, I felt a little neglected.

"Very," Archer answered. "I think we've developed a pretty strong program that will address the complexities of familial dynamics and…"

I zoned out. I'd called to tell him all the frightening things that had happened in the past day, but I was starting to wonder if we were even on the same page anymore. Anyway, if I told him, all he'd do would be worry about me and suggest I lock myself behind a guarded wrought-iron fence topped with barbed wire until he could come to the rescue.

I wanted him home. I needed him. But I wanted to be able to rely on myself, too.

Just as I was about to tumble headlong into my own pity party, Bump pressed his nose to the passenger side window and snorted. The windows were partially fogged, but I could tell by the rumbling muffler that Selma had just pulled in behind me. She got out of her car and wiggled her fingers in a wave. Her hair had that unwashed, slept-on look, rather than her usual carefully coiffed hairdo. Bump yipped an ear-piercing greeting, and Selma blew him a kiss.

At least I had these two hooligans. Which wasn't the most comforting thought, when I considered someone's life was at stake.

Selma tapped on my window, then lifted a tub of mint chocolate chip ice cream out of the paper bag she was carrying. I signaled with my index finger that I needed a minute. She gave me a thumbs-up, clacked on her high-heeled zebra-print boots up to her front door, and unlocked it. She was the best kind of best friend a girl could ask for. And she was here, and Archer wasn't.

"Listen to me," Archer said, "going on and on. How are things on your end?"

"Me? What... Why are you asking?"

There was a pause.

"Sam, is everything okay?" His voice sharpened in concern. "Has something happened? Are you in any danger?"

"Danger? No..." I lied. "Everything's fine."

Fine like china. Just don't drop it.

I wanted to tell him what had been going on lately, but the moment I thought about how to explain the incident at Clint's, I went blank. It would've been easier if he were here with me.

"Sam, do you want me to send Marco by?"

"Marco with the tattoos and roving eye? Thanks, but no. Anyway, I talked to him already. Something about his mom and he can't come by to finish the job until later in the week."

"That's right. I forgot about her issues. He's a good guy. Just a little rough around the edges." He went quiet for a few moments. "Sam, I love you more than anything, and I don't want anything bad to happen. I'll be home before you know it. Just stay safe until then, okay?"

THREATS AND THREADS

"I'll try."

We muttered perfunctory goodbyes and hung up.

A broken sigh tumbled out of me. Inside, I was crumbling into a million pieces. I covered my face with my hands. Tears wet my palms. Whimpering, Bump licked my face. What I really wanted right now was a good soul-purging cry, but Selma was waiting on me.

She'd lifted the little café curtain on her front door and was staring at me. I blew my nose and went inside, gym bag in tow.

Bump barged through the door in his usual reckless fashion. His tail sweeping away everything within two feet of his hind end, he galloped to her sleep sofa and flopped down with a grunt.

Dropping my belongings by the door, I squeezed past Selma and settled beside Bump in a space twelve-inches wide. "Hey, are these new throw pillows?" I pulled loose the one beside me to give myself more space and set it on the floor, then clicked the TV on and started surfing.

Selma blocked my view of the TV. "Sam, have you been crying?"

"Me?" I dragged a hand under my nose. "No, no... just allergies."

"You don't have allergies. That's your ugly crying voice. I recognize it. Did Archer break up with you?"

"What? No!"

"Then tell me what's up, 'kay? I don't like knowing my BFF has been balling her eyes out."

I sniffed the air. "Selma, did you really give up smoking? It smells so... fresh in here."

"One whole week smoke-free. Turns out Newt has asthma. Now out with it."

"All right." I let out a breath. I had to tell somebody. "TrueLuv just threatened to harm someone close to me."

"Who?"

"She wouldn't say."

"No, I mean *who* is TrueLuv?"

"I don't know for sure, but she's a reader who was unhappy with my last story. She's been sending threatening e-mails and texts."

"Oh, dear. That's terrifying. Is Tara all right?"

"She's at school right now, but she's been staying with the Mullinses'. I asked Judy to keep the girls at home when they aren't at school."

"Move it, buddy." With a glitter-flecked fingernail, Selma poked at Bump's ribs. He rolled off the sofa with a disgruntled *woompf*. She shimmied down beside me. "'Kay now, give me *all* the details. Don't skip any. No matter how boring or outlandish. As your bestest bestie, I should know more about you than anyone."

So I told her. Not that she could fix anything. But it did feel good to confide in someone.

Somehow, we ended up watching an episode of *The Brady Bunch* while downing the full half-gallon of ice cream.

When a commercial came on, Selma tapped at her temple. "It *has* to be someone you know. Someone who lives here in Wilton."

To me, her observation was, well, obvious, but I was curious to hear her logic. "Why do you say that?"

"They know practically everything about you."

"Like my pen name *and* my real name?"

"Exactly!" She went all of six feet to the fridge to retrieve a couple of root beers. "So, any suspects?"

"Maybe."

Selma handed me a bottle. "Name?"

I opened the cap with the tail of my shirt. "Well, I did run into Birdie Swinson in Chicago."

"Hmm, that *is* a strange coincidence. The chances of you two running into each other there are what?"

"About one in a hundred million."

"Case closed then. Call Driscoll and tell him you know who it is."

"Can't."

"Why not?"

"I don't have any evidence she did anything, that's why."

"She knew where you were going, Sam. Need more evidence than that?"

"She's a librarian and an avid romance reader, that's all."

"Why don't you let me dig up some dirt on her?" She clapped her hands together. "Ooo, I feel like a genuine sloop."

"A what?" I took a longer chug. Carbonation gurgled in my stomach. I'd probably have gas and a bloated belly later, but sometimes you had to live a little.

"A sloop. You know, one of those private detectives who solve murders. I like the thought of being a female sloop. It—"

I burped, then patted my sternum to coax the rest of the air bubbles upward, but they stayed trapped in my esophagus. "Sleuth," I muttered.

"Sleuth? Hon, that's one of them really slow animals that hangs upside down. You and I need to visit the zoo soon and brush up on animal names. Anywho, how could anybody have found out about you?"

Ignoring my heartburn, I sat up straighter. It was all starting to snap together. "Maybe somebody let it slip—somebody who has firsthand knowledge about me?"

Shaking her head, she blew across the neck of her bottle so it made a faint foghorn sound. "Naw, that'd be nobody."

I narrowed my eyes at her. "*You* know."

"Yeah, so?" Then she flinched like someone had smacked her with a flyswatter. "Wait... you aren't inseminating that I..."

I refused to even let that picture form in my brain.

"No, just no." She stomped her foot. "I swore I'd keep it to myself and I did. I did! How can you even—"

"I'm not saying you did it on purpose."

Tipping her bottle up, she drained it completely, then put it on a wooden cable spool that served as an end table and let out a belch loud enough to put any beer-guzzling biker to shame. "I didn't do it accidentally, either. I'd remember if I did."

Her wounded look was a punch in the gut. Having just accused my BFF of betraying me, I felt lower than a slug. She had every right to kick me out. So I stood and saved her the trouble. "I'm sorry. I shouldn't have said that. I'll go."

She blocked the door. "Where?"

"I don't know." Hoisting the bag onto my shoulder, I waited for her to move. Confused, Bump tilted his head at me, but didn't budge. "Out of town, maybe?"

"So you'd abandon your daughter? Run away?"

Not only had she pierced my stubborn resolve, but she was also perforating it like a sieve.

"Of course not. I'll... I'll..." Lost for an answer, I tossed myself back onto the sofa and clutched one of the pillows I'd set aside, then buried my face in it.

Was it possible to suffocate myself—or would I pass out before I was starved of oxygen? I didn't have a clue what I was going to do. Maybe the Humboldt County sheriff's department had a witness relocation program.

"Well, if you're going anywhere, I'm going with you."

I glanced up. "What?"

"I can't let you go off alone." She sank down beside me, tilting the cushion. I rolled toward her involuntarily. Like the good friend she was, her arm went around my shoulder. She leaned her head against mine. "Somebody has to look out for you."

Bump rested his chin on my knee, gazing at me with sad puppy-dog eyes.

"See there." Selma raked at the back of his neck with her nails. "You sure can't leave him. That dog loves you more than peanut butter."

THREATS AND THREADS

On cue, Bump raised himself up and hitched both paws over our shoulders in a group hug. This was what it meant to have friends. They loved me no matter how horrible I was to them, because they understood that life could be messy and we sometimes acted out of fear and anger and frustration. I didn't deserve their devotion, but I was sure glad I had it.

My heart melted from the inside out.

SELMA CANCELED HER DINNER date with Newt, and we gabbed late into the night while gorging ourselves on microwaved pizza rolls and pumpkin-spice eggnog. Bump kept guard by the front door while Selma and I slept until noon, comatose on a cocktail of fat and sugar.

We woke to Bump slurping greedily from the toilet bowl. Before Selma went off to work, she made me promise to stay put until it was time for the book club meeting that evening. She'd meet me there as soon as she could get off.

Although I hadn't heard from TrueLuv in almost twenty-four hours, I, by no means, felt beyond her reach. To alleviate my anxiety, I did busywork—washing Selma's dishes, dusting her furniture, and running the vacuum. It was the least I could do for her putting me up at a time like this. Bump followed me around the whole time like all those mundane chores were the most interesting thing in the world.

Worn out, mentally and physically, I decided it was time for a nap on her 1980's brown plaid sofa. First, I needed to get the big marrow bone from my suitcase to occupy Bump. I pulled out the plastic bag in which I'd wrapped it. Five seconds later, he was lying beneath Selma's dinette table gnawing away.

Then, I saw it—the manila envelope.

"No time like the present," I said to myself.

The couch nearly swallowed me, body and spirit, as I sank onto its worn cushions. For half an hour, I sat with the envelope in my lap, distracted by a soap opera with characters I wasn't familiar with.

Finally, I opened it. The flap of the envelope sliced the pad of my thumb. I winced. A bead of blood welled, scarlet and gleaming. I stuck my thumb in my mouth and pulled the contents free. Another envelope, addressed to my mother's parents. The stamp was plainly French, but the postmark was too blurred to make out. When I was eighteen, I'd buried it on a shelf in my closet and forgotten about it. With each move, I'd repacked it. But I hadn't been ready to look inside. Not when I got it. Not when Kyle and I married. Not when Tara was born or Kyle died or I'd first moved back to Wilton.

The truth was that I'd never be ready.

Somehow, I opened it one-handed. A typewritten letter in French. I'd taken two years of the language in high school, but that had been decades ago. I only recognized a handful of words. So I consulted the all-knowing Google.

My dear Ann,

I have tried so long to find you. I said things in anger. I did not wish for you to go away. I have learned of the child. While I cannot claim my paternity, let me do what is right. I have set aside money for her. Enough to take care of her for the remainder of her life. The information you require is below.
Étienne

"Enough to take care of her for the remainder of her life…" I said aloud.

What did that mean? Enough to buy a house? To set up a trust fund for Tara and pay her college tuition? Enough to purchase a yacht and cruise the Rhine?

At the bottom was the name of what I surmised was a bank, an address, and a series of numbers, most likely for an account. There was also a full name, which, until then, I'd never known—Étienne

THREATS AND THREADS

Renard.

Étienne. My biological father. He'd tried to take responsibility. Yet, my mother had never opened the letter. Why? Had she been too ill by the time it reached her? Had she wanted nothing more to do with him? Had he loved her as much as she'd loved him? Or had she been merely a plaything, conveniently whisked aside when she became pregnant. Then again, later, when another, even younger woman came along?

Most likely, I'd never know.

There was money for me in France. Did I want it, given that he'd never been a part of my life? Heaven knew I could put it to good use. I made enough to live on, but it was a constant struggle. I no longer had a car of my own. The house I'd come to know as my home would soon be reclaimed by its rightful owner.

If I accepted that money, would I be betraying the man who'd raised me? And yet—if he never found out, did it matter at all?

As much as I'd been pining for the support of loved ones lately, this was one matter I had to take care of entirely on my own.

chapter 24

AN OVERSIZED BROWN BUICK jutted out into the street, its front end angled out. I veered around it, trying to avoid the other car on the opposite side of the street.

Bump tipped sideways, plowing into my right arm. Strings of drool dripped from his jowls. Instead of righting himself as I corrected course, he crumpled like an old dishrag beside me, his head squarely in the center of my lap.

I lifted his snout, then tucked it between the outside of my leg and his paw. Another reason I needed to go car shopping as soon as possible. Having Bump right next to me in Dad's truck was an accident waiting to happen. I'd opted to drive to Cleora's rather than walk because the forecast had predicted rain turning to snow. Judging by the blustery wind and the dampness in the air, it would be rolling in any minute. At any rate, I didn't feel safe walking alone, dog or not.

The entire block around Cleora's house was choked with cars. I inched along, searching for a spot of my own.

Was this because of the Apple Pie Bibliophile Society meeting?

Couldn't be. There *had* to be something else going on like a baby shower or a Bible study.

A shadowy figure stepped out between two cars, slightly ahead. I slowed to let him cross the road. He flipped the hood of his winter coat up over a green-and-red knit cap. It was Lionel. I was about to wave as I passed by, but his back was already turned as he got into his car.

Big drops splattered on the windshield. I cranked the wipers up. As I made another turn, Bump sat up, his upright ear perked forward. A yellow Chevy Spark whipped around the corner and swerved toward us, crossing the center line. I tapped on the brakes, throwing my arm out to keep Bump from flying through the front windshield. The Spark rocketed down the middle as if it were the only car on the road.

Hitting the horn, I made a hard right into a driveway just in time to avoid getting clipped. The car buzzed past, Gladys Detwiler hugging the steering wheel as she waved in my general direction.

After my heart rate returned to normal and I was sure Gladys was beyond striking distance, I resumed my quest. One more turn and half a block later, I found a parking spot. I hopped out, pushed the button to open my umbrella, then led Bump down the street.

By the time we arrived at Cleora's front door, my shoes were soaked and so was my dog. I was also frozen to the core and my teeth were clacking.

"Oh, dear." Cleora opened the door wide to let us in. The house was packed. "Did you walk all the way here?"

"I might as well have, considering how far away I had to park." I shook my umbrella out before propping it next to the others just inside the door. The warmth from the furnace enveloped me. I shed my coat, then hung it on the antique coat rack just inside the door. "I had to park on Nightingale."

"That far? I am surprised. *Really* surprised."

Bump twitched his shoulders side to side.

"No, Bump, don't!"

But he was already committed. He shook full force, water flinging outward from his body in a rotating arc. It hit the walls, the front door, the umbrellas, the little side table with the hard caramel candies... Mostly, though, it hit Cleora and me.

"I'm so sorry. Maybe I should just take him home now." I tugged at Bump's leash, turning toward the door.

"Don't be silly." Cleora dug into the hall closet, then handed me two towels. "One for you, one for the dog. I always keep these handy for after our walks."

I gave Bump a good rub down. He still smelled like wet dog, but at least he wasn't a walking wet mop.

"Sam!"

Selma wedged herself through the crowd at the end of the foyer. There had to be upward of fifty people crammed in the narrow living room. I couldn't even venture to guess how many were mingling in the kitchen or dining room. Last time, there weren't even two dozen.

"Hey, Sel."

Her hair sparkled with iridescent glitter. She had on a white chenille sweater with pearly sequins, a pair of dark gray tights woven with metallic thread, and tall lace-up boots. She must've changed at work, because that wasn't what she'd had on earlier. The amazing thing about her fancy get-ups was I never saw her wear the same one twice. I was pretty sure she combed the thrift store on a weekly basis, donating all her once-worn clothes before exchanging them for new ones. That, in itself, had to be a full-time job. Besides, there couldn't have been room in her mobile home to store that many clothes.

Bump lifted his nose in the air, sniffing. He whined. On cue, Fancy trotted to him. His entire hind end wagging, Bump dipped the front half of his body in a play bow. Soon, they were both prancing playfully and batting at each other.

"Why are there so many people here?" I asked.

Cleora fanned her neck. "Believe it or not, over three-fourths of American women read an average of twelve books a year. Of course, some may only read one how-to book, while others read a book a day.

The most avid readers consume romance novels."

"Yeah, but I got the impression the meetings weren't usually this well-attended."

"They usually aren't."

"So why—"

A frosty white fingernail poked at my sternum. "Honey," Selma added, "they're here because they all heard how good your—"

I squinted at her. Threateningly.

"They all heard how good that S.A. Mack book is. Everyone's talking about it. Buy the Book over in Oil City sold out of copies and had to order more. The ladies who couldn't wait caved in and bought e-readers or downloaded it to their phones."

That just didn't make sense. This was Wilton, Indiana. People here thought the *National Enquirer* counted as journalism.

"Why don't I take Bump and Fancy to the laundry room to play?" Cleora said, as if eager to escape the commotion. "It's not very spacious in there, but they can at least keep each other company without getting in the way. I hadn't counted on quite so many people. There won't be enough punch or snacks to go around."

"Not to worry, Cleora," Selma said. "I got it all covered. Newt let me have all the almost-expired snacks for free. They're on the counter next to the fridge if you run low."

"Oh, Selma, I couldn't—"

"Sure, you can. Now go play hostess. Sam and I will put the dogs in their playroom. Let me see that baby of yours." Crouching, she clapped her hands. Fancy leaped into her lap. She lavished kisses on the little dog, which Fancy returned excitedly. "You wuv your Auntie Selma, don't you? Don't you?"

Fancy gave a little yip of agreement, then Selma tipped her on her back to cradle her like a baby.

Cleora clasped her hands together in a gesture of gratitude, then returned to her other guests.

Most I didn't know. I would have preferred they didn't know me either, but chances were they knew my name, what street I lived on, and who I'd dated in my few short months here, as well as who'd tried to kill me.

"What did you do?" I asked as we made our way through the crowd with the dogs. "Bus a crowd here from Fort Wayne?"

"No, Newt took me to church this last Sunday."

"Church? On a date?"

I shooed Bump into the laundry room. Selma set Fancy down beside him before I closed the baby gate. They started playing instantly, unconcerned they might miss out on the party.

"Kinda. It was a carryover from our Saturday night activities. If he'd been a Catholic, he would've been at confession, if you follow me."

"Got it. Did anybody ask why you two were there together?"

"Couple of the ladies here. I said Newt and I were talking at work and I'd let slip I hadn't been to church since I was five, so Newt offered to take me to his. No one suspected a thing about us."

"So these are church ladies?" We started back toward the living room, but I lingered in an empty corner.

"They are. Just as nice as they can be, too." A fiftyish woman with a mahogany-brown bob waved at Selma, and she waved back. "That there's Lindalou Buckminster. Or maybe Buckingham... or is it Bucketmaster? Ah hell, starts with a B anyway."

"Which church?"

She bit her lip. Her eyes rolled up toward the ceiling. She was thinking. "The Humboldt Something-Something-Something of Something."

"The Humboldt Brethren Evangelical Sanctuary of Worship?"

She held a finger up. "That's it! You know—the big one on Route 379."

"I'm familiar with it." Hooking her elbow, I reeled her in close.

"Do they *know* what kind of book we're reading?"

"Know?" She wrinkled her nose. "Are you kidding me, Sam? They were raving about it at the refreshments table between Sunday school and the service. Well, Lindalou was telling one of her friends how your series helped rekindle the romance in her marriage, then I chimed in." She waved a hand at the throng. "The rest is history."

"I... I don't know what to say."

"Thank you," she whispered.

"For what?"

"No!" She smacked my forearm lightly. "That's what *you're* supposed to say—to me. Thank you, Selma, for using word of mouth to save my career."

"Okay, one small point. It wasn't exactly tanking. Things were going just fine."

"But great?"

"Well, no, but—"

"Then, there you have it. You're welcome."

"Thank you." I started toward the living room, and she trailed after me.

Everyone was moving in clumps in the same direction. Several women were holding dog-eared hard copies of my book. A few others were clutching e-readers and tablets.

Somewhere in the crowd, I bumped into Cleora's twin sister.

"Hi, Cordelia," I said. "You look so professional."

"Why, thank you, Sam." As she straightened her red blazer, the badge with her name and the realty company on it caught a gleam of light.

"Say, maybe Cleora's asked you already, but did somebody buy Miley Harper's house?"

Cordelia tapped a fingertip on her chin, pensive. "Mmm, no, I don't think it was ever listed. That means it would have been a private sale. Or it could've been sold at the monthly sheriff's auction. Or been transferred to a relative."

"How do I find out who owns it now?"

"They'd have the records at the county courthouse, but those aren't necessarily public information. Have you tried, you know, just knocking on the door and introducing yourself in a neighborly way?"

"I was just curious. Thanks, though." I *could* have asked around the neighborhood, but that would've entailed talking to other people I didn't know. Odd to think anyone would want to live in a house that someone was murdered in, but then it probably went for cheap. Which gave me a thought. "Say, I might be looking in the near future. If you come across any steals…"

She took a business card from her blazer pocket and handed it to me. "Sweetheart, I will call you first thing. Too bad I didn't know last week. There was a four-bedroom on ten acres in pristine condition on the south end of the county that went for under four hundred thousand. It was way underpriced."

"I was thinking more, uh, quaint, cozy, fixer-upper, that sort of thing. Closer to a hundred, if that."

She winked. "I'll keep an eye out."

A final glance around the room revealed Selma's old BFF, Amy Sue, tucked in the far corner next to Gladys Detwiler. They seemed wrapped up in Gladys's latest crocheting project. If it hadn't been for Amy Sue, I'd have marched over and chastised Gladys for nearly running me off the road. Amy Sue sniffled into a tissue. Her eyes seemed a little red and irritated, indicating she might be fighting a cold. I decided to keep my distance for now.

"Quiet! Everyone, please quiet down." Cleora, standing in the middle of the living room, clapped her hands in that attention-grabbing authoritative way only a librarian could. "We need to get started. Please take a seat."

There was a brief spat of jockeying for the best seats. Selma and I ended up wedged between the dining table and the wall.

THREATS AND THREADS

Cleora leafed through her paperback, the spine broken from wear. "We left off at chapter—"

"Excuse me." A gray-haired lady with a bun stood abruptly, an e-reader crushed to her bosom. Her denim skirt reached her ankles, and her paisley blouse was buttoned all the way to her collar. She raised her chin, and, in the mousiest voice imaginable, spoke. "I-I-I... I would like to say s-s-something important—if I may."

Cleora gave a nod of approval.

"My husband thought I'd been reading a book about the French Revolution." She lowered her eyes suddenly, as if regretful she'd spoken aloud.

"Why would he think that?" someone near her said.

"Have I been reading the wrong book?" Gladys peered over her bifocals. "Did we start another one?"

"Are you?" another added. "Reading about the French Revolution, I mean. Because if you are, then I'm not—"

"No, no." Gray Bun flapped a hand in denial. "I hate history. So... boring. Dreadfully, dreadfully boring."

"And everyone dies at the end, when you think about it." Gladys had a lapful of yarn, a section of it already knitted into a child-sized sleeve. When several people looked her way, she added, "Well, if it's more than, say, a hundred years ago, don't you think?"

They all pondered her observation. Several shook their heads.

"Why would you tell him that?" Stacy said as she gently rocked the infant seat on the floor beside her with a foot. Aster was sleeping blissfully, and Stacy seemed far more engaged with her surroundings than she had at the last meeting.

"Read about the French Revolution? I haven't. I just told him that."

"So you lied?"

Gray Bun nodded feebly. "It worked. For a few days. But then... then he turned my e-reader on. I didn't even know he knew how."

"My word…" Cordelia flattened a hand over her heart. "What happened?"

"Nothing happened for ten minutes or so." She glanced around the room, her eyes pausing on one face, then another and another.

"You mean he was *reading* the book?" Selma said.

Gray Bun nodded again. "When he realized I'd been standing there all along, he asked me to read it to him."

Gasps resounded.

"He didn't take it away?"

"Chastise you?"

"Schedule a counseling session with Pastor Matt?"

"Oh, no." The tiniest of grins tugged at the corners of Gray Bun's thin lips. "He wanted to… I was… We… we, you know." Blushing, she lowered her eyes. "Let me just say he was late for work the next morning." She'd broken out in a full smile by then. It made her look ten years younger. "I haven't felt this desirable since my wedding night."

"Same for me," came a voice from over by the hallway.

"Me, too!"

"Best thing to happen to my marriage since birth control."

"Maynard's been calling me his 'mistress'," said a thirtyish woman in a navy sweatshirt, "We've been pretending we're having an affair—with each other!"

"How titillating!"

"Did you wear fancy lingerie?" Stacy teased, grinning.

"Did you pretend to be a…"—Gladys giggled—"dominatrix?"

One of the church ladies covered her mouth with her hands. Another covered her ears and closed her eyes. Several began fanning themselves with their books.

"Oh, no," Gray Bun said. "It wasn't like that. It was very… intimate. Like falling in love all over again."

A collective "Aww" went around the room.

THREATS AND THREADS

Gray Bun turned toward her congregation sisters. "Yes, I felt exactly like that. It was like being a bride on her wedding night. Makes you realize it's how we see our husbands that matters—and how they see us. We all start our relationships off thinking of them as Prince Charming—handsome, hardworking, strong, and brave. But somewhere in there, we stop seeing those things and focus on what they're doing wrong. Sure, we all change as we get older. We sag and get wrinkles and lumps and go gray. But the person we are deep down inside… that person is still there. Just tired and more worn, but still there. I looked at Clem with new eyes this past week. And when I did that, he did the same with me."

"Good for you," Maybelle grumbled from the comfort of the recliner. She must've arrived early to snag the best seat in the house. "Not all of us are so lucky."

A couple of women rolled their eyes at Maybelle, but the rest ignored her surly comments.

"Honestly," Gray Bun began, "I've never read anything like this in my life. I thought all romances were filthy dirty pornography. But this book, this book treated the acts between a couple with dignity. It left something to the imagination. And trust me, Clem has plenty of that."

Emboldened by all the nodding in the room, Gray Bun squared her shoulders and glanced from face to face. "But it also deals with what happens when we let ourselves be led down the path of temptation. It may feel right at the time, but you know that in real life, no good will come of it. Sometimes reading about things that are wrong doesn't mean you condone them. It just serves as an example of what *not* to do and why. But let me tell you this, ladies—don't give your man a reason to look elsewhere. See the good in him. Always."

My thoughts instantly swung toward Archer and how much I missed him. The ache had been so great that I'd desperately wanted to fill it. Gray Bun may as well have been speaking directly to me.

I hadn't meant to seek out Clint's solace, but I hadn't exactly tried to stay away from him while Archer was gone. Granted, in a town this small, I couldn't avoid bumping into Clint, but maybe I'd taken a step too far in asking him to watch Bump.

Which reminded me, I hadn't heard the dogs making their normal play-growling sounds. Maybe Cleora had given them bones to keep them busy. I'd have to check on them the first chance I got.

"Did you read the part to Clem where Alexander is kissing Felicity's neck," Stacy said, "and he thinks she thinks it's actually his twin, Axel, but she knows it's him all along?"

"Eventually, I did. But that first time, I read him the passage about Felicity and Gerard in the moonlit garden."

More gasps.

"That one?"

"Oh, my."

"No wonder you two are a couple of lovebirds."

It had taken me a while to realize Birdie wasn't at the meeting. Regret filled me that I might have somehow offended her. But I was also relieved because I wasn't entirely convinced she wasn't my stalker.

"So do you think Clem fantasizes... about other women?"

Gray Bun's brow twitched. "Don't you ever imagine yourself with another man?"

These modest, tightlipped, small-town women—stay-at-home moms, librarians, receptionists, postal workers—they had feelings and desires as real as my own. Suddenly, and shockingly, I realized I had more in common with them than differences.

That didn't mean I was going to start inviting them to card club parties or join the local bowling team just to have a reason to dish out gossip once a week. After all, I was still an introvert. But it did make me less inclined to be aloof and cynical.

For the first time since moving to Wilton, I felt like I belonged. That my storytelling filled a need. I had a purpose bigger than just providing for myself and my daughter.

I'd helped these women understand that true love didn't stem from an inherent physical beauty or flow from some mystical source. It began from within and grew when you focused on the good in another human being. If you didn't believe yourself deserving of love, if you couldn't see the qualities in someone else worthy of loving, then you would never, ever know true love.

Wow. I needed to write that down before I forgot it. I scanned around me for a pen and a scrap of paper. Never mind—I could type a memo on my phone. I pulled it from my pocket and saw there were two texts from Archer.

Sam, all day long, I've been thinking of you. Of us.

My heart swelled with love.

Can you call me? We need to talk. There's something important I want to discuss with you.

And then it cracked. Right down the middle.

chapter 25

'WE NEED TO TALK' was seldom good. Unless you were having a disagreement about which sofa to buy, it was the beginning of all breakups.

For the next ten minutes, while the women of Wilton bubbled with excitement over a book about the complications of love, I tried to think of scenarios that would've put a positive spin on Archer's texts, but nothing came to mind. I knew I ought to call him, but I was afraid of what he might say. I didn't want to ugly-cry in front of half of Wilton.

My phone dinged with another text. It was my dad.

Samantha—this is your father, Walter Schimmoller. Still alive, miraculously. Interpol and pickpockets everywhere. This is supposed to be fun? Can't wait to toss a ball for Bump. Here's hoping we make it home.

Half a minute later, Ida followed up.

Ida here. The 'pickpockets' are children who ask for a dollar to pose in a picture with you in their native dress. They're adorable and quite harmless. Walt is convinced they've been set loose on the tourists to steal phones and sell them on the black market. Despite his paranoia, Walt is enjoying himself. He can now curse in Spanish and Portuguese, and he has acquired a taste for a drink called pisco, which makes him more affable. See you soon!

THREATS AND THREADS

Out of the corner of my eye, I saw Selma curl a finger at me. She was standing in the hallway, jaw clenched, nostrils flaring. A look that screamed, "Get over here *now*!"

As inconspicuously as I could, I slid my chair back and wedged my way around the back of the crowd. Fifteen excuse-me's later, I reached her.

She grabbed my sleeve, hauled me to the end of the hallway, then thrust me into the bathroom. Before I could wheel around and ask her what the bleep was going on, she shut the door and locked it.

"Selma, what—"

"Shh!" She flapped a hand at me, pressing her ear to the door.

I waited five seconds. "Is this important? Because I need to call Archer about something. And I really ought to check on the dogs. They haven't made a peep since Cleora—"

She produced a cigarette and a lighter from a small case in her pocket. When she put the cigarette in her mouth and flicked the lighter, I grabbed it from her.

"You can't smoke in Cleora's bathroom."

Grabbing the lighter back, she put it and the cigarette away with a huff. "You're right, you're right. I've been trying to quit, but whenever I get anxious, I want to smoke. It calms me down."

"Glad to hear you're trying to kick the habit, but what's bugging you?"

"Did Amy Sue say anything to you when you got here?"

"No, I barely even realized she was here. Why?"

"You didn't notice?"

"Notice what?"

"She's been giving me the evil eye."

"Like how?"

"Like this." Selma's left eyebrow arched high onto her forehead, while the right eye squeezed down to a slit, quivering. The effect was very menacing.

"Did she say anything to you?" I asked.

"No. Her look says it all."

"And what does it say?"

"I don't know. But it's not nice."

"Are you sure she wasn't having a problem with her contacts?"

"She doesn't wear corrective eyewear, Sam."

"Maybe she had a bug stuck in her eye."

"It's practically winter. Bugs are all dead."

I shrugged. "She has a facial tic?"

She stomped her foot. "I'm serious."

"I know you are, but I sure don't know what it means. Has she been looking at you that way the whole time?"

"Just at first. The last few minutes, it's been more of a smirk. Like this." She curled her lip.

"You said a smirk. That's more of a snarl."

"What?"

"Watch." I took her by the elbow, swiveling her toward the mirror so the two of us stood hip to hip. It was a tiny bathroom, the vanity barely wider than the sink. The mirror on the front of the medicine cabinet was even narrower. We leaned our heads closer. I made a face.

"What is that—a grimace?" she asked.

I checked. It was. I made a lopsided grin.

Selma shook her head. "That's a sneer."

I tried again, this time with more smugness to my grin.

"Yeah, like that!"

I tilted my head sideways, thinking. Selma mirrored my action so our heads were touching.

"Why would she give you that kind of look, Sel? I thought you two used to be best friends." Until I came along, anyway. "What happened? You never said."

"She asked to borrow money. A lot of money."

THREATS AND THREADS

"For what?"

"She was out of a job. Had been for months. Claimed a coworker framed her and got her fired. I told her straight out I didn't make loans to friends. That was about when you came along."

"Ah, I see. Well, I don't blame you. They say loaning friends and family money is a bad idea. What was she asking for—a few hundred bucks? A thousand?"

She pumped a thumb upward.

"Ten thousand?"

She repeated the gesture.

"Six figures? Seriously? How long did she plan to stay unemployed?"

"Tell me about it. I'd say that chick is on crack if I didn't know better. Said she wanted to buy a fast-food franchise. Don't know what made her think I'd fork over such a big chunk of my savings."

I squeezed between Selma and the sink, twisting around to meet her nose to nose. "You don't actually have that kind of money... do you?"

She stepped back, her lower lip pinched between her teeth. Then she flipped the toilet lid down and took a seat. "Maybe."

I squatted in front of her. "How did I not know this?"

"It never came up. Not like in between bites at Suds and Grub, I'd suddenly blurt out, 'I've got a quarter mil tucked away for a rainy day. How 'bout you?'"

"A quarter mil?" I clamped onto her knees. If anyone were to open the door right now, this would look extremely odd. "You're just grabbing a number, right? I mean, you live in a trailer, shop at secondhand stores, drive a clunker, and work at the grocery store." I laughed. "Where would you get a quarter-million dollars?"

"Sam." She looked me dead in the eye. "Why would I exasperate about something like that?"

I bit my tongue. With Selma, I had to go by context. Letting go—

literally and figuratively—I sat against the wall. "How though? You're like one of those recluses you read about in the newspaper who lives alone in some slum apartment in New York City and dresses like a bag lady. Then, when they die, the authorities go inside the apartment and discover bundles of money stashed in the mattress."

She bristled. "Thank you for that pretty picture. Never knew I looked like a 'bag lady'." A few seconds later, she perked. "Wait, did you mean like a Gucci bag lady—or a shopping bag lady? 'Cause that might determine whether I give you a smooch or wallop you."

"Please don't kiss me. If anyone walks through that door, we'll be the new talk of the town—and not in a good way."

"Right, I forgot about you being a thespian."

Let it go, Sam, I told myself. "Okay. Anyway, explain. How did you get so rich without me knowing, huh?"

"My daddy. Course, some say he came upon his money by unlawful means, but truth is he was just a good businessman. Just don't ask me what kind of business, if you follow me."

"Not really, but go on. What did he do for a living?"

"Lots of things in his lifetime. But later on, he made his money with a trucking company. He sold it just before he was killed in a hit-and-run accident. They never did find the person who ran him over."

"So you and your half-brother, Virgil, got the money from the sale of his company?"

"Nope. Just me. Virgil still thinks the company went bankrupt and Daddy sold it for what he owed on his debts. They had a falling out when Virgil was about seventeen, and Daddy kicked him to the curb. Virgil went through a rough patch, but he and I stayed close. Eventually, he did get his act together. He and Daddy never reconciled, though. Men can hold a grudge just as long as any woman."

Wow, there was a lot more to Selma's life than I knew. "So you inherited all this money, but you really can't use it because you're afraid your brother will find out, huh?"

THREATS AND THREADS

"Oh, no. I don't care if he knows. I'd give him some of it, but if Dylan ever found out, he'd find a way to cheat him out of it. I'm just waiting until he wises up about Dylan Hawkins."

"How did Amy Sue find out about the money?"

Selma's lips parted, but before she got a sound out, we heard the creak of floorboards in the hallway. In the crack beneath the door, a pair of feet were shadowed against the light from behind. Selma and I shared a glance. I pressed a finger to my lips, then crept toward the door, but before I could turn the knob, our eavesdropper scurried off.

Selma stood and flushed the toilet.

"Sorry, force of habit." She lifted the lid, then gently dropped it for added effect. "Probably just someone who needed to pee."

"Right." I turned the water on in the sink and washed my hands—out of habit.

"Anyway, I didn't want them to think we were in here talking about people."

"We kind of were."

"I know, but I thought I'd make it look legitimate."

"The two of us?"

"When you gotta go, you gotta go, honey. Company or not. Anyway, girls are always going to the ladies' room together."

"Yeah, but they usually don't share a stall." Turning the faucet off, I whispered, "Let's rejoin the party, shall we?"

She took my hands, squeezing them. "Sam, I don't even care if anyone—even Amy Sue—thinks you and I are an item. You're the best kind of friend a girl could have."

"Thanks, Sel." Before she could crush me in an awkward hug, I flung the door open. A couple of women stood at the far end of the hallway, their backs to us. "Ladies' room available," I announced, "if anyone needs it."

But no one made a move. They were all sharing stories about how different scenes in the book related to some episode of their lives. At this point, I figured I'd had more than enough feedback, and it was time to go.

I also needed to talk to Archer. Privately. The thought set big hairy moths loose to flop around in my stomach.

Selma hovered at the back of the room. Assured Amy Sue was nowhere in sight, she glommed onto Stacy, whose baby was now sitting in her lap trying to pull her tiny socks off. After giving me the universal signal for 'call me later,' Selma engaged in a game of peek-a-boo with the baby girl.

When I couldn't find Cleora in the living room, I wound my way into the dining room. She was there, carrying around a tray of cheese and crackers.

"Cleora?" I tapped her on the shoulder.

She set the tray down. "Would you like something to drink, Sam? Chips and salsa? Cookies?"

Her words said, 'perfect hostess,' but the frazzled look on her face shouted, 'overworked'. "Thanks, but no. I'm about to head home."

"So soon?"

"Yeah, sorry, but I have a ton of stuff to do. I know I was only gone three days, but it seems like three weeks."

"That's all right. I understand. Careful out there. Bye now."

"Goodbye, Cleora."

We exchanged smiles. I turned away, but before I could get out of earshot, she added, "Oh, I just remembered—I let the dogs out to relieve themselves. That was ten minutes ago. They're probably a mess. You might want to collect Bump at the side gate next to the garage. I'm going to have to dry Fancy's little snowshoes off with a towel as is. Feel free to grab a spare one. They're above the dryer. And don't worry about returning it—I have a dozen."

"Thanks, I think I might."

"Bring Bump back when the weather's better, will you?"

"Of course." I started to go, then turned back. "Hey, you see Birdie at work, right? Did she say anything about not coming to book club tonight?"

"As a matter of fact, she did. Said she's still unpacking from a recent move. Oh, and her cat had urinary issues. I understand they're particularly susceptible to them."

Sounded like a flimsy excuse to me, but whatever. "Next time you see her, tell her I said I hope her cat feels better."

After grabbing a spare towel, I put my coat on and pulled my hood up, then went outside. The rain had turned to snow and a fierce wind was kicking up. A single porch light in front emitted a weak cone of light that didn't reach past the side of the house. I stumbled through darkness around the side of the house as bare shrub branches grappled at my coat sleeve.

I stood at the gate to the backyard, peering into the darkness. "Bump! Come on. Let's go home."

A few seconds passed. I called again. He probably knew that coming meant he'd have to leave his sweetheart. "Bump, let's go. Time for a walk!"

Nothing. No sloshing of feet across spongy earth. No playful growls from the far corner of the yard.

"Bump? Fancy?"

The only sound that reached my ears was the rising rush of wind from a brewing storm.

"Buuuuump?"

In the time it had taken me to walk around to the back gate, Cleora had to have opened the back door and let Bump and Fancy in. I went through the gate into the yard, then shut it behind me.

Daggers of sleety snow pelted my face. I pulled my zipper up as high as it would go, then drew the drawstring of my hood tight—so tight I had only a small circle to peer through. Out front, the ladies were funneling out. Cars were starting and creeping down the slick street as they headed home to beat the worst of the weather.

I stepped onto the concrete sidewalk that ran along the back of the house, thinking maybe the dogs were huddled beneath the overhang of the roof, waiting to come in. But they weren't.

Shivering, I went inside and pulled my hood back. The kitchen was empty, the snack tray depleted, and the garbage near to overflowing. One by one, the last few women were putting on their coats and venturing forth into the storm.

"Thank you for coming," Cleora said flatly, repeating it over and over again as she stood by the front door, waving goodbye. "Thank you. Thank you…"

The baby gate was open, the laundry room empty of dogs.

My heart sinking but not yet ready to ring the panic alarm, I put my hood up again and went outside. They had to be out here. *Had* to be. I just hadn't looked hard enough. Or in the right place. It was dark. The weather made it hard to see far.

Maybe they'd discovered a mole hill and started digging. Or found rabbit droppings to roll in. Or were busy munching away on a stick. Or hiding beneath the wheelbarrow by the garden shed to wait out the storm.

I searched everywhere. Found no pawprints. Heard nothing. Hands cupped to my mouth, I called and called… and called. Ventured farther into the unlit yard. No dogs resting behind the tree. No dogs hiding in the hedge. None behind the trash cans or under the patio furniture.

Cleora's yard was enclosed on three sides by a privacy fence—only the portion facing the street was contained by chain-link—so I couldn't see into the adjacent yards. They could've tunneled out and were just on the other side of the fence, but if that were true, they would've heard me calling and barked in response.

My heart was galloping as I walked the perimeter. A queasy feeling writhed around in my stomach. Something was wrong. But

THREATS AND THREADS

what—

The gate in the far back corner. I went to it. Saw it was open.

"Oh, no," I whispered. "Just... nooo."

"Sam?" Cleora called from the back steps. "Where are the dogs?"

"They're..."

Shoes squished hurriedly over soggy ground. She came up beside me, holding the front of her coat closed, too rushed to button it up.

"They're what?"

I turned to her. Slowly. "Gone."

chapter 26

"'GONE' AS IN... NOT here?" Cleora said. "Missing?"

I nodded. Sleet stung my face.

All the Apple Pie Bibliophile Society attendees were long gone. Cleora and I were standing at the far end of her fenced-in yard, next to an open gate.

"But, but... how did they get out?" Her hands fluttered over her breastbone. "I checked that gate just this afternoon while I was cleaning up Fancy's doo-doo—and no one has gone through it since."

"No one that you know of."

She grabbed my coat sleeve with bare fingers. "What do you mean, Sam?"

The possibilities were leaping through my brain left and right. But considering what had been happening lately... "Someone let them out."

"By accident?"

"I doubt it."

"Why would anyone just let them out to wander? They weren't making any noise. They hadn't even been out here that long."

"Which means someone was waiting for them to go outside. Someone in the neighborhood." I turned to her. "Or someone in the book club who holds a grudge."

"A grudge against who? I can't think of anyone who holds a grudge against me, if that's what you're insinuating. I have charged some people with hefty overdue fines, but I can't imagine—"

"Not you."

"Who are you talking about then—you?"

I didn't answer her. It would take too much time to explain, and we didn't have that luxury right now.

Pushing the gate wide, I peered through. On the other side was a yard with no fence. That house stood at the end of a dead-end lane. To the right were other houses on either side of the street. But to the left stretched a field thick with underbrush and beyond that dense woods.

They could have gone either way. If they were still in the neighborhood, we might have some luck. If they'd headed toward the woods...

I called for both dogs. Soon, Cleora joined me. We hollered until our voices cracked with strain.

"Why would anyone do this?" Cleora was close to tears. She searched franticly around a hedgerow in the neighbor's yard, then behind their garden shed, kicking up slush as she did so. "I don't understand. Why?"

"Maybe it was just someone who hates dogs—the same person who poisoned Grace Hazelton's dog."

Her eyes snapped to me. "Poisoned? Is that what Dr. Clint determined?"

"Not exactly. But he said it was possible."

She gave me a skeptical look—like I was the crazy one, not my stalker or the person who went around killing the neighborhood pets. The more I thought about it, though, the more I was starting to think it could be the same person.

Then I remembered TrueLuv's message—the one about hurting

someone I loved.

Maybe 'someone' wasn't a person.

"Cleora, it's possible someone has it out for me, and they figured the way to get to me was through Bump. If that's true, Fancy was merely collateral damage."

"Good heavens, why would anyone have anything against you, Sam? This is all sounding so ridiculous. Like some crazy TV show or the wild plot of a second-rate novel. It's not even worth thinking about. Not right now, anyway. We need to… to…"—she clenched her fists at her sides, lost for an answer—"do *something*."

She was one hundred percent right. We had to act, not stand around and speculate about someone's motives.

"Do you want me to drive, and you can be the lookout?" she said. "Or would you prefer to drive?"

"Actually, I think it would be better if you stayed here. Someone needs to remain at home base, just in case the dogs find their way back. It's possible the gate got blown open accidentally, and they're just on a walkabout. One of us needs to sweep the area. The sooner I get out there and start looking, the better."

"All right. Is there anyone else who could help us?"

"Will you let Sheriff Driscoll know they're missing? He can tell whoever's on patrol to keep an eye out for them."

We went back into Cleora's yard, but Cleora left the gate open, just in case. The sleet was turning to heavy snow.

"Should I organize a search party?" she asked as we reached her back door. Stepping inside the house, a wall of heat greeted us.

While I had no doubt Cleora could summon the masses, I wasn't sure I wanted everyone in on it just yet. It took a few moments for my teeth to stop chattering, so I could say, "I'll get Selma to help."

As I opened the contacts on my phone, Cleora surveyed the after-party clutter. Half-full cups of punch and soda sat on end tables and paper plates littered a teakwood sideboard in the dining room.

THREATS AND THREADS

She let out a weary sigh, then wrapped me in a hug. "Have faith, Sam. Over ninety percent of all lost dogs find their way home. Sadly, only seventy-five percent of cats do."

Then it hit me. I flipped over to my apps. "I bet the chances are even greater if one of said lost dogs is wearing a tracking collar."

Thankfully, the app walked me through step by step, first asking for my password, followed by my contact info. It pulled up Bump's info.

Cleora stepped to my side to see. "Will that tell you where he is?"

"If I recall, close enough to narrow down the search to visible range."

After a few more taps, it started searching for Bump's location. A map of Humboldt County popped up, along with a pin for our current location. Then, an arrow inside a circle appeared. The point on the arrow dipped, then began rotating. It spun and spun and spun.

"How long does it take to work?" Cleora asked.

"I don't know. This is the first time I've tried it." I paced the length of the kitchen, but nothing changed. I hit refresh, then waited some more.

A minute later, the arrow blipped a few times, then disappeared. Finally!

A message popped up. *Weak or no signal.*

What? How could that be? It hadn't been more than twenty or thirty minutes since they'd left the yard. I clicked on the information icon. It took me to a troubleshooting page. The only solution listed was *device out of range or battery not fully charged.*

I banged my head on the wall. On purpose.

Cleora rushed to peer over my shoulder at the screen. "What... Oh, dear. Did you charge the battery before you put it on him?"

Face to the wall, I said in a small, regretful voice, "No, not recently. But..."—I turned to her—"when I put it on him this morning and hit the 'test' button, it showed green."

"What does that mean?"

"That it was charged at the time. It's possible the charge could've drained between then and now, but not likely."

If something terrible happened to him... No, I couldn't think like that. I had to hold onto hope.

Still, a vision of my house without Bump in it flashed before my eyes. A clean house, a quiet one, with a miserable teenager sprawled on the couch blowing her nose, and, draped over the recliner, a grouchy old man clutching a tennis ball. I felt heartsick. That dog had bonded us like Super Glue.

"So he's out of range already?" Cleora asked, her voice sinking. "How big of an area does the service cover?"

"Anything within range of a satellite, which should be the majority of the state. The country even. Unless..." I tapped through the app again until I found the FAQs. "Crap. Just what I thought."

"What is it?"

"It says that some more rural areas may have spotty satellite coverage. I suppose Wilton falls under that umbrella."

"That's possible. Sometimes when I'm talking to Cordelia on my way to or from work, the call gets dropped on Hilltop Road. I've even had it happen on the west edge of town and over by the fairgrounds. Then, thirty seconds later—"

A balloon blipped on the screen so briefly I almost dropped my phone in surprise. "There! Right there."

I pinched in tighter on the screen, but all that did was send it into search mode again. Finally, a tiny red balloon showed Bump heading northeast from Route 379 on a rural road. One more blip flashed, then disappeared before I could see which road they'd turned on.

The *out of range* message scrolled down again. At least I had a direction.

"I'm going. I'll call you if I find them."

"Or any sign of them. Anything at all." She clamped her hands together. "I'm so worried about Fancy being out in the cold. She's not road-wise, either."

Neither was Bump, but I didn't say it. That was how I'd found him. He hadn't been vigilant enough to steer clear of my headlights, and I'd hit him.

I tried to console her. "Bump loves Fancy. He wouldn't let anything happen to her if he could help it."

Even as I said it, my stomach lurched. Bump was part Husky, meaning he was born to run for long distances. Out there with no boundaries, who knew how far he'd go or where. And his little BFF Fancy would follow faithfully.

Zipper up high, hood drawn tight, I grabbed my umbrella and tromped out into the sleet.

I *had* to find them—and fast.

chapter 27

A SALT TRUCK BARRELED down Route 379 as I lingered at the stop sign coming out of Bluebird Estates. Allowing the salt truck a head start, I hit Selma's number on my speed dial. She answered on the first ring. After putting her on speaker so I could grip the steering wheel of my dad's truck two-handed, I gave her the abridged version of the story and pulled onto the highway.

"Oh no, Sam," she said, her voice echoing in the car. "Poor pooches. They must be frozen solid and terribly afraid. It's wicked out there."

"You're telling me." The salt truck was already out of sight. "I'm creeping at thirty miles an hour, tops—and even that seems dangerously fast. Can't see more than fifty yards in any direction either."

"How will you ever find them if you can barely see?"

"Bump's tracking collar. He keeps going in and out of satellite coverage, but, occasionally, I can get a location."

"So you think someone left the gate open on purpose?"

"I know it. Cleora said she checked that gate shortly before the book club meeting. I have a good idea who did it, too."

"You do? Who?"

THREATS AND THREADS

"Birdie Swinson."

"Birdie? She wasn't even there tonight."

"Exactly."

"Then why would you think she did it?"

"Just a hunch, but it all adds up. Besides, she would've known I was going to be there and that I might bring my dog."

She didn't say anything for so long I thought the connection had dropped. "Selma, you still there?"

"Yeah." A long pause, then, "Birdie, huh? Are you sure about that? Like a hundred percent, bet-your-granny's-wedding-ring-on-it sure? Because my institution is telling me—"

"Okay, maybe not a hundred percent, but sure enough." I decided to change the topic before I forgot why I called her in the first place. "Say, are you still driving, or did you make it home?"

"Well, um... I kinda had plans."

I made a rolling stop at a four-way, praying another vehicle wouldn't appear out of the frozen darkness and ramrod me, then continued. "Selma, I hate to ask, but I could really use your help right now."

"I know, Sam. I know. But... I can't."

"Can't?" What could she possibly have to do that was more important right now than help me find Bump and Fancy?

"Look, Sam, hon... I have to go now. I'll call you back as soon as I can."

"Tell Newt I said 'hi'." But I wasn't sure she'd heard me. The line went dead.

Why was Selma avoiding me lately? Her fling with Newt was no secret to me. She had to have something else going on I didn't know about—and that made me worry even more.

I pulled to the side of the road to get a better look at the tracking app.

"That's odd." The tiny red balloon had taken an abrupt left at

Runyan Road, almost as if the dogs were following a street map. I'd have thought they'd just cut across fields and meander through backyards. Dogs usually followed their noses, not the yellow line down the center of the road. Maybe trotting down the road was just easier. I calculated the distance. They were less than two miles away.

I headed in that direction. Snow was piling on top of ice. The thin blanket of white was deceptively pretty, crystals of snow glistening like sequins in the glow of my headlights. Since I'd left the neighborhood, I'd passed all of two cars. Everybody else had the good sense to stay home.

The phone rang. It was Cleora.

"The sheriff says everyone on duty has been told to watch for the dogs. I told them Fancy might be scared and run if a stranger approaches, so if there are any sightings, they'll notify us right away. Oh, and by the way, the dispatcher says hi."

"Thanks, Cleora."

"Do you still have a signal?"

"I do. They aren't far now."

"Oh, thank goodness, thank goodness."

She gushed with relief. I told her I'd call her back in a few minutes either way.

I glanced at the app again. The indicator signal hadn't moved. Good, that meant they'd stopped to rest, and I could catch up with them. Even if I had to get out of the car in this nasty storm and hike across a marshy meadow, in less than five minutes, they'd be with me again and this horrible night could be over.

I turned onto Runyan, dense stands of leafless trees on either side of the road. In a wooded area like this, it made sense why the dogs hadn't cut through, but why would they have even come this way?

The closer I got to their signaled location, the more I started to doubt my first assumption. What if Bump wasn't just sitting somewhere dry so he could rest? What if... what if he'd been hit by a car?

THREATS AND THREADS

My heart drummed in my chest. A fresh surge of anxiety flooded my gut.

The tires lost traction. My stomach lurched. Three-and-a-half tons of rusty pickup skated over icy asphalt. I tapped at the brakes. Nothing happened. Except the truck was now headed on a diagonal toward the ditch on the opposite side. I hit the brakes more firmly. One of the front tires hit a patch of gravel and bit into it. The backend fishtailed. The truck careened at an angle in slow motion. Straight toward a row of mailboxes.

Think, Sam. Think!

Unable to halt momentum, I had to change the trajectory. My reflexes responded to some long-ago driving lesson from my dad. I turned the wheel—the wrong way, apparently. The truck spun in a counterclockwise direction.

The world rotated dizzily around me. My head whipped one direction, then another as I searched for an object, any object, to gain my bearings. The lineup of battered mailboxes loomed closer, posts as thick as telephone poles.

Ever so slightly, I reversed direction on the steering wheel. The truck straightened, but it was still skidding slowly toward the ditch—and, beyond it, a rusty six-foot chain-link fence that leaned to the side. Again, I tapped a staccato on the brake pedal. The tires chattered over scatterings of salt before finding purchase on a patch of slush-free pavement.

I punched firmly at the brake, the left-side tires of the truck plowing deep into the gravel shoulder and sending a spray of pebbles outward. My phone slid off the passenger seat, then fell to the floor with a thunk and a clatter.

By the time the truck came to a full stop, the beams of the headlights were shining through a latticework of metal fencing at an old tractor salvage yard. There was less than two feet to spare between the front bumper and fence.

After shifting into park, I took a few moments to catch my breath. Cautiously, I turned my head, then twisted side to side. No whiplash. At least not that I could tell. I reached for my phone, but the seat belt dug into my abdomen in an impromptu Heimlich maneuver. My torso ricocheted back reflexively. I unclipped my seat belt to grope around for my phone.

My fingers closed around something hard. I brought it up. An old CD case. Willie Nelson. Huh. Never would've pegged my dad to be a Willie fan. I swept my hand back and forth, finding a lot of stuff—an old electric bill, a coupon flyer, a dried-up pack of hand wipes, and… my very wet umbrella. I retrieved it, then laid it on the seat. With the sleet-snow now coming down hard and the wind getting stronger, it would be pretty useless as far as keeping me dry. I flailed a hand above me to search for the button for the overhead light. I flipped it on, and did a survey. No phone in sight. It had to have slid under the seat.

Exasperated, I turned the truck off, leaving the headlights on, and shoved the door open to go around to the other side. Ice balls pelted my face. Clinging to the bed of the truck, I worked my way around. Nothing on the outside of the truck appeared to be damaged. I pulled on the handle of the passenger side door, but it was locked. Dang it!

I groped my way back around, reached across the seat, and unlocked it. Then I repeated my treacherous trek once more. I pulled on the handle. The door popped open, swinging wide and almost taking me down with it.

There was a faint glow under the seat before the screen dimmed. I grabbed my phone, then hurriedly pulled it into the light. The screen was cracked. At least the app still appeared to be working because the signal was flashing big and bold. He had to be within earshot.

Grabbing the umbrella to use like a ski pole, I called out. The only sound was the *plink-plink-plink* of sleet as it bounced off the frozen ground. I called again. "Bump? Buuuump! Fancy? You there, Fancy? Come here, Bump!"

THREATS AND THREADS

I took a few steps forward, the tip of the upside-down umbrella planted before me. Ice crackled. Rusty links glinted in the headlights. I twined my fingers through the wires and peered through a descending veil of ice, calling until my voice was hoarse. Hope dimmed with each syllable.

The place appeared abandoned. It was nothing but tractors, farm implements, and a few pieces of outdated heavy-duty construction equipment. A weed-infested breeding ground for rats and insects. In the middle of the metal graveyard squatted a small pole barn, which was probably an office building. The front window was smashed, and the entrance door stood agape. Had they gone in there to seek shelter?

To my left, about forty yards back the way I'd come from, was a huge gate. I made my way unsteadily toward it, clinging to the fence for support. A thick chain, fastened by an oversized lock, was wound tightly between the two gate panels. I shook the gate, hoping something would loosen, but it held strong. I scanned up and down the fence line for another opening. It was hard to see much beyond the scope of the truck's lights.

Calling at intervals, I returned to the truck, but, again, there was no sign of them. My teeth chattered. I climbed back in, grateful the truck hadn't been damaged. After I started the engine, I cranked the heater up to thaw my feet. My duck boots were the low, slip-on kind, meant for gentle strolls down the driveway to fetch the newspaper, not for tromping through slush-filled ditches. My socks and pants legs were soaked halfway up my shins.

As much as I wanted to go home, I couldn't leave here without checking inside the grounds. If I had to guess, the locating app was telling me it was highly likely they were inside that building. Chances were that due to the sleet pinging on the metal roof, they couldn't hear me calling. They must've found a gap in the fence big enough to squeeze under. I had to find a way in.

I put the truck in drive, then drove slowly toward the far corner of the fence along the road. No other entrances that I could tell, but there was a section where two fence posts were leaning precariously inward and a big portion of the links had separated. I stopped there. Looked like someone had hit it some time ago. Wouldn't take much to knock it over.

Hands locked on the steering wheel, I backed the truck up a ways, then gunned it. The bumper slammed into one of the posts with a metallic crunch. The fence caved like a popsicle-stick fort. Two panels to either side collapsed, falling flat. The truck rolled over the fence, jostling my insides as it bounced over the center post. Like a professional demolition-derby driver, I made a turn and braked just in time to avoid crumpling the truck accordion-style into the bucket of a front-end loader.

When Dad asked how I'd wrecked his truck, I'd blame it on the icy conditions. He wouldn't give me flack for being out in it, though, because I was looking for Bump.

Dad... Bump... I couldn't give up now.

I shifted into reverse, hoping to aim the headlights toward the office building, but something seemed caught underneath. I put it in park, turned off the engine, and searched in the glove compartment for a flashlight. Found one, but it was suspiciously lightweight. I flicked the switch. No light. Unscrewing the end, my fears were confirmed. No batteries.

I checked the app one more time before switching my phone to flashlight mode, noting as I did so there was a low-battery warning.

On my knees, I swept the light underneath. A sizeable section of the chain-link was caught up in the undercarriage. There was no way I could undo it. I'd have to call a tow truck to—

A strained *yip-yip* rang out. It was Fancy's bark.

After grabbing the umbrella, I did a quick search for a tire iron to use as a weapon if needed, but found nothing under the seat. Nothing behind it or in the bed, either. Probably stowed away with the spare, if there was one, but I didn't have time to retrieve it.

"Fancy! Fancy," I called, working my way through the junkyard. "Here, girl! Where are you?"

She yipped again. Higher pitched. Like she was in distress.

I took off running, the umbrella clutched in my left hand, the light from my phone in the other shining a bouncing path before me as I dodged giant discarded tires and wove around rust-pocked relics from days gone by.

I *had* to find them. Had to keep going.

A pipe covered by snow tripped me. My ankle rolled. I tumbled sideways. The umbrella fell from my grasp. A blanket of slush broke my fall. The landing was soft, but shockingly cold. Lying on my side, I moved my foot in a circle. A little stiff, but not broken or sprained this time.

Pulling the umbrella to me to use as a cane now, I struggled to my feet. I was wet, freezing, and sucking air.

The bark sounded again, but, somehow, it was either more distant or muted, I couldn't tell which. I spun in a circle, totally disoriented as to where I'd abandoned the truck or in which direction the little office building was. The farm machinery hadn't been arranged in neat rows like a car dealership, but they were haphazardly grouped—older general-use tractors in one collection, bigger combines in another huddle, and backhoes lumped in a loose circle somewhere else.

My first impulse was to sink down and cry. Not that it was going to help. It just seemed like a hopeless situation. Still, I couldn't give up. They were here somewhere.

The battery icon on my phone told me I only had five percent left. I turned the flashlight off and started a group text to Cleora, Selma, and Clint. Clint wasn't in the loop yet, but he'd catch on.

Bump and Fancy still lost. I think I'm close, but I can't see them. Truck went off the road. I'm fine. At an old trac—

I heard a voice. A woman's voice. Someone was here.

Without any lights to see by, I could only make out objects by their shape. I walked around a small bulldozer, trying to discern where the voice was coming from. Fancy whined again, and I started that way. Not running, but walking as quietly as I could, stopping intermittently to listen.

Hinges squealed. A door thudded softly. Feet tamped over a solid surface. I continued toward it.

Soon, the small metal building came into view. It was actually a mobile home made into an office unit. About fifty feet from it, I ducked behind a disc plow and quieted my breathing the best I could, watching and waiting. The only sound was the hiss and ping of sleet. Maybe I'd only imagined the voice?

Then, I heard Fancy's whine.

I broke from behind the plow and went straight to the door. A cement block was holding it closed. I shoved the block out of the way before pulling the door open wide. Blackness stared back. Bravely, I stepped inside. Glass crunched underfoot.

A glance at the locator app indicated I was practically standing on top of Bump. Hooking the umbrella handle over my wrist, I tapped the flashlight on. Yellowed floor tiles, faux-wood paneling, an old filing cabinet with papers sticking out, a chair with cracked vinyl... Everything you'd expect in an abandoned office. But no dogs.

"Fancy?" I called softly, hopefully. Then, more loudly, "Bump?"

Silence, except for the weather outside.

I swept the flashlight around again. The light dimmed slightly. Four percent on the battery. I hit *send* on the text before my phone completely died, not remembering if I'd finished it or not. I stepped farther inside the building, shining my light into the corners and around furniture. The locator app was going crazy.

Metal glinted in the beam of light. Between the filing cabinet and slanting desk lay Bump's collar—the tracking device still attached, the clasp undone. Had someone taken it off him and left it here? Or had he scratched at the collar, and it just popped open and fell off?

"Bump?" I called again. "Bump?"

No Husky yodel in answer. The tiny spark of hope I'd felt sputtered and died.

There was only three percent battery left now. I disconnected from the tracking app and turned the data off. Still no reply texts.

I was about to book a retreat so I could turn the flashlight off, get back to the truck, and wait for a response when the faintest whimper sounded from the back of the office. Swinging the light that way, I noticed, for the first time, a door.

The light bounced off a mirror as I pointed it at the opening. Then I noticed the toilet through the barely open door. A bathroom.

Tiny paws scratched at something solid. Fancy. She had to be stuck in there.

I rushed to it, then set the umbrella just outside the bathroom. Inside, through a glass sliding door, I saw Fancy, standing on her hind legs. She raked at the glass again, bouncing in relief. Aside from being wet, she didn't seem any the worse for wear.

"Oh, Fancy," I whispered. "How did you get in there?"

She must've been looking for a place to curl up before accidentally knocking the door shut.

I hit the switch on the wall. Light from a single incandescent bulb filled the small confines. I turned my flashlight off, then set my phone on the sink counter beside the door. On top of the toilet tank was a… Good heavens, was that a manual typewriter? I hadn't used one of those since junior high. On the floor between the toilet and sink cabinet sat a box of paper. Strange place to store supplies.

Fancy bounced higher, her front paws swinging in a begging motion. I popped the door open. She leaped into my arms, all wiggles and slurpy little kisses.

"Let's go back to the truck. Okay, Fancy?"

She licked my neck and chin, her tongue tickling me. I had to turn my head so she wouldn't French kiss me. Her nose poked inside my ear, and she gave a little snort. I hugged her gently. An almost-imperceptible grumble shook her belly.

"Did I squeeze too tight, sweetie?" I pulled back to study her.

Her lip quivered. Soon, her little grumble morphed into a full-blown growl. I heard my phone slide across the counter, then whipped around in time to see the umbrella handle hook around the doorknob and the door slam shut. A sliding bolt on the outside clunked into place.

My phone was gone.

I set Fancy down and rushed at the door, banging on it. "Hey, what's going on? Let me out of here! Keep the phone. I wasn't trying to steal anything. I just came for the dog. That's all—honest."

No matter how much I begged and bargained, there was no response. I spun around. No other door, no window. I opened the cabinet doors, searching under the sink for a secret panel, as ridiculous as that was. I yanked on the knob, threw my shoulder at the door, searched for something to smash it down with... There wasn't even so much as a toilet bowl brush.

Even as I pounded my fists at the door and shouted for help, I knew who'd done this. Knew that she'd lured me here by dognapping Fancy and stealing Bump's collar. Knew she'd planned this all along.

"TrueLuv? TrueLuv, I know it's you! Come on, please. Just let me out of here. Give me my dog back. Pleeeease!"

I stopped my caterwauling long enough to listen. Footsteps. Glass crunching. She was still there.

"TrueLuv?" I knocked three times. Like I expected she'd just fling it open. "Tell me what you want. Whatever it is, I'll give it to you. I don't have much money, but—"

A handwritten note slid under the door.

start writin

"Write what?" I said to the door.

THREATS AND THREADS

A pencil scratched at paper. Another note.
a better endin
"What does that mean?"
u know
"No, I don't. Tell me." I was hoping she'd start speaking, so I could put a face to the voice and learn her true identity. She gave no reply. "What if I write something and you don't like it? You have to tell me what you want so I don't screw it up. Please."

I pressed for more details—like which story, at what point I was supposed to start, what kind of ending she had in mind.
u hav until mornin
"Morning as in what? Nine o'clock, ten?"
sunrize
By my best recollection, that was about seven at this time of year.
"I can get you money," I offered, "if that's what you need."

Frigid wind rushed under the door. Fancy shivered violently. I picked her tense little body up again, then tucked her inside my coat. "What if I can't?"
ur dogs a goner
"You're lying," I risked. "He got away from you, and you're just bluffing."

She didn't answer. I wasn't even sure she was still there. Because no more notes appeared under the door. No more footsteps sounded.

The only sounds were the howl of the wind as it blasted through the partially open exterior door and Fancy's whimpers. And eventually… the distant rumble of a car starting up and driving away.

chapter 28

IF I HAD ANY regrets right now, they had nothing to do with careers or relationships or other life choices. It was that I hadn't charged my phone and kept it in my pocket.

How could I have been so dumb? Why had I turned my back? Why hadn't I brought a real weapon? Did I think I was going to spear an attacker with my umbrella? Plus, the more I thought about it, the more certain I became—I hadn't added my location on the text.

I hadn't called Archer back, either. He probably figured I was avoiding him.

My back to the door, I slid onto my rump. Loneliness and hopelessness went hand in hand. I'd never felt more of either. Kind of like finding myself in a deep, dark hole with no promise that anyone was going to throw a rope down any time soon.

And the more I sat there, the lonelier, more hopeless, and colder I got. Shivering, I pulled my knees to my chest and buried my head beneath my arms. Fancy's tiny body warmed my chest.

Why hadn't TrueLuv just used that photo of Clint and me for bribery? Why do this to me, too? Was she going to kidnap Tara and demand a ransom next? And where was she hiding Bump?

Eventually, I got up and pulled an overturned trash can up to the typewriter. Fancy wriggled from my lap before settling herself in a corner. I wasn't sure how long I stared at that typewriter, but with each heartbeat, I sensed time ticking away. I had one night to rewrite a book. One. Night. How was I supposed to manage that when I couldn't finish one in less than six months? Did TrueLuv not realize these things took planning? Storylines scribbled on a whiteboard and plot points laboriously outlined, rough drafts, final drafts, and multiple rounds with an editor? The best writing came when I allowed my characters to lead the way. Felicity and Alexander weren't going to cooperate very well if I held a gun to their heads.

It didn't matter, though. I had to give TrueLuv what she wanted. Or I was going to die here—alone and frozen.

A tear rolled down my cheek. A sniff turned into a sob. Fancy toddled to me and climbed into my lap, snuffling and whimpering. I cradled her in my arms.

"Oh, Fancy. I'm so sorry she did this to—"

My own words sounded far away. Like someone else was speaking them.

I couldn't feel Fancy in my lap anymore. I wasn't in the office bathroom...

Not again.

IT WAS DARK. A radio played loudly. I had the sensation of flying at an incredible speed. How I loved car rides! Were we going to a dog show? My tummy felt queasy. I used to love dog shows, until... until that one terrible time I was attacked. I might have died if Cleora hadn't snatched me up.

In the backseat of an unfamiliar car filled with many scents accumulated over the years, I stood on my hind legs to look out the window, but I couldn't quite reach. All I could see was a dark sky through glass smeared with icy rain. Sometimes, a light would appear from ahead, sweep past, then disappear behind us with a *whoosh*.

A sudden jarring caused me to tumble sideways. I landed on a massive lump of fur. Bump lay on the other end of the backseat, drool dripping from his tongue in long globs. I nuzzled his chest, but he gazed back with a hazy look. Worried, I curled up beside him and licked the underside of his chin.

For a long time, the windshield wipers slapped out a frightening rhythm. In the front seat sat a woman with hair past her shoulders. Someone not Cleora. A long scarf dangled from around her neck.

Nervous, I scooted toward the middle of the seat to sniff the air. The nails of my front paws curled into the edge of the seat. I inhaled more deeply, letting the scent molecules swirl inside my nose as I sorted through memories. The faint, offensive odor of cat tickled my nostrils. I'd smelled this woman before. Seen her. Not all that long ago... But from where? When?

The car hit another bump in the road. I toppled forward. Hit something hard. Chilly air wrapped around me...

WHEN I CAME TO, returned to my human form, Fancy was huddled beside me, her tongue swabbing my cheek. I was lying on my side next to the toilet on the grungy bathroom floor of the abandoned office. I shivered. Every bone in my body felt so cold it could break.

I forced myself to move, to get up. My clothing was still soaked. If I stayed on the floor, I'd freeze to death.

Under the sink, I found an old hand towel. It was stiff and scratchy to the touch, but I swaddled Fancy in it and set her in a cardboard box for warmth while I tried to figure out how to get out of there. I dug deeper into the contents beneath the sink, past rolls of toilet paper, trash-can liners, empty aerosol cans of disinfectant, and half-full bottles of ammonia. Just when I was about to give up, I found a rusty length of old pipe pressed into the back corner.

It was so corroded I was afraid it would crumble into pieces or cut me and give me a nasty case of tetanus, so I wrapped it inside a plastic bag. Then I began whacking at the walls with resolute strength. Made of a cheap metal, they dented easily, but they wouldn't give. I started on the door. It only took a few blows to figure out it was metal, too, but a sturdier metal. Running out of options, I began banging at the floor, hoping to discover a weakness in it.

In her box, Fancy quivered violently. I dropped the pipe and sat on my knees, fighting back tears. The longer I stayed locked away in here, the closer to death Bump became—if he wasn't already dead. Which was a very real possibility.

With frantic desperation, I searched through the vanity drawer. Hidden among old boxes of air freshener dispensers were a few bobby pins and a metal nail file.

I inserted the point of the file into the head of a screw on the lowest hinge of the door. It turned easily. A few minutes later, I had all three screws undone. I started on the middle hinge. But there, my fortune ran dry. Two of the screws were rusted in place. The slots of the third were completely stripped.

Channeling my inner MacGyver, I started on the top hinge. The first screw loosened easily. But on the second, I got overzealous. The file snapped in my hands. I picked up the two pieces. The small pointed end was too short to get any leverage on to turn it, and my fingers were too numb from the cold to grip it even if I could. The end with the handle was too thick across to fit in the screw head slots. It was useless now. I tossed it in the corner and took the truck key out of my pocket. Its blunted end wasn't even close to fitting.

Then I heard it—my phone, the ringtone playing "Stayin' Alive". It was in the office somewhere. She probably left it there just to taunt me. It beeped to indicate it had gone to voice mail.

Defeat hit me like a brick to the forehead. There was no way out of here. None. I was trapped in a metal box in Siberia. I had electricity, but all that got me was one bare light bulb to see by. There wasn't so much as a hairdryer to warm my hands, let alone a space heater. The only upside to my futile endeavors was that moving around had warmed me up a little. Fancy, however, was turning into an icicle. I moved her box to the side of the vanity where the draft wasn't as strong.

My surroundings were about as austere as they could get. I did have a toilet, should I need it. I turned the faucet handle. Brown water reeking of sulfur dribbled out. It cleared up somewhat after a minute, but, judging by the smell, it wasn't potable. Good enough for flushing anyway.

Settling to the floor, I rolled a sheet of paper under the typewriter carriage and warmed up my fingers by testing the keys. More than once, I jammed my fingers between the raised, rounded keys, pinching them. The spacing was different from my computer keyboard, and it took a certain measure of strength to depress each key. Another fifteen minutes later, I was finally getting the feel of it, but my hands were cramping from the effort.

Three more calls went to my phone and probably a few texts—it was hard to hear the little beep above the clacking of typewriter keys and crinkling of paper. Someone was trying hard to reach me, but the calls soon stopped. Either they'd given up or the battery had died. Or both.

Aware time was ticking away, I wrote faster than I'd ever written before. Lives depended on it.

Halfway into the night, I stopped to count how many pages I'd written. I'd managed only twenty-nine, single-spaced pages, the right-hand margin sometimes stretching to the edge of the page. I'd pecked out two pages of a vague outline to get my start, but I hadn't stopped to correct any typos or revise a single paragraph since then. I wasn't about to sweat the small stuff. TrueLuv would just have to accept whatever I gave her.

After another hour—or maybe it was two, or three, I wasn't sure—I got up and paced around to let my joints warm up. I was exhausted—physically and emotionally. Then I tucked Fancy inside my coat again, as much for my benefit as hers. If I rested for just a little bit, maybe I could get this done. I sank downward. The moment my rump hit the cold, hard floor, I was once again sucked into a vortex of memories not my own.

They were Fancy's...

THE BACK GATE OPENED, the wind snatching it wide. A figure in a hooded raincoat appeared. Bump trotted toward them, his tail wagging in welcome.

I ran after him, but my legs were short and he was much faster than me. He sat before the person, sniffed their outstretched hand, and took a cookie.

I barked in warning, sensing something was not right. Bump ignored me and took another cookie. It was a woman, judging by her build. Slipping her hand beneath his collar, she led him away. Toward the street. Where a car with an open door waited.

He was willing but unsteady on his feet and slow. I followed along, yapping at him to come back, but he was too foggy to resist. She dragged him through the icy rain, then shoved him inside the car. Before she could slam the door shut, I leaped in after him, landing on his rib cage. He toppled over with a yawn, unfazed.

She reached for me, but I summoned my fiercest growl. A smirk tilted her mouth as she yanked her hand back.

Oh, aren't you scary? With a triumphant laugh, she slammed the door shut, then got into the front seat and started the car. *You'd be cute if you didn't have such a big mouth.*

Tires screeching, we lurched forward, and I tumbled to the floor…

ADRENALINE SHOT THROUGH MY heart like the jolt of a defibrillator. I sat up with a start, thinking my heartbeat had slipped into arrhythmia, but it was only Fancy shivering against my chest.

In a blink, all the energy drained out of me. Sleep beckoned.

chapter 29

WHEN I WOKE UP, what I noticed first was the absence of wind and that the *ping-ping-ping* of sleet was gone. What I noticed second was the nearing *crunch-crunch* of shoes on frozen ground.

My breath puffed in an icy cloud before me, sluggishly drifting upward. Even though the light bulb was still on, I could discern the faint peachy glow of sunrise slipping through the gap beneath the door.

With stiff fingers, I patted my coat, then the floor around me. Fancy had wiggled free. It took some effort, but I rolled over and lifted my head to look around. There she was, lying in the shower stall, curled into a tight ball. Not moving.

My heartbeat stalled. *No, please no...*

Outside, the plodding of feet grew louder. The front door groaned open. One of Fancy's ears twitched. Her head snapped up. Her little button eyes peered suspiciously at the door. Feet clomped across the office floor, scattering pieces of glass in their wake. But instead of coming directly to the bathroom door, TrueLuv circled the office, pausing in places as she yanked open drawers and filing cabinets. Why was she doing that? She'd been here just last night. Had she forgotten something?

Holding my breath, I concentrated on Fancy. Her ribs lifted ever so slightly. Her lips fluttered in a soft snore. Relieved, I exhaled. And waited.

A drawer banged shut. Something fell onto the floor. She muttered a curse word. Shuffled closer.

I didn't move.

The only thing within arm's reach was the typewriter. Hefting that dinosaur over my head to clonk her with would be next to impossible.

Then I saw it. The rusty pipe. Lying right next to the door where I'd left it.

On my belly, I slithered toward it. Stretched an arm.

A shadow moved across the slanted rectangle of light spilling from beneath the door.

Closing stiff fingers around the end of the pipe, I slid it free of the plastic bag. Cold metal. Heavy. Lethal if I struck with force. All I needed was to hit her hard enough to knock her to the ground so I could escape. After I locked *her* inside here.

I wouldn't make her suffer the cold all night long like she had me, however. No, she'd be plenty toasty in the back of a cruiser when Sheriff Driscoll and his fleet arrived.

She turned the doorknob. Then, as if remembering after the fact that the lock was in place, she jiggled it.

As quietly as I could, I grabbed the edge of the vanity and pulled myself into a stand. The lock on the outside of the door slid, released. I pressed myself into the corner between the door and the vanity. Raised the pipe above my head.

The knob rotated. I squeezed the pipe tighter until my fingers were bloodless. The door cracked open, a hand adorned with acrylic nails and glittery rings still gripping the outer knob.

"Anybody in here?"

Before I could fully connect the voice to the person, Fancy shot across the floor, her nails scrabbling for traction on the linoleum. Her warning rang out. "Yap-yap-yap-yap!"

The door slammed shut.

"What the bleep?" The person outside scampered away, little shards of glass clinking as she retreated.

Fancy jumped at the door, her silky tail now wagging with glee. It wasn't TrueLuv out there after all—unless Selma *was* TrueLuv.

There was one way to find out.

"Selma?" I dropped the pipe. Pounded on the door. "Selma, it's me—Sam! Let us out, okay?"

"You sure there isn't a rabid wolf in there?"

"I'm sure. Just Fancy and me freezing our derrieres off in here. Selma, can you let us—"

"It's not locked, hon."

"Right." I swung the door open. Fancy rushed out, then commenced doing laps around the office desk.

Selma was sitting on top of the cluttered, dusty desk, her legs tucked up to the side. She flourished a can of pepper spray in Fancy's direction. "Sam, hon, can you pick up the dog? As much as I'd love to play kissy face with that angel, she has sharp little claws and I don't want her to tear my leggings. I paid full price for these at Wally World."

Same tights she'd been wearing at the book club last night.

"You haven't changed," I remarked.

"Since high school? Lots of people tell me that. But how would you—"

"Since last night. Those are the same clothes you had on last night."

"Look who's calling the kettle black." Her gaze slid from my crazy hair to my crumpled coat to my mud-splattered boots. "You look like you haven't gotten a wink of sleep."

I braved a step forward. "How did you know where to find me?"

"Long story. I'll get to it." Setting the can down, she picked up a cell phone from the desk. "Anyway, lookie at what I found just now. This yours?"

"Only one person knew I was here."

"Sam... I'm here to save you. *Trust* me." She frowned, like she was crushed that I'd suspect her of trying to hurt me. Fancy bounced around the desk, barking happily. "The dog, please. I love her, but I love these leggings, too."

I wasn't entirely ready to let down my guard, but I decided to trust the dog for now.

Crouching, I patted my legs. Fancy bounded across the floor, stirring up clouds of dust. She vaulted into my arms. I stood, surveying my surroundings. Hard to imagine, but this place was even creepier in the daylight. Yellowed papers lay everywhere, scattered by the wind that was gusting in through the broken window. The wind had died down since last night, but it was even colder than yesterday. I couldn't wait to get in a warm car—any car, even Selma's—and crank the heater up to full power.

Selma hopped off the desk, and I exchanged Fancy for the phone. Hopeful, I hit the power button, but nothing happened. Dead.

"I tried to call you last night about five hundred times," Selma said, rocking Fancy in her arms, "but it kept going to voice mail. I went to Birdie's house to—"

"You what? Why?"

"Because you were sure she was TrueLuv. I had to find out if that was true."

"And?" I slipped the phone in my coat pocket.

"She's not."

"How do you know it's not her?"

"She told me so."

"Oh. Great. That's good to know." I clamped onto Selma's shoulders, shaking her once good and hard. "Get a clue. If she was, she wouldn't tell you."

THREATS AND THREADS

"Relax, Sam. I didn't ask if she was your stalker, exactly. But I did gather enough evidence to be satisfied it wasn't her. Turns out she had a perfectly legitimate alkali for missing book club."

"Alibi, you mean?"

Selma flapped her eyelashes.

I'd lost her. "Okay then, where was she?"

"Who?"

"Birdie!"

"Oh, right, Birdie. I went straight to her place right after book club. I had to figure out once and for all if she was your stalker."

"So you weren't at Newt's last night?"

She set Fancy on the floor. "You assumed I was going there, Sam. I never said I was. But I couldn't tell you what I was up to or else you would've told me not to go. Honestly, sometimes I don't think you think I'm smart enough to figure stuff out on my own. Anywho, Birdie claimed she went to urgent care yesterday right after work. Had a sinus infection. That's why she didn't go to book club."

"How do you know she wasn't making that up?"

"Here." She pulled a piece of paper from her back pocket, then flapped it at my face.

"What's this?"

"Her bill from Fullbright South Urgent Care Center. I stole it off her counter when she went into another room to grab a box of tissues. Look at the time."

She was right. According to the time stamp, Birdie hadn't been checked out until just about the time book club was breaking up. Given the distance, there was no way she could've been responsible for stealing the dogs. Fancy was meandering around the office, searching forlornly for her friend Bump.

I gave the paper back to Selma. "Okay, so it's not her. But I still don't know who did this."

"What did happen last night, anyway? You look like hell. You aren't hurt, are you?"

"I'm okay enough. Just exhausted. And cold. TrueLuv lured me here by planting Bump's tracking collar over there." Pointing, I swung toward the place I'd last seen it. "It *was* there, anyway."

"Does she have Bump?"

"I'm sure of it. She drugged him, but my guess is he was too heavy for her to drag in here."

Fancy was shivering again, so I picked her up. She licked my chin. Her kisses were so much daintier than Bump's. Gawd, I missed that big lug. "Anyway, it was all a ploy to lock me in that room and get me to write a new ending to my last book. One more to her liking. At least I didn't die here." I walked to the broken window, frigid wind biting at my exposed skin. It was well past dawn, and TrueLuv hadn't returned. Probably never intended to. "I'm glad you were looking out for me and tried to figure out if Birdie was TrueLuv, but"—I pivoted to face Selma— "how *did* you know where to look for me?"

"Cleora called me this morning. The sheriff's department has been on the lookout for you. There was even a segment on the morning news with your mugshot and all, saying you were a missing person and there was suspected foul play."

"What?" By now, Tara had heard about it and was probably having a total meltdown. "You still didn't answer me, though. How did you know to come here? This is about as remote as you can get in this county."

She tapped her temple. "Because after I went to Birdie's and figured out she wasn't your stalker, I did some hard thinking. I know who it is, Sam."

"Who?"

Fancy's ears perked at my voice. Her body tensed.

"I figured it out from the text you didn't finish. You said you were at an 'old trac-something'. I knew there weren't any race tracks in this county. The only other thing that came to mind was tractor. An old tractor salvage yard. Then, it hit me. Sam, your stalker is the gal whose crooked family owns this junk pile—Amy Sue Bradley."

Before I could extract any details from her, the front door groaned on its hinges, then banged shut as the devil herself strolled in.

"Took a while for you two to catch on." A scowling Amy Sue flipped the tail of her scarf over her shoulder. A green-and-red scarf. With a distinct snag in it where a thread had come loose.

Fancy jumped out of my arms and charged, six pounds of shampooed fluff snapping and snarling. Amy Sue kicked a small trash can at her. The little dog turned tail, but it clipped her hind leg. Yelping, she limped to me. I scooped her up.

"You," Selma growled. "I *knew* it was you."

"Karma's a bitch, isn't it?" A smug smile tilted Amy Sue's mouth. "You know, I thought you were my friend, Paradiso. But not only would you not help me out with a tiny loan, you also cheated on me."

"What are you talking about?"

"With *her*." Amy Sue speared me with a gaze that could've lasered through solid rock. "The bitch who's living my dream."

Selma flicked her hand in my direction. "You're jealous of her? Really? Why?"

"Let's see… She wasn't in town a month and hopped in the sack with Wilton's most-eligible bachelor, Dr. Clinton Chastain. Then she dumped him just as quick. I would never treat him that way. Never! I've been trying to get his attention for *three whole years*! Do you know how miserable my life has been? I'm allergic to pet dander, but I adopted a cat, so I'd have a reason to see Dr. Clint. I've been getting allergy shots just so I could breathe."

"You have a thing for Dr. Clint?"

"Who wouldn't?"

Selma held up a finger. "You got me there, hon."

"I've run out of reasons to take my cat to the clinic. There are only so many shots, nail clippings, ear mites, fleas, and teeth cleanings

I could manufacture. He started hiding from me whenever I got out the cat carrier. I dreaded touching him as much as he dreaded getting in the car. I even took Batman to get anti-anxiety meds."

Batman?

She was the one living in Miley Harper's old house? All this time my stalker had been just a couple of streets away?

"Geesh!" Selma exclaimed. "He probably thought you had that Munchkin by paradox syndrome."

Unable to help myself, I muttered, "Munchausen syndrome by proxy."

Amy Sue sneered at me. "Aren't you a smarty-pants?"

"Clint and I aren't together anymore," I tersely reminded her as I stroked Fancy's neck. "Why didn't you just ask him out yourself?"

"Because nice girls don't do that sort of thing. But then, you wouldn't know about that." Arms crossed, she sighed in disgust. "I had to take up jogging, so I'd see him on the bike path. Jogging! Perspiring is not something I do willingly. But I think he was starting to notice me. He smiled a couple of times. Big sexy smile. Too bad he had that mangy mutt with him, or I would've stopped him to chat. I detest dogs even more than cats. That's why I poisoned that stupid beagle to shut him up for good."

She'd probably killed Grace Hazelton, too.

Amy Sue refocused her attention on Selma, like there was still a chance of convincing her to ditch me. "Anyway, not only did she steal my one true love, she also stomped on his heart. And then she had to go and get rescued by the fire chief like she's some damsel in distress. And while she's pretending to be the girl next door, she's pounding out steamy romances that—"

"They're not—" I started to protest.

"You, hush! All my life, I've dreamed of being famous, but a stay-at-home kind of famous novelist, with a handsome husband who adored me and a nice brick ranch with a flower garden and two kids named Morgan and Blaze... Instead, I did the sensible thing. I paid my own way through tech school to learn about computers and went into information technology for an e-commerce company. But I did learn a few useful things. Amazing how easy it is to lift someone's private info off the internet with one little password."

"Okay, so you hacked into my accounts," I said. "But how did you know my pen name?"

"That tidbit was a little harder to come by, but while you and Dr. Clint were an item, I happened to be in his office and mentioned I'd seen the two of you at Wild Bill's Western Eatery. I straight up asked what you did. He told me you wrote love stories. I eventually figured out your *nom de plume*."

So Clint *had* let my secret slip! Then again, I couldn't recall ever asking him to keep it a secret.

"I still don't get what the point is," I said. "You could've ruined my professional reputation. Stolen my identity and lived off my credit cards and savings for a while. Why make me write a different ending and threaten to kill my dog?"

"Because you ruined *everything*! I lost my job and my chance at my dream man. I figured if I couldn't have Clint, I'd get the story I wanted, skim some money off your income, and punch you in the gut, all in short order. Even though my boss couldn't prove I'd done anything wrong—I was sure to cover my tracks—they let me go because they'd had suspicious activity reported. Try getting a job after you've been fired. I've barely been able to afford the rent on that dive I've been living in. Only reason I got Harper's old house was because no one else would touch it with a ten-foot pole. So I had nothing to do but read your stories and dream of how it could have been between Clint and me. When you yanked Felicity and Alexander apart, you crushed a part of my heart." Tears pooled in her eyes, but she dashed them away. "You deserve to suffer, just like me."

She dug her hands in her coat pockets. One was definitely bulkier than the other. Did she have a gun in there?

"Oh, sweetheart. I didn't know how bad it was for you." Selma started toward her. "Why don't you and I just go down to Bub's Place and cry into a few beers? We may have had a few tiffs and drifted apart, but we have a history—you and me—Amy Boo Bear. She'll never take that away from you."

Her expression softening, Amy Sue nodded. "Yeah, you're right. You always were. You were there for me so many times..." She leaned against the wall next to the door. "So... we could be friends again? Hang out, have one of those all-night talks like we used to?"

"Sure, hon. Why not?" Selma held her arms wide, offering a hug of sympathy. "Now let's—"

Clunk!

Selma's phone flew from her coat pocket and tumbled forward. Right toward Amy Sue.

Before Selma could react, Amy Sue pounced on it. She clutched it in her fist, gloating for a moment before sliding it in her own pocket.

"Then if you really *are* my friend, Paradiso"—Amy Sue drew back—"help me tie her up and lock her in that bathroom. Then we can get the hell out of here. Let's let her rot in there. No one has to know. It can be our little secret. Just between us gal pals."

Selma hesitated.

Amy Sue scoffed. "That's what I thought. Once a traitor, always a traitor."

Possibly for the first time in her life, Selma was at a loss for words. Amy Sue had called her bluff. We were screwed.

"Look, I said I'd be your friend, not your partner in crime." Selma turned to me. "Come on, Sam. Let's get out of here."

She spun around and made for the door.

Before I could even take a step, Amy Sue threw her arms out, bracing her hands on the doorframe. "No, you don't. Little Miss Perfect here owes me something."

THREATS AND THREADS

Fancy growled at Amy Sue. I shushed the little dog, or tried to, but the rumble in her throat only increased in volume.

"It's sitting next to the toilet." I hooked a thumb toward the bathroom. "Help yourself. It's a little rough yet, but nothing a good proofread can't clean up." Rough was an understatement. It wouldn't make the grade for a freshman class in creative writing. I gravitated toward Selma.

"Don't even think about it," Amy Sue warned, one hand in her pocket. "Or the dog dies."

"Oh, come on now." Selma threw her hands up. "Why would you hurt Fancy? What's she ever done to you?"

"I couldn't care less about that yappy mop. I'm talking about *her* dog—Bump." She seemed to be taking perverse glee in terrorizing me. Of all her taunts and threats, I was sure she meant this one. She took her phone from her coat pocket, jabbed at the screen, and flashed an app at us. A countdown clock showed. My heart sank.

"Looks like you better hurry home, hon," Selma joked halfheartedly. "Cake's due to come out of the oven."

"Haha," Amy Sue replied dryly. "No, you idiot. Your friend there had better cough up a satisfactory novel ending like she promised or she's going to condemn her dog to a slow death."

"Where is he?" I shrieked. "What have you done to him?"

"Oh, sweetie, I haven't done anything to him… yet. This app is connected to a remote start on a 1970's Mustang my daddy left me—may he rest in peace—that belches carbon monoxide by the cubic yard. It's sitting in a garage, oh, let's just say somewhere in the county. I hit the start button just before I stepped in here. By my calculations, your mutt has about half an hour's worth of air before asphyxiation gets him." Back in control now, her tone had calmed. "Now, where's that ending you promised me, Miss S.A. Mack?"

"In the bathroom, I told you."

"And why should I trust you, seeing all the grief you've caused me?" She swept her fingers toward the bathroom door. "You two march back in there. Hand it to me. I'll determine if it's good enough. If it is, I'll set you free. If not..." Her hand wandered back to her pocket.

My body rigid with horror, I was barely aware of Selma's right hand tucked at the back of her hip, her pointer finger waggling directly at the can of pepper spray on the desk. If I went for it, even if I hit Amy Sue square in the face and we got away, Bump might very well die. If I didn't, if we let her lock us up, chances were damn good *we* were going to die in there.

She might also shoot one of us before I could get within range. *If* she had a gun.

Selma turned a pleading gaze on me. "Sam, we can't—"

I rushed forward to pull my friend into a one-armed hug, holding Fancy to the side. "We'll be okay, Sel. We'll be okay. Promise." I turned her by the elbow. "Trust me. Now come on."

It took a good tug to get her moving, but she came. I angled past the desk, scooping the canister into the pocket where my dead phone was as I twisted to look over my shoulder at Amy Sue. She stood her ground in the doorway, one hand clutching the bulky lump in her pocket.

At the door to the bathroom, Selma stopped dead. "Sam, if we go in there..."

"She's got a gun," I said, just loud enough for Amy Sue to hear.

"Oh my God." Selma clutched my arm. "I don't wanna die, Sam."

"Me, either."

Handing Fancy off to Selma, I walked into that frozen dingy bathroom. Then I picked up the stack of papers and plopped that ugly sucker just outside the door. With a hand on the small of her back, I ushered Selma inside.

"Now you keep *your* word," I said to Amy Sue.

"Cross my heart." She put a hand briefly over her heart, then brushed me off with a wave. "Bye now."

Joining Selma, I closed the bathroom door behind me.

"How are we going to get out of here?" Selma whispered as she set Fancy down.

Amy Sue's footsteps resounded in the brittle chilly air as she crossed the room, crunching over wads of crumpled paper and bits of broken glass. Halfway across, she paused. Desk drawers slid open one by one, then banged shut.

"Where's *your* phone, Mack?" Amy Sue demanded.

"I have it. It's dead."

"I don't trust you. Slide it underneath."

Taking the pepper spray from my pocket, I placed it in Selma's hand, then tipped my head for her to stand back, out of eyesight. At first, she looked so paralyzed I didn't think she'd comply, but then she moved out of the way, pressing her back to the wall.

"I could really use a cigarette about now," Selma muttered.

"I don't think that would help our situation," I whispered.

"I know, but—"

"The phone," Amy Sue barked. "Or the dog dies."

I knelt and tried to slide the phone underneath, but its bulky case, the one Tara had insisted I buy to keep it from getting damaged, stopped its progress.

"It's too big," I objected. In reality, all I had to do was remove it from its case.

"Fine then. Open the door. But just enough to set the phone on top of the papers—and make it quick."

I flung the door open, tossed it haphazardly, causing some of the top papers to go tumbling off the stack, then slammed the door shut again.

Amy Sue approached. As soon as she got within a few feet, I pulled the door open again and dropped to my knees to gather the papers. "Sorry, I didn't mean to—"

"No!" Amy Sue shouted.

All I heard was the hiss of aerosol. I covered my head with my arms. Amy Sue's body hit the floor with a clumsy thud. She screeched.

A sharp, acrid scent scoured my nostrils. Selma leaped over me and rushed at Amy Sue, who was writhing on the junk-littered floor, screaming profanities.

Instead of going to Amy Sue, Selma veered toward an old lamp sitting atop a tall filing cabinet. She yanked the cord from the wall, ripped the lampshade free, and raised the base over her head as she bore down on Amy Sue. But Amy Sue was mad as a hornet. She'd heard Selma coming and rolled to the side, just as Selma slammed the lamp downward. Its ceramic base broke into shards, leaving nothing but a short, slim metal post through which ran the electrical cord.

On hands and knees, I scrambled to grab my abandoned umbrella, barely aware of Fancy's tiny paws scrabbling over the floor as she headed straight for Amy Sue. The tiny dog launched herself through the air just as Amy Sue yanked what looked like a toy gun from her pocket. But it was yellow. And plastic.

It was a taser.

Amy Sue pulled the trigger. The probe shot into the air, a tiny needle of paralysis seeking its target, its highly charged wire trailing behind like the tail of a comet.

Leaping to my feet, I swung the umbrella like a baseball bat, knocking the probe away, and let go. The probe and its wire fell to the floor in a tangle, little sparks of electricity cracking and popping.

Amy Sue screamed.

Fancy had chomped down on the meat of her thumb, causing her to lose her hold on the taser. I kicked it away and grabbed Fancy before Amy Sue could take a swat at her.

With lightning swiftness, Selma grabbed Amy Sue by the scarf, then flipped her onto her stomach. Seconds later, she had her hogtied with the electrical cord. By then, Amy Sue was sobbing.

THREATS AND THREADS

"When and where did you acquire that talent?" I asked.

Smiling, Selma pulled her phone from Amy Sue's pocket. "Sam, honey, I was the Humboldt County calf scramble champion my senior year." When Amy Sue lifted her head and spat in my direction, Selma slammed a palm into the back of her skull and smooshed her cheek against the floor. "You've been underestimating my abilities all along. Give me a little more credit, will ya?"

"From now on, Sel, I will." If there was one thing I'd learned during my time in Wilton, it was that more people than I ever imagined had my back. As much as I may have felt ostracized in this town at times, I'd also discovered security and trust. Sometimes, I had to learn those things the hard way.

"Now, hand me your phone," I said. "I need to call Misty."

chapter 30

FANCY WAS TROTTING BEHIND me as the first ring went through. On the second, a familiar voice answered.

"9-1-1. How can I help you?"

"Misty! Thank God it's you." With Selma's phone pressed to my ear, I paced the floor to warm myself. Selma had hiked out to her car to fetch some blankets she kept in the trunk. She'd done an impressive job of incapacitating Amy Sue, even duct taping her mouth shut when she started to threaten us with a lawsuit for bodily injury.

"Ms. McNamee... Sam?"

As quickly as I could, I filled Misty in on the situation. Then, after pinning my location down to A & B Salvage on Runyan Road and assuring me she was sending the closest deputy, Misty asked, "So you have your dog now? Is he okay?"

"No... I mean, I don't know." I slumped against the desk for support. Between the bone-shattering cold and the lack of sleep, every muscle in my body was beginning to seize up.

"Where is he?"

"Check any properties Amy Sue Bradley or her father may have owned—businesses, storage units, houses... Wait! She was living in a house in Bluebird Estates. Send someone there!"

"Do you know the address?"

"Hang on." I tromped over to Amy Sue, then ripped the tape off her mouth. "Tell me your address, so they can find Bump! Or they're going to add animal cruelty to your rap sheet. I hear it's a felony in this state."

She spat at my boots. "Nice try, but I'm not squealing."

"This is your last chance at redemption, Amy Sue. Tell me where he is, and I'll ask them to go easy on you."

"Oh, well... in that case"—she flashed a wicked grin—"it won't matter. You're too late."

I didn't want to believe her, but she'd almost killed *me*. What was a dog to her?

I yanked a fresh strip of duct tape off the roll and slapped it on her mouth. Fancy stood in front of her, yapping bravely.

"You tell her, girl," I said to Fancy. Then, to Misty, "I don't know the house number, but I think it's on Cardinal Drive. It's the house Miley Harper was killed in. On Cardinal Drive."

"All right. I'll look into it and send an officer over as soon as one's available."

"As soon as... But he's running out of air!" Or maybe he already had.

"I'm sorry, dear. There was a pile-up on the interstate. Someone will get there as soon as they can, though. Meanwhile, do you need an ambulance?"

"No, I don't think so. Just tell them to find Bump, *please*."

Misty quickly confirmed all the details, then told me to keep the phone at hand and ended the call.

Selma yanked the door open. Outside, the snow had stopped, but it was piled deep. She handed one blanket to me, then wrapped Fancy in the other one. "Someone coming?"

"Yeah." Defeated, I set her phone beside me on the desk and cocooned myself.

She rubbed my shoulder. "Soon?"

"I don't know," I mumbled. "Lots of accidents, not enough deputies, I guess."

"It's a mess out there. I almost went off the road a couple of times myself on the way here." She checked Amy Sue's bonds, tugging at one to tighten it, then returned to me. "What about Bump? They're sending someone to get him, aren't they?"

"Amy Sue told me... he's already... gone." I burst into tears. It all seemed so hopeless. Selma had saved my ass, but there just hadn't been enough time to save Bump, too.

She wrapped her arms around me, gentle and comforting. "Shh, shh. There's still hope, hon. I wouldn't take that bitch's word on anything."

I wasn't so sure. That dog had turned my life around, taken me down a road better than any I could've planned. I owed that dog *so* much. Couldn't imagine my life without him. Dad would be devastated. Tara would be grief-stricken. I sobbed harder into Selma's shoulder.

Suddenly, Selma thrust me away. "Why don't you take my car and go—"

Her phone rang. She picked it up, looked at it.

"Who is it?" I rubbed my sleeve across my upper lip to wipe away the tear-snot.

She answered. "Hello? ... Oh, hey, honeybunch! Can't tell you how happy I am to hear from you! ... Uh-huh, uh-huh. ... Yep."

"Who is it?"

"Yeah. ... Yeah. ... Hold on, she's right here." She handed me the phone.

"Hello?"

"Sam!" It was Clint. "Where are you?"

"A salvage yard on Runyan."

"Ah, I know the one. Cleora called me just before dawn. She told me you went out looking for the dogs. Are you okay?"

"I suppose, b-b-but..." Then it hit me. "Clint, you have to go to Miley Harper's old house. Amy Sue left him in a car there in her garage. She's trying to asphyxiate him!"

"Sam," he said, "I already did."

"Already did what?"

"Went to Miley's house. Sam, I have Bump. He's okay. A little woozy, threw up just a minute ago, but he's conscious. I'm on my way with him to the clinic. Likely, it'll take a little time for his system to rebound, but he should be okay within a day or two."

Relief crashed through me. "I don't know how to thank you. But how... how did *you* know where to find him?"

"The app for the tracking collar. Turns out there's a feature that not only tells you where the collar is, but where it's been. Just like your phone, it pings at regular intervals. The signal started at your house last night, went to Cleora's until the meeting ended, then took a detour to the house where Amy Sue was apparently staying. She must've driven there with him in that old Mustang, then parked it in the garage and taken his collar out to where you are. It was a two-car garage, so I'm guessing she had another car to get to the salvage yard. I couldn't decide whether to head to the salvage yard or the house she'd stopped at, so I took a gamble and came here since it was closer. I'm glad I did."

"You didn't get my text last night?"

"I left my phone in another room, so I didn't see it until early this morning when Cleora's call woke me up. She told me you'd gone out looking for the dogs and hadn't returned. Then I got a text from Selma that she was going to the salvage yard to see if you were there. By then, I was already at Miley's old house. I broke into the garage when I heard the car running. No one answered when I tried both you and Selma, so I called the sheriff. Someone should be on their way."

I gazed out through the broken window of the office trailer.

Sitting in a muddy lane that hadn't been visible the night before, there was a silver-gray compact car. I'd seen that car before. More than once. A car so nondescript it could easily have been overlooked.

Everything made complete sense now. She'd planned out all the details. Stalked me relentlessly in an attempt to scare me and drive me out of town. When that hadn't worked, she'd tricked Bump into getting into her Mustang, then left it at her house while she took her other car and brought Bump's collar out here to lure me away. All to get back at me.

"Why?" I said. "Why would anyone do something like this? It's sick. Maybe her life wasn't great, but was terrorizing me really the answer to her problems? I mean—why *me*?"

From somewhere, I heard the familiar cry of a siren.

There was a telling pause on the other end. "I, uh, may have mentioned you were a romance writer to her when she brought her cat in once."

"I know, Clint. She told me."

"Oh... Look, Sam, I'm sorry. I really, *really* am. If I'd thought for a second she—"

"I didn't ask you to keep it a secret. It's not your fault she's crazy. Her life hadn't panned out, and she needed someone to blame."

"Then I'm sorry it was you. You could use a break from crazy."

"Amen to that."

"Hey, Sam, I'm pulling in at the clinic now. I have to go. Can I talk to Selma for a moment?"

I handed her phone back.

"Yeah, sweetie, we're fine. Really," she reassured him "'Kay. Bye-bye."

Footsteps hammered erratically on icy snow. The deputies were picking their way through the maze of rusted metal. Plucking Fancy up, Selma rushed to the door and hollered for them.

"Over here! We have the dognapper!"

THREATS AND THREADS

There was one thing I still had to do before the cops hauled Amy Sue away. I picked up the stack of papers I'd pecked out with numb fingers until every joint in my hands ached. Then I crouched in front of Amy Sue. "Should I read you some of it?"

Her curses were muffled by the tape.

"That's right. You're a little tied up right now. Let me get to the good part." I leafed to the last page and read, "As she watched Alexander's jet ascending into an eternal blue sky, Felicity understood that you couldn't *make* someone love you, no matter how much you wanted them to. When you found love, though, you had to find a way to make it work, no matter how hard that was or how long it took to get it right. For true love might not always come easily, but it was always, *always* worth fighting for. And the harder the fight, the greater the love."

Something between rage and confusion boiled behind her eyes. She mumbled angrily beneath the tape, her nostrils flaring as she drew air between words.

"What's that?" I ripped the tape off. "I couldn't quite understand."

She sputtered. Tears of pain trickled from her eyes onto the dirty floor. "All you did was change a few sentences. The ending's still the same."

"True. But I did add that bit about true love—an homage to you, of course. And Alexander left in a jet. So much more dramatic and final than driving off in his Porsche Carrera like he did originally. He could've turned his car around and come right back. A jet, not so much."

"It's the same. They're *still* not together!"

"No, maybe not. But their story's not done yet, either. And they do still love each other. Very much."

"Miss Paradiso?" Deputy Strewing stepped into the trailer, surveying the scene.

A few seconds later, Deputy Ecklund followed. She stomped the snow loose from her shoes. "Ms. McNamee, good to see you in one piece."

I slapped the tape back on Amy Sue, then rose and stepped back.

Deputy Strewing circled Amy Sue, then bent to inspect her scarf. "This the person who has been causing you all the trouble, Ms. McNamee?"

I nodded. "Make sure when Sheriff Driscoll interrogates her that he asks her about Grace Hazelton and Miley Harper, too."

He took out his notepad to jot it down while Deputy Ecklund replaced the knotted electrical cord with handcuffs on Amy Sue. "We'll look into it."

Then he directed the two of us to sit tight while they escorted Amy Sue to the cruiser to read the woman her Miranda Rights.

The moment she was out the door, exhaustion hit me hard and heavy. Tonight, I'd sleep well. I wouldn't have to worry about whether my stalker was outside my door or draining my bank accounts. I'd be safe at home—or at least the place I called home for now.

There was a lot more about my crazy life to unpack, but I wasn't going to worry about it now. Not one bit. I'd figure it all out. Eventually. Until then, I'd count my blessings.

The important thing was that I was safe. And so were the people —and the dog—I loved.

chapter 31

As grateful as I was for the officers of the Humboldt County Sheriff's Department, I hoped it was a long time before I ever saw any of them up close and personal again.

After they released Selma and me, she dropped me off at Ida's house and waited until I'd gotten the keys to Ida's Camry and started it up. It purred like a kitten. We waved goodbye, then went our separate ways. I sat at the end of Ida's lane for a few minutes, letting it all sink in. I wasn't looking forward to telling Dad about his truck, but I knew he'd be glad that both Bump and I were okay.

By the time I pulled into the parking lot at South End Animal Hospital, it was midafternoon. I'd already texted Clint that I was on my way to pick Bump up and asked how I could bypass the front guard, Janelle. He'd told me to shoot him another text as soon as I arrived, and he'd meet me by the back door.

I'm here, I texted.

His answer came within seconds. *Be right there!*

As I killed the engine on Ida's car, I gazed out over a world frosted in wintry white. I hated driving in snow, hated how it turned to a gritty black slush on the roads after a couple of days, and how it melted into patches of ice on the sidewalks. As far as I was concerned, winter sports were best enjoyed from the comfort of one's own living room with expert commentary running on the TV.

My phone rang. When I saw the caller ID, my heart paused. It almost went to voice mail before I answered. "Hey... I wasn't expecting you to call."

"No? You're happy to hear my voice... aren't you?"

It was Archer.

"Of course." I both longed for him and dreaded to know what it was he wanted to tell me. By now, I'd convinced myself it wasn't good news. "It's just... we keep missing each other."

The back door to the clinic opened and Clint walked out, his coat unzipped. Beside him, Bump ambled unsteadily. Clint led him to a bush and the dog lifted his leg to pee, almost toppling over sideways before he finished. Afterward, instead of bounding to life, Bump leaned against him for support. Clint beckoned for me. I held up a finger to let him know I needed a minute. Giving me a thumbs-up, he began slowly walking Bump in a circle, probably to see if he needed to empty his bowels.

"Sam? You sound... I don't know. Did something happen over the weekend?"

"A lot. But I'm okay. Can I call you back in a few? I have something I need to do, then I can talk more."

"Yeah, I'll be here." He'd gone from sounding genuinely happy to gravely concerned. "Are you sure you're okay? Is Tara all right? Your dad?"

"They're all fine. I'll call you back. Promise." Then I ended the call and tossed the phone on the seat. Kicking the door open, I jumped out and rushed toward Bump. "Hey, Bumparoo, buddy! How ya doing?"

He gazed at me with foggy eyes, his head tilting as if he wasn't sure he recognized my voice at all. Slowly, his tail begun swinging like a lazy pendulum. A low chortle of glee emanated.

THREATS AND THREADS

Dropping to my knees, I wrapped him in my arms. He threw his front paws on my shoulders, returning the hug. Together, we fell sideways into a bank of snow.

"Um, I *think* that snow's clean," Clint said, "but I wouldn't swear to it."

I planted a giant smooch on Bump's head before rolling free. After checking to make sure the snow wasn't yellow, I sat on the ground with my dog while he licked my face and did a slow-motion version of his happy dance.

"He's still kind of groggy," I noted.

Clint crouched, balancing on the balls of his feet. "A little, but he's getting better by the minute. He still shows signs of dizziness, and he has trouble keeping food or water down. On top of the carbon monoxide poisoning, he has some kind of sedative in his system. I'm not sure what, but whatever it was, she gave him a hefty dose of it. He's been sleeping a lot. It's going to take some time yet for things to work their way out of his system. I could keep him overnight for observation, but he seems to be past the worst of it."

"He can come home, then? You're sure?"

"We can't yet rule out the possibility of complications, but based on his improvement so far, I'd say yes. I'd expect him to sleep a lot, but, of course, if you observe anything unusual"—Clint handed me the leash— "call me."

Ruffling Bump's mane, I kissed him on the nose. "I'm so tired I could fall asleep right here."

Clint helped me up. "I'm sure you could, but I wouldn't recommend it."

Bump yawned, then sat on my feet, his head drooping like he was about to fall over. I scratched between his ears. "I feel the same way, buddy."

We began to walk with Clint to the back door.

"Have you talked to Danielle since she came back from

Chicago?" I asked.

"I have."

"And?"

"She's seriously considering adoption."

"That's good!" When he didn't respond, I added, "Isn't it?"

He stopped abruptly, turned to me. "She's contacted an agency that handles orphan refugees. Her work abroad, it seems, had a profound effect on her." His gaze slipped to the ground. Something about him was suddenly incredibly sad. "She's accepted an out-of-state job offer already. And soon, she'll have a family of her own." He met my eyes then. Stirred that part of my soul that had been deeply buried for too many years while I tried to cope with Kyle's loss.

"Goodbye, Sam." He tipped his head at the building behind him. "If you ever need me…"

I said nothing. Smiled. Watched him disappear inside while the wobbly mutt, who'd been nothing but trouble since the day I ran into him, leaned against my knee.

As for Clint—he'd come into my life precisely when I needed him. I hoped he'd forever be a part of it. Something would be missing if he wasn't.

And just like that, everything clicked together. Everything. My life had needed to be shaken up, turned upside down and inside out, in order for things to fall into some kind of order. Or maybe instead of denying what I felt and where I was going, I was finally embracing it all—good, bad, and in-between.

Whatever happened from here on, I'd deal with it. More than anything, I needed tranquility and stability. I needed to feel safe and know I was loved. Wasn't that really all anyone wanted? Even if Archer and I went our separate ways, I already had a support system I could depend on. No matter what, I was going to be all right.

Oddly calm, I walked back to the car. Lifted Bump into the passenger seat. Got inside and shut the door. Sat in the peaceful cold next to my drowsy dog for a good five minutes before I summoned the courage to pick up the phone again.

Four rings. An eternity. And then—

"Sam? Wow, I almost missed you *again*." Archer's words spilled out. "It's so loud in here I almost didn't hear my phone. Hey, guess what? I'm on my way home."

"Home?" I echoed, taken off guard. "When?"

His voice pitched in excitement. "I'm sitting at the airport right now, waiting on a flight. I... I can't wait to see you."

For a moment, I didn't breathe. Couldn't. Had I interpreted everything *completely* wrong?

"I couldn't find anything direct to Indy. I have two plane changes with a few hours' layover in Dallas. It'll probably be close to midnight before I can make it back to Wilton, so maybe I'll just wait until tomorrow to—"

"Archer..." I started up the car. Put him on speakerphone. Backed up and headed for the exit to take the road home. "You said we needed to talk. About what?"

"I did?" He sounded genuinely perplexed—or distracted, maybe. There was so much background noise, mostly voices breaking over the public address system, that it was hard to hear him. Then, after a few more moments, it came to him. "Oh, right. Now I remember. I do, but it can wait until after I get back. Will you be home tonight? It'll be late, but I can come directly to your place if you want. I'm pretty burned out after a week's worth of meetings, but I'm sure I can catch a few Zs on the flight. Just a few more hours until I can see you. Well, more like nine or ten. Soon, anyway."

He didn't sound at all like a guy prepping me for a breakup. He sounded like a guy who couldn't wait to be with the woman he loved. Which only made what I had to say that much harder. I had to tell him the truth. All of it.

"Sure, come on over. Before you do, though... there's something

I should probably tell you. A lot, actually."

An announcement broke through in the background. Something about 'final call' and 'Dallas'.

If he'd heard me, he didn't let on. Because the next thing he said was, "Oh, hey, they're getting ready to close the gate. I have to go. Love you, Sam!"

And then, he was gone.

chapter 32

I TRIED TO IMAGINE Amy Sue Bradley in an orange jumpsuit, sitting at a table in the mess hall, eating her rations with a spork while surrounded by hardened criminals. Frankly, I didn't feel the least bit sorry for her. According to Sheriff Driscoll, she'd likely be charged with multiple felonies. Chances were, if convicted on all counts, she'd get up to twenty years, although the sheriff warned me she could get off for good behavior in half that time. Although she'd be forbidden to come near me or Selma, that wouldn't necessarily keep her from hunting us down for revenge.

Right now, I needed to relax. With Amy Sue in the county slammer while she awaited her hearing, I could treat myself to a quiet night at home without fearing for my life. And I had just the thing in mind.

Sitting on the side of the tub, I dipped a toe in the water. Too hot. I turned the cold-water knob some more, then flipped through the pages of my new reading material—a romance novel, heavy on the physical. Definitely not a how-to on building relationships, but it could rival the *Kama Sutra* in the how-to-please-your-partner section.

My purse was sitting beside the hamper where I'd shed the rest of my clothes. I reached for the leather strap, pulled it to me, and looked in the outside pocket for my phone. Dang. I'd left it charging on the nightstand next to my bed. Oh, well. As long as no one called in the next fifteen minutes, I didn't need it, anyway.

It had been several hours since I'd spoken to Archer. Soon enough, Archer and I would be face to face. I'd tell him the whole truth about Amy Sue stalking me, me asking Clint to watch Bump while I went out of town, how I'd ended up at his place for the night...

He'd either believe me or he wouldn't.

I knew how I wanted things to turn out. But it always seemed like the universe was working against Archer and me.

If it was true that what didn't kill you made you stronger, after the last few months' trials, I had become an Amazon warrior princess. I'd battled and conquered. I could survive anything.

Except, maybe, a broken heart.

I swirled my fingers in the tub water as it reached the half-full point. Getting too cold now. After adding some more bubbles, I twisted the hot-water knob to compensate and continued to thumb through the pages for the titillating parts—which was about every fifth page in this particular book, entitled *Love Me Hard and Fast*. Meanwhile, the intoxicating scents of jasmine and hyacinth wafted from the steamy water.

When the temperature was just right and the level high enough, I eased myself into the tub. Warmth flowed over me. Flowers and spices permeated my senses. A trio of candles flickered on the vanity countertop. For music, I'd chosen some easy-listening jazz. Beside the tub sat a tray of asiago cheese slices and dollops of pesto artfully arranged on sesame crackers, plus a glass of cabernet sauvignon. The bottle was within arm's reach for easy refills. I'd saved that lone bottle of wine for over a decade, figuring as long as I was strong enough to resist it, I had a handle on things. Tonight, though, I drank it in celebration. I nibbled, sipped, read, lost myself in the music, and sipped some more. My arms and legs floated in the sweet-smelling salty water. I hadn't felt this relaxed in a long time.

After a few chapters from the book, I got bored and tossed it at the trash can, but it landed in the hamper. I'd fish it out later. My music on a loop, I sank down deeper until the water came up to my chin.

The last two weeks had been exhausting. But it was over now. Finally over. Once the police interrogated Amy Sue and went through her computer and house, they'd find the evidence to link her to Grace Hazelton's death and who knew how many others. The chick was a psychopath.

I drained the last drop from my third glass of wine. As the water cooled, I thought about getting out, but it seemed like so much effort. And I was tired. Exhausted. Bushed, beat, and completely unmotivated to move.

I closed my eyes. Drifted off. Dreamed wine-soaked dreams.

Of wading into a warm salty ocean until my toes and fingers were wrinkled. Of lying on the beach to dry, the sun beaming down on me. Of a man sitting on the seawall, playing a saxophone. Of a giant stomping toward me, the earth shaking beneath his feet.

The stomping paused. Came closer. A door clicked shut—

Wait. There weren't any doors on the beach. And you couldn't exactly stomp on sand.

My eyes snapped open. One of the candles had gone out. Then I noticed how cool the water in the tub was. How long had I been sleeping?

Worry compressed my chest. Had I turned the alarm back on when I'd come home? I couldn't remember. I'd been so exhausted and concerned about Bump, I hadn't been thinking straight. The more I thought about it, the more I doubted I had. What if—

A draft of air brushed past me. The flames on the two remaining candles fluttered, then sputtered. A second one went out.

I could barely see. A single candle was burning. Hands on the bottom of the tub, I started to push up to get out. The long, faint creak of floorboards sounded. My muscles locked in place. A shiver shot up my spine.

This was an old house. It made all kinds of weird sounds. I was making too much out of this. If the wind blew, the gutters rattled. When it poured rain, water dripped around the roof vents and plopped into a wastebasket I'd had to put in the attic. Sometimes, the old stick frame cracked and groaned like an old woman's bones for no reason at all. A lot of little things needed fixing, and I had no intention of doing that on my dime if I didn't own it. Melissa was welcome to have it back. By week's end, I'd have a new car and could start looking for a new house. One of my own.

I reached for the towel on the floor, water dripping down my arm to pool on the linoleum.

The vaguest of shadows moved across the far wall of the bathroom.

I froze. Held my breath. The hardwood planks of the hallway groaned unmistakably under the strain of a weight.

It was the dog. It had to be.

"Bump?" I whispered. Then, a little louder, "Come here, buddy."

Silence.

"Bump?"

Nothing. The last I'd seen of him, he'd been fast asleep on Tara's bed, recovering from his own near-death ordeal.

Tara, maybe? No, she would've called first. I'd made sure my ringer was on, so even from here, I would've heard someone calling me.

If someone had broken in, then who? Amy Sue was locked up, but there were half-a-dozen others in this county who had a vendetta against me. Multiply that by their number of friends and family and my odds of being knocked off were pretty high.

Goose bumps rose on my arms. Cold fear filled my chest.

Think, Sam. Think, think, think!

All I had to do was jump up, slam the door shut, and lock it, then squirt myself out the tiny second-story window and land cat-footed on the leafless forsythias below. Then I remembered that this past summer, on a ninety-degree day, we'd discovered this bathroom window had been painted shut.

I was trapped in here.

If I could at least lock the door, I could call the sheriff and wait for help to arrive. Easy enough. Except… my phone was in the bedroom, being charged.

A footstep, undeniable. The shadow grew larger. The room darker. Another wisp of a draft—and the last candle was snuffed out.

Oh, shit.

A hand crept around the doorframe. Groped for the switch. Flipped it. Light flooded the room. Exposed me. A very nude, very cold me.

Shit, shit, shit.

The intruder moved into the doorway. Into the light.

A very wide person. A woman with an unmistakable scowl.

"Maybelle?" I grabbed the towel. A tsunami of scented bathwater cascaded onto the floor. Maybelle Purnell had just trespassed into my home, then crept up my stairway unannounced. This was so beyond bizarre my head was about to explode. "What are you doing here?"

Just as I started to rise out of the tub, she shoved me back. My right hip hit the edge, then my elbow. As water sloshed over the side and spilled onto the floor, the back of my head thunked against the tiled wall.

Dazed, I lay in a half-full tub of chilly water, only vaguely cognizant of Maybelle towering above me.

"You shoulda left town a long time ago." She dropped something small and shiny on the floor. "Harmon doesn't need your house key, you whore."

It was my key. He'd never returned it because she'd taken it from him.

Coughing, I tried to push myself up. "What are you talk—"

She pushed me back down, the weight of my body pinning my left arm beneath me. Her hands went around my throat so fast I could barely register what was happening.

"You and your kind. No shame. No shame at all. Hussies, all of you. Trying to tempt my man. Pretending to be his friend so you can flaunt your young skinny body in front of him."

My right arm was numb from my elbow hitting the edge, but I flailed it wildly, trying to fend her off. My palm glanced off her padded rump. Her anger flared. Her fingers tightened against my trachea, clamping my windpipe shut. I let out a strangled croak. Her thumbs dug into my jugulars. The edges of my vision darkened, then narrowed. I felt lightheaded, disconnected from my own body.

One last time, I tried to swing my free arm at Maybelle. But I could barely lift it. My muscles were being starved of oxygen. All I wanted to do... was breathe.

I was going to die. Not by gunshot. Not from being beaten until my brains were jarred loose and my ribs punctured. Not from smoke inhalation before gasoline-fueled flames consumed me. I was going to die at the chubby hands of Maybelle Purnell—the neighbor who'd never liked me for reasons that, until now, I had never understood.

Most of us had no choice in how or when we died. I just never imagined it was going to be so inglorious.

Maybelle's eerie grin widened to show her coffee-stained, slightly crooked teeth. Her eyes were wide, maniacal, and possessed. She looked as though she would break into a mad cackle like a hyena's laughter at any moment. Yet, she made no sound. Said nothing.

I couldn't let her win. Wouldn't.

Too weak to beat her back, I twisted my body, desperate to

loosen her grip on my neck. Her weight pitched to the side. One of her hands slid from my neck and plunged into the water, splashing water into her eyes. Reflexively, she turned her head, giving me a momentary reprieve. I gulped in air, but it wasn't enough to fill my lungs or clear my head. I was still struggling to think or even act.

Muttering curses, Maybelle let go of my neck. But before I could fight back, she planted both hands on my chest and pushed me underwater. I stared at her through a blurry mosaic of bubbles. Soap stung at my eyes, and I closed them. I didn't want her face to be the last thing on my mind.

I thought of Archer and what we might have had. Thought of Clint and how, despite all his faults, he had so much capacity for love. Of Dad and Ida and Selma. But most of all, I thought of Tara. Dear, sweet, almost grown-up Tara. At any moment, she could walk into the house and come looking for me. I didn't want her to find me like this.

I wanted so badly to open my mouth and breathe, but I knew if I did, water would rush into my lungs. I fought it. Forced my mouth to stay shut.

In my fading moments, I also thought of Bump—a crazy, overzealous mutt who'd stumbled into our lives by accident. If not for him, I might never have met Clint or Archer. If not for him, my relationship with my father would still be tenuous, at best. Even now, I could imagine him romping through the house, shoving his nose under the couch or the bed, looking for his much-loved and slobbered-on ball, then dropping it in my lap as I sat at the computer trying to work.

I could even envision his loveable, grisly face… like he was right there, that very moment.

Something soft and round dropped into the water. I pried my eyes open.

Saw Maybelle. And to her left, a pointy gray snout, a tongue hanging out over jagged white teeth. A wolf?

No... Bump.

He shoved his nose in the water. Snapped at something beneath the surface. Maybelle turned to look at him, her face rife with fear.

As she did so, her weight shifted once again. Bump's appearance and the brief ease of pressure from my chest afforded me just enough of a chance to gather the last shred of my energy and pull my head out of the water.

I sucked in air. Precious, life-giving air.

Bump slurped his tongue across Maybelle's cheek. She shrieked. "No! Don't touch me, you filthy beast! Or I'll kill you, too!"

He licked harder, drool dripping from his tongue. She recoiled until he had her practically pinned against the wall at the end of the tub. Bursting upward, I slammed my palm into her collarbone. I threw myself over the edge of the tub and onto the floor just as she toppled sideways—into the bathwater.

I had to incapacitate her before she recovered, so I rolled over to grope for my purse atop the hamper. Found the strap. Pulled it to me. Reached inside.

"Damn you, you slut," she raged as she came up and grabbed my dripping wild mess of hair to drag me back. "No different than that foxy little imp, Miley Harper, or that sly divorcée, Grace Hazelton. No morals, any of you."

My fingers dug past a bulky wallet and a pack of tissues before my nails hit the metal canister. I wrapped my fingers around it. Felt for the trigger.

Bump was blowing bubbles in the bathwater as he bobbed for his ball. In that moment, I resolved my next dog was going to be a Doberman. I felt my hair being pulled from its roots. With my free arm, I rammed my elbow backward, connecting with ribs buried beneath fleshy padding.

Maybelle grunted. My eyes still stung from the mineral salts in the water. I couldn't focus well. I swung the canister around. Sprayed it back and forth.

She let go of my hair, clutching both hands over her eyes as she screamed in pain.

I scrambled to my feet. Blinked to clear my vision. Looked down at her. Her screams were now broken by hysterical sobs.

In the other room, the ringtone on my cell played. It went to voice mail.

I threatened Maybelle with another squirt of pepper spray. "Shut up or I'll hit you again!"

She instantly shushed, although her jaw quivered terribly and tears streamed down her face.

Bump brought his head out of the water, turned to me, and spit a thoroughly soaked tennis ball at my feet.

"Later, buddy," I promised. "Later."

I yanked the cord of Tara's hairdryer from the outlet, then wound it around Maybelle's ankles. Taking a sharp pair of hair scissors from the drawer behind me, I cut the electrical cord just below where it attached to the hairdryer and tied it off.

Maybelle lay blubbering in shallow water, her feet bound. She wasn't going anywhere. But just in case, I sprayed her again. Just as Bump stepped forward to offer her the ball.

He yelped. The ball plopped into the bathwater. And then he ran from the room.

Right between the legs of Harmon Purnell.

"Maybelle? Oh, Maybelle..." he lamented.

If I'd temporarily forgotten about my nakedness in order to save my own life, the awareness returned with a jolt. I grabbed a spare towel off the towel rack, pulled it around me, and tucked the tail end tightly at the top. Not very secure, but at least my modesty was spared for the moment.

"Harmon, what are you doing here?" I wasn't sure whether him showing up was a good or bad thing. Especially since he just stood there staring at Maybelle.

"Harmon? Is that you, snookums?" Maybelle said. "Help me, Harmon. I came in here to talk to her, and she tried to blind me. My eyes are burning!"

He shook his head slowly. Looked at me. His brow wrinkled in confusion. "What did you *do* to her?"

"Harmon!" Maybelle flopped around in the tub, her hands flailing about. She found a washcloth lying on the soap shelf and swiped at her eyes, but that only seemed to exacerbate the pain. Finally, she threw the washcloth in Harmon's direction. "Will you do something before she kills us both?"

Harmon's sad, droopy eyes wandered from Maybelle to me. He froze in indecision.

Maybelle kicked her legs. The cord loosened. She reached down, found the knot, and freed a foot.

Still clutching the pepper spray, I wrenched the shower curtain rod loose one-handed with a single jerk and swung it at Harmon. All I needed to do was throw him off balance so I could rush past him. He dodged to the side. I rushed at the gap between him and the doorframe. But the shower curtain, trailing on the floor, tripped me. I tumbled to Harmon's feet, my forehead smacking squarely against his shins. The curtain rod fell to the floor with a clatter, the can of spray lost somewhere in the floral drapes of cloth.

I rolled over, scanned for the can, but I couldn't see it. The rod was tangled in the curtains. My feet were, too.

Maybelle's eyes, surrounded by a mask of red, flapped open. "Do something, Harmon! Don't just stand there!"

The expression on Harmon's face was utterly frightening. It was as if his body had been possessed by evilness. The man standing before me was not the gentle soul I'd come to know. Could *he* have been the one behind Grace's and Miley's deaths?

The faint plink of glass on tile sounded. Maybelle lifted my wine bottle up. Blinking wildly, she brandished it in my direction. Huffing and grunting, she got her legs beneath her and stood in the tub.

"We've got her covered, Harmon. Just do her in."

He picked up the curtain rod, standing tall and resolute.

"Don't be swayed by her good looks and tempting ways, Harmon. You should know how these wayward women operate by now. They just want to use you and toss you away like yesterday's laundry. You know I'll never leave you. I'll always love my snookums." She squeezed her eyes shut. Tears of pain poured down her cheeks. Her face contorted in agony. "Just... do it, damn you!"

Harmon's chest swelled with an indrawn breath. He gripped the rod in both hands, his arms so stiff with tension they shook. He brought it back to his shoulder. And then—

He swung it.

The impact of metal on bone resounded, a sickly, dull sound. Maybelle went down like a lucky spare in the last frame of a championship bowling match.

"Oh, no. Oh, no." His brow crumpled with shock. "Maybelle, Maybelle... I didn't mean to... You know I..."

Grabbing the top of my towel in one hand, I got to my knees. But before I could crawl past Harmon, he whipped around.

"People shouldn't hurt other people—ever," he said dolefully. "It's bad to hurt other people."

"What? No, I didn't... You don't understand, Harmon. *She* tried to drown *me*."

He frowned. "I know."

Slowly, I stood. I still wasn't sure what he was capable of. He looked very confused and conflicted. Maybelle lay face down. There was no blood seeping from her head that I could see. I inched toward the door. "You do?"

He nodded. "She was going to finish you off just like she did Miss Harper and Miss Hazelton. They didn't deserve it, either."

By now, I was beyond the threshold, in the hallway. "*Maybelle* killed them both?"

He sighed. "Yep." Then he shuffled to her. Nudged her with a foot. She didn't respond, but I could see her chest expanding with the faintest of breaths. She was still very much alive, just out cold.

"Ah, Maybelle. Why'd you have to go and cause so much trouble? It was all innocent. They were my friends. Just friends. I kept telling you that." Dropping the curtain rod, he snuffled. His chest rattling with a sob, he crashed to his knees beside her.

Before the murderess could regain consciousness, I ran into the bedroom, grabbed my phone, and dialed 9-1-1. Cold and still dripping, I returned to the bathroom as I spoke to Misty the dispatcher. I saw the pepper spray and reached to pick it up.

"You'll never believe this," I told her.

"Actually," she said. "I probably will. Tell me—what happened *this* time?"

"SAM? SAM, ARE YOU here?"

Ears perked, Bump's head swiveled toward the voice. Standing in the upstairs hallway with a wet towel around my middle, phone in one hand, pepper spray in the other, I was so wracked with shivers it took a few moments for recognition to register.

Archer was here.

The side door to the kitchen closed. Still blinking and sneezing, Bump scooped up his wet ball and galloped down the hallway and stairs. Apparently, I hadn't hit him directly with the spray. Just close enough that he'd inhaled some of it. Poor guy had quite a day. And yet, he still maintained a happy-go-lucky attitude. Maybe I wouldn't get that Doberman after all.

"Hey, pal. Whoa there! Slow down," Archer commanded—

unsuccessfully, because I heard the unmistakable sound of paws hitting a body and the ensuing grunt of air being ejected from the upward thrust of Archer's diaphragm.

In the upstairs bathroom, Harmon was seated on the closed lid of the toilet, elbows on his knees, face in hands, muttering gibberish. He wasn't the one I was worried about, though. Because a minute ago, Maybelle had stirred from her comatose state. While she'd been out cold, I'd retied the cord around her feet, but I hadn't found anything close enough to bind her hands. I figured as long as she couldn't move about, I had an advantage. When she'd finally come to and seen me with the pepper spray in my hand, she'd decided to stay put.

"Up here, Archer," I called. "Hurry, I need help!"

The tucked end of the towel slipped loose and fell to the floor at my feet.

Grasping at her chance, Maybelle planted an elbow beneath herself in an attempt to get up.

I aimed at her face again. "Don't even try."

"My head's throbbing. My throat's burning. I can barely see." With a whimper, she sank down. "And I'm freezing to death."

"Too bad. Maybe the sheriff will get here before hypothermia sets in."

My arm was shaking visibly now. I could tell by the weight of the can there was little-to-no spray left in it.

As if she knew I was low on ammunition, Maybelle wiggled toward the empty wine bottle.

I rushed forward and kicked it away. "I said stay put!"

She grabbed at my ankle, but I'd already retreated and was pointing the canister at her.

"Sam, what's going on?" Archer bounded up the stairs. Seconds later, he was standing in the bathroom doorway. He took one look at me, then his gaze slid to Maybelle. "What on earth..."

"She's trying to kill me," Maybelle said. "She's a harlot and a murderer!"

"Oh, come on, Maybelle. You tried to kill me first. Just like you killed Miley and Grace."

"Her? Really?" Archer pointed to Maybelle. Before I could elaborate, he peeled his Pittsburg Penguins sweatshirt off and exchanged it for my can of pepper spray.

I slipped the shirt over my head. "You said you weren't going to be back until midnight."

"I was able to sweet talk an airline employee into letting me have an empty business-class seat on an earlier connection in Dallas." The canister aimed at Maybelle, he took a step closer to her. "I may have said something about needing to get home because my wife was going into labor early."

Maybelle shrank beneath his glare. A giant red blotch marked one of her cheeks, and a faint purpling hinted at the bruise to come. I was sure I had a few of my own, not to mention my throat and entire rib cage hurt like the dickens.

Archer glanced at Harmon. "What's up with him?"

"After he put two and two together, he hit her with the shower curtain rod. Harmon wouldn't hurt a fly, but he couldn't let her go on doing what she'd done. He saved me, Archer—and he almost killed Maybelle to do it."

Extending a hand, Archer started to help Maybelle up.

"What are you doing?" I tugged his sweatshirt down as far as I could, but it barely covered my bum.

"Checking her out to see if she needs an ambulance." Somehow, he managed to heave her off the floor and set her with her back against the wall. She grunted, her hands fisted like she was going to pummel him. Ignoring her, he peered into each of her pupils, then proceeded to check her head for bumps. She winced as he touched a spot just above her left ear. "Looks like she ended up the loser in this brawl."

"What about me?"

"Fine, are you hurt?" he said without looking.

"I'm okay." Physically, maybe. But on the inside, I was crumbling.

He gave me a skeptical glance. "You do look like you've had a rough day."

"This isn't even the half of it."

"I hesitate to ask. I trust you called the sheriff?"

"They're on their way. Do you want me to call an ambulance for her?"

Shaking his head, he flipped the lever to drain the tub. "I don't think she'll need one. No concussion, no broken bones... Just a nasty lump the size of a lemon."

My teeth started to chatter so hard and loud I sounded like a machine gun.

"Sam, go ahead and get dressed, then go downstairs to let the deputies in when they arrive. I'll keep an eye on her—and Harmon here, although I don't think he's going to budge."

I started to go, but his hand on the back of my leg stopped me. I turned around. Met his eyes. Dissolved inside.

"You're a tough gal, Sam McNamee."

I shrugged. "Right now, all I know is I'm cold and tired and my ribs ache and... and..." If I uttered one more syllable, I was going to completely fall apart.

"You are. Tough, that is. Brave and strong and independent, too. The bravest woman I know." He smiled—a smile of admiration and a million other unsaid things. "And here I thought I'd always be the one to rescue you. Looks like you're perfectly capable of doing that yourself."

I tried to smile back, but tears were making me choke up. I needed him. Needed his strength and his support. Needed someone like him to laugh with and long for, to take comfort in and to lift me up at times like this. To have and to hold. Forever and ever.

Sirens breeched the quiet. Outside, doors slammed. A fist pounded on the front door.

"Please, *please* stay for a while this time, Archer."

"Don't you worry, Sam." Standing, he pulled me into his arms. "I'm not going anywhere. Not any time soon, anyway."

"Are you sure?"

"Positive. Turns out, saving the rest of the world doesn't mean much if you can't be with the person you love."

chapter 33

"When you told me tonight's date was going to be a surprise," I said as we turned onto yet another country road, "this wasn't quite what I envisioned."

It had been five months since Amy Sue and Maybelle both tried to kill me on the same day. I hadn't seen the sheriff or his deputies since, except when driving the opposite way on Route 379.

Bump, sitting in the back of my new-to-me midsized SUV, pressed his nose to the glass. Today, Archer had insisted on bringing him along on our date. He'd also offered to do the driving, since only he knew our destination.

Tractors were out in the fields, busily churning up the earth. Beyond a line of treetops to the west, a thunderstorm threatened, carrying the promise of rain on a steady breeze.

"Looks like we're going to get rained out," I said. "If we're going hiking, that is."

"You're assuming I made outdoor plans."

"Why else would we bring Bump along? Unless we're headed to the pet store in Fullbright—in which case, I'm sorry, but that's not quite my idea of a date."

"Mine either. But don't worry—we'll get where we're going…

eventually."

We'd left my house fifteen minutes ago, dropping Tara off at Ida's along the way for their weekly game night. Shortly after Thanksgiving last year, Dad and Ida had returned from South America more in love than ever. Already, they were planning their next adventure, this one to Iceland to take in the geological wonders before the super volcano blew its top. Dad justified it by stating he'd taken up photography again, thanks to the new digital camera Ida had bought for him.

"Why *are* we going this way, though?" I asked. "Seems like we're halfway to Fullbright already."

Archer had been working there on a treatment center to combat drug addiction on a local level. It was due to open in three weeks, and he'd already resigned from the fire department in order to give it his full attention.

"I want to show you something."

Thunder clapped. I flinched instinctively. "What?"

"You'll see when we get there."

No matter how much I pleaded, he wasn't giving in. Finally, we pulled into a gravel drive. There was a house so far back off the road it would've been easy to miss if I hadn't been looking.

"Lost?" I asked, figuring he was about to back up and turn around, but he kept going.

Halfway down the driveway, he stopped the car and turned the engine off. His chest expanded with an indrawn breath. The more I stared at him, the more I realized he'd been a little nervous since he'd picked me up.

"Sam... I haven't exactly been honest with you."

A squirrel scampered up a nearby tree trunk, and Bump whined.

"What... what do you mean?"

"When I told you I had to work extra hours because of the rush to get the center up and running, well... sometimes... I wasn't *at* work. At least not the whole time. I've had... something going on."

I couldn't look at him. "Who is she?"

"She? You assumed I... No, Sam..." He got out of the truck, came around, and opened my door. "Let me show you what I've been up to."

After gathering Bump's leash, we walked down a lane framed by maples. On the left was a freshly tilled field stretching for hundreds of acres. To the right was a fenced-in yard, the grass a little too tall to be considered lawn. The house was maybe two hundred yards from the road. Not as far as I'd first thought. It was an older home, two story, although not large, with white siding, red shutters, and a black roof. A small barn stood to the side, and an attached garage was situated to the rear.

We stopped about thirty yards back where the details became more apparent. Bump sat automatically. He still remembered his lessons from Clint, even though they didn't see each other much anymore. The paint on the house was fresh, the roof new. The windows still had the manufacturer's stickers on them.

"This," he said in a very unceremonious way, "is where I've been."

It was an older house that had been lovingly restored. "You did all this?"

"Not by myself. Marco helped. It was his house."

"Was? You bought it?"

He nodded. "He hasn't been here much since his mom's health went downhill."

"It's gorgeous... and so peaceful out here." I turned to him. "But why didn't you tell me about it?"

Hand in hand, he led me up the freshly cemented sidewalk and onto the covered porch. "Because it's the most important thing I've ever done... so far."

"More than Everly's Foundation?"

"Yes, even more than that. You see, I realized as important as that is, it doesn't mean much without someone to share my life with. Marco had just started to think about selling this place when you and I got serious. At first, I was just helping him fix it up to sell, but the more I came here and worked on it, the more I thought about buying it. So I did. I figured you could have all the peace and quiet you need out here to write."

He unlocked the front door. I unclipped Bump's leash, and he paraded in like he owned the place.

The hardwood floors had recently been refinished. There were still plenty of tools strewn about, but not a stick of furniture that I could see. Still, it was easy to imagine this being someone's home. There was a brick fireplace perfect for winter nights and a ceiling fan for hot summers. I'd already circled the living room and was on my way to the kitchen when I noticed Archer was still standing in the doorway.

"Aren't you coming in?" I said.

Bump trotted once more around the living room, then down the hallway, stopping to poke his head in every open door before continuing on.

"Not yet."

I started toward him. "Why? Is something wrong?"

"No, not wrong. I'd say something's right. Very, *very* right."

"Meaning?"

"You're here. In this place. With me." He entered. Drifted toward me. Took my hand again and drew me to him. "I almost lost you twice in one day, Sam. It took that to make me realize the gift I'd been given when you stood in line next to me that day at Garber's Groceries. Until then, I'd somehow convinced myself that falling in love wasn't in the cards for me. That I had work to do. Needed a purpose to make up for my past mistakes. Turns out, all that time, I'd simply been waiting for you to come along."

THREATS AND THREADS

I laid my head against his chest, listening to the steady beat of his heart. Absorbed the warmth of his skin. Let his strength become mine.

There was safety and support in the circle of his arms. A soft place to land and a solidness from which to launch myself toward the stars.

Nose to the ground, Bump raced past us and up the stairs, like he was on a mission.

"Can you imagine yourself here, Sam?"

"Sure, I—" I stepped back. "Wait, this is your house. Are you suggesting we... move in together? Is this still even Wilton schools? I'm not expecting Melissa back for—"

"Sam, I didn't mean right away. I thought maybe you could move in here first, and later..." He stalled. "Later, we... I thought maybe someday, if we..."

A funny little tickle started in the pit of my stomach before fluttering upward.

"Ah heck, Sam, will you—"

A high-pitched bark sounded overhead. We both glanced up at the ceiling. It certainly wasn't Bump's bark.

"Archer, did I hear another dog?"

"Not *exactly*."

"Sure sounded like a dog to me."

He pointed at me. "Wait here."

A minute later, he came down the stairs with a fuzzy puppy cradled in his arms. Mostly black, with tan eyebrows, cheeks, and feet, and a white patch on her chest. Instead of a long plume of a tail like Bump, she had a short little bobtail. Bump trailed after them, his entire body gyrating in excitement.

"I thought Bump could use a buddy to help burn off some of his energy. She's an Australian Shepherd."

Bump's eyes hadn't left the puppy for a second. He was in awe. Or love, maybe.

"What's her name?" I squeezed a paw. The pads of her feet were velvety soft.

"She doesn't have one yet." He held her out. "Any suggestions?"

I started to reach for her, then stopped myself. "Oh, no. No, no. no. I see what you're doing. You're distracting me with a puppy. You were about to ask me something."

"I was?"

Arms crossed, I glared at him. "You were. And I got the sense that it was something… important, maybe?"

"All right," he began a little timidly. "Sam, will you—"

The puppy kicked and squirmed, wanting to be let down, but Archer held her tight. He tried to shift her to one arm, but she only wiggled more.

Impatient, I grabbed the puppy from him. She climbed up my chest, then hooked her paws over my shoulders. Her tiny tongue flicked at my ear and cheek. My toes and fingers began to tingle.

"Will I what?" A funny sensation came over me. Like I was detached from my body, my spirit floating on a cloud.

Archer leaned in close, the fluffball scrunched between us, his gaze shifting from my eyes to my lips and back to my eyes. "Will you marry me?"

My knees went weak. I wobbled. Archer snatched the puppy out of my arms just as everything around me went fuzzy.

I LIFTED MY NOSE. Smelled earth and damp wood and the looming threat of rain. It wasn't spring, but summer. And I was not a small puppy, but a full-grown dog, living a life before this one.

Ahead of me ran a young man with legs that were lean but well-muscled. His arms swung rhythmically, his shoes barely touching the ground. The skin beneath my fur prickled. The air vibrated, rumbled.

THREATS AND THREADS

He glanced over his shoulder at me, his face brown from the sun, his hair dark and thick.

"*Rapido! Apurate!*"

I hurried to catch up, stumbling before I realized I had four legs, not just two. With compact feet, I dug my claws into the soft dirt of the trail and bounded forward, my speed increasing with each stride. I ran hard until I was at his side, then ahead of him, through a tangled archway of tree limbs. The path climbed a series of hills and diverged several times, but I knew the way. We'd done this before.

Just as I reached the top of the incline into a place where the trees opened up, lightning flashed at the periphery of my vision. I stopped, looked back for the young man.

His eyes met mine for the briefest of moments. Until his toes caught beneath a root. His chest continued forward, his hands flying out before him. His body hit the ground hard.

Spinning around, I rushed to him.

"*Basta, basta, basta.*" He swatted me away. Tried to raise himself up on an elbow. His face contorted in agony. He collapsed, moaning in pain, then rolled to his side as he drew one arm in protectively.

Concern filled me. Nothing to offer but comfort, I licked his face.

"*Pronto, mi amigo. Pronto.*"

Again, my skin tingled. The fur lifted from my neck.

The boom and the flash came as one.

The world around me faded.

NOT ONE TONGUE, BUT two swiped repeatedly across my face. Bump's halitosis mixed with the bologna scent of puppy breath.

I swatted at Bump. "Stop it, stop it, stop it."

He whimpered. Sat and cocked his head.

Archer knelt beside me, touched my cheek and temple as he

gazed into my eyes. "You okay, Sam? We were talking, and you just dropped to the floor. Are you susceptible to low blood-sugar levels? Have a heart problem? Ever had a seizure before?"

"None of the above," I said.

He gently probed my head for knots, then checked to see if my pupils were dilated. "Then what—"

"Migraines, sort of. I'll fill you in later. It's a long story."

After he determined I wasn't permanently damaged, he helped me sit up, then brought me a can of sparkling water from the fridge.

"Do you remember what we were talking about?" he asked.

"I do. And I have an answer."

He raised both eyebrows. "Okay, what is it?"

"Pronto."

"Excuse me?"

"Her name is Pronto. You asked me for a name, and that one came to me. It means 'quick' or maybe 'soon' in Spanish, doesn't it? I'll ask Tara. She'll know."

Disappointment dragged down the corners of his mouth.

"Oh, you don't like it," I said. "We'll come up with something else."

"No, that's not it. I like the name, but I think we should get you to the hospital. Do a more thorough check to see if you have a concussion."

"Why?"

"Well, you can't remember the last thing we were talking about, so—"

"Yes."

"Yes, what?"

"You asked me if I'd marry you. The answer is yes."

His mouth slowly curved into a smile. He leaned in and kissed me. Until a small, leaping puppy and a big, goobery mutt invaded the space between us.

THREATS AND THREADS

We both laughed. I touched my finger to the tip of Archer's nose. "You did ask me more than one question. I just wasn't sure what order you wanted them answered in."

chapter 34

I OPENED MY MOTHER'S jewelry box and beckoned Tara closer.

She peered at the contents, tracing a finger over a long strand of pearls, turquoise rings set in sterling silver bands, oversized brooches, and dangly hoop earrings. "Did you get that at a garage sale or something? Or is this what you used to wear in the seventies?"

We were sitting on the edge of Ida's bed, which was covered by a handmade quilt. A late summer breeze lifted the lace curtains. Outside, a flock of starlings landed on the roof and began to quarrel.

"The eighties, pumpkin. Don't age me an extra decade. But no, they weren't mine."

"Then whose were they? Anybody I know?" My little girl wasn't so little anymore. She looked so grown up in her off-the-shoulder dress and with her fancy up-do with a few springy tendrils grazing the back of her neck.

"No, nobody you knew."

It was the truth. There were times when Tara was small, though, that I used to wonder how my mother would have been with her. Even as vain as she had been, she'd been a fun mother who'd delighted in running barefoot with me through the backyard as dandelion seeds exploded in the wake of our laughter-driven stampede. We'd danced together to the hit tunes on American Bandstand. She'd let me play dress-up in her clogs and peasant tops. From the bottom right drawer of the jewelry box, I took out a pinkie ring and placed it on Tara's little finger.

Her face lit up. She tilted her hand to catch the light. "Oh, that's pretty. I like it. It's sort of ten colors all at once—shimmery white and minty green and sky blue… I'm not a diamonds and gold sort of girl, but this is gorgeous. I could look at it all day long."

"It's an opal."

She started to slide it off, but I held up my palm. "It's yours. Keep it."

For several moments, she said nothing. Then, "It was your mom's, wasn't it?"

I nodded. "Gramps gave it to her on her birthday the first year they were dating. He said up until then, except for his car and his camera equipment, it was the most expensive item he'd ever paid for. He wanted to impress her. She ran with the rich crowd. She was a rising model, and he was just some middle-grade photographer. But she chose him." For a while, anyway. I hadn't talked much to Tara about my mother, the assumption being I didn't remember much about her. Mostly, I remembered how it felt to be without a mother. How the other kids' moms accompanied the class field trips and sent in cupcakes on their birthdays and how every time those things happened, I felt the stabbing ache of rejection. Dad had been there physically, but not emotionally. So I'd buried myself in books and studied my heart out, seeking the approval of my teachers and later my bosses.

Time had broadened my perspective. The truth, eventually, had made me more forgiving of my father's shortcomings. My daughter was old enough to know the truth now, too. "Tara, there's something I have to tell you."

"About what?" She went to the door, peeked out in the hallway, and closed it. "I think they're waiting on us."

"I'll be quick. It's about Gramps… He's not your biological grandfather."

She cocked her head at me, face scrunched like I'd just spoken to her in ancient Latin. So I explained, as devoid of judgment and emotion as I could, how my mother had left him for an old flame in France, then gotten sick and died. I told her about the DNA test I'd had done, and that Gramps didn't know the actual results. Then I gave her the envelope I'd kept in storage for all these years, yet only recently opened.

"His name is Étienne Renard. His address is at the bottom. It took some effort to track him down, as it's his oldest daughter who lives there now, but I spoke to him two days ago." I paused to take in her reaction.

She was surprisingly calm. "That must've been awkward."

I exhaled in relief. I'd half expected histrionics. "You could say that. It was a long talk. Luckily, his English is better than my French. But anyway, I assured him I didn't want any of his money, that I was just reaching out and I didn't want my dad to know. The dad who'd raised me, that is."

"That's good, I guess. I'm glad you got it sorted out." She leafed through the papers from the envelope. "What are these, anyway? They're all in French—I can tell that much. I see a lot of numbers, but what are they for?"

"It's money he set aside for me. I told him I didn't need it, so it's yours now. I asked him to put it in a trust for when you turn eighteen. It's more than enough to get you through a good college and then some."

She blinked, like it was going to take some time for all of this to soak in. "You said he has a daughter in France?"

"Two daughters, actually. And a son. They're all doing very well. And it turns out they already knew about me. He told them after his wife died."

"Wow, okay... Thanks. I... I don't know what to say. This is like some kind of strange soap opera. But..."

"But what?"

"It doesn't really change anything. I mean, Gramps is still *my* grandpa. He is kinda grumpy, but to me, that's how grandpas are supposed to be. I love that he taught me to sing along to old songs and likes to go fishing and drives a truck that's thirty years old—or used to until you crashed it into that fence. I'd never trade him for another."

I pulled her into a hug.

A knock sounded at the door. Tara cracked it open. A long snout wedged through the opening. A ball dropped to the floor, rolling until it hit Tara's feet.

"Hey, Bump. Hi, Pronto." She opened the door a little wider and gave the ball back to Bump. "Gramps."

Dad poked his head in. Bump stood next to him, the ball in his mouth. Pronto tugged at his tail. She'd grown a set of giraffe legs in the last couple of months. The puppy fuzz was gone, but she was still cute in that innocently awkward way of teenagers.

"You two gals are holding up the works." Grabbing Bump by the collar to pull him back, Dad shut the door without waiting for a response. Then, just as I stood up and started to smooth out the wrinkles in my dress, he opened it again. He surveyed me, head to toe. Tears glinted in his eyes. "You look beautiful, Sam. Just... beautiful. You, too, Tara. My daughter... getting hitched. Makes an old man happy."

Before he could dissolve into a puddle of emotions, he quickly shut the door.

"Wait for it," Tara muttered. "Waaaait for it..."

The door sprung open again. Behind Dad, the two dogs were having a wrestling match in the hallway. He jabbed a finger at us.

"Now don't be thinking that Ida and I are getting any fancy ideas. Things are fine the way they are. I might keep on courting her forever. Keeps things fresh. Besides, I don't want her thinking she's stuck with me. Makes me work a little harder to keep impressing her. And she forces me outside my"—he waggled two fingers of each hand in air quotes—"comfort zone, whatever the hell that is."

"Dad?"

"What?"

"You *do* look good in a tux."

"Not happening, Sam. I'm not wiggling into another monkey suit like this until Tara walks down the aisle—and don't you even think about that until you're twenty-two, you hear me?"

"Make that twenty-five, Gramps," she said, "or thirty, maybe. I plan to do some globe-trekking with you and Ida when I'm out of high school, if you don't mind me tagging along."

"You're taking Spanish in school, right?"

"Yes. I'll have had four years of it by the time I graduate."

"Then you're in." He winked at her. Then, to me, "I'm going to start the processional. You might want to get a move on. The guests are getting twitchy."

A moment later, my daughter and I were alone again.

Circling me, she tugged at the hem of my dress to straighten it. Then she gathered my bouquet from atop the dresser and placed it in my hands. I inhaled the perfume of roses and lilacs. Downstairs, music from an old record player started up.

"I thought Gramps lost all his records in the fire," Tara said.

"He did. He's been buying replacements from the vinyl store over in Oil City. Dad said he learned he didn't need as much stuff from his old house as he'd always thought, except for the things that made him happy. Music was one of those things. You and I were the others."

Tara tilted her head. "That song... It sounds familiar."

I listened more closely. Al Green's melodious voice drifted up from the living room. ""Let's Stay Together"."

"Was that their song?"

"Gramps and my mom's? No, that would be too ironic. Theirs was "Let's Get It On"."

"Really?"

"They were children of the sixties, sweetie. Free love and all that. Anyway, I think this one is supposed to be for Archer and me." I took a deep breath. "Shall we?"

Tara's head bobbed in an enthusiastic nod. Then she scrunched her mouth thoughtfully. "If I ever get married—*if* being the operative word—do you suppose Archer will, you know, stand in as my dad?"

I kissed her brow. "Without a doubt."

We both grinned. She opened the door for me. Dad was standing there at the top of the stairs, waiting. He handed Pronto's leash to Tara, then moved Bump to his right side. I hooked my hand through his elbow.

When we reached the bottom of the stairs, Selma was there waiting by the front door for Tara in a matching bridesmaid dress and hairdo. Today's theme was apparently 'twinning'.

Russ Armentrout was standing next to the record player. He and Dad had set aside their differences when Russ invited him out for a day of fishing in his new boat. They still argued, but that was the whole point of getting together. There was a pause as Russ switched out the songs and "Always and Forever" by Luther Vandross began playing.

Through the picture window overlooking Ida's front garden, I could see the chairs set up there, filled with all the friends I'd made since I came to Wilton. In the back row was Birdie Swinson, Cleora, and her sister Cordelia, along with her husband Hubert. Over to the right were Keisha and William and the Mullins family. To the left, I caught a glimpse of Stacy and a couple of other women from the Apple Pie Bibliophile Society. I also saw Misty seated next to Marco.

Rumor had it they were dating. Even Sheriff Driscoll was there with his wife. Toward the front was Newt. Selma waved at him. Even that made his cheeks redden.

Danielle Townsley had already flown off to the Sudan in search of her new family. She promised to send pictures.

Peeking around the crowd from the front row was Ida. Dad blew her a kiss, and she flung a hand out like she was catching it and brought it to her heart.

Dad squeezed my hand. "Ready?"

I nodded. Selma led the way down the front steps, followed by Tara with Pronto bucking and leaping beside her. The guests laughed, which was how I wanted it—to be in a place filled with laughter and loved ones. According to Sheriff Driscoll, I'd singlehandedly cleaned up Humboldt County, so even though I may have crossed a few people along the way, there were a whole lot more who were grateful that I'd made the community a safer place to live.

Archer waited beneath a trellis woven with daisies and baby's breath, his hands clasped before him in a boyish way. At his shoulder stood Clint, his best man.

Russ held the door open. The guests all turned, stood. Gazed on with beaming smiles. Snapped photos with their camera phones.

My father... *my* father and I, with Bump beside us, strolled onto Ida's front porch, then down the aisle to the man I loved—and a life full of unexpected adventures.

about the author

N. Gemini Sasson has worked as an aquatic toxicologist, an environmental engineer, a teacher, and a cross country coach. A longtime breeder of Australian Shepherds, her articles on bobtail genetics have been translated into seven languages. Her Imagineer line of Aussies has earned ASCA's Hall of Fame Excellent distinction. She lives in rural Ohio with her husband and an ever-changing number of animals.

Long after writing about Robert the Bruce and Queen Isabella, Sasson learned she is a descendant of both historical figures.

If you enjoyed this book, please spread the word by sharing it on Facebook or leaving a review at your favorite online retailer or book lovers' site.

For more details about N. Gemini Sasson and her books, go to:
www.ngeminisasson.com

Or become a 'fan' at:
www.facebook.com/NGeminiSasson

You can also sign up to learn about new releases via e-mail at:
http://eepurl.com/vSA6z

Made in the USA
Columbia, SC
24 June 2023